# HIS CONTRACT

REBECCA GRACE ALLEN

Rebecca Grace Allen Enterprises

His Contract

Copyright © 2015 by Rebecca Grace Allen

Print ISBN: 978-0-9978792-8-5

Print ISBN: 978-0-9992066-6-9

Digital ISBN: 978-0-9978792-6-1

Editing by Christa Soule

Cover Design by Syd Gill

First Samhain Publishing, Ltd. print and electronic publication: October 2015

*Lawyers know when to play by the rules...and when to break them.*

*Legally Bound, Book 1*

Harvard law professor Jack Archer once balanced his professional life with the private world of dominance, surrender, and trust he shared with his wife. Since cancer stole her a year ago, finding love again—her final wish for him—is the furthest thing from his mind.

From his empty house to the classroom, grief follows his every move. Until he meets a young woman with shadows in her eyes even darker than his own.

Once a shining star at law school, Lilly Sterling's dreams died when the Dom she trusted left her heartbroken and lost. She's starting fresh in a new city as a paralegal, but meeting Jack reawakens all her old demons—and her lingering desires.

Jack offers to become Lilly's mentor for both the courtroom and the playroom, but tells himself it's not a relationship. Their carefully worded contract guarantees that. But when their trial agreement starts heating up, both Jack and Lilly must decide what will tip the scales: the letter of the law...or love?

*Warning: All rise for a book that contains a wounded submissive and a Dominant who wants to retrain her while retaining control of his heart. Discovery phase may involve spankings, bondage, edging, and blindfolds. Is it hot? You be the judge.*

# PRAISE FOR HIS CONTRACT

★ Amazon Kindle Top 10 in Romance
★ Amazon Kindle Top 100 Bestseller
★ Barnes & Noble Nook Top 20
★ Barnes & Noble Nook Top 10 in Romance

*"An explosive, deeply personal love story."*
—RT Book Reviews, 4 star review

*"As soulful as it is sexy. This book is everything 50 Shades wanted to be, and wasn't!"*
—5 star Goodreads review

*"[A] beautiful, heartbreaking and heartwarming love story...His Contract is a 1-click you don't want to miss."*
—The Book Hammock, 5 stars

*"His Contract is an incredibly well-written love story with chemistry in spades."*
—Pretty Sassy Cool

*"Beautiful, emotional, thoughtful BDSM het romance."*

—Duke Duke Goose

*"This is how erotic romance should be written."*
—Bookaholics Not-So-Anonymous, 5 stars

*"Fifty Shades of Grey was my first introduction to the BDSM lifestyle... This is the book I should have read as an introduction... I absolutely fell for this book and couldn't put it down!"*
—Kilts and Swords Book Blog

# PROLOGUE

*J*ack Archer counted the seconds between his wife's shallow breaths. The rented hospital cot cradled her wasted form, but to Jack, it felt more like a casket than a bed. He ground a fist against his palm, a reminder to stay strong. Being Eve's rock had been his job since her diagnosis—the only way he'd survived as the happy life they shared melted into chaos. That strength had begun to falter during the vigil he'd kept by her side the last few days. Her organs had shut down, every cell riddled with cancer, the purple shadows under her eyes as dark as the wintry Massachusetts sky at dusk.

Another breath. Jack counted again. The silence before her next inhale lasted too long.

"Joshua," the hospice nurse said.

Jack's son looked up from the sofa. Tears stained his cheeks, angry splotches left behind from where his hands had been holding up his head.

"It's time to say good-bye now."

Although he was already a man, Josh's face crumpled like a child's.

He stood and advanced toward his mother. Sitting on the

ottoman a few feet away, Jack felt the same agony he saw in his son's face, the same force of will that was keeping his own muscles rigid. Josh crouched down as Eve's eyes opened and twin pairs of bright blue eyes found one another. Josh was a duplicate of his mother, inheriting her eye color instead of Jack's blue-gray. Matching golden hair framed their faces, although Eve's had dulled to flaxen wisps before falling out altogether.

"You apply to that PhD program now," she said, her words coming out with a wheeze. "Or I swear I'll haunt you until you do."

Jack let out a pained laugh. Even in the face of death, Eve found a way to joke. She beckoned Josh closer and tenderly kissed his forehead.

"I love you, Mom." Josh's voice broke. The sound was a knife to Jack's heart.

"Me too."

Another difficult breath was followed by a pause. Jack caught the nurse's gaze. Her sad but rapid nod signaled it was time to do the impossible. She wrapped an arm around Josh and led him out of the room.

Jack worked to control his breathing as he started toward the cot, but had to stop and brace a hand against the wall. There was no way to prepare for this moment. He'd have pleaded with Eve to stay with him, but he refused to fill her final moments with sadness. It wasn't a request she could grant him now, anyway.

She tried to lift her head as he neared.

"Don't—" he whispered sharply, then winced. Regretting his tone, he bent down to kneel beside her. It wasn't a position he was accustomed to, but he didn't care about the role reversal now.

He gathered one of Eve's cold hands in his and ran his thumb over the finger that used to bear his ring. It slipped off the month before, when the last cruel waves of the disease took hold. She'd asked Jack to link it onto the silver chain she wore around her neck, the meaning of which only they knew. It represented the secret intimacy in their marriage, the cherished bond they'd always kept private.

Eve lifted her free hand and began tracing her fingers along the chain. "Do something for me?"

Her voice was thin and reedy. She sounded so far away already.

"What is it, love?"

That made her grin—the use of her pet name, only spoken during their play. Jack smiled, the moment a brief respite from the bleak reality in front of him.

She tapped her finger against the chain. "Don't bury me in this."

"What?" he sputtered. "Why?"

"Because," she said slowly. "It will keep you bound to me for the rest of your life. I don't want that for you."

Jack was stunned into silence. Tears threatened to brim over. He had to clench his jaw to force them back. Refusing to let her see him fall apart, he bowed his head, his forehead meeting the bony knuckles of her hand. She tried to soothe him, a quiet *shhh* coming out on a ragged exhale, and then Jack was crying. He hated himself for breaking down, for being so terrified of losing her that he was gripping her fingers tightly enough to break them, while she was setting him free.

He dragged his head up. "I can't, love. I can't."

"You have to." She paused as she tried to swallow. "Promise me something?"

"Anything."

She looked at him with the same eyes that had seen through him since he was a teenager. "Promise me that someday, you'll fall in love again."

The last shreds of Jack's composure unraveled.

He shook his head, his heart caving in, everything inside him locking down. He couldn't promise her that. It would be impossible to love anyone again, to care for another woman the way he'd cared about her for the last twenty-five years. But then Jack saw the hope shining from Eve's tired eyes, suddenly filled with more life than he'd seen in weeks. It was as if she'd summoned all the strength she had left for this one last request, and he couldn't let her go without saying something to ease her pain.

"Okay. I'll try."

She smiled, and her eyes drifted closed. Her muscles went slack, relief seeming to settle through her.

"Love you," she whispered.

"I love you too," Jack rasped, but she was already gone.

# 1

———

"*L*illy, why don't you take the bar exam already?"

Lilly Sterling winced and looked out the windows lining the associate bullpen. Boston's jagged skyline glittered against the murky purple horizon. It was late. Ten thirty on a Tuesday night and the hallways were dark. Even the Ivy League graduates hoping to make junior partner had left for the day. There was nothing to distract Gabe from his favorite line of questioning.

He leaned over the partition separating her desk from the other cubicles. "Hello?"

"I told you. I'm not sure this is what I want to do with my life."

"That's what you said when you blew off taking it after law school, and I got you this job for some—" he made air quotes with his fingers, "—real life experience."

Lilly cringed at the reminder. Gabe was acting like her request had been an excuse. A stay of execution, so she could decide if being a lawyer was what she really wanted.

As if that had ever been the case. "I remember, Mr. Hartley."

Gabe rolled his eyes. He hated it when their boss called them by their last names, which was precisely why Lilly did it. "So I call bullshit, since it's glaringly obvious you love working in law."

"Exactly how is it glaringly obvious?" Lilly began rearranging the files on her desk, but had to stop when Gabe held out his hand in front of her.

"A bachelors in pre-law. File clerk for the district attorney," he said, ticking reasons off his fingers. Each one felt like a tiny stab wound. "A note in the Northwestern Law Review, a summer internship, then a JD. And now the hardest working paralegal on staff. Come on, Lilly. Bite the bullet and take the damn bar!"

"Hey, go easy on her."

Lilly glanced up as Gabe's junior associate Cassie came down the hallway in her coat, a hat tugged over her short brown hair. She elbowed Gabe and threw Lilly a grin.

"Be happy Lilly's such a diligent researcher instead of the last moron Forrester hired."

Gabe snorted. "Don't remind me. That idiot couldn't even find the file room."

The sound of his phone beeping stopped Gabe from what was sure to be a bitter diatribe about the incompetency of the latest new hires. He pulled it from his pocket and frowned.

"Is my stupid big brother freaking out again?" Lilly asked. Only a panicked text from Nick could make Gabe's face look like that.

"He's having another *I-can't-do-this, they're-all-going-to-hate-me* meltdown. Maybe if you tell him the opening won't be a total flop, he'll actually believe it."

"I thought talking him down from ledges became your responsibility when you married him."

"I suppose so, but he listens to you. And since you moved here, I've considered ledge-talking a joint responsibility."

They shared a smile. Lilly really did adore Gabe, had ever since Nick met him, even though she never suspected her brother was gay. He'd been the small-town football hero with expectations of going pro, so his coming out had been quite a shock to her parents, her mother especially. But it never mattered to Lilly who Nick loved, as long as he found it with someone. Especially considering the price he'd paid for it.

Gabe's phone beeped again. He looked at the screen and grimaced. "Oh Lord, he won't stop."

Lilly laughed. "Tell him to call me later."

"Fine." Gabe picked up his briefcase and started down the hall. "But you're going to have to become a lawyer so I can sue your brother for driving me crazy."

"I think that's a conflict of interest."

"You could always represent yourself," Cassie added. When Gabe was out of earshot, she turned to Lilly with an apologetic smile. "Sorry he was giving you a hard time again. It's only because he cares."

"I know." Lilly closed the file she was working on. "I think it's time to call it a night."

They walked out together, and Lilly recoiled from the harsh blast of wind that greeted them outside the doors. They parted ways at the corner, heading to their separate T lines. A runner jogged past and Lilly looked away, searching through her bag for her headphones. After finding them stuck inside a folder of briefs she'd been drafting, she plugged them into her phone and blasted the same music that used to propel her through her own daily runs. When she reached Downtown Crossing, she double-checked the signs before boarding her train. She still felt out of her element in Boston—a little like Dorothy in Oz.

Head down, music on, she kept her arms tight around her middle until the train pulled to a halt at her stop. Her boots left prints in the snow as she walked toward the aging building where she rented her small one-bedroom apartment. Boston wasn't cheap. Even with a decent salary, the only place she could afford on her own had nothing more than a galley kitchen off a combined living and dining area. But it was hers, and far away from the life she'd left behind.

Her cat greeted her when she stepped inside, winding his way around her feet and purring loudly enough to remind her of how she'd come up with his name.

"Hey, Rumbles."

She poured his food, switched her suit for sweats and pulled her long, blonde hair free from the tight braid it had been woven into all day. Too exhausted to cook, she chose from one of the many microwave dinners she'd stashed in her freezer. It had just finished cooking when her cell phone lit up, Nick's name on the screen.

She ran a thumb over it to accept the call and tucked the phone between her ear and shoulder.

"So I hear I have a ledge to talk you down from. Again."

"But there's an actual reason this time," Nick insisted. "The gallery owner has connections at *Framed* magazine. Reviewers will be there, and some big buyers too. They say it sucks, and then poof! There goes my career."

"I don't think that's going to happen."

"It could. I'm freaked and it's making Gabe crazy. I wouldn't be surprised if he leaves me. I'm living in the darkroom lately."

"Dahkroom," she said, mimicking his accent. "You don't even sound like you're from Illinois anymore."

"I've lived here for years. Don't worry. Soon you'll sound like a New Englander too."

She hoped so. Starting fresh was why she moved here.

"You need to relax," Lilly said as she retrieved the plastic tray from the microwave and carried it to the table. "The show is going to be great. And Gabe loves you."

"If I promise to stop having meltdowns, will you come to the pub with us on Friday? Brady was there last week by the way. He says hi."

"Bonding with Brady. That must've been fun. And loud." Nick's college football teammate could really fill a room, but Lilly didn't think badly of him. He did save Nick's life, after all. "I still think about what could've happened if he hadn't shown up in time."

"Well, he did. And it was over a decade ago. So stop thinking about it."

It didn't matter how much time had passed. Nick's assault had been the defining moment of her teenage years. He'd made the mistake of coming out to Brady within earshot of his teammates. All he remembered after that was getting slammed into a wall as he tried to leave the locker room, the words *faggot* and *queer* accompanying blows to his head. He'd woken up in an ambulance with Brady beside him, half beaten too for trying to defend him.

It was the first time he'd told Lilly he was gay.

"I think you'd have fun, Lil," he added, jolting her into the present. "I miss you. You've been here six months, and I never see you."

She chewed dryly, swallowing over the lump that guilt formed in her throat. She'd moved to the East Coast to join him, but she'd spent nearly every day since then in the same monotonous cycle, working herself to exhaustion so there was no room left for anything else, even thinking.

Especially thinking.

"Sorry," she said. "I wanted to go last week, but it was late."

"I've been with Gabe long enough to know that nine isn't late. For a lawyer, it's early."

"Good thing I'm not a lawyer, then."

"You should be."

"I like being a paralegal," she said. "You talked to Mom and Dad lately?" A subject change was definitely necessary. Hearing it from Gabe had been enough for one day.

"Just Dad."

Lilly frowned at her dinner. Their father had accepted that Nick was gay, but Mom had become more distant with each passing year, especially after Nick met Gabe. She'd only been to visit Boston once in the last decade, begrudgingly attending their marriage with a polite yet restrained smile. They hadn't spoken much since.

"Mom will come around," she said, hoping it was true.

"I'm not holding my breath. Anyway, I really want you to come with us. The pub has a pool table, and I need a rematch from last time."

She didn't answer.

"It's a sports bar near Fenway," he continued. "With lots of single, straight guys."

"You going straight now? Mom will be thrilled."

"I'm talking about you, doofus."

"I don't have time to date."

"That's what you always say. You should be out meeting people. Not staying home every night with your cat."

"I'm working on it."

Nick let out a frustrated sigh. "I'm not buying this 'it was just a bad breakup' crap, Lilly."

Lilly dropped her fork into the tray, her appetite gone. She wasn't talking about this with Nick now. Or ever. If she confessed the real reason why she never took the bar and left Illinois, she was sure all she'd see in his eyes would be disappointment.

"Can we drop this, please?"

He sighed again, this one short and clipped. "Fine. But you're coming with us. If nothing else, just to spend some time with me."

"Fine," she said, stretching out the "i", hoping the teasing sound would placate him. "I'll go."

When they hung up, Lilly trashed the contents of her dinner, flopped onto the couch and turned on the television. Rest didn't come easy for her lately, and she hoped a mindless sitcom would lull her to sleep. Eventually her eyes closed and she drifted off.

*"Right here, Lilly. This is why you can't walk away. This is why you're mine."*

She bolted up at the familiar voice in her head, the words that crept into her mind like tendrils of ivy, dark and poisonous. She'd moved twelve hundred miles to get away from those memories, but they'd followed her here, taunting her every night in her dreams.

Lilly squeezed her eyes shut and burrowed deeper under the blanket, wishing her demons would leave her the hell alone.

## 2

---

*J*ack pulled his glasses from his face and rubbed his eyes. It was only midweek, and he was already exhausted. He'd spent the day refreshing his memory for the upcoming week's lectures. There'd been a "welcome back" faculty luncheon that afternoon, but he'd avoided it, not wanting to deal with the sad smiles from his co-workers. He'd seen enough of that last semester when he picked up two of his classes after a year and a half off.

A year and a half. That was all it took for the cancer to claim Eve, spreading like a brush fire.

Now for the first time since before she got sick, Jack was back to teaching five classes. It was the last "first" of the many he'd had to endure: the first Valentine's Day not celebrating his anniversary, the first summer sunset at the Cape without her by his side, the first Christmas he hadn't bothered finding a tree. And a few weeks ago, he'd spent New Year's Eve home alone, congratulating himself that he'd made it through a year without her.

A sharp stab of loss cut through him. He pressed a hand to his chest to try to force away the pain, but it didn't help. Deciding he'd had enough for one day, he threw on his coat, trudged outside and drove to the campus athletic center. He was early for his weekly tennis match, but he had nothing left to do, and staying in his office any longer didn't sound like he was adjusting to his "new normal".

The court he reserved every Wednesday was empty. A quick change and some practice serves later still left him with too much time on his hands. Jack sat down on the bench by the net, pulled out his phone and called Josh. Once again, he was answered by the blank void of his son's voicemail.

"Hi, it's Dad again. Just wanted to see how you're doing. Give me a call."

He dumped the phone in his bag. A month had passed with nothing more than a few short emails. Josh was working hard, but Jack didn't think it was schoolwork stopping his son from returning his calls. Not that he blamed Josh for not wanting to deal with the loss of his mother. Jack and denial had become close friends too. He hadn't been to Eve's grave once since the funeral.

"Hey, sorry I'm late." Jack looked up as his childhood friend, Patrick, strode onto the court. "I left on time, but opportunity knocked on the way over."

"By opportunity, you mean getting phone numbers from unsuspecting females."

Patrick pulled a few business cards from his pocket. "Willing, not unsuspecting, my friend." He flashed a lewd grin from behind his goatee, his hair as dark as it always had been, with no signs of gray. They were the same age, but Jack had started to feel decades older.

"You'll have slept with the entire female population of Boston if you keep this up. What will you do then?"

"Move."

Jack huffed out a laugh. "No one would know there's a good guy under all that bullshit."

"I'm insulted. Why would you say that?"

"You know why."

"Because I'm the one who locked up your liquor cabinet and hid the key? That makes me sound like a dick, not a good guy."

Jack studied the white paint outlining the edges of the court, remembering the hole he'd fallen into after Eve died and alcohol became his closest companion. "You're not, even though you act like one half the time."

"Don't tell anyone. You'll blow my cover." Patrick dropped his bag on the bench next to Jack. "How's work going? You sure you're up for a full course load?"

His tone was light, but Jack knew the real question behind it. "I need work. Not more time off."

"Gotchya." Patrick retrieved his racket and spun it around. "You ready to lose?"

"Keep dreaming."

A short time later, however, Jack watched his last shot fly into the net and bounce uselessly toward the other balls pooling at the mesh wall base.

"Out," Patrick called gleefully and jogged to Jack's side of the court. "I win, sucker."

Jack would've punched him in the face if he weren't his best friend.

Hell, he wanted to punch him a little bit anyway.

"How do you have so much energy?" he asked. "Shouldn't you be worn out with all your extracurricular activities?"

"Sex gives you energy, man. You should try it some time."

Jack ground his jaw and rubbed the vacant space on his finger where his wedding ring used to be. He'd had that kind of drive before, had craved the nights when he and Eve would go out, her collar a silver line across her throat, a secret they'd held close with quiet smiles and knowing glances. They'd return home to nights filled with sex so passionate he was sure it would burn them both alive. But that part of his life was gone now, reduced to nothing but cinder and ash.

Patrick spoke first. "Sorry. But I think it's time you got back in the game."

"Don't start."

"Come on, Jack. It's been a year. You've got to get out of the house at some point."

"I know how long it's been. I'm not ready. And I can't do what you do."

"Can't what? Talk to a woman?"

"No. I can't just meet someone and bring her home for a night. Don't you find that kind of empty by now?"

"Do you think I'd keep doing it if it was?" Patrick grinned and folded his arms, the picture of confidence Jack used to possess. "These women know exactly what they're getting into—a night of dirty, hot sex, no strings attached. That's not you. But no one's talking one-night stands here. Just a date."

"Dating at forty-four. I'm not exactly a great catch."

"Are you kidding? You're a good-looking, single, law professor. The chicks'll be lining up to buy you a drink."

"Widower, not single. There's a difference. And even if they were..." Jack tapped the net with his racket. "It wouldn't work out."

Patrick smirked. "There's plenty of kinky women out there, trust me. I've had a few ask me to tie them up myself."

Jack grimaced. "I really wish you didn't know about this."

"Hey, it's not my fault you guys didn't clean up after yourselves. What's a drunk best friend supposed to do when he finds wrist restraints hanging from the guest room bed? Other than tease you about it?"

The memory from years ago tugged at Jack's heart—the night Patrick discovered the bedroom in their vacant basement apartment was actually a playroom. They all had a good laugh about it, and then he and Eve had sworn him to secrecy.

"If you're not comfortable at a bar," Patrick continued, "there are other options."

"We're not having this conversation."

It wasn't the first time Patrick suggested Jack join a local BDSM group, but he'd never been interested in opening up his personal life to strangers. Part of the excitement had been in hiding the devious other life he and Eve had. Dozens of boring events had been made more exciting by the invisible mask of their roles. No one had any idea. It was something she always understood, accepting his need to claim her as well as his need for privacy, never once questioning why he wanted to keep both sides separate.

He was a professor. At Harvard. If word ever got out that he got his kicks smacking his wife around, Jack's credibility would be shot to hell.

"But—"

"No. I didn't want to before she died, and I don't want to now." It was worse than that, though. He wasn't sure he was a Dominant at all anymore without her.

Patrick grew quiet, his face taking on an uncharacteristically solemn expression. "It's what she wanted, right?"

Jack's vision blurred. He closed his eyes and waited for the moment to pass, wishing he'd never confessed Eve's final request during a moment of weakness over a bottle of scotch.

"Can we get back to the game?"

"Fine. But I'm sick of your moping. We're going out Friday night. We'll hit that pub Brady's always blabbing about."

"He's turned out more like you than me," Jack muttered. His younger brother, Brady, had worshipped Patrick since he and Jack met in the ninth grade, following them around like an eager puppy in the form of a hyper five-year-old. Little had changed since then.

"Brady's a family man. We couldn't be more different." Patrick cracked his knuckles. "It'll be a nice change of pace. It's been a while since I worked the Fenway scene."

"I'm really not up for this."

"What if I promise to help? I'll be your wingman. I won't talk to a single woman until I've snagged one for you."

"Patrick," Jack warned, but it was pointless.

"We can watch the Celtics game there. It'll be exactly like watching it at home. Only with bigger TVs. And more beer."

"I'll think about it."

He didn't plan on thinking about it at all, but Patrick's idea lingered as he got home and searched through his fridge for something edible. He was sick of frozen dinners, but he had no desire to cook, and he'd already eaten the meals that Brady's wife, Samantha, had brought over, something she'd done often during the past year.

He slammed the fridge shut and ordered a pizza. When it

arrived, he retreated to the den, turned on the TV and flicked through channels. The silence surrounding him was oppressive.

Jack closed the greasy box and dropped his head against the couch. Things weren't like this before. Once his kitchen was well-stocked. He and Eve would prepare lavish meals that sometimes were forgotten when he got lost in wanting more than just food. Now his only company was the ticking clock in the kitchen. The house was empty, devoid of life, with nothing greeting him every night, save for the exterior post light set on its timer. He needed companionship, but he hadn't so much as noticed another woman, let alone found one attractive since Eve passed. And the thought of being in a noisy, crowded bar, of trying to make small talk with a stranger...

Jack preferred the ticking clock.

He stashed the rest of the pizza in the fridge and went upstairs, his eyes immediately falling upon Eve's nightstand. It was a practiced move, really. He often looked at it, sometimes opening the jewelry box inside when the loneliness became stifling.

He pulled the drawer open and ran his fingers across the box's lid, pausing before flipping the top up and brushing his thumb over the cool metal of her ring. Her collar was still looped through it.

*"It will keep you bound to me for the rest of your life. I don't want that for you."*

Jack let out a heavy breath. His solitude was slowly killing him, and Eve saw that coming, even with death staring her in the face.

"I miss you," he whispered. "So much."

Unable to fend off the grief that tugged him down like quicksand, Jack sank onto the bed and closed his eyes. When he opened them again, sunlight was streaming through the windows. He'd never even undressed.

Groggy, he rubbed his eyes, sat up and pushed himself through the motions of another day.

## 3

"*You're my submissive, slut. Tell me what that means.*"

*She was trapped face down, her legs splayed open, arms bound, a blindfold over her eyes. She couldn't see. Couldn't breathe.*

*He slapped her rear, and what had been pleasure erupted into pain.*

"*It means you can do whatever you want to me, Sir.*"

"*Correct.*" *He slipped a hand between her legs and laughed.* "*You're wet.*"

*Shame made her eyes burn. Why did she like this?*

*She shouldn't like this.*

"*Right here, Lilly. This is why you keep coming back to me.*" *His other hand gripped her hair, jerking her head up.* "*This is why you're mine.*"

Lilly woke up startled, a cold sweat lacing her skin. Shaking, she pulled the covers back and tried to catch her breath. Rumbles cuddled closer, and she scratched his fur, attempting to ground herself in the present.

Thursday. It was Thursday, and she needed to get to work.

She was still unsettled when she got off the T. She walked quickly, the air frigid despite the rising sun. The cold seeped into Lilly's bones, clutching her with icy fingers that held on as tightly as her nightmares did.

She pulled off her headphones at the corner and looked at the towering wall of glass in front of her. The law offices of Forrester, Schaeffer and Pierce were located in the tallest building in Boston. Appropriate, given it was the city's biggest firm. Cassie was waiting at the coffee cart out front. She motioned Lilly over and handed her a cup as they walked inside.

"We've gotta move. Forrester wants us in the conference room."

"Us? Meaning me too?"

"Apparently."

That couldn't be good. They needed to get up there fast, or their boss would be sending out a search party. Or having security dump their things in the lobby.

They hurried into the elevator, and Lilly's phone chirped with a text. She read the message and dropped the phone back in her bag.

"What was that?"

"Nothing. Just Nick reminding me I can't back out of going to the pub tomorrow night."

"How about I go too?" Cassie suggested with a bright smile. "I'll stick by your side and make sure no cocky third years try to ply you with tequila shots."

"So protective. Must be the Latina in you."

"Half," Cassie reminded her, the same way she corrected Gabe when he poked fun at her for lapsing into her mother's native tongue. She pushed Lilly's hair away from her face, the mothering gesture part of the role she'd taken on when they became friends, even though she was only ten years Lilly's senior. "You can't stay home forever, you know."

"I know." She knew she couldn't. It was just so much easier that way.

Gabe was waiting when the elevator door opened. Lilly yanked off her coat as they raced toward the glass-enclosed conference room.

"What's Forrester on the warpath about this morning?"

"A new case," Gabe replied. "And from the way he's acting, it's a big one."

Lilly slid into a chair and pressed her fingers against her hot coffee cup. William Forrester entered the room a moment later, his forehead lifting with the ever-present accusing tilt of his eyebrows.

"Holbrook Laboratories. Our newest client." He dropped a thick maroon folder on the table. "Simon Holbrook is a scientist who's discovered a new way to test blood, making pre-screenings for diseases more accurate. However, his former employers at Giordano Diagnostics claim he stole the formula from them."

"Giordano?" Gabe asked, reaching for the folder.

"Salvatore and Francesca Giordano. Alleged members of the Lombardo family."

"Lombardo," Lilly repeated. "As in Antonio Lombardo? The Godfather of Boston mafia?"

Forrester nodded. "He's their uncle."

Gabe grinned so wide that Lilly had to stifle a laugh. He loved mobster movies. This case was right up his alley.

"Mr. Holbrook is concerned," Forrester continued as he began pacing around the room. "He claims he didn't steal the formula, and contacted us after receiving a cease and desist. But he doesn't have a great deal of money."

"Then he probably can't afford us," Gabe said. "Why are we taking this on?"

"Because I decided this was a noble cause and offered our services at a discounted rate." He halted at the window. "And because Giordano Diagnostics is represented by Charles Mahoney."

"There it is," Gabe sang.

Confused, Lilly leaned toward Cassie and asked quietly, "Who is Charles Mahoney?"

"He's Forrester's arch nemesis from law school," she whispered back. "We've never lost a case to him."

That explained it. Pro bono work was not exactly the firm's top priority.

"We're starting on this immediately. Ms. Sterling—" Lilly immediately straightened up as Forrester pivoted around to face her. "I want you to work closely with Ms. Allbright and Mr. Hartley on this."

It was a good thing their boss was focused directly on Lilly. It meant Gabe's eye roll at the use of his and Cassie's last names went by unnoticed.

"There's a great deal of information to sort through," Forrester added. "I have a feeling your knack for detail will be a valuable asset."

"Of course," she replied. It was the first time he'd acknowledged her skills. This was going to be her trial run, a chance for her to prove she'd been worth hiring. "Thank you, Mr. Forrester. I won't let you down."

"See that you don't. I have a meeting now, and I'm sure you're all eager to get started."

Forrester left the room without another word. Gabe rubbed his hands together.

"Get your game faces on, ladies," he said. "We're going to the suitcases."

Cassie narrowed her eyes at him. "The line is 'the mattresses', Gabe."

"Suitcases, mattresses, potato, potahto."

There was pure joy on his face at Cassie's scowl. Intentionally screwing up movie lines was Gabe's favorite way of irritating her.

Lilly shook her head and reached for the file.

* * *

They were still sitting there hours later. Gabe leaned back in his chair and stretched. "I'm starving. You two want to grab some lunch from that new Italian place?"

"Has the paint even dried at this one yet?" Cassie asked with a shake of her head. "You've really missed your calling as a mob-movie-obsessed food critic."

"You ladies know I'm a slut for innovative cuisine."

*"Dirty fucking slut."*

Lilly winced, suddenly nauseous. She took a shaky breath and stared at the floor.

Cassie moved in front of her, making a show of reaching for her purse. "Why don't you go ahead and get a table, Gabe. We just need to freshen up. Meet you there in a bit." When he'd left the room, she bent down next to Lilly's chair. "What happened?"

"Nothing." There were a lot of things Cassie knew about her past. The word that had been used to demean and humiliate her wasn't one of them.

Cassie didn't budge. "Damien hasn't tried to find you again, has he?"

Lilly's stomach lurched, the same way it did last November when Damien's name appeared in her personal inbox for the first time in months. Staring at the message as if it were something poisonous, she'd deleted it without reading, then immediately ditched her account and opened a new one. She made sure he was blocked on Facebook, checking her privacy settings for the umpteenth time. And even though she'd changed her phone number once already, she did it again. Cassie was the one who found her in the office bathroom afterward, splashing water over her tearstained cheeks.

The simple question of "Who was he?" had opened the floodgates.

She'd given Cassie the highlights, needing to confess it to *someone*. Cassie hadn't known the lofty expectations Lilly had grown up with, and hoped her new friend wouldn't judge her too hard for her failure.

She hadn't said a word, only dried Lilly's tears and told her she understood. Now Cassie was the single person who knew why Lilly hadn't taken the bar, and exactly what she and Damien Brooks were to one another.

"No," Lilly admitted quietly. "Not since the email on my birthday."

"Okay. Just checking." Cassie stood and nodded toward the door. "You want to eat? Italian does sound good."

"I'm not hungry."

"I'll grab you something and stash it in the fridge?"

Lilly nodded and forced a smile until Cassie reluctantly left the room. Then she took a deep breath and went back to work.

# 4

*J*ack had just gotten home Thursday afternoon when his phone rang. He answered, not bothering with a greeting.

"Not planning on chickening out, are you?" Patrick asked.

He'd hoped Patrick would forget about his nefarious Friday night plans for him.

It didn't look like that was working out.

"I guess not. What the hell am I supposed to wear, anyway?"

"It's not the senior prom, Jack. Just find some clothes and put them on."

"Thanks, asshole."

"No problem. See you tomorrow."

Jack pocketed his phone and sighed. The liquor cabinet beckoned, seductive with its ability to drown out the past. Staying away from it was nearly impossible, but he had work in the morning, and didn't have the luxury of showing up to his own classes hungover.

Forcing himself in the other direction, Jack walked down the hall and was drawn toward another vice—a door that had been closed for a long time. The one leading down to his basement, and the playroom.

Jack laid a hand on it. Converting their basement into an apartment and renting it out was what got them through the years when he was in law school, living off Eve's teacher salary with an infant to feed. They stopped needing the extra income by the time Josh was a teenager, and once he'd left for college Jack and Eve meandered down there, needing a different space than their bedroom to fall into their newly found roles.

They only played on weekends, leaving behind the titles of husband and wife to become "Master" and "love". She showed him what true submission was, allowing him to let loose his most perverse desires. When her stubborn streak came through in occasionally defiant responses, he'd discipline her by tying her up and whispering everything she liked in graphic detail until she was ravenous for him. She was able to read him so clearly, perfectly anticipating his needs, and she never needed to safeword because Jack knew her so well. He had to; he was her protector, after all.

But he couldn't protect her from cancer. Or death.

She'd been willing to play after the disease hit, when the radiation made her honey locks wither down the shower drain. Apart from the gentle, easy sound of her laugh, Eve's hair was Jack's favorite thing about her. He'd barely been able to keep it together when the last of it fell out, or when a gentle spanking left welts on her skin that wouldn't heal. And even then, she'd been the one to lament her failing body's reaction.

She amazed him every single day. How was he supposed to fulfill her dying wish when the only thing he wanted was to have her by his side again?

He turned around and pulled out his phone. Patrick was only trying to help, but he couldn't do this. He'd just started to dial when his doorbell rang. Jack glanced down the hallway. His niece Allegra was waving at him through the glass window by the front door.

"Hi, Uncle Jack!" she said when he opened it. "We're here with your dinners."

Out on the driveway, Samantha was pulling several tinfoil containers from the back of their Jeep. His weekly meal drop-off was often accompanied by impromptu visits from his brother's clan.

"That's great. How's the fourth grade going?"

"Good. My spelling bee is tomorrow." She clasped her hands together, bringing them beneath her chin. "Say you'll come, please?"

Relief flooded through Jack, happy to trade a night at a bar for one filled with family.

"Of course Uncle Jack will come," Brady said before Jack could answer, walking toward them with his other daughter, Hope, in his arms. She was six, but Brady could have lifted both his children in the same arm with ease. "That way he can't say no to going out with me afterward."

Jack's shoulders slumped. "Patrick called you."

"Hell yeah, he did."

Allegra gasped. "Daddy, you said hell."

"Shh," he said as he let Hope down and glanced over his shoulder, no doubt to make sure Samantha hadn't caught another one of his frequent slips of bad language in front of the children. "Go inside and wash up."

The girls stomped snow off their shoes before running down the hall.

"So you're in, yes?" he asked Jack. "Barrel 'n' Flask, home of babes, beer and basketball. I can't wait to watch Patrick work that scene" Brady's dimples showed with his wistful smile. "The eternal bachelor. He's got the *life*, man."

Jack shook his head. Thirty-five years old with a steady job and family who loved him, and Brady had no idea how good he had it.

"The grass is always greener, little brother."

They filed inside, and Allegra asked everyone to test her spelling while they ate. When the meal was finished, the girls colored in the kitchen as Samantha started on the dishes.

Brady scraped his fork against the remnants of pie on his plate. "Heard from Josh lately?"

"Not since Christmas. School is keeping him busy."

"Your side sure did get the brains of the family."

"That's not true."

"It is. After all, you're the one Dad sent to Harvard and recruited to his firm, not me."

"And I'm the one who left the corporate life to teach, while you became the boss of a huge IT company."

"True. So why is it that with all my technical know-how, I can't get you to use Facebook once in a while? Your last status update was in August."

As if Jack cared about that. "I'll work on it."

"You're a shitty liar."

Sam yelled something from the kitchen about him watching his mouth. Brady snickered silently and carved out a second piece of pie, his appetite as endless as it had been when he was spending all his time being a quarterback instead of staring at lines of code.

Jack watched him swallow a mouthful the size of his fist. "I don't know how you can take bites that big without choking."

"Practice. So, pick you up at five tomorrow? I'll be designated."

It was an artful suggestion, offering to drive so Jack could drink. It also meant he wouldn't be able to duck out early when Patrick started lining up the women like planes on their final approach into Logan.

"There's no getting out of this, is there?"

"It's no big deal, Jack. It'll just be us, Nick, Gabe, his sister and one of his co-workers."

"A night out with my philandering best friend, my little brother and friends," Jack grumbled. "Can't wait."

* * *

A day later, Jack found himself entering a noisy pub on the outskirts of Fenway. He steeled himself as they stepped inside. Baseball season was months away but the pub was packed anyway, the games on the flat screens loud and the conversations even louder, ricocheting off the brick walls and cherry wood tables. They found Patrick at the bar, clearly several drinks in.

"I thought you were my wingman tonight," Jack said. Not that he was complaining. He'd get through this quicker if his friend was too drunk to make good on his promise.

Patrick raised his glass. "Flying toasted makes it more of a challenge."

"Hold up, did someone say wingman?" Brady asked. "I thought we were just getting some beers. What am I missing?"

"We are going to get your brother a date tonight."

"For real?" Brady looked to Jack, then responded with a hesitant, "O-kay."

Jack ordered a draft and knocked back a heavy gulp as two women squeezed next to them. Patrick offered to buy them a round of shots, but they seemed to only have eyes for Brady. When he apologized with a flash of his wedding ring, they pouted and turned away. Patrick began working his magic on another pair, and Jack tried to participate in the conversation, but the words *I don't want to be here* were beating a chorus in his head.

They moved on and Patrick glowered at him. "You want to put in a little effort?"

"Sorry."

"Bullshit. You're not even trying."

"Ease up, Patrick," Brady said. "He's here at least, right?"

"Barely."

Jack pushed back from the bar. "I need some air."

He walked away with the intention of merely stepping outside, but the entryway was so thick with people he could barely muscle his way through the crowd.

Screw this. He didn't want to be here. And he was going the fuck back home.

Jack started to reach for his phone, planning to text Patrick and Brady that he was getting a cab when something a few feet away stopped him—a shock of blonde hair, long and curling at the ends. His breath caught. For a moment he wasn't sure if what he was seeing was real. She looked so much like Eve once did it was eerie. He knew he was staring, but he couldn't stop, not even when the young woman's gaze shifted and met his. She blinked rapidly before looking away. Her stare slowly crept back, though, and when their eyes met again, her cheeks colored with a rosy flush.

Fuck.

A spark kindled in Jack's belly, his body awakening with needs he thought all but dead. The hint of a fantasy ignited, his mind tripping over itself like a cold engine starting after a long winter. Dormant for so long under a cloak of grief, his sex drive roared to life. The attraction was intense and unexpected.

She broke the connection when a brunette linked arms with her and led her through the crowd. Forcing himself not to look to where she'd gone, Jack returned to the bar.

"You get your air?" Patrick asked.

"Yeah," Jack lied.

Brady slapped a twenty on the bar. "Great. Next round is on me."

From behind them, someone said, "You always were ready to foot the bill for a keg."

Jack turned around as Brady's friend Nick pulled him in for a one-armed hug. Brady slapped him on the back and motioned to Patrick.

"Patrick, this is Nick Sterling, my buddy from college. He's a hotshot photographer now. Nick, meet Patrick Dunham. He works in publishing and has slept with half the women in Boston." Patrick saluted at the joke before Brady put a hand on Jack's shoulder. "And of course, you remember my brother, Jack."

They'd met once long ago when the boys were in college. He vaguely recalled seeing Nick at Eve's funeral. Jack braced himself, waiting for the inevitable questions about how he'd been doing, but all Brady's friend did was smile.

"Of course, it's good to see you. Gabe went to find a table. You want to join us?"

"Oh thanks, but—"

Patrick picked up his glass and stood. "We'd love to. There's a redhead by the dartboard who needs some attention."

Jack sighed and followed behind them, twin flags of dread and desire planting themselves in his stomach when he located the blonde again. She'd taken off her coat, revealing a skirt and sweater that clung to her body in all the right places, her legs endlessly long.

He ground his jaw. Jesus fucking Christ.

"So, Jack, how are classes going?"

Nick's question shook Jack out of his stupor. He cleared his throat, trying to get the blood to rush back to his brain and not about three feet south of there.

"They're all right so far," he said, his eyes still on the blonde and the table she was sitting at. The table they were, without a doubt, walking toward.

Nick stopped just shy of her chair and smiled. "Let me introduce you around: my husband Gabriel Hartley, and his associate Cassandra Allbright."

They waved. Jack gave an abrupt nod back.

"And this—" Nick tugged on a lock of the blonde's hair. Jack's heart started to pound as she turned and looked up. "—is my little sister, Lilly."

5

—————

*J*ack's eyes locked with Lilly's. Her golden hair and creamy skin were the same as Eve's, but that was where their similarities ended. Her eyes were hazel, more green than brown, and dark around the irises. Her face was full and heart-shaped, her cheeks dusted with freckles. With her arms wrapped around her middle, she seemed nervous and guarded—not at all like the confident woman his wife was.

And she looked young. Very young.

God, the first woman he'd found attractive, and she was his brother's best friend's little sister.

"It's nice to meet you," he managed to say.

She offered him a small smile. "Likewise."

"Lilly Sterling, in the flesh," Brady called out, barreling past Jack. "I thought Nick was lying about you moving here, since we never see you."

She laughed, a short, tight sound. "I've been busy working."

Nick turned to Jack, beaming proudly. "She's a paralegal, a graduate of Northwestern School of Law. And a bit of a workaholic."

She made a face. "Takes one to know one. At least I see the light of day once in a while."

29

"Darkrooms are supposed to be dark." Nick tugged on Lilly's hair again, and she playfully shoved him off.

Brady jerked a thumb at Jack. "My brother's a workaholic too. He's a big shot Harvard Law professor."

"Harvard," Lilly said. "Wow."

Jack caught something in her gaze, something like admiration, or even attraction. Maybe she wasn't as young as he thought. She'd graduated law school, which meant she was at least old enough to be in her mid-twenties.

The relief he felt over that needed to vanish. Now.

He turned to look for Patrick, finding him with that redhead in his lap. Resigned to being here for a while, Jack pulled out a chair and kept his eyes locked on the television. The Celtics' point guard missed a shot, and the crowd around them exploded into jeers. Then, across from him, Gabe said, "Three, two, one..."

Nick groaned and buried his face in his hands.

"You drunk already?" Brady asked.

"No. It's this gallery opening," Gabe answered for him. "He's worried it's going to be a bust." He put his arm around Nick. "You've got to stop this. Your stuff is great."

Lilly nudged her brother and smiled. "He's right. I don't know why you can't see what we all see in you."

Nick lifted his head and bumped his shoulder against hers. "I could say the same about you."

Her grin faded and she looked down at her lap. Her sudden unease was so apparent Jack was surprised no one else at the table noticed it.

*Drink your beer. Watch the game. Stop staring at her.*

"I appreciate your votes of confidence. I expect you all to buy my most expensive pieces," Nick said, then nodded as Gabe pointed to someone on the other side of the room. "There's a rep over there I need to mingle with. Be right back."

After Nick stood and stepped away, Brady hopped into his empty seat. "So, Lilly. You enjoying Boston so far?"

She smiled, but it didn't reach her eyes. "I haven't seen much of the city. Work takes up most of my time."

"Have you always wanted to be a lawyer?"

"Since you guys were in college. Since..." She waved a hand toward where her brother had gone.

"Since our dipshit teammates tried to beat the crap out of Nick?" he asked. Lilly nodded, and some of Brady's usual teasing manner melted away. His jaw went rigid. "I still kick myself for not pushing him to press charges."

Jack remembered what had happened to Nick years ago. He'd always been proud of what Brady did. It was the first time Jack had seen him as a man instead of his kid brother.

A second later, however, Brady's dimpled smile returned. "But I guess one good thing came out of it, right? Turned you into one of those optimistic types who wants to help people? Right the wrongs of the world?"

She gave a slight laugh. "Pretty much."

Cassie leaned in. "She's the best paralegal around. Crazy organized. Never misses a detail."

Lilly's lips turned up in a shy smile as she ducked her head. "I like the research," she said. "Catching the things no one else finds. It's like solving a puzzle."

"Then why haven't you become a lawyer like the rest of these clowns?"

Lilly paled slightly and shoved her hand into her hair. "I just decided not to take the bar yet. After graduation, I wasn't sure I was ready to make the commitment."

Something didn't match up. Her casual tone wasn't meshing with her body language. Jack wondered what she was trying to hide, but she seemed so uncomfortable that he was overcome with an instinctual need to protect her, to make her feel safe.

"Not everyone who goes to law school becomes a lawyer," he said. "I'm an example of that."

Lilly glanced up, confusion barely hiding the pain in her eyes.

"Yeah, Jack thought being a lawyer was overrated," Brady said. "He was the youngest attorney to make partner at our dad's firm, but he turned it down for Harvard."

Jack shrugged. "I'm more comfortable in the classroom than the courtroom, so I teach."

"What subjects?" Cassie asked.

"Finance and trade. The corporate life wasn't for me."

That changed the topic of conversation. Gabe and Cassie began to reminisce about their finance classes in law school, and Brady turned his attention to the game. Lilly's hand was still buried in her hair, but her eyes had become clearer. Brighter. Her chin dipped in a silent thank you. Jack gave her the tiniest shake of his head in return, but as the seconds dragged on he didn't look away and neither did she. There was something irresistible about her inability to break their link, and it made him crave more. He wanted to keep her like that, to make her hold his gaze a beat longer, to coax that blush back to her face.

Jack watched her intently until she released her grip on her hair, her hands sliding into her lap. Blinking rapidly, she swallowed, and then her cheeks rushed with color. It was the reaction Jack was waiting for—expected, somehow, and he felt a surge of victory. He chuckled softly, which only seemed to make Lilly's blush deepen even further.

Then Nick returned to the table, and reality hit Jack like a cold shower.

"Did I miss anything?"

Brady vacated the seat next to Lilly, letting Nick take his spot back. "Nah. Just boring lawyer conversation."

Jack stared at his beer, the rush he'd felt instantly shorting out. He shouldn't have been looking at Lilly like that, shouldn't have tried to entice anything from her youthful face. She could only be in her twenties, and he was barely out of mourning. Was he going straight from grief into a fucking midlife crisis?

The redhead in Patrick's lap let out a loud giggle. Patrick pushed her to her feet and stood, grinning devilishly as he towed her toward the table.

"Hey, everyone. Sorry I didn't get to say hello."

Patrick wasn't remorseful. If anything, he was sorry he had to make niceties before taking his conquest home.

"I'd love to stay and chat, but I think...Lisa and I are going to call it a night."

He looked at the redhead for verification, as if to make sure he'd gotten her name right. She gave him a hungry smile in return. Jack wanted that same look on Lilly's face. To see her eyes grow wide. To see the color rise on her cheeks again, and peel off the layers she'd wrapped around herself.

He needed to get the hell out of here.

"I think I'm ready to head out too," he said, giving Brady a look that said he'd had enough for one night.

"Actually I'm pretty tired," Lilly said, a silent exchange passing between her and Nick before he agreed to take her and Cassie home. They settled up, and Jack kept his distance from Lilly as he led the pack, his eyes on Brady's Jeep.

"I say we make this a tradition," Brady bellowed when they reached the curb. The wind whipped at their faces, the towering presence of Fenway doing nothing to block its assault. "Friday nights by the Green Monster. Who's in?"

Nick wrapped an arm around Gabe. "We are."

"Me too," Cassie added, then raised her eyebrows at Lilly.

"Sure," she said. "Sounds good."

Brady hooted and unlocked the car. "Jack?"

Jack didn't look up as he opened the passenger door. "I'm not sure yet. I'll let you know." It wasn't a good idea to be back here next week, not after whatever had just happened.

He sat down and slammed the door, waiting for Brady to get him as far away from Lilly as possible.

# 6

---

*L*illy climbed into the backseat of Nick's car and watched Brady's Jeep disappear around the corner. Her pulse was racing, her joints loose-fitting somehow, her limbs flushed with an odd combination of bonelessness and excitement that started when Jack locked her in his gaze. For those few seconds, she felt safe, but imprisoned somehow too.

She'd never felt anything like it.

Cassie sat down next to her. "You okay?"

Lilly blinked a few times, trying to break out of the bizarre fog she was in. "Yup. Totally fine."

She looked out the windshield as Nick started to drive, compelled to seek out Brady's car again, but she couldn't make it out. It blended in with the mass of taillights underneath the neon colors of Boston's famous Citgo sign. She leaned back and sighed. It wasn't as if Jack had paid her any interest. He'd barely talked to her at all. Then again, he didn't speak to anyone until that moment when he saved her from the spotlight, taking the group's attention onto himself.

Cassie reached over and squeezed her hand. "Hey, how about I hang out at your place for a bit? You look like you could use some company."

"Okay," she replied, but her mind was still on Jack's stormy gray-blue eyes, so intense and yet so gentle. There'd been a few lines stamped around them and a sprinkling of gray in his sandy blond hair, but those signs of age had only made him more attractive.

Lilly shook her head. She needed to stop thinking about him, and that *look* they shared. It seemed to mean something, as did the half smile he gave her afterward, which vanished as quickly as it came. She was probably imagining things. And she wasn't interested anyway. In him, or anyone else.

Once Nick had dropped them off and they entered her apartment, Rumbles pranced toward them, rubbing against their legs. Cassie bent down to scratch his head.

"You want to watch a movie?"

"Sure. You choose." Lilly sank down on the couch and handed over the remote. Cassie picked a romantic comedy, and Lilly tried to watch but she couldn't focus. She missed half the jokes before they'd gotten halfway through.

Cassie turned it off. "Okay, that's it. Spill."

"What do you mean?"

"Don't try to play me. You're totally out of it." Cassie narrowed her eyes, as shrewd as if she were questioning a witness. "You're telling me the truth, right? Damien hasn't tried to worm his way back into your life?"

Lilly winced, a sudden burning path of acid slicing up her throat. She picked at the seams of the couch. "He's engaged, remember? He doesn't need to talk to me."

Cassie fell back against the cushion with a huff. "I can't believe he called to tell you he was getting married the night before the freaking bar. I mean, who does that?"

Lilly tried to reply, but the words got stuck in her throat. It had been Damien's final act of cruelty, the runner-up to breaking things off on her graduation day. She hadn't known what to make of his call at first, but there was some small, stupid part of her that hoped he missed her. Wanted her. Needed her. She'd never anticipated his news or the way he seemed to be baiting her with it, gauging her response—testing her, like he always had. All she could do was utter her congratulations before ending the call.

But it wasn't Damien's announcement that made her skip the bar. It was what happened afterward that truly destroyed her.

"Selfish assholes do that."

Cassie snorted. "True. Thank God you'll never have to be in a relationship like that again."

"Never," Lilly agreed, but the word mocked her. It was a fallacy she felt every morning, after her nightmares looped into her fantasies before shifting back into shame.

After a quick hug, Cassie saw herself out with a promise to call tomorrow. Lilly made her way to her bed and tried to sleep, but the angry dreams came like they always did.

*"You seem so sweet. So innocent." Damien coiled his hand around her hair and pulled. Hard.*

Lilly sat up and put her head in her hands, but the recollection of the first night he took her home with him lingered like a ghost— the sensation of his fingers against her scalp, and the way he looked at her, lust in his sharp green eyes.

*"Anyone ever done that to you before?" he whispered, his words hot, naked and treacherous.*

*"No."*

*His fingers tightened. It felt so good. So unbelievably, ridiculously good.*

*"Sir," he said, the veiled threat in his voice as exciting as it was terrifying. "I want you to say, 'No, Sir.'"*

If only she'd had the sense to recognize how dangerous he was underneath his polished exterior, that she'd never wanted to flirt with the darkness he offered. But she was the dumb, gullible lamb, and he was the wolf, seducing her to her own slaughter. In one night, he answered the question of why sex with other guys was always missing something, his handprints marked on her flesh like a brand. By the next morning she was a junkie craving her next fix.

He'd told her his conditions, and she'd accepted them without a second thought, too hungry for what he could do to her to question why she was never allowed to tell anyone. Too desperate for the way he'd tell her to kneel and make her beg, then reward her by turning her inside out with pleasure.

Too trusting in him to wonder if he was being honest when he said, "*This is what good submissives do.*"

For a year she followed his rules, always remembering to address him as Sir in private, despite the way he kept his distance in public. Despite how he'd always abandon her after the passion ended, locking the bathroom door to shower while she was left to the cold confusion of empty sheets.

She'd been so fucking naïve, believing she was his. No matter how many times Damien called her *mine*, it was a ruse, a line that snapped the second their play was over. Lilly knew better now, enough to know there was nothing to love about being submissive. All it meant was that you could be humiliated, used and thrown away.

She burrowed deep beneath the blankets, praying for a dreamless sleep.

That world wasn't for her and never would be again.

---

## 7

*C*ampus was busy despite the early sunset, students spilling out of lecture halls and dorms, their conversations carrying across the snow-covered quads. With his office door closed, Jack was able to block out the noise, which would've been excellent, if he'd been able to concentrate worth a damn.

He pulled off his glasses and rubbed his eyes, but it only made his recollection of Lilly's face even clearer. It was more than physical attraction that had her on his mind the last few days—there was also a curiosity he couldn't smother. A desire to unravel her, to know more about the past she seemed to need to keep hidden. But she was far too young, and he had no business thinking anything about her. He wouldn't be seeing her again, anyway. He'd already made the decision not to go to the pub this Friday.

Problem solved.

He reopened his eyes as a rap sounded on the door.

"Office hours aren't until Thursday," he said, but the door swung open anyway, revealing Patrick with a wide grin, his tennis bag slung over his shoulder.

"I'm going to have to meet you here before our games more often. I never realized how many Ivy League girls are looking for a sophisticated older man."

"If they were looking for sophisticated, they wouldn't be talking to you," Jack said. Patrick flipped him the bird. "Did you come here to hit on my students, or to be a pain in my ass?"

"Both." Patrick plunked down into one of the chairs. "You still working?"

"Noticed that, did you?"

"Well, get it out of the way now. Free up your weekend hours for the pub."

"I'm not going."

Patrick waved off his rebuttal. "So you didn't score. This week will be better."

"Repeating the process won't make it any more of a success. There was no one there I wanted to talk to."

"No one."

"Yup. You saw me. Total waste of time."

"Yeah, I saw you." Patrick paused. "That Lilly was a cute one."

Jack flashed him a warning glare.

"What? You were looking at her."

"And how would you have noticed, since you spent the night with your face in Lisa's breasts?" Jack asked. Patrick smiled proudly. "She's ancient history now, I assume?"

He snorted. "Duh."

Jack gathered his papers into a pile and sighed. "Fine. Yes, Lilly was...cute, but she's Nick's little sister and probably not much older than Josh. So you're dropping the subject. I'm not going, and that's final."

"You have an entirely overdeveloped sense of morals, my friend."

He was about to say something about exactly how underdeveloped Patrick's morals were when his cell rang. Jack looked at the screen, both shocked and thrilled at who was calling.

He hit send. "You must be calling to ask me for money."

There was a familiar laugh on the other end. "No, Dad, I'm not."

"Sure, sure."

Patrick's eyes lit up. "Is that Josh?" he asked. Jack nodded. "Put him on speaker."

Jack shook his head, but Patrick angled an arm out, nearly snatching the phone from his hand.

"You're a dick," he mouthed. "Patrick is here. He wants to say hi." He hit speakerphone and put the phone down on his desk.

"Hey, runt," Patrick said. "It's a good thing you finally called. I was going to tell your father to cut off your tuition."

"I haven't been avoiding him, I promise. This program is kicking my ass," Josh insisted. "But I had to call when I saw what Uncle Brady said on Facebook. Dad, were you actually out at a bar last weekend?"

"I was." Jack shifted to face his computer and opened a browser. "Why?"

He waited for judgment, for the words *have you forgotten about Mom already?* but Josh only laughed. "There's no 'why', Dad. I'm just happy to see you out."

Jack navigated to Brady's page and read his status from Friday: "*Kicking it old school style at Barrel 'n' Flask! A good time was had by all.*"

He'd tagged everyone who was out that night, including Lilly.

"Did you have fun?" Josh asked, but Jack was distracted, his mouse hovering over the link to Lilly's profile. He should've ignored the impulse to learn more about her, but the chance to peek into her life was too enticing.

He clicked on the link, the simple act feeling strangely illicit, but her profile was private. All he saw was a photo of her in graduation garb, her cowl in Northwestern's purple and gold. She should've looked happy, but her smile seemed forced. As if it hurt her to even try.

*What happened to you?*

"Dad?"

"He had a great time!" Patrick answered. "We're going again on Friday."

Jack glowered at Patrick, but it was too late. He sat back in his chair, smug.

"That's awesome," Josh said. "Man, talk about role reversal. You're out at a bar while I'm stuck in the library all the time."

Jack quickly closed the browser. "You're working hard. I'm proud of you."

"Thanks," Josh said. "On that note, I've got to get back to studying. Sorry."

"That's okay. I'm glad you called."

"Me too. Hey, Patrick, keep getting my dad out of the house. It's good for him."

Jack yanked the phone from the table, taking it off speaker before Patrick could say anything else. "Don't go another month without calling again, okay?"

"I promise. Love you, Dad."

Jack's throat went tight. "Love you too."

He ended the call and took a breath. Patrick gave him no time to recover before starting in on him.

"Looks like you'll be seeing Lilly again after all. Doctor Archer's orders."

Jack glared at him. "You drive?"

"Took the T."

"Let's go."

Outside, the inky sky was clear, the air a piercing cold. Jack stalked toward his car and wrenched the door open.

"Something crawl up your ass when I wasn't looking?" Patrick asked as they climbed inside.

"You want to back off?"

"See, now this is why Josh wants you to get out more. You're way too uptight—"

"Your version of 'going out' is not what Josh meant. He meant have a few beers, watch a game. He didn't mean stare at a woman half my age."

"At least now you admit you were staring at her."

"Damn it, Patrick. Just leave it alone."

"I'm only trying to do right by you. By what you said Eve wanted."

"This isn't what Eve meant, either."

"And you know what Eve meant."

"Like hell, I do!" Jack gripped the steering wheel until his knuckles turned white. "She wanted me to fall in love again. Not guzzle beer and gawk at a fucking teenager!"

He closed his eyes and waited for his breathing to calm.

Patrick was quiet for a moment. "I'm not going to tell you what I think anymore. You obviously know what you need more than I do, so just come to the bar, have a beer and pretend Lilly doesn't exist."

Jack opened his eyes and started the car. "That's exactly what I'm going to do."

\* \* \*

When they arrived at the pub on Friday, it was even more crowded than the week before. They found Brady playing pool with Nick. Lilly was nowhere in sight. If Jack was lucky, she wouldn't show up at all. He was actually starting to relax when she arrived with Gabe and Cassie. She was dressed in a blouse and a neat, slim skirt that showed off her figure, smoothing over curves that seemed softer and more inviting than he remembered.

*Fucking hell.*

Fine. She could be here, but that didn't mean he had to talk to her, or look her way. He fixed his eyes on the pool table as Nick took his last shot, winning the game.

"There's nowhere to sit tonight?" Cassie lamented. "Can't we go someplace else next week? A place where my shoes won't stick to the floor?"

"Well, you're all coming to my show on Tuesday, right?" Nick asked. He looked over at Cassie. "The floors there are squeaky clean."

"Tuesday?" she asked. "That's Valentine's Day. Won't people be going on actual dates?"

"*You* won't," Gabe teased.

Cassie wrinkled her nose at him. "I'd smack you, if you weren't right."

"The show is called Sex, Love and Bromance," Nick continued. "It's the perfect Valentine's Day outing for couples and singles of any sexual orientation."

"Open bar?" Cassie asked. Nick nodded. "I'm in."

"Good. Brady, you and Sam are coming, right?"

"Already got the babysitter lined up."

Nick looked to Patrick next, who shook his head. "I'll get back to you. I'm not sure about my status yet." He and Brady exchanged fist bumps as Nick turned to Lilly.

"It is a weeknight," she said. "But I guess I can manage to take a night off."

"I'm so honored." Nick stuck his tongue out at her, and she grinned. It was a real smile, full and beautiful.

So much for not looking at her.

"Jack?"

A quick swig of his beer gave him a second to think. Valentine's Day was his wedding anniversary. Last year, he'd spent it with a bottle of scotch. He'd hoped to ignore it this year.

He lowered his drink. His eyes found Lilly's.

"Sure," he said. "Sounds good."

"Great. I'm going to call the gallery owner and give her a headcount." Nick handed Lilly his pool cue. "Play for me? I plan on schooling Brady when I get back."

She looked bewildered for a moment, and then slipped the rod between her fingers, deftly running a block of chalk over the tip. Jack swallowed and tried to focus on the television. On the people around him. On anything but her.

"I've gotta get my game on," Patrick announced. "Next round's on me as long as someone's my wingman."

"Where's the girl you went home with last week?" Cassie asked him.

"Home? Aruba? Afghanistan? How the hell should I know?"

She looked horrified until Brady said, "Patrick never goes out with the same woman twice."

"Wow. You must be running out of options at your age."

"Hey now, don't hate the player—" Brady began, but before he could finish the sentence, Cassie pushed past both of them.

"Hate the chauvinistic pig? I think I will. Now if you'll excuse me, I need the ladies' room."

As she walked off, Jack readied himself for another tour at the bar, but Brady stepped up.

"If you're buying, I'm game," he said to Patrick. "Don't tell Sam I'll do anything for a free beer." Brady offered Jack his cue. "Take my turn. I want that rematch with Nick."

Feeling as if his brother had presented him with a hot poker, Jack took the cue from him and threw a dirty look at Patrick, who smiled and walked away. Jack turned around, but wasn't at all prepared to see Lilly racking the table, her open blouse giving him an enticing glimpse of cleavage peeking out from a lacy white bra.

Christ. Keeping his distance from her was impossible, let alone keeping his eyes off that body, or his mind off what was hidden behind that smile.

When she looked up, however, her smile had vanished.

# 8

---

"*D*o you want to break or should I?" she asked.

"I'm a little rusty. You go for it."

The words "Yes, Sir" formed on her lips, but she managed to clamp her mouth shut before she said them out loud. That would've made things even more awkward, given how obvious it was that Jack was annoyed at being stuck with her.

Well, she was annoyed now too. At him, at how Damien's training was drilled into her, at Nick for dragging her out and then leaving her alone with someone who wouldn't even look her in the eye. God, what an idiot she was for thinking about Jack last week. She smacked the cue ball hard in her frustration, but she knew what she was doing. Her shot sent several balls scattering into various pockets.

"Nice shot," Jack murmured, his tone approving.

Lilly hid her smirk. Pool was a pastime she'd grown up with. Her dad had a table in the basement, and had spent many an evening teaching her and Nick how to hold their own.

"Solids," she declared as she sank another with little effort. When she scored a third time, Jack's eyebrows rose but he remained withdrawn, his lips pressed together in a tight line.

Lilly frowned back. She wasn't about to stand here with him and not say anything at all until the others came back.

"How was your week?" she asked. It wouldn't kill him to talk to her. And a part of her wanted to challenge him. To see if she could dig under that gruff exterior and get a repeat performance of last week's look.

"Busy," he answered.

"Busy's good." Lilly scratched and stepped back. "I like staying busy too."

"I gathered from Nick's comments." Jack put down his drink and began rolling up his sleeves. "How long have you worked at the firm?"

"Six months. How long have you been at Harvard?"

"Fifteen years."

He lined up his shot, and her body went molten at the sight of him stretched out long and lean. Older or not, this man was *fit*. She would've asked if he worked out, but that was a stupid line, and besides, the flexing muscles in his forearms were proof enough that he did something athletic in his downtime. She watched as he pulled his right arm back, and caught a glimpse of a small arc of white that crossed his wrist. It was curved, raised and angry looking. Whatever caused it must have hurt a lot.

Jack scratched, and when he stood, he glanced down to where she was staring. He quickly jerked his sleeve down.

Lilly's cheeks flamed. "I'm sorry. I didn't mean to...I'm sorry."

He looked away, shook his head and let out a heavy exhale. "No, I'm sorry. It's nothing. Just an old injury."

She blinked, oddly soothed once again by the soft cadence of his voice. It curled around her like a ribbon, making her knees go a little rubbery. A moment passed before Jack filled the silence.

"So," he said. "Quite a change, coming from Illinois to Boston."

"It was, but I needed to get away."

Her sudden honestly surprised her. She blamed his voice and that weird, wobbly feeling in her legs.

Scanning the table for her next move, she asked, "Have you lived here long?"

"Massachusetts, born and bred. We moved from Springfield to Boston when Brady was little. He's been following me around ever since."

"We younger siblings are the worst, aren't we?" she asked, happy to feel the conversation shift into more comfortable topics. "I was like that with Nick. I'd chase him everywhere."

"My wife once joked that Brady would've come with us on our honeymoon if he could."

Lilly's stomach plummeted. "You're married?"

Jack cleared his throat. Seconds felt like hours. "I *was* married. She passed away."

An odd mix of relief and sadness filled the void in her belly. "I didn't know." She peered up at him. "Can I ask what happened?"

"Cancer."

The grief on his face made her heart ache. "I'm sorry."

"Thanks." He took a breath and exhaled heavily again. "So, why the no-go on the bar exam?"

Lilly stiffened, her muscles going rigid. "It's like I said last week. I'm not sure I want to be a lawyer," she said, hoping he'd drop the subject.

He didn't.

"And yet you apparently have the reputation of a workaholic." Jack looked at her quizzically, as if she were a puzzle piece he was trying to fit. "Something must have happened to change your mind."

*"Did you actually fool yourself into thinking I belonged to you?"*

Hot tears pricked at her eyes. Lilly looked at the floor.

Jack moved next to her. "Did something happen?"

His voice was so warm and calming. It brought her back to the present and anchored her there. "Yes," she whispered.

"Can you tell me about it?" he asked, but she shook her head. "Lilly, look at me."

His tone hadn't changed, but the timbre of his words echoed with a strength and confidence she couldn't place. Without thinking, she looked up at him, and found herself unable to move, locked in his stare.

"Whatever's haunting you, you need to let it go. I know a thing or two about being chained to your past, and it's no way to live." His gaze drifted over her like a caress. "Don't be like that. You're too beautiful to be so sad."

For a second, she couldn't remember how to breathe. "Thank you," she said softly.

"You're welcome." He was looking at her so intently it almost made her feel naked. "I have to ask—how old are you?"

"Twenty-eight. Why? How old are you?"

"Forty-four."

She smiled, happy to finally have that question answered. Jack smiled back and raised an eyebrow, his expression playful. "Does that bother you?"

"No—" *Sir.*

Shit, she'd almost said it again.

Lilly's face rushed with heat, and Jack's eyes grew hooded. His gaze traced her cheeks, the shape of her nose, her lips, slow and deliberate, before meeting hers again. He licked his upper lip, and that slip of tongue made Lilly's breathing quicken. She imagined what his mouth would feel like on her neck, if his stubble would rasp against her skin. The thought made her lick her own lip in response. It was a move Jack caught, and suddenly his gaze was no longer mischievous.

It was hungry.

"Geez, you'd think they'd have more than two stalls in this place," Cassie announced, returning to the table.

Her arrival broke their connection. Jack quickly stepped away.

Lilly faced the pool table again, feeling like she'd lost a chance at something. She wanted it back again, even though her flying heartbeat told her that *something* might be better off left alone.

* * *

Jack closed his front door and leaned against it, as if doing so could shut out what he'd felt tonight. As if it could shut Lilly out. He'd wanted to murder Patrick for leaving him alone with her, and yet, during that short time, he'd forgotten how for the last year it had hurt to do anything more than breathe.

Hearing she was at least older than Josh was a small comfort. His age, however, seemed of no consequence. He'd thought she hadn't read anything into the question, that the attraction that was driving him out of his mind was all one-sided, but Lilly's blush said otherwise. As did the quick pass of her soft, pink tongue over gorgeously full lips.

Jack groaned and scrubbed his hands over his face, then looked at his scar. He could only imagine what Lilly would think if she knew where it came from, what kind of life he'd lived. The Dominant he once was.

He closed his eyes and saw Eve in their playroom, the two of them beginning their scene with practiced words.

*"You are mine, love."*

*"I am yours, always, Master."*

Grief shouted from the past. But the image was quickly replaced with one of Lilly looking up at him in the bar. How would she react if he ordered her to strip for him? Would all of her skin bloom with the rosy hues he'd seen on her cheeks? Jack's mind traveled to a place where he had her bound and naked, telling her to bare everything to him—body, mind and soul.

Realizing where his thoughts had strayed, he tried to shut the fantasy down but it was too late. Lilly had flipped a switch in him, waking the part that had been buried under the ashes of Eve's death. And now that he'd opened that door, he didn't know how to close it again.

## 9

*I*t was late into the afternoon on Valentine's Day when Lilly finally glanced up at the clock. She'd been staring at her computer screen for so long she could still see lines of text before her eyes.

She'd spent the day poring over the Giordanos' laboratory database. It contained a ton of information—months of data from the company that hosted their logs. It was nothing more than an internal logging system, but after hours looking at it, she felt like she'd taken the LSAT in Hungarian.

Lilly studied the column containing the random lines of numbers she'd been pondering all afternoon. It bugged her, not being able to figure out what they stood for. There were about ten numbers on each line, too long to be dates or social security numbers. The column was titled "MOD_dt", which she'd tried googling, but everything she found was technical garbage.

Frustrated, Lilly turned toward the window. Snowflakes were falling softly, white laced with pink from the waning sun. Across the cement horizon, Cambridge and the redbrick buildings of Harvard camped against the Charles River Basin.

It made her think of Jack, and how he'd looked at her with burning eyes and told her she was beautiful. She'd barely been able to think about anything else since. The way he stuck in her thoughts was a complete mystery to her, as was her reaction when he told her to look at him. She'd obeyed his command without thinking. Damien had ingrained that response in her, but she didn't know why Jack triggered the impulse. He'd confirmed his age, so it must have been his older, more powerful presence that caused it. Nothing more to it than that.

She picked up the dress hanging from the back of her cubicle and headed to the ladies' room to change, slipping the sheath over her head. The fitted, ruched fabric clung to her body, a lover in the form of a little black dress. It hugged her shoulders and stretched out along her collarbone, the hem licking above her knees.

The dress reminded her of what it was like to feel sexy and strong. Confident.

It had been a splurge—a reward for procuring the summer associate position at Damien's firm. She'd worn it the night he and her colleagues took her out for drinks to celebrate. Later that night, it was in a ball on his bedroom floor.

The sharp tang of memory made Lilly cringe. She could've worn something else tonight, but the dress fit the event, and she wanted to wear it. Maybe if she did, she'd be able to find that confident version of herself again.

Downstairs, Lilly flagged a cab. She texted Cassie that she was on her way during the ride over to Newbury Street and the row of brownstones where Nick's gallery opening was, but didn't get a reply. When the driver pulled up to the curb, Lilly eyed the line of people going in and out of the building. She could hear a trance beat vibrating all the way from here.

She paid for her trip and went inside. The narrow space was lit with hot track lights, dozens of people standing around in clusters of excited conversation and clinking glasses. Lilly checked her coat, slipped her black wristlet purse over her arm and searched for a familiar face among the crowd.

She wasn't looking for Jack. She wasn't.

A server passed by and offered her a glass from a tray of decadent-looking beverages. She took one and sipped slowly, relishing the sweet burn. Glass in hand, she concentrated on getting lost in the art hanging on the whitewashed walls. She paused by one of an elderly couple holding hands as they reclined on a park bench, completely absorbed in the contented looks on their faces when someone tapped her shoulder. She whirled around to see Nick's smile, the tips of his hair turned to a shining halo by the bright lights.

"Hey," he said. "I thought I'd never find you."

"I'm not surprised. This place is packed." She beamed at him. "The turnout is incredible."

"Did you see my photos?"

"Not yet."

Nick took her hand, drawing her to where his work was displayed, and stepped back to let her take it in.

His work was exquisite, each shot offering only a snippet of the moment he'd captured: a man's hand tenderly cupping a stubbled cheek, two masculine fingers curled around one another, a baby girl being kissed on each cheek by two pairs of fatherly lips. They were intimate, quiet, the emotions reflective of the kind of love she'd always been proud to watch him celebrate.

"They're amazing," she said.

"You're biased."

"I'm right."

"I've already sold six pieces. And *Framed* wants an interview with me."

"Congratulations! I told you this would be great."

"Yeah, yeah. You're a genius." He kissed her on the cheek. "Enjoy the show. Gabe and the others are around here somewhere. I'll find you later."

Lilly watched him disappear into the crowd. She was so proud of him, but a tiny part of her was jealous. She wished she'd done something by now that he could be proud of too.

A server passed by, and she handed him her empty glass, hesitating before plucking another one from the tray. What the hell. It was Valentine's Day, she was single and her career was dead-on-arrival. Drinking under those circumstances was a moral imperative.

After wandering through the rest of the gallery, she ran into Brady at the bottom of a staircase. A striking redhead she recognized as his wife stood by his side.

"Hey, Lilly. I don't know if you've ever met my wife, Samantha. Sam, this is Nick's sister, Lilly."

Samantha's smile was even more stunning than her hair. "It's nice to finally meet you," she said.

"You too." Lilly tilted her head to look toward the second floor, where heady music pulsed. "What's up there?"

Brady winked at her. "The sexy pictures. You coming?"

She glanced up again. The music thumped and echoed, the bass deep and intoxicating. She took another swill of her drink, then downed the rest of it and placed the empty glass on a tray.

"Sure. Why not?"

She followed them up the steps and stopped on the balcony, held up by a line of people streaming in and out of a room guarded by maroon velvet drapes. Cassie hurried out from behind them, lines scored into her forehead, lips pursed with tension.

The alarm on her face was quickly replaced with a smile when she saw Lilly. "There you are. Come downstairs with me?"

"Now? But I want to see what's in there."

Cassie looked from Lilly to Brady and back. "I don't think those photos are to everybody's liking."

"Why not?" he asked. "I heard they're hot."

The curtain rippled and Gabe wandered out, grinning. "Damn straight they are."

Emboldened by alcohol and curiosity, Lilly stepped toward the entryway, turning around once to smile at her friend. "They're only pictures, Cass. How bad can they be?"

She pulled the curtain open, and her eyes adjusted to a room that was darker than she expected. Red and white lights hung from the ceiling, setting a feverish hue to the photographs spread out on black walls. As soon as she saw them, she understood why Cassie tried to stop her. They were frozen reflections of wrists held roughly down, of faces drowning in ecstatic pleasure, exuding the delicate balance of control and abandon found in dominance and submission.

It was everything she'd learned to crave and ran away from.

*"Spread your legs. Show me what's mine."*

She drifted toward a snapshot of a finger on an upturned chin, the owner's other hand holding the chain to a studded choker. Lilly ran a finger along her neck, feeling the absence of the exquisite pressure of a collar.

Held down. Chained up. Fingers on her throat. Tongue against her clit.

Another photo, filled with the ravenous expression of a submissive on her knees, looking up at her Master with both desire and fear. Lilly had kneeled like that under the heavy command of Damien's stare.

*"I know how badly you want to come, but not yet. Not yet."*

She moved on, each picture tiptoeing through her memories and dragging them into the light. Hands locked in cuffs. A fistful of hair being grabbed by masculine fingers. Her scalp tingled, her wrists longing for the splintering pleasure of that leather embrace. A palm print painted onto someone's backside, and ghostly sensation whispered across Lilly's flesh, reminding her how long it had been since she felt the delectable pain of a spanking.

*He gripped her hair, and she hated how much she loved it.*

*God, she loved it.*

A dam collapsed. There was no denying that she ached to feel this again. Even in the face of Damien's lies and deceit, Lilly remembered how, within the blinding release of his restraints, she actually felt whole.

Her trance gave way when Brady called out, "Jack, where've you been?"

She felt him before she saw him. The sensation of being watched drew her eyes to where Jack was standing in the corner. His gaze traveled down the length of her dress and back up again, his body taut and motionless.

"Here," Jack replied, his eyes focused on hers.

"Uh, guys?" Gabe said. Lilly turned, and the effort it took for her to break from Jack's stare was almost painful. "We should go downstairs. They're going to toast the artists now."

"Be right there," she said, but didn't move as the room began emptying out.

"You coming, Jack?" Brady called over his shoulder.

"In a minute."

Brady shrugged and walked through the curtains. Cassie gestured to Lilly, but she waved her on, promising she'd follow. She didn't want to leave yet. She wanted to stay a little longer and drink in the imagery around her.

She *wanted* Jack.

Turning to face one wall of photos, she felt his gaze on her. He stalked closer, until he was right behind her.

"Joining the others?" he asked softly.

She felt out of control, her body flying apart where she stood. "Not yet."

"Still looking?"

"Yes, Sir."

The instant the word slipped free, Lilly winced and bowed her head. It came so naturally—she couldn't help it. But through the haze of humiliation, she heard Jack's breath catch.

"What did you say?" His voice was gravelly. Husky. She didn't answer—she couldn't—and he stepped around to face her. "Lilly."

He captured her chin with his forefinger and thumb, lifting it gently. There was a question in his eyes as they searched hers, and then his expression shifted into something else.

Something she recognized.

"I want to take you someplace quiet," he said.

It wasn't a question. It was a command.

It suddenly became clear what had drawn her to him. Why he'd stepped in and taken over her thoughts.

Jack was a Dominant.

ack couldn't believe what he was seeing.

From the minute Lilly parted those drapes, he couldn't take his eyes off her. It wasn't only because of how incredible she looked in that tiny black dress, so goddamn sexy it was almost painful. It was because of the barbed wire of worry lancing his thoughts, wondering how she'd react to photos of the lifestyle he'd embraced.

Her reaction wasn't at all what he'd expected.

Somehow, he'd missed the signs—her lowered glances, quiet blushes, and how she'd responded so easily, so sweetly to his commands. Even when her face flushed as she moved throughout the room, Jack still didn't recognize it. But then she'd said "Sir" in a way that was practiced. Trained. And now she was looking up at him as if she'd follow him anywhere.

"Okay," she whispered.

All rational thought escaped him. He wanted her alone, now. If she was a submissive, he had to find out.

Jack released her chin. "We're leaving. If anyone asks, you've had too much to drink, and I'm taking you home. Understand?"

"Yes."

*Sir,* he thought. *Say "Yes, Sir" again.*

She turned toward the steps. Driven by instinct, Jack slid his palm down the back of her dress to the delicious curve below her waistline, fanning his fingers out to brush the swell of her rear. Lilly shuddered softly, and arched back against his hand. His cock pulsed, his entire body hungry for her. But when she peeked over her shoulder at him, her eyes wide, she looked almost...lost.

Jack reassured her with a gentle press of his palm. He needed to soothe her, to let her know she was safe.

"Don't worry," he said. "I've got you."

They reached the first floor landing as everyone was cheering the artists, holding up flutes of champagne. It would be easy to duck out without anyone noticing, if they were quick. Not wasting any time, Jack guided Lilly toward the coat room. She pointed to her jacket, and he pulled it from the rack, wrapping it firmly around her before grabbing his own and leading her toward the door.

They slipped outside. Once they were in his car, she fingered her purse, then pulled her phone from it.

"I need to let Nick know I left."

Shit. He hadn't thought this through. Nick would notice their absence and so would Brady. Damn Patrick for finding his own plans tonight, the one time Jack could've actually used a wingman.

"Of course. I understand."

He took his phone from his pocket too, sending Brady a quick explanation.

*Went home. Tired. Call you tomorrow.*

The lie only bothered him for a moment until he saw Lilly tap out another text. "I have to tell Cassie too. She'll worry."

"Cassie seems very protective of you."

Lilly lowered her phone to her lap. "She is."

The urge to protect her flooded through him again. Jack reached up to brush his knuckles against her cheek. She made the barest press of her face into his hand—a hesitant little nuzzle. It was such a sweet motion, one that made him long to find whatever it was that had hurt her and make it go away.

"I'd like to know what happened," he said. "If you'll tell me, I want to hear it all."

Lilly's eyes sparkled with tears. "There's a diner we could go to that's open late. Rosie's. It's near my apartment."

He put the car in gear, and she directed him to a small suburban eatery. Jack asked the hostess to seat them at a secluded booth in the corner. They ordered coffees, and Lilly didn't say anything at first, her fingers dancing around the rim of her mug.

"How are things at work?" he asked. She obviously needed help calming down. Talking would be easier if he distracted her with safer topics first.

"Good. I've been put on a case, but I'm not having much luck finding what I need."

"What kind of case is it?"

"Trade secret."

"That's my specialty. I'd be happy to help."

"I might take you up on that." Lilly sipped her coffee, her posture relaxing. "Why did you stop practicing?"

She seemed a little more at ease, so he indulged her in the story. "My father was a lawyer. He went to Harvard Law, so it was a given that I'd be going there too. Brady was much younger and a computer whiz, so Dad didn't push him along the same path."

"You didn't want to go to law school?"

"I wanted to be like my father, but then I realized anyone who wants to go to law school is a complete masochist." That prompted a giggle from her. "It's true. No one tells you before you go in how bad it is."

"It's like *Fight Club*. First rule about law school—you don't talk about law school."

"Exactly."

A grin that matched his spread over her face. Her real smile.

God, she was beautiful.

"Anyway, I liked school, but it was difficult to study with an infant at home."

"You have kids?"

"A son. Joshua. He's twenty-two and getting his doctorate at Stanford." Jack toyed with the handle of his mug, gauging Lilly's reaction. There wasn't one. "My wife and I met when we were seventeen. We got married right out of college."

"So young."

"It wasn't as unusual back then. Eve got pregnant right away, so once I graduated, there was no option but to go straight into my father's practice." He drummed his fingers against the table, remembering the long hours, the meetings, the feeling that no matter how much billable time he put in, it was never enough. "I loved law, but not the reality of the work. I ended up devising a restructuring plan to package and resell bad debt, but it didn't sit right with me. It did get me an offer for partner, though."

"And you turned it down."

"Yup. I wrote something about the plan that got published in *The Harvard Business Review*, and they offered me a chance to teach. I liked the idea of mentoring future lawyers, so I left."

"How did that go over with your father?"

Jack laughed. "Not well. But I knew I needed to follow my heart."

"You sound like Nick, pursuing photography instead of going pro like everyone expected."

He sipped his coffee, watching her. "You became a lawyer because of what happened to him?" She'd said as much to Brady the first night at the pub, but he wanted to hear more.

"Yes," she started, then paused and dug a hand into her hair. Jack recognized the nervous habit. He'd seen her do it before.

"You don't have to tell me if you don't want to."

"No, it's okay." She lowered her hand and took a slow, deep breath. "When Nick was practically bludgeoned to death, and his teammates got away with it, I knew I had to become a lawyer. I never wanted to see anyone taken advantage of like that again. My parents couldn't afford law school after sending us both to college, so I clerked for a few years to save up. I was twenty-five when I started at Northwestern but jumped right into it."

"Workaholic," he said with a grin.

"Yeah, yeah."

She rolled her eyes, her nose scrunching up, a smile pressing at her lips. It was adorable, and yet, he couldn't stop thinking about how much fun it would be to take her over his knee and show her what those bratty little eye rolls could cost her.

"Anyway, during my second year, we had a lecture series on gender discrimination. The lawyer giving it was an alumnae who specialized in civil rights. After what happened with Nick, I couldn't wait to meet him."

"Naturally."

"I read all of his articles, and thought he was brilliant, but then I saw him." The amused look on her face fell away, replaced with one filled with regret. "He was the kind of tall, dark and handsome a small-town Midwest girl dreamed about. Worldly, refined. Older than me too, by six years." She shrugged. "Age was never an issue for me."

Good to know, but this wasn't the time for that. "Go on," he coaxed softly.

She inhaled again, deeply. "I went to every one of his lectures. We'd chat afterward—and flirt—but it was never more than that until I got a summer associate position at his firm. My first night, we went out for drinks, and the way he looked at me..." Her speech slowed, her words drawn out like taffy on a pull. "It was like he could eat me alive and I'd love every second of it."

Her words conjured up images of Jack doing exactly that, of his head between her luscious thighs, tongue licking a stripe up her drenched pussy lips while her legs and arms were spread-eagled, chained up on his bed.

Jack clenched his jaw and forced himself to concentrate.

"What happened then?" he asked.

Lilly dragged her gaze upward. Her eyes were unfocused, drowsy. "I went home with him, and he did things to me no one had done before."

"What did he do?"

She paused, her lips pursed in her hesitation. "He pulled my hair, held me down and spanked me."

Fuck. "And did that frighten you?"

Lilly shook her head, slowly, that damn blush painting her cheeks. "No. I loved it."

Jack's mouth went dry. There it was. The proof he'd been waiting for.

"It was like he'd lit a match inside me that no one ever struck before. The pleasure and the pain, the way he could play my body. The feeling that I was his, and he was mine too." Her gaze dropped back down to the table. "That part was all in my head, though."

Jack frowned. "Why do you say that?"

She curled her arms around her middle, as if she were trying to physically protect herself from what she was about to say.

"We kept meeting up after the job ended. He was teaching my third-year clinic at school, and asked me to keep things quiet. I was of course completely in love with him by then, so I said yes, thinking things would change after I finished school. But at my graduation, we got into an argument. I asked if we could go public now, but—" Lilly winced, then regained her composure, taking a breath. "He laughed at me. Told me I was a fool for thinking he belonged to me. That he wasn't mine and never would be."

She stared hard at the table, her jaw tight with the effort of holding back tears. Jack leaned toward her, an instinctual response that spiraled out of his gut.

"I hope you punched him in the jaw."

Her sudden laughter was a welcome relief. She smiled and shook her head.

"Sadly, no. I went home, tried to put him out of my mind and study for the bar. But the night before the exam, he called to tell me he was engaged. Someone he'd met over the summer."

*Oh, Lilly.*

She lifted her chin, a show of strength Jack respected the hell out of. "So then I did what I should've done on day one—I researched BDSM and discovered a whole slew of things he never told me. That I was entitled to a checklist. And limits. And a safeword."

"You played without one?"

She glanced at him. There was so much pain in her eyes. "I never knew I could have one."

Jack's stomach lurched, his jaw going tight with anger. "He sounds like an irresponsible, selfish prick."

61

That earned him a faint smile. "Yeah, but I was the one who was stupid enough to believe him."

"You weren't stupid. You trusted him."

She laughed again, but there was no mirth in it. "Well that was pretty stupid, wasn't it?"

Lilly uncurled her arms to wipe her tears away. Unable to hold back the urge to comfort her, Jack reached out, took her free hand in his and stroked her palm with his thumb.

"It wasn't your fault. It sounds to me like this guy knew what he was doing. Most girls are easily swayed by a man like that."

"I wasn't a little girl. It was only last year."

Jack cringed. Yeah, that sounded patronizing as hell.

"I didn't mean it like that. I just meant with your age difference and the kind of relationship you were in, it isn't surprising that you trusted him so completely." He gave her a teasing grin. "And I didn't say you were a 'little' girl. You added that part."

Her eyes cleared, lips curving up into a small smile. He liked having that effect on her, and seeing the fire in her despite her pain.

"Sorry. I overreacted," she said. "Anyway, that's my story. I wasn't in any shape to take the bar after that. I'm not really sure I ever will. I mean, I had all these dreams about protecting the innocent and defeating the bad guy, but how could I ever defend anyone else's rights when I'd been unable to defend myself?"

Jack sighed. It seemed a little extreme to give up years of hard work all because of a guy, but it wasn't his place to judge.

"Does Nick know?"

"Not really. All I told him was that I'd had a bad breakup and needed a fresh start. Gabe got me a job and I came out here."

He squeezed her hand. "I'm sorry. That's not how it should be."

"How—" She stopped herself. Looked up at him. "How was it for you?"

He sat back, stunned he'd revealed something so private after years keeping it hidden. Jack gently released Lilly's hand and stared out the window. Eve's ghost filled the room like a fog.

"It's not something I talk easily about. My wife and I were very private."

"I don't mean to pry."

"You're not." Jack turned back to meet her gaze. "I always knew I was...different. Even as a teenager, I had these fantasies about spankings and bondage, of depriving a woman of pleasure and then giving it at my will."

Lilly's eyes dilated slightly. God, she was responsive.

"I thought something was wrong with me, that I was sick and twisted. I tried to bury it, but it didn't work. We were married for ten years before I looked up BDSM on the Internet and discovered I wasn't such a sicko after all. Suddenly this door opened up to a world I never knew existed."

"Did you tell your wife?"

"I wanted to, but I was scared shitless to mention it." They shared a quiet laugh. It was the first time the recollection didn't sting. "She pulled it out of me, though. Got me to admit wanting to tie her up. I was sure once we'd acted out the fantasy, then that would be it. But neither of us knew how much I'd like it."

"How much was that?" Longing flashed in her eyes, the color on her cheeks returning, spreading to a blush that made him hard for her all over again.

"So much that I knew I couldn't live without it."

She nodded. He could hear her breathing quicken. "I know what you mean. That moment when you realize this—"

"—is what's always been missing." Their eyes locked.

Fuck.

Jack cleared his throat. "So, I understand how addictive it can be. I'm sorry your experience was so bad."

"Thanks. What I don't understand is why I still...I mean, how could I want to..."

She trailed off, and what she was trying to say dawned on him.

"You still want to be dominated."

Her gaze dropped to her lap. "Yes."

A spike of desire pounded through him. He wanted to hear her whisper that word again, naked and kneeling on his playroom floor. A wet mess barely able to remember her own name.

He was halfway ready to suggest it when her phone rang.

She wrenched it from her purse. "It's Nick," she said before accepting the call. "Hi... Yes, I'm fine." She paused and frowned. "No, I just drank too much. Jack took me home."

He bristled at her lie. Home was where he should've taken her. And it was where he was going to take her, right now. His thoughts were already completely out of line, his body vibrating with hunger when his brain knew better. An unspoken attraction was developing between them, crackling in the air like static on a cold night, and igniting it was a mistake he couldn't afford making.

Jack waved down the waitress for the check. By the time Lilly said good-bye and ended the call, he was standing, holding out her coat.

"We should get going."

She silently slipped her arms into the sleeves and they walked to his car, saying little else as she directed him to her apartment.

He cut the engine in front of it. "I'll see you inside."

It was the right thing to do—to make sure she was safe.

Inside the building, Lilly led him up a creaking set of stairs, stopping to face him when they reached her door. "Thanks for the coffee."

"You're welcome." They were close to one another. Too close. "Have a good night."

As Jack turned, he saw something mischievous in her eyes.

"You too," she said. "Sir."

Jack couldn't stop himself.

Before Lilly had time to gasp, he had her pressed against the wall, her purse clattering to the ground as he pinned her wrists on either side of her head. She was playing with fire, using that title again, and he wasn't going to let her get away with it.

"Do you know what it does to me to hear you say that?"

Lilly shook her head, her eyes wide.

"No? You don't know how crazy it makes me?" He pulled her hands above her head and trapped them together in one of his. "Because I think you do."

Jack pushed his hips against hers. She arched and whimpered.

"Oh, yes. Your body is telling me you do, *little girl*."

Her legs buckled. Jack's grip was the only thing keeping her from slipping down the wall. He grasped her chin, brought a fingertip to her quivering lower lip and pulled down on it, opening her mouth to him.

"This is what you like, isn't it?"

Lilly whined. It was a desperate, needy sound. Jack wanted all her sounds, to hear her beg. To see what she'd look like when she came. He freed her mouth and stroked down her jaw to the column of her throat, leaning in to brush his nose along hers.

"Isn't it?" he repeated, putting a little more pressure on her neck.

She nodded quickly, a tight movement she seemed barely able to make. Jack dragged his nose over her cheek and breathed against her ear.

"Tell me you want this."

Lilly shivered. Her dress rode up an inch, and Jack slid his thigh between hers to rub against the damp fabric there. Her whole body bucked off the wall, her need palpable, but she still didn't answer. Something was stopping her, making her fight to keep the words inside.

Impatient, Jack drew her hair into his fingers and made a fist, twisting her head so she had no choice but to look at him.

"Tell. Me."

He searched her eyes, his stare hot and unwavering until she finally succumbed.

"I want this, Sir," she whispered. "I want you."

His mouth open, lips poised against hers, he said, "Good."

Then Jack kissed her, slipped his tongue into her mouth the way he wanted to fuck into her body. She kissed him back, hungry and eager, and Jack groaned, a deep, guttural noise of satisfaction. Letting go of her wrists, he drove both his hands into her hair and kissed her deeply, tasting her, teeth against teeth. He could feel her heat through his jeans. He wanted inside her, and if they did this a second longer, he was going to break down her door and fuck her in her hallway, safeword or not.

No safeword. Fuck!

Jack broke off the kiss. Released her hair and took a step back. "We need to stop."

His voice was hoarse, and he glided his fingers over his mouth despite his uncertainty, as if he could rub their kiss into his skin. Lilly was breathing fast, her palms pressed into the wall. He itched to soothe her, but he couldn't. She'd been through hell, and here he was about to take her with no limits, no boundaries set.

If he went near her again, he'd lose it.

"I have to go," he told her. "Before anything else happens."

"Okay." Her gaze dropped to the floor. God, she looked so confused. He couldn't leave her like this.

Wrestling back his control, he moved in and kissed her tenderly on the forehead. "We'll talk tomorrow. Go inside."

Lilly picked up her purse and fumbled for her keys. When she was through the entryway, she turned, one side of her mouth lifting in a meek smile as she gave him a tentative wave. Jack nodded briskly and turned away.

He didn't look back. He thundered down the stairs and slammed the door behind him.

## 11

---

*J*ack dropped his things in the kitchen and reopened his bottle of scotch, on the island where he'd left it last night. It was a slippery slope, but he was desperate for the distraction. He'd do anything to kill the ache of wanting Lilly.

He'd been such an ass. It had only been after two drinks the night before and several brutal passes of his hand over his still-pulsing cock that he realized how much he'd fucked up. Being a Dominant meant keeping his head on straight, and he'd been far from that. He was out of his goddamned mind. He should never have kissed her, let alone booked it out of her building afterward. He'd wanted to contact her all day, to make sure she wasn't regretting the desires he forced her to face, but he didn't have her number, and asking Brady for it wasn't an option. He'd found her firm's phone number online, but calling her there wasn't a good idea. Receptionists had a tendency to talk, and whatever happened between him and Lilly needed to stay private. The only way he could reach her was through Facebook. It was absurd to have to resort to that, but he didn't have any other choice.

Jack poured himself three fingers for company and was heading upstairs to his computer when someone's fist pounded on the front door.

"You'd better have a good excuse for cancelling tennis at the last minute!"

Damn it, he'd hoped his rain-check text would get Patrick off his back. Jack banged the glass on the island, walked down the hallway and yanked the door open.

"You look like shit," Patrick said. "What the fuck's the matter with you?"

Jack gripped the edge of his doorframe. He could have made something up, but he wasn't exactly quick on his feet at the moment. Maybe if he told the truth, Patrick would be able to talk him out of how badly he wanted to go back to Lilly's apartment and finish what they'd started.

"I kissed Lilly."

"Seriously?"

Jack didn't answer. He turned around and went back to the kitchen.

Patrick dropped his tennis bag in the hallway and shut the door. "I thought you were staying away from her."

"Yeah, that didn't work out so well."

Jack took a long sip. Relief fired down his throat, hot and burning. Patrick came into the kitchen, made himself comfortable on a stool and eyed the level of scotch in the bottle.

"So, we're drinking again?"

"Fuck off."

"Drinking and cursing. Definitely Harvard's finest. Well, *Professor*. You want to tell me how you went from not wanting to go near Lilly five days ago to having your tongue down her throat?"

Jack lowered his glass. "She's a submissive."

Patrick's jaw dropped. Then he smacked one hand down on the island and laughed so hard he nearly fell off the stool.

"What's so goddamned funny?"

"It's not funny. It's just that it's the best news I've heard in a long time." Patrick lifted the bottle and held it up in a toast. "To your luck."

"My luck?"

"Yeah, your fucking luck. The first woman you've shown any

interest in, and she's into exactly the same shit you are. I'd say that's pretty lucky."

It was an unreal coincidence, but that didn't make any of this lucky.

"You don't understand. Her first Dominant fucked her up. She confided in me, and then I couldn't stop myself from mauling her in her hallway."

"Nice."

"Shut up."

"It wasn't nice?"

Jack sank down onto the other barstool. "Nice doesn't begin to cover it."

He'd tried to block out the feeling of satisfaction that permeated the whole thing. How calling her "little girl" had been a whim, an impulsive move with the intent of putting her in her place, and yet it made her practically melt to the floor. He seemed to know what would coax out her submissive side—he could practically smell the kink on her. But, God, the way she looked when she admitted what she wanted. How she'd called him Sir again, and meant it. The vicious, primal urge that word sparked became all that was driving him, and while he'd tried to harness it, to put it back in its cage, it was pacing behind the bars, wanting to be set free again.

Jack rubbed his hands over his face. "I can't believe I did this."

"It was just a kiss, Jack. Don't make a fucking soap opera out of it."

"Remind me why we're friends?"

"Because you're a pervert and I'm a pig," Patrick said. "So if kissing her was so unbelievable, what the hell are you waiting for?"

"What am I waiting for? She and I can't have a relationship."

"Who said anything about a relationship?"

"We're back to this, now? One-night stands?" Jack reached for the bottle and topped off his glass. "I can't do that. I'm involved in her life now. She trusts me."

No doubt she'd trust him right into his playroom. But no matter how crazed he was to see her kneeling before him, she might be too hurt by her past to handle it, even for a few dark, passionate hours. And then where would that leave them?

"It doesn't have to be one night," Patrick said, grinning like the day he discovered his father's porn stash.

"What do you mean?"

"Why couldn't you come up with some kind of agreement? Talk your shit out beforehand, and then go for it."

"A contract?" Jack considered the idea, but shook it off. "You're out of your mind."

"I'm telling you—people do this."

"How the hell do you know?"

"How the hell do you not know?"

"Because, damn it, Eve and I didn't have a contract!"

It was something he'd researched, along with the checklist of limits he'd presented her when they decided to make BDSM a part of their lives. But Eve had simply shrugged and said if there was anything she was uncomfortable with, she'd let him know.

"Well, think about having one now. You both get what you want, and there's no baggage to deal with."

Jack stared at his glass and thought about Lilly's tortured little noises. The desperation in her kiss. It was an enticing proposition, but he couldn't entertain it. There was too much at stake for both of them.

"She wouldn't be interested," he insisted, needing it to be true. "Not after what she's been through."

"Really? She let you kiss her after meeting you—what? Twice? I'd say anything is fair game."

"And what if Nick found out? Or Brady? Or Josh? They'd hate us."

"Oh, please. How would Josh ever know? He's thousands of miles away. Brady would be happy you're finally getting some. Means you'd be less of an asswipe once in a while. And you and Lilly are consenting adults. Her brother doesn't have a say in who she sleeps with."

*Sleeping with Lilly.*

Jack's body stiffened, from his jaw through his spine and down to his dick. But it wouldn't be just sex. He'd want all of her, want her to lay herself bare so he could dismantle all those walls she'd put up. Would she be ready for that when behind those walls she was hurting, her wounds pink and raw?

Jack swirled the amber liquid in his glass. "Who am I to teach her anything about submission?"

"This isn't torts class, Jack. You're not getting graded."

He laughed, but it was a tight, uncomfortable sound. This wasn't a lecture, wasn't something he could give her readings to prepare for and discuss. Then again, maybe he could do that. She knew so little about the lifestyle, and he'd certainly read more than his share.

No. That was crazy. She didn't need a professor. She needed someone to heal her wounds. "It wouldn't work. I can't be what Lilly needs."

"I think you might be exactly what she needs. And maybe she's what you need too." Patrick shrugged. "This is who you are. Denying that isn't doing either of you any favors."

Denying it would be impossible. He certainly couldn't be around her again, wanting her like this. But...

"That's not the only reason," Jack said quietly. "You know this isn't what Eve wanted."

Patrick took Jack's glass from his hand. "Maybe you have to put Eve aside and do what's right for you for a little while." He knocked back all that was left and then grinned. "After all, kissing Lilly made you forget about your anniversary."

Jack blinked, shocked. Grief stabbed him, his breathing tight with shame. For a year he'd felt as though he was missing a limb, unable to take a step without Eve in his thoughts, and yet somehow yesterday he hadn't spent a single moment recalling the day he'd bound his life to hers.

"But if you're in no rush to tap that fine piece of ass," Patrick continued, "I might just move in and do it for you. I know my way around a rope and a spanking."

A flash of anger seared across Jack's vision. The idea of Patrick, or anyone else, touching Lilly made his blood boil. He wanted to be the one to make her beg and cry with painful pleasure, to be responsible for the flush of her skin and feel the wet heat between her legs.

Patrick held up his hands in surrender. "I'm kidding. Jesus, Jack. You looked like you were about to rip my throat out."

Jack looked down to discover clenched fists. Shit.

Patrick whistled and shook his head. "Sex with a girl in her twenties. Man, you're gonna be glad I kept dragging your ass to tennis all these years." He picked up the bottle and stood. "Come now, Master. Let's get this back where it belongs. I don't want to have to put you on lockdown again."

When his friend finally left, Jack retreated to his home office in the attic. It was Josh's old room, but he'd been using it as a study for years. After booting up his computer, he signed into Facebook and navigated to Lilly's profile. Once again, he focused on her photo, this time understanding the heartbreak in her expression, and why her smile didn't seem genuine.

He sat back and sighed. She thought of herself as broken, but underneath her scars she was courageous and brave. She proved it at the diner, and in how she baited him in the hallway. She bit back, and it made him want to bite her even harder.

Biting Lilly. Fuck.

Could he do this? The idea of writing up a contract with her sounded so shallow, but then again, she was a submissive. He was a Dominant.

This was who they were.

Jack closed his eyes. Eve knew being dominant was a part of him, both when she agreed to wear his collar and when she insisted he take it off. This wasn't what she'd asked of him, but maybe that was okay. This had nothing to do with falling in love. Lilly simply wanted to be dominated again, and he could offer her that.

It didn't have to be a long-term thing. They could just do it once—scratch this itch and satisfy the hunger between them. And then he'd kiss her sweet, pouty lips until she was begging for his touch.

Until he'd driven her into a trembling wreck of sex and submission and made her come for him over and over and over again.

Cracking his knuckles, Jack opened his eyes, straightened his posture and began to type.

## 12

The words on Lilly's computer screen had started to swim. Her eyes burned, and she squeezed them shut to force them to focus. It didn't help that she barely got any rest the night before. She'd been taunted by different nightmares, ones that reminded her how she'd wanted Jack to do the very thing she swore she'd never allow anyone to do to her again.

It had all happened so fast. She'd guessed what Jack might do if she called him Sir again, and she'd been right. She loved his reaction, and as much as she couldn't believe it, the feeling of being so helpless too, trapped between him and the wall. She'd felt unbearably free somehow. With a look that felt as if it reached into her soul, he allowed her permission to give in to the part of herself that wouldn't be quieted. And the way he kissed her. *God*, she would've done anything he asked, even fallen to her knees right there in the hallway. But he'd pulled away so quickly, practically bolting out the door. Only his explanation that he had to leave before things got even more heated had stopped her from thinking he regretted it.

At least, that was how she'd felt before half the day had gone by and she hadn't heard from him.

She glanced at her work phone for what felt like the fiftieth time, confirming that she hadn't missed a call, nor had she put on her *do not disturb* without realizing it. She'd been waiting for his call all day, but now it was nearly dinnertime, and her hopes had finally faded. She'd cried silently in the bathroom stall a hour ago, half-angry at him for getting her hopes up, half-furious at herself for being so upset over the whole thing. She'd lived through worse than this. Not hearing back from a guy a day after he'd kissed her shouldn't have bothered her so much.

"I can't believe I'm just getting here when it's dark out."

Lilly's head shot up at the sound of Cassie's voice. Both she and Gabe had been at client meetings all day. Lilly had hoped to avoid them, not wanting to answer any questions about her disappearance the night before, but that wasn't likely if either of them got a look at her post-sob-fest eyes. She bent down behind her screen and tried to look busy.

"I swear if I see another cup of coffee, I'm going to puke," Cassie continued as she neared Lilly's desk.

"I thought you liked client meetings because they got you out of the office," Gabe said.

"I'd like them a lot better if it weren't freezing outside."

"Maybe it's time for you to take a trip down to Miami and pay *la familia* a visit."

"And be harassed by my mother about the lack of productivity of my uterus? No thank you."

They stopped at Lilly's cubicle. Gabe crossed his arms over the partition. "How's our star doing?"

"The usual," she replied, not looking up. "Working until my eyes bleed."

"It looks like you're halfway there already."

Lilly quickly rubbed her eyes. "They're dry. From staring at the screen."

Cassie leaned down by her desk and caught her gaze.

Busted.

"Coffee," Cassie suddenly said. "I need coffee. Lilly, come with me?"

Gabe raised an eyebrow. "Didn't you just say you'd vomit if you had any more coffee?"

"I changed my mind. And I could use some fresh air."

"I thought you said it was freezing out."

"Are you a lawyer or a detective?" she snapped. "Lilly?"

Gabe held up his hands, and Lilly allowed Cassie to tow her past him and down the hall. Once they were outside, Cassie threaded an arm through hers. The evening was laced with a bitter chill, and Lilly braced herself against the cold, burrowing deeper into her coat and closer to her friend.

"I knew you weren't drunk last night," Cassie said. "Those pictures were awful. They should've had a sign by the stairs. A warning or something."

"They weren't that bad."

A *pfft* sound came out from between Cassie's lips. "I tried to stop you from going in there. I wish you'd listened to me."

Lilly kept her head down as Cassie chattered on. She wanted to tell her friend what really happened, but couldn't bring herself to talk about it. When her cell buzzed in her pocket, she pulled it free with numb hands, expecting a work email, but it was her personal email announcing a Facebook message. From Jack.

Her pulse began to race. With a sideways glance to check that Cassie wasn't looking, she opened the message.

*Lilly—I'm sorry I haven't been able to reach you until now. I hope you don't think I've been ignoring you. I wasn't happy with how we left things last night, and I'd really like to talk, but I'd prefer to do it in person. Is there a good time for us to meet?*

Her stomach somehow found its way up into her chest. Lilly read the message again, her body warming from the inside out, the tension she'd felt all day evaporating like steam. Angling the phone away from Cassie's line of sight, she opened the Facebook messenger app and covertly typed a response.

*It's okay. I should be able to leave the office in an hour. Would that work?*

His answer came through a few seconds later.

*Let's meet at Rosie's again. Eight thirty.*

A sudden burst of happiness made her hands shake. Unable to hide her smile, she quickly replied, telling him she'd be there. She needed to get back to the office and finish some things up, but Cassie was still droning on.

"Cass, I'm fine," she said when she could finally get a word in. "I was surprised by the photos, but they didn't upset me. I just had too much to drink."

She eyed Lilly warily. "You sure?"

"I am. I promise. Can we go back now? I can't feel my hands."

Back at the office, Lilly got through the remainder of her work as quickly as possible, then booked it out of there. At twenty past eight, she entered the diner. The walk from the T station had left a chill on her cheeks, but the cold became a distant memory when she found Jack in their booth and his eyes met hers. It was heat, plain and simple. A fire that reached into her bones. She'd told herself to be cautious on the trip over, but it was hard to keep her wits about her once she was seated across from him.

"How was your day?" he asked.

"Fine. Busy."

Jack's brow creased. "Your eyes are red."

She hadn't expected him to notice. It was startling how much he seemed to catch. But she didn't want to tell him she'd been obsessing over him all day like a teenager. She waved it off and smiled.

"Just a long day staring at the computer. How about you?"

"Busy too. Classes full of terrified first years who have no clue what they're getting into, then meetings with panicked advisees." He frowned and looked at her intently again. "Eyes don't get that red from too much screen time, Lilly."

She glanced at the table, part of her pleased that he cared enough to push the subject, and partly uneasy at what felt like an admonishment. It forced her to be honest with him.

"I was a little upset when it started getting late. I was hoping you'd call earlier."

He sighed. "I don't have your cell number and I didn't want to contact you at work. I thought Facebook was the best way to keep things...private."

"Oh." Her gut twisted at the word, although she wasn't sure why. She wasn't exactly blabbing about this either. "I understand."

"I had every intention of talking to you today, though. Don't doubt that."

His voice softened and he tilted his head, as if to say *I'm a man of my word*. The chivalrous gesture deflated her anxiety.

"I believe you," she said. "So...what did you want to talk about?"

Jack sat forward and clasped his hands on the table. "First, I need to apologize for yesterday. I didn't handle myself very well."

"It's okay—"

"No. It's not. I shouldn't have left you like that."

Something like hope fluttered in her stomach. "You wanted to stay?"

"Of course." He leaned closer to her, his voice low and soft. "You don't make it easy for me to control myself around you, little girl."

Desire curled through her, so intense she had to press her thighs together. "I didn't want you to stop."

Jack inhaled—a long, deep breath that he took in through his nose.

"Clearly we're very attracted to each other, and we both have needs that are currently unfulfilled." He studied her for a moment before asking, "Did you mean what you said? About wanting to submit to someone again?"

Lilly swallowed. "Yes."

The answer came to her more quickly than she expected, but it was the truth. How else could she explain how easily she'd given in last night, how swiftly she'd fallen back into the mindset she'd put aside long ago, sure it wasn't for her?

"Okay then." Jack reached down beside him and handed her a stack of papers. "I have a proposition for you."

She glanced cautiously at the pile. "What's all that?"

"Just read."

Lilly scanned the first page. It was titled "Negotiation for First-Time Play".

It was a contract, laying out the terms of a proposed arrangement between Jack Archer, a.k.a. "the Dominant", and Lilly Sterling, a.k.a.

"the submissive". She examined the agreement, her heart starting to pound when she reached item six: *The submissive's limits (See checklist)*.

He must have known what she was reading because he said, "It's three pages in."

She flipped ahead and discovered the most comprehensive list she'd ever seen, followed by several articles on BDSM. The last page had blank lines for the date and time of play, as well as Jack's signature, address and phone number. There were spots next to it for hers. Lilly shoved a hand into her hair, her nerves taking over. Part of her wanted to say yes without reading anything else, and part of her wanted to run away.

As if he could sense her unease, Jack gently took the papers from her hands and placed them face down on the table.

"I'm not suggesting commitment. Just a day, to help you get comfortable with this again. And I don't want you to give me an answer now. Think about it. But in case you're wondering, I've been tested and can provide you with the results. If you decide you want to do this, I'll expect the same from you."

He brought his hand to her chin, tilting her face up until their eyes met.

"I will respect your limits, Lilly. Even if your answer is no."

A tiny sigh of relief escaped her. Not only was he offering her time to absorb everything, he was *telling* her to take it. To be sure this was what she wanted. There was no pressure, no expectation from him, and some of the ice that had caged itself around her heart melted away.

"Okay. I'll think about it."

He paid for his coffee and they walked outside, stopping at his car.

"Can I drive you home?"

Remembering what happened the last time they were alone together set her teeth on edge, yearning clawing its way up her spine. She wanted to say yes, but a repeat of the previous night wasn't going to help her think things through.

Lilly nodded toward the T. "Thanks, but my line is right there."

Jack moved closer, his height a reminder of all the masculine strength she'd felt the night before. "I want to argue with you and see you home safely. But it's not my place to give you orders. Not yet."

Lilly shuddered. Somewhere deep inside she wanted him to overpower her. To press her up against his car and insist she go home with him. To burn away her demons and make her forget everything but him.

But all Jack did was press his lips to her forehead. His breath formed a warm cloud in the frigid air between them, the vapor kissing her face. A tingling sensation raced down her body, and Lilly closed her eyes briefly at the contact, reopening them when Jack pulled back. He gestured toward the station.

"Go. Call me when you've thought things through."

Lilly walked backward a few steps before turning to cross the street. She paused at the corner and looked over her shoulder. Jack was by his car, watching her. It was so unfamiliar to be cared for like this.

He gave her a little nod, wordlessly telling her to go on. Lilly hugged the papers to her chest and hurried into the subway.

*he purpose of this contract is to allow the submissive to explore her sexuality safely with respect and regard for her needs, her limits and her well-being.*

Lilly curled up under her blanket, Rumbles purring loudly by her side.

*The submissive is to serve, obey and please the Dominant.*

A hot flush stole up her neck. The idea of serving Jack, obeying his commands and submitting to his will sparked an ache between her thighs that begged for her attention, but it scared her too. The simple act of reading through this felt like hazardous territory, a minefield of her past that could blow up at any moment.

She turned the page. The section entitled "Play" was first. It had been left blank, with a note to discuss it beforehand. A series of questions followed.

*Does the submissive have a history of seizures? Of fainting?*

*What will ensure the submissive's safety if the Dominant becomes unconscious?*

She'd never thought of half these things before. Maybe Jack had gone to some kind of Dominance Safety 101 training. He seemed so meticulous; she wouldn't have put it past him, if something like that even existed. At the end of the section, there was a spot to list a "safety call" person, with a note that said "to be determined". Her breathing went tight at the idea of telling someone. Nick was her usual in case of emergency contact, but there was no way his name was going down here. Maybe she could make something up about a blind date and ask Cassie to call in case the guy turned out to be a total psycho, but that didn't seem appealing either. She left it blank and moved on.

*Is it acceptable to the submissive if the play leaves marks?*

God, yes.

Trepidation changed swiftly to longing as she imagined Jack strapping cuffs around her wrists, turning the skin there pink. Striping her ass with his hands, leaving it heated and stinging.

Lilly turned the page, ready to read more, but halted at the next heading.

*Safewords.*

A blank space was beneath it.

She had no idea what to write. "No" probably wasn't a good option. The one time she'd said it to Damien, pleading with him to stop, he'd been so mad that he'd refused to speak to her for a week.

Putting the contract aside, she reached for the articles on "Risk Aware Consensual Kink" and "Safe, Sane and Consensual Play". She read through them, her mind stalling over the word consent every time she saw it. It was a term she knew well from her legal training, and yet she'd never truly given it to Damien. How could she have consented to anything when she never knew what was coming? It was crazy to willingly give up control of your body to someone, and yet here she was, about to let Jack do the same thing.

This was totally different, though. It was one day, and she had some say in what was going to happen. Knowing she could say no, that she could tell him to stop, changed things.

She turned over and retrieved the checklist from the pile. Each term had several columns next to it where she was supposed to enter in a rating: curious, love, like, dislike, soft limit, hard limit. It was a strange kind of thrill—to be offered a chance to choose her surrender and in what ways. It was almost like Christmas, but with far more dangerous toys.

She started checking off the things she loved first. Teasing, fingering, dirty talk, oral—they all made the pulse between her legs grow even stronger. She paused at anal play and put a check mark under "curious". Ropes? Cuffs? Chains? Yes, yes and more yes. She scanned through the different types of bondage, flogging and spankings. Whips were kind of scary, but she'd always wondered what a flogger felt like. Damien never used one on her, preferring to see his own handprints on her skin. Which, at the time, she hadn't minded so much.

Checking "curious" under flogging and writing in the word "very" next to it, she squirmed and pressed her hips against the mattress, aching for some release.

Her mood changed, however, when she came across some of the things that Damien had used, and not in pleasant ways: the medieval-looking Wartenberg he'd brandished when she was tied up. Nipple clamps that bit into her skin so hard it brought on waves of nausea. The blindfold he used to make sure she stayed vulnerable and weak.

Lilly checked "dislike" for all of them, starring them to drive the point home. Then she starred blindfolds a second time.

The next heading was labeled "Edge Play". There was a lot she wanted Jack to do to her, but choking her and using knives weren't among them. She checked "hard limit" for the whole section. When the list was complete, she did one last read-through, and her pencil hovered above one item.

Sex.

It was the most basic thing on there, but it made her pause. She was already on birth control, preferring the regularity it provided, however that wasn't the problem. It was because it was during those intimate moments when Damien was inside her that she'd fooled herself the most. If she and Jack had sex, would she believe this was more than it was?

It wasn't a risk she was willing to take.

Erasing the check she'd put under "love", she replaced it with one under "soft limit". That category was defined as something the submissive has placed strict conditions on, but might still be up for discussion. Lilly knew what her answer in that discussion would be. She turned back to the final page, but her hand froze over the signature line. Putting her name down, actively signing her rights away, felt so...official.

Maybe she should sleep on it. It was late. She had a busy day ahead of her tomorrow, and things might seem clearer in the morning.

Lilly leaned over, dropped the papers on top of her briefcase and shut off the light.

\* \* \*

"Have you found anything useful in those logs?" Cassie asked.

"Not yet." Lilly climbed out of the company car and followed Cassie and Gabe down a broken sidewalk toward Holbrook Laboratories. The cold bit through her stockings. It hadn't been such a brilliant idea to wear a thin skirt and sweater when it was freezing outside, but it was the best option she had when she'd rushed to get ready that morning. She'd overslept after an even more fitful night's sleep than usual. "I did, however, find an entry from June that implies Simon came up with the formula while he worked for the Giordanos."

"That won't help us." Gabe stopped in front of a dilapidated storefront and checked it against the address on his phone. "How discounted a rate is Forrester giving this guy?"

Cassie peered around the side of the building. "Maybe he's paying us in livestock. I wouldn't be surprised if there's a chicken coop back there."

Gabe snorted and yanked open the door. A few minutes later, they were seated in Simon Holbrook's office. It was a dark, cramped space with a red shag carpet that probably hadn't been replaced since the seventies, and Simon looked as disheveled as the room. The frayed edges of a button-down shirt hung loosely over his worn corduroy pants. He sat at his desk and tugged on his thinning hair, the lines above his bushy eyebrows bunching up on his forehead.

"Why don't you start at the beginning?" Cassie suggested. "The facts from your point of view."

Simon pushed up his large glasses over an even larger nose. "For five years I was the Giordanos' chief scientist. They were extremely paranoid. Everyone had to make daily logs in their database, chronicling every detail of the day's work."

As Simon continued to talk, Lilly reached into her briefcase and retrieved a printout of the database file. A few papers slipped out with it. She leaned over to grab them, only to realize they were Jack's checklist and contract, most likely thrown into her bag in her haste to get ready that morning.

Panicked, she snatched them off the ground and shoved them back into her briefcase. Gabe and Cassie were too involved in what their client was saying to notice.

"I hated their business practices and the way they intimidated their employees, so I left," Simon continued. "I opened this lab last summer and finally developed my new formula."

"Our opponents have a different story," Gabe said. "They say you created the formula in their lab and took your research with you. They even have a log entry to prove it."

"They're lying!"

"We know you're upset, Mr. Holbrook," Cassie said calmly. "But we need to figure out what happened."

"Yeah, or I'm going to get whacked."

Gabe stifled a chuckle, covering it with a very overt clearing of his throat.

"You won't get whacked," Cassie insisted. "But they might be able to put you out of business. Can you think of any reason why your former employers would accuse you of stealing?"

Simon sighed. "Because of Jacqui."

Gabe glanced at his notes. "I assume you mean Jacqueline Broussard. The Giordanos' current chief scientist?"

"She was my lead project scientist and friend," Simon explained. "She was promoted after I left, but she didn't belong there. When I made my discovery, I invited her to lunch and offered her a job. I thought she'd jump at the chance, but I was wrong. She needed money. Her mother is sick and the Giordanos pay her more than I can."

"Do you have a receipt from that lunch?"

"Somewhere."

He pulled open a drawer and searched, throwing pieces of paper on the floor and rummaging deeper.

Cassie wrinkled her nose as she watched him. "Do you have any logs of your own notating the creation of the new formula?"

"I do, but it's a hand-dated notebook." Simon stopped hunting. "Please don't let them put me out of business. This is my life's work."

Gabe gave him an understanding smile. "We'll do our best."

They headed out, telling him they'd be in touch. Once they were back in the car, Cassie grumbled, "This is looking better every day."

Lilly tried to focus, to discuss the case and brainstorm ideas, but she couldn't stop thinking about Jack's offer, waiting for her signature in her briefcase. When the driver let them out in front of their building, she paused on the sidewalk.

"I'm going to grab some lunch."

Gabe turned around, eyebrows skyrocketing to his hairline in shock. "You haven't taken a lunch break since you were hired."

Cassie took a step toward her. "You want some company?"

"Nah, I'm just going to look over the files someplace else. See if it helps me think."

Lilly backed away and crossed the street before either of them could say another word. Once she was settled at a café a few blocks away, she took the contract out and read over it again. It seemed less menacing in the light of day, but she still hesitated over signing it.

She pulled her phone from her bag, thumbed over the screen to unlock it and brought up Jack's Facebook profile. As soon as she saw his photo, her body instantly reacted, limbs softening at the memory of his touch. The warmth of his breath. His kiss.

*"I will respect your limits, Lilly. Even if your answer is no."*

Did she want to say no?

There was only one way she'd be able to decide.

# 14

*J*ack glanced at the clock in the back of the classroom.

"Looks like it's time to wrap up," he said. His students began gathering their things. "I'm sure none of you need the reminder about next week's reading. I'll be expecting some lively analysis. If you have questions, you know when my office hours are."

Although he wished they weren't today.

Almost twenty-four hours had gone by since he'd seen Lilly, and the strain of waiting for her answer was driving him crazy.

He collected his laptop and the text he'd been reading from, then left the room and walked down the hall toward his office. The department secretary stopped him before he reached it.

"You've got someone waiting," she told him.

"Already?"

He'd hoped to have a few minutes to himself before the parade of students arrived. He rounded the corner and froze. Lilly was standing outside his office. She was pacing, one hand tugging on a braid that spilled over her shoulder. Concern for her gripped Jack like a vise.

She went stock still when she saw him. Jack neared her and murmured, "This is a surprise."

"I know. I'm sorry. I looked up your office hours online. I thought you might be free, and I...needed to talk."

"Is everything all right?" Lilly nodded but said nothing else. "Let's go inside."

He opened the door and ushered her inside. Heat sputtered from the faintly hissing radiator, glare from the snow-glistening campus shining in through the windows. Jack placed his things on a small table by the door.

"You can put your bag here," he told her. "Let me take your coat."

She put down her bag, took off her coat and handed it to him. She'd been dressed for work—both professional and sexy as hell in a soft cotton sweater, stockings, a skirt and heels. He hung her coat on the back of the door, closed it behind him and locked it.

"What did you need to talk about?"

"I want to. I think—" Lilly blurted out, then winced. "The contract, I mean. I want to. With you."

His cock pulsed, but Jack ignored his body's reaction. He needed to focus on Lilly. "You think, or you know?"

There was a difference, one she had to be sure of.

She fingered her braid again, twisting it even tighter. That nervous habit of hers was out in full force. Jack wondered what it would be like to coil that silky rope around his own fingers, then beat the image back. She was anxious, and needed comforting right now.

He lifted a hand and stroked her cheek with his thumb. "Relax."

"I'm sorry. I'm not sure how to process everything." She took a breath and released her hair. "It's hard to believe you're giving me so much freedom. My ex never did."

"I'm not him," he said simply.

She searched his eyes for a long moment. "I know."

Jack encouraged her to take a deep breath, then another. When she finally seemed calmer, he lowered his hand.

"You read everything I gave you?" he asked. Lilly nodded. "Did you bring the checklist?"

"I did."

"Good girl."

She smiled briefly, a tiny curve of her lips. He put that smile on her face, and he wanted to keep it there. She liked being praised. He'd have to remember that.

Jack held out his hand. "Let me see it."

Lilly went back to the door and retrieved the papers from her bag. When he took them from her, he let his fingers brush along hers, his touch lingering until she blushed.

"Have a seat," he told her, and Lilly sank into a chair.

Checklist in hand, he strode toward the window and flipped the blinds shut. He started at the last page, scanning through some of the riskier stuff, relieved to see she'd put hard limits on all edge play. That had never been his thing. He continued flipping backward, his eyes drawn to the items he most wanted to read. She'd checked "curious" for flogging. Good. He'd love to introduce her to that, to hear her startled gasp at the heavy thump of the tails. It seemed she liked being restrained too, and he relished the image of her shackled in his cuffs.

Corralling his concentration, Jack scanned through the rest, noting her dislikes and limits. He stopped short, though, when he reached the first page.

She'd put a soft limit on sex?

That was a surprise, but then again, how much did he really know about her? No matter what she'd admitted in the diner, he was pretty sure he'd only heard a small part of her story.

Jack turned back to face her.

"I'm proud of how thoroughly you've gone through this, and I want you to know how brave I think you are." He moved to a spot between where she was sitting and his desk, leaning against it. "Would you mind explaining the reasons for some of your dislikes?"

"Which ones?"

He glanced at the list. "The nipple clamps, for example."

The color drained from her face. "They hurt a lot when my ex used them. The Wartenberg wheel too."

"Did he use them for punishment?"

"No. I think he just liked hurting me." She laughed softly. "In a multitude of ways."

It was obvious there was more to it than that, but he didn't want to push. "What about blindfolds?"

"I just haven't had good experiences with them." Her shoulders curled inward. She took a shaky breath. "I don't like being in the dark like that."

The look on her face was so heartbreaking that Jack wanted to pull her into his arms.

"And the limit on sex?"

She cringed. "I'm sorry."

"You have nothing to be sorry about. I just want to know why."

"I didn't think it was a good idea, since this isn't a relationship."

"Hmm." That wasn't quite an answer. "Is there something you're not telling me? Did your ex ever force you?"

"No, Damien did a lot of horrible things, but he never raped me."

Damien. What a perfect name for someone who sounded so evil.

She picked at her skirt. "I understand if it makes you not want to do this."

Jack put the paperwork down and reached for her hands. He pulled her up to stand and looked her in the eye.

"I want to."

She awarded him with another tiny smile. "I can get you the results of my last STD test. But you should know I left a few things blank on the contract."

"Like what?"

"I didn't pick someone for a safety call," she said. "I think I'd rather keep this between us."

That was a relief. He'd have given her the option if she needed it, but telling someone would make this a hell of a lot more complicated.

"Me too." Jack rubbed his thumbs over the tops of her hands. "What else did you leave blank?"

She shifted her weight and looked at the floor again. "The safeword. I didn't know what to write."

A deep V had formed between her brows, a frown on her lips that spoke of shame. Jack slid his hands up her forearms and stroked her shoulders, her hair, the sides of her neck. Cupping her cheek, he moved in close and kissed her softly. Slowly. So slowly that when he pulled away, Lilly's eyes were still closed, her mouth open, her body leaning into him for more.

"Let's figure one out for you then."

She opened her eyes and smiled, big and wide and bright, hope like a ray of light on her face. The sight did things to him that it shouldn't have, tugged at an empty space inside him.

He put that thought aside.

"Colors are commonly used," he explained. "Green to tell me you're okay and you like what I'm doing. Yellow to tell me you're nearing your limit. Red for stopping the scene entirely. Do those work?"

"I like that."

"Good. I also think it's important we don't use our names in my playroom. It will help to keep us in the right frame of mind. I liked calling you little girl. Are you comfortable with that, and with calling me Sir?"

A tiny tremble was coupled with a quickened breath. A rush of pink colored her cheeks. "I'm comfortable."

Jack grinned, enjoying the high he got from her reaction. Now that she felt more secure, it was time to push her a little. To make her hungry with anticipation. He needed her desperate, not only to be in his playroom, but to crave giving over power to him.

"Do you want to put a date on the contract?" he asked.

"Sure...I guess? I mean, when did you want to do this?"

"As soon as you're ready. Because you know what it means when you are, don't you?"

Lilly hesitated, an even deeper blush covering the freckles on her cheeks. He'd love to see where else those adorable little marks ran across her flesh.

"What does it mean?"

He brought his lips to her ear and whispered, "It means for one day, your body will be mine. Your skin, your moans, your scent, your taste. They're all mine."

Lilly inhaled sharply. Seeing her so turned on was a delicious image, one he wanted to savor. But there was something he needed to take care of first.

Jack clasped his hands behind his back and began walking around her.

"First, however, we have to discuss the error you made."

That startled her. She turned back to look at him, her brows high and pressed together. Jack raised his chin and pointed to the floor. Her gaze obediently fell to the carpet.

Perfect.

"Do you want to tell me what you think your mistake was?"

"I—" She halted. Jack watched her closely as he continued to circle her. Underneath the soft fabric of her sweater, her nipples had stiffened. She was confused but not scared, turned on even in her uncertainty.

To help her understand, he grabbed her braid and tugged her head back. "I don't like surprises, Lilly."

She gasped when he let her go. "I came to your office without contacting you first."

He let that sit for a beat. "And why might that be a problem?"

"You could've been busy. Students could've been here."

She knew the answer now but didn't realize he was simply testing her, employing the same method of questioning he used with his students—another question for an answer. Only with her, the game was much more fun.

Moving to her side, he clasped her chin in a grip just shy of rough and drew her face up. "And what could you do differently in the future, so as not to displease me?"

"I should get your permission first, Sir."

Smart girl. And fuck, he loved it when she called him that.

"Yes. You should." He caressed her cheek, then stepped behind her once again and leaned in close. "How to punish you."

She stiffened, her arousal edged out by sudden fear. Jack clucked his tongue.

"I'm not going to hurt you." He tugged down the edge of her collar and ran his lips over her neck, biting below her jaw line. She went up on her toes, breath hitching. "You'll be in pain, all right, but not the way you think."

He gripped her by the hips and pushed her toward his desk. Seizing her wrists, he locked her hands down on the surface.

"Stay," he whispered, nipping at hear earlobe. Lilly moaned softly. "Oh no. We can't have that. Can't have everyone hearing you."

He covered her mouth with one hand, and the beast within him yanked on its leash at the sensation of Lilly held captive. But Jack was in control. Nudging her lips apart, he gave in to the pleasure of sliding the cage door open, of letting his dominant side take over, and plunged his thumb into her mouth.

"Show me," he ordered, grazing it along her tongue. "Show me what you are."

He waited, needing to break her down, to see her give in and become the submissive he knew she wanted to be. Lilly groaned and licked once along the intrusion before sucking hard, rhythmically drawing his thumb deeper until her cheeks hollowed out.

"Good girl." Jack kissed the side of her face. "Such a good little girl, sucking my thumb like it's the sweetest thing you've ever tasted."

He slid his other hand around to her belly. Pressing the heel of his hand into the soft hollow above her pelvis, he gently increased the pressure until Lilly's hips flexed and she panted out a sharp breath through her nose. Unable to stand the inch of space that remained between them, Jack brought his hips flush against her ass. She was all heat and lush curves, and he let himself have a moment to feel it, to let the pleasure roll through him.

Lilly groaned again and pressed backward, seeking more.

"So needy. Are you wet?"

She whimpered around his thumb. It was a pitiful, wonderful sound.

"I bet you are. I bet you're dying for more. I bet you're aching for it."

Jack dipped his middle finger over her pubic bone and searched for the top of her slit through the thin fabric of her skirt. He found the cleft with a practiced touch and rubbed it in a tiny, teasing circle.

Lilly sagged toward his desk even as she kept working herself against him.

"That's right. I know what you need. You need my hands on you, holding you down. Making you come."

She was shaking so hard she was probably close to coming already. Jack withdrew his thumb from her mouth and cradled her throat with one hand, continuing to stroke her through her clothes with the other. Pulling her upright, he tilted her chin back. Her eyes were pinched shut, her mouth open as she writhed against the movement of his hand.

"Do you want to come, little girl?"

"Yes, Sir." Her answer came out in a high-pitched whine of pure, unadulterated need. Which was exactly where he wanted her.

He released her and stepped away. Lilly whipped her head around. Her face was a mask of agony, her hands gripping his desk. Jack smirked. Sure, it was torture for him too, but leaving her like this had been his plan all along.

"Your punishment will be no orgasms until you're in my playroom." If she was this wound up, he could only guess what a few days without any relief was going to do to her. "I think that will be suitably painful, don't you?"

Her mouth opened in protest, but she said nothing.

"Good girl. Now, did you want to put a date on that contract?"

## 15

*J*ack drove home with an energy he could barely contain, his fingers tapping on the steering wheel. He was still buzzing off everything that had transpired in his office, off Lilly, off the fact that in two days he'd have her on her knees in his playroom.

When he'd asked if she wanted to put a date on the contract, she'd grabbed it and asked if Saturday was too soon. She'd agreed to the rest of his terms—that she wear her hair loose and down, her body prepared by either waxing or shaving, and arrive at noon with her schedule cleared until five. All his concerns that she might not be ready were eradicated, and now Jack's mind was full of the things he wanted to do to her.

He cut the engine in his driveway when his cell rang. Hoping it wasn't Lilly having second thoughts, Jack looked at the screen. Not her.

"Yes, Brady?" he asked once he'd answered the call, both relieved and annoyed.

His brother started to answer, but female shrieks in the background cut him off. "Hope, let go of your sister's hair right now!" he bellowed, then resumed a normal decibel. "Jesus, how long until these two are in college?"

"You've got a while." Jack climbed out of the car. "Was there a reason for your call?"

"I can't make it to Barrel 'n' Flask tomorrow night. Sammy's planned a family campout in the basement." Brady sighed dramatically. "She's already got me pitching a tent."

"You love it."

"Yeah, yeah. So, you good on your own?"

Jack let himself inside and set his things down. Brady being a no-show fit in perfectly with his plans.

"Actually, I was planning on staying in."

Lilly had said she wouldn't be going to the pub tomorrow either, which was a relief. It would've been difficult to stop himself from joining her, and he had preparations to make.

"Aw, come on, Jack. You were finally getting out. Don't bail on that now."

"I'm fine. I just have some things to do. I'll go next week. Promise."

Mollified, Brady let it go. After they hung up, Jack went to the basement. Anticipation rolled through him as he walked downstairs through the darkened apartment and pushed the playroom door open. He expected to be greeted by a cold, stale wall of empty air, but was enveloped by warmth instead. Jack flipped on the light switch and checked the thermostat, remembering how he'd always set it higher in here than the rest of the house. Nudity and chilly temperatures weren't a friendly combination.

He turned and surveyed the room. It wasn't like the dungeons he'd seen advertised online with everything ensconced in black, nor was it similar to the playrooms he'd read about in novels, walls and linens swathed in red. It was painted a creamy beige, with drapery on the rectangular, high windows set to match. A simple queen-sized bed dominated the middle of the room, bookended by nightstands. A mirror and a tall armoire sat across from it. With the hand and foot restraints tucked under the mattress, and the armoire full of toys locked, no one would've guessed that this space was anything more than a guest room.

He ran his hand over the bed, then headboard. The pads of his fingers came up with a thin layer of dust. He grabbed a towel from the neatly folded pile in the closet and cleaned it off, then did the same to the panel for the built-in stereo tucked away on a shelf. He flicked the power on, testing the speakers, then checked that the mini-fridge was still running and stocked with bottles of water.

After cleaning off the remaining surfaces, Jack found the key to the armoire in its hiding place, hanging on a ribbon behind a piece of artwork. His pulse quickened as he unfastened the lock and opened the doors.

Wrist and ankle restraints hung from hooks on the left side, followed by chains to link them, then a furl of silk rope. He touched the smooth wood of his paddle next, then his long, black riding crop. The memories stirred by the woodsy scent of leather and the tinny chime of metal made his body stir. He pulled open the drawer at the bottom, where the smaller objects were kept, most notably the items Lilly disliked. Jack fingered the blindfold, then the clamps. It was a shame she had such a strong distaste for them. He'd love to see her senses heightened from lack of sight, to watch her reaction as he tugged on the chain.

His gaze was drawn to the opposite door, the one with all his floggers. Jack fingered each one with reverence: first the fur-tipped and velvet ones, then deerskin and suede, followed by heavy leather. Jack smiled at his beautiful arsenal. He knew these instruments well —what reaction he could get from the lightest touch with some, how much force to use with others, and the surprising pleasure the littlest ones could bring.

Seduced by the urge to feel its power, Jack picked up the suede flogger. It fit perfectly in his hand, spots worn into the leather handle from frequent use. He practiced twirling it, easily picking up the motion. Stepping back and facing the wall, Jack dragged the tips back with his other hand and snapped the falls out across the wall. The thumping sound of the impact gave him a rush. He could almost see Lilly's body rolling as the stinging strike bloomed into pleasure. The idea thrilled him to the point of being painfully hard. Jack retreated to the bed, flogger in one hand, the other drawn to the stiff shape in his pants.

He closed his eyes and pictured Lilly waiting for him on all fours, her legs spread, ass on display, rising up to him as he palmed each rosy cheek. She'd be so perfectly vulnerable, so open to him. He could trace her spine with the riding crop. Listen to her sharp intake of breath as he swatted it against the swell of her bottom.

No, if he was going to spank her, he'd rather feel her flesh against the palm of his hand.

Fuck.

Jack unbuttoned his pants and freed his cock. Dragging a tight fist over his hard flesh, he replayed the sounds of Lilly's desperate whimpers in his mind. She'd broken down so beautifully with his thumb in her mouth, but he wanted more. To hear her cries of pleasure as he stroked her bare slit. He pumped harder, imagining climbing on the bed behind her and the blissful slide into wet flesh as he drove himself inside her.

But sex with her wouldn't be happening. Not with a soft limit on it.

Jack squeezed his erection with a groan. He'd gotten an idea of how to push Lilly's buttons, and had a feeling he could get her worked up enough that she'd be willing to go past it, but that wouldn't be right. No matter how badly he wanted her, he told her he'd respect her limits, and pushing this one was no way to treat her. Not after what she'd been through.

Jack blew out a breath and looked up at the ceiling, staring at his surroundings to ground his thoughts. An empty planter hung from the steel hook he'd soldered in the corner, planning to experiment with suspension before Eve got sick.

Eve.

He'd been so overcome with wanting Lilly, he didn't think about the fact he was bringing her here, the space he'd created and shared with his wife. His hard-on subsided as guilt stabbed, but he fought back the feeling of betrayal. He and Lilly were only going to be doing this once, and they definitely wouldn't be having sex. He wouldn't even let her touch him.

Satisfied with the justification, Jack buttoned his pants, stood and tucked the flogger back in the armoire.

* * *

*He was ignoring her again, and she hadn't even done anything wrong yet.*

*"I'm not ignoring you," Damien had insisted, his tone distant and cold. "This is the way it has to be if you want to keep doing this. No one can know."*

*This was the way it had to be, if she wanted to be his.*

Lilly's nightmare woke her up early on Saturday. She sat up and thumbed her phone to check the time. She wouldn't be meeting Jack for hours, but she couldn't go back to sleep now. That particular memory of Damien stung more than all the others, although she couldn't put her finger on why. There were a million more painful things he'd done to her than pretend she didn't exist.

At least she didn't have to worry about Jack casting her aside like that, because what they were about to do was totally different. It was consensual, all the rules written down on crisp pieces of paper. She knew what was expected of her, and in return she was going to get five hours of Jack's undivided attention.

Lilly touched her lips, remembering his thumb inside her mouth. The pressure of his hand below her belly, and the sweet agony of his almost-there caress. It was the most aroused she'd ever been, and he'd barely even touched her.

Yes, today would be totally different. And she couldn't wait for it to start.

She got up to shower, unprepared for how the rush of hot water would feel on her recently waxed skin. Her appointment Friday night had been her excuse to get out of going to the pub, although she could've used a cocktail afterward. She hadn't had to withstand that particular brand of torture in a while. It had been months since her skin was this exposed, and after the initial pain subsided, she lingered under the stream, letting the water tease her smooth, bare crevices. An ache quickly flared, the same restless, frustrated desire she'd felt since she left Jack's office. The need for release clawed at her.

He wasn't kidding about her being in pain.

Keeping her mind busy with getting ready, she dried her hair, then donned the nicest lingerie she had, covering it with a pair of black leggings, an oversized ivory sweater and her sheepskin-lined boots. After eating breakfast and spending some time working through briefs she'd brought home, Lilly poured extra food for Rumbles and went out into the day. Jack had offered to pick her up, but she'd insisted on getting there herself. Too edgy to sit, she stood as the T rolled its way toward Cambridge. The doors opened at Harvard Square, and she followed the directions Jack had given her. The temperature was barely above freezing, typical for Boston in the dead of winter, but the sun made it feel less bleak outside, snow shining in the midday light.

A few blocks up Massachusetts Avenue, Lilly turned down a side street and stopped in front of a sprawling Victorian home. A wraparound porch hugged it close, each window framed by dark green shutters. It looked so safe, so sturdy and welcoming.

Just like Jack.

"I see you found the place."

She jumped at the sound of his voice and found him standing at the door. It was obvious from his smirk that he'd been watching her, and Lilly's cheeks heated as she went up the walkway, half at having been caught gawking and half at Jack's appearance. He was barefoot, dressed casually in worn jeans and a white tee. A long sleeved flannel was halfway buttoned over it. He'd rolled the sleeves up to his elbows, showing off the cords of lean muscle that flexed as he held the door open for her.

God. *God.*

"Did you have any trouble getting here?" His voice blanketed her as much as the breath of heat she felt in the foyer as he closed the door behind them. She shook her head. "Good. Let me take your coat."

Jack lifted it from her shoulders, and she shivered from the contact when his fingers brushed over her neck. He hung her coat in a closet, then showed her where she could toe off her boots, stowing them in an entryway bench that was lined with cubbies. The sight of their bare feet on the dark wood floor together was oddly intimate. Jack held out his hand and smiled.

"Let me show you around."

Lilly slipped her hand into his. His fingers were strong and reassuring as they curled around hers. He led her past a staircase, pointing up to where his bedroom was on the second floor, his office on the third. Next was an inviting living room, filled with cushy sofas, bookshelves and a fireplace, then an archway leading into a grand kitchen. It was filled with natural light, windows everywhere. An island sat in the middle, with enough counter space to prepare food for a dozen people.

For a moment, she felt unwelcome, like she was intruding on the space that his wife spent long hours in. The table where his son might have done his homework.

*One day,* she thought to herself and the ghosts she imagined around her. *I'm only here for one day.*

Jack pulled out a barstool from the island and gestured for her to sit. "Can I get you anything? Coffee?"

"No, thank you." She was jittery enough.

He sat down next to her. "You could have let me pick you up at the T, you know. You didn't have to walk."

Lilly smiled. It was nice how he wanted to look after her. "It wasn't that far. And I used to run, so it was good to get some exercise again."

Jack cocked his head to the side. "You ran...marathons?"

"Hah. No, I was never that good. But I was a pretty valuable member of my high school track team. I kept up with it all the way up through law school."

"But you said 'used to'."

Lilly confirmed his verification with a quick nod. She didn't want to get into all that right now. "I work crazy hours. I don't have time for it anymore."

He studied her for a beat longer. "Got it. How's that case you mentioned going?"

"Still frustrating." Giving him a sideways glance, she added, "The last two days have been *especially* frustrating."

"I'm guessing you don't mean with work."

"Nope."

Jack laughed. His voice was husky when he added, "If it helps, I've felt the same way."

Desire rushed over her, and Lilly shifted on the stool. The idea of Jack as frustrated as she'd been was too much to handle, as was his gentle touch when he stroked her lightly up her arm.

"Before we start, I want to make sure you're comfortable with what we discussed."

"I am." Gooseflesh rose and spread in the wake of his touch. "Do I get to see your checklist?"

"You can if you want, but I assure you they match up. Perfectly."

She was probably supposed to reply, but the movement of his hand was distracting her. Jack smirked and her cheeks went hot again.

"I'll take your word for it," she said, embarrassed. Jack was all too capable of making her blush. And by the pleased smile quirking up his lips, she was pretty sure it was a fact he was aware of.

"Good. I've planned a scene within your limits. We can discuss it beforehand, if you'd like."

His hand drifted over her shoulder and into her hair, fingering the strands, a hint of what was to come but sweet at the same time. It made her dizzy, how tender he was with her. For the first time in so long, she felt calm. Safe.

"We don't need to," she said. "I trust you."

A pause followed. "Good."

Jack's gaze grew intense, firm, his demeanor shifting. He stood and waited for her to do the same, then walked her down the hallway, stopping in front of a closed door. He pulled her in front of him, and Lilly's heart stuttered.

"Now, Lilly," he said. "Now, you're mine."

## 16

*"Mine."* Lilly's breath caught at the feeling of Jack's touch, his body so warm and solid behind her. She melted into his heat, wanting more than anything to be his, just for a few hours. He marked the flesh below her ear with a kiss, then moved around her and opened the door.

"Follow me."

Without another word, he led her downstairs. The area was dimly lit, with just enough light for her to make out a kitchenette and a small living area. Sensual music got louder as he guided her toward the back of the space and into a room lit with candlelight.

It would've seemed like nothing more than an ordinary bedroom, if it weren't for the gleaming chains that had been stretched between the foot and headboards of the bed. Two pairs of leather cuffs and a feather tickler had been placed on it. A pillow was on the floor.

Panic sparked. Her pulse started to race. She drew in what was supposed to be a steadying breath, but it didn't help. She crossed her arms and tried to calm down, to recall how confident she felt in the kitchen, but she couldn't.

Jack walked ahead of her and sat down in an armchair. "Take your clothes off and put them in the closet. Keep your eyes on me."

Lilly inhaled another shaky breath. Her arms felt rubbery as she peeled off her sweater and leggings, her hands trembling so much she had trouble unclasping her bra. She struggled to keep eye contact as she hooked her thumbs in her panties and tugged them down, turning back to face him after she'd stashed it all in the closet.

"What's the pillow for?" Her mouth had gone dry, and her voice came out hoarse. "Sir."

"So you don't get rug burns on your knees."

"Oh." Which meant he planned on having her down there for a while.

Jack stood and pointed to the cushion.

"Kneel. Your bottom on your heels, arms behind your back."

Lilly knelt down and tucked her feet under her rear. She crossed her wrists at the small of her back, posture straight, eyes on the floor. The position felt familiar, natural, and yet, she couldn't stop shaking.

A paralyzing doubt gripped her, dread a heavy weight in her stomach. Jack could do whatever he wanted to her, and she'd have to take it. She had no idea how long she knelt there, time seeming to stretch on and on. Lilly tried to concentrate on the music, on her breathing, on anything other than how naked and exposed she was, but all she could hear was the frantic pounding of her heart.

Jack's footsteps were quiet as he stepped in close behind her.

"Are you ready to play, little girl?"

Lilly swallowed. "Yes, Sir," she said, even though she wasn't. It was too late for doubt now.

He circled her in a slow prowl. "Do you know how often I've thought about you like this?"

She clamored for another breath. It was like breathing through a straw. "No, Sir."

"Too often. More often than I should. And now here you are, just as I imagined." He continued walking around her, a hunter lying in wait. "Now I get to see the part of you no one else knows about. See you so crazed with hunger you're begging for relief. But as lovely as you look on your knees, I want to see all of what belongs to me. Stand up."

She rose as gracefully as she could, her joints sore from kneeling, limbs awkward with her arms behind her.

"Spread your legs," he ordered. Lilly complied, widening her stance. "Look at you. So eager and willing."

*"Dirty fucking slut."*

The memories slashed through her mind, making her tense and shiver.

Jack chuckled. "Oh, yes. You'll shiver, and harder than that. You will whimper and plead. Your skin will be raw, your throat raspy from screaming. And I'm going to enjoy every fucking second of it."

His hands finally met her bare skin in a caress along her shoulders, and Lilly jolted from his touch as sharply as if she'd been shocked with a cattle prod. A sob burst out before she could stop it. She ripped her hand from behind her and covered her mouth, but it only managed to muffle her cry.

Jack was quiet for a moment. Then, softly, "Where did you go?"

Lilly dropped her hand but shook her head, unable to answer. Jack stepped around to face her, dipping his head in an attempt to catch her gaze, but she couldn't meet his eyes. She couldn't bear to see how furious he must be with her.

"Lilly." He cupped her face in his hands, breaking the mood like a spell. "Talk to me."

She found the strength to look at him. "I'm afraid."

"Of me?"

"No, not you. Not really." She hugged her arms close to her and glanced around the room. "Of this. Of what's going to happen."

His brows drew together. "Why didn't you safeword?"

The safewords. She'd completely forgotten about them. "I didn't remember I could."

Jack cringed. He lowered his hands to her shoulders, and Lilly waited for his disappointment. For him to tell her she'd wasted his time.

"It's my fault," he said.

She blinked. "What?"

"I should've known you'd have trouble with that. I should've reminded you."

"You're not...mad at me?"

"Of course not."

Jack rubbed his palms up and down her arms in a hypnotic rhythm, and the clutch of terror lodged in her chest loosened. His touch was an anchor, a reminder of how much she'd wanted this, and she exhaled, her arms dropping to her sides. But as her fears ebbed, embarrassment took their place.

Lilly stared at the ground. "I felt so brave before."

"You are brave. It took a lot of courage for you to come here today, didn't it?"

"I suppose."

Jack cupped her face again. "Look at me."

She lifted her gaze and found only comfort in his eyes.

"Don't be so hard on yourself. You're much stronger than you give yourself credit for."

His tone was gentle, his words soothing. It seemed silly now to have gotten scared. She'd never felt anything but secure with him.

"Thank you," she said, then quickly added, "Sir."

Jack tenderly kissed her forehead, and the move drew her eyes to his bare torso. She hadn't noticed that he'd removed his shirt. The haze of anxiety she'd been clouded in started to lift as she watched his arms flex, saw the strength within them. The sculpted planes of his chest, his muscles ropy and notched where they met his shoulders.

His eyes sparkled when he caught her looking at him. "Do you want to continue?"

Her heart rate sped up, but there was no panic. She wanted this, wanted him. "Yes, Sir."

"Do you trust me?"

She did. She didn't know why she'd forgotten that. "I do, Sir."

"Then close your eyes."

Lilly obeyed. Jack's lips brushed against hers, soft and reassuring, before he deepened the kiss, teasing her mouth with his tongue.

"Tell me your safewords," he murmured.

The words they'd agreed on came back to her slowly. "Red, yellow and green, Sir."

"Good girl." Jack stepped behind her once again and trailed his fingers over her neck, her shoulders, her back. "Relax. Let go of your past. There's no room for ghosts here."

He gathered her hair, lifted it up, and pressed an open-mouthed kiss to the back of her neck. Heat bloomed and rushed down her spine.

"You're here with me," he said. "And while you're with me, while you're naked in my playroom, you're mine. Every part of you is mine."

His words put her into a trance. Jack pulled her to him, and his body was a wall of strength along her spine. She could feel the thick, hard line of him through his jeans. He nipped at the juncture of her neck and shoulder, a small bite that sent a staggering blaze of need through her. Lilly rose up on her tiptoes, trying to gather more of the sensation. She pouted when he pulled back, feeling the air shift as he stepped around in front of her, his hands gently bracing her shoulders.

"Open your eyes."

She did, and found herself under the weight of mischievous, dangerous blue. His eyes were hungry, a skillful predator staring down his prey.

"Tell me who you belong to."

"You, Sir. I'm yours."

He wrapped one hand around her neck, collaring her with his fingers. "What color?"

"Green, Sir."

Jack smiled wickedly and released her throat. "Now, little girl, we play. Hands behind your back."

He retrieved the restraints from the bed and wrapped one cuff around each of her wrists, then did the same to her ankles. He stood back to look at her, then kissed her fiercely, thumbs grazing her nipples. When he bent down and took one taut bud in his mouth, she almost toppled forward, the sensation sending a spark from her breasts to her clit. He paid the same attention to the other breast, then pulled back and retrieved the feather tickler, twirling it between his fingers as he looked her over.

"I want you to stay perfectly still."

Jack waited until she nodded, then chased the feather between her breasts. He fanned it over her nipples, wet from his mouth. Lilly strained to keep motionless, her nerve endings firing. Every limb was quivering by the time he'd stroked it from her shoulders down to her ankles, up her thighs and between her legs. She instinctively bowed toward the feeling, and Jack immediately stopped. He raised an eyebrow.

"I told you not to move, didn't I?"

"You did, Sir."

But he wasn't angry. He simply waited until she was settled before bringing the feather between her legs again, grazing it along her clit. Lilly shuddered, her arms trembling as she fought the urge to rock against it. Jack pulled the feather away, and she let out a helpless whimper. He mimicked the noise she'd made, and the sound of him making fun of her was demeaning and seductive all at the same time.

"You want more, don't you?" he asked.

"Yes, Sir."

"Do I have to ask if you've been good? If you've suffered through your punishment?"

God, couldn't he tell? "I've suffered, Sir."

Jack brought his lips to her ear. She could feel the shape of his smile pressed against her skin. "Then I look forward to rewarding you. Get on the bed, on your hands and knees, facing the headboard."

Lilly scrambled onto the mattress. Desire coursed through her as he linked the cuffs on her wrists and ankles to the chains, binding her to the posts.

"Do you have enough give?"

She tested the slack. "I do, Sir." She was comfortable, her arms close enough together that she could stay balanced. Her legs were wide open, her body completely exposed, but instead of shame and fear, she felt only want. An aching emptiness, the tender bud between her legs throbbing. Lilly squirmed, desperate for relief.

"Patience, little girl. I didn't say I was rewarding you yet."

He danced a fingertip along her thighs and rear, taking his time, his touch skirting right past where she needed it until he brushed her sensitive flesh in a glancing touch, then swiftly moved away. An endless amount of teasing followed, his fingers spread as he traced the insides of her knees, up the backs of her legs and over her rear. When he brushed along her pussy lips again, Lilly rocked backward into his hand, keening in need. By the third taunting touch, her head dropped, a low groan escaping her.

"Is this frustrating you?" he asked. "Is it making you wet?"

"So wet, Sir," she blurted out, but her words melted into a moan as Jack finally sank a finger inside her. He pumped once—one delicious, maddeningly slow thrust, before sliding it free.

"Very wet, indeed."

Lilly made a noise she wasn't sure sounded human.

Jack chuckled and skirted his touch up to rub her swollen clit. She cried out, shocked at how easily he found her most sensitive spots. With tight circles, he worked her quickly. Too quickly. She felt her release bearing down on her at the same instant he stopped. She moaned loudly at the loss.

"My poor, aching girl. I haven't given you permission to come, have I?"

"No, Sir," she whined, shaking her head. Jack landed one light swat on her ass. It wasn't enough, not nearly enough, and she arched up for more.

"How long has it been, hmm? How long since you were properly spanked?"

She yelped when he swatted her again. "Too long, Sir."

"Is that what you want? To be spanked?" His hand dipped down to her wet flesh again. "Or do you want to be fucked by my fingers?"

Lilly closed her eyes and groaned. "I want both, Sir."

"So greedy. You want both?"

"Yes, Sir."

"Then beg me."

Lilly stiffened. She never imagined she'd let herself beg for this again. "Please, Sir," she whispered.

"Please, what?"

"Please give me both, Sir."

His finger circled her opening. "You can do better than that."

"Please, God, I need it."

He smacked her harder, a blissful sting that morphed into pleasure. He kept his hand against her freshly spanked skin, stroking her burning flesh once before pulling away again.

"No!" she cried.

"I told you to beg."

"Please, please, please!"

"Not good enough," he said through clenched teeth.

Lilly clutched the sheets, her sanity crumbling. The need to obey, the need to please him and the blinding, frantic need for release made her entire body buckle down.

"Please, Sir, spank me, touch me, anything, fuck! God...just... please."

Jack grabbed a fistful of her hair and dragged her head back. The look in his eyes was wild. Feral.

"There it is. That's what I wanted to see," he hissed. "When you wake up tomorrow with your ass screaming, you will think about me. My hands on you. Nobody else's."

He kissed her then, a rough, searing kiss that claimed, their teeth clashing before he abruptly let go of her hair. He slid two fingers inside her as his other hand came down on her ass, hard.

"God, yes." Lilly bowed her head, sinking into the sweet torture. "Thank you, Sir."

Jack started a pattern, lashing her over and over as he pumped faster, working her into liquid fire. When her release started to rip through her, Jack slowed his strokes and slipped his fingers free, leaving her trembling, right on the edge.

"You want to come?"

The agony of holding out for this moment washed over her. "I want to, Sir. So bad."

"Two more spanks and I'll let you. These won't be gentle, though."

She tried to prepare herself, but when his palm cracked against her ass, Lilly cried out in real pain, nausea crawling up her throat along with the sickening worry that she'd been wrong all along. That this was when he was going to hurt her.

Then she felt Jack's lips over her skin, kissing where he'd struck.

"Such a beautiful, brave girl, giving herself to me like this."

Her heart skipped a beat, his intimate touch and words of reassurance reaching a place inside her that had been broken for so long. He might hurt her, but he wouldn't harm her, and Lilly realized that she could take more. She *wanted* to take more, for him.

She didn't wait for him to ask what color. She simply whispered, "Green."

Jack exhaled softly, then smacked her hard enough to propel her forward on the bed. A tear trickled down her face, but it wasn't from the pain—it was in relief and pride that she'd taken what he wanted to give. He freed her from the chains and rolled her onto her back, somehow preventing her sore bottom from rasping against the sheets. Her breathing hitched when he climbed onto the bed and maneuvered her legs over his shoulders, lowering his face between her thighs.

"Come for me."

He slid his tongue along her clit, his fingers pushing, thrusting, and Lilly's hands found their way into his hair, her eyes slamming shut. It was too much. Her legs involuntarily clamped together, but he wedged his arm across her thigh, a steel cable pinning her down and opening her up even more. He pressed his free hand down gently on her belly, sharpening the sensation of every lick and thrust, until she finally, blissfully came apart. Lilly cursed and thrashed, helpless to the pleasure that barreled through her, arching off the bed with the force of her release.

She was sure she'd died by the time the last spasm ripped through her, but Jack didn't stop. He replaced his tongue with his fingers and demanded, "Again."

She shook her head—it wasn't possible, not after coming so

hard, but he worked her relentlessly until a second, even more intense, orgasm took hold.

Spent and shuddering with aftershocks, she was vaguely aware of Jack moving her body, urging her face down on the bed. Of him unbuckling the cuffs, massaging her wrists and ankles. The liberation was a strange discomfort. He spread something moist and cool along her backside, and Lilly whimpered, feeling adrift. Like she didn't know how to come back to herself again.

"Shhh." A blanket came over her and Jack pulled her into his arms. "I'm here."

Her mind glazed over. Her eyes closed.

Sometime later she awoke with a start. With her body sore and tender, she expected to be greeted by an empty bed and the sound of the shower in the background, the clock ticking the seconds down to her obligatory quick exit. But she wasn't in Damien's bed. She was in Jack's, and he was right there, holding her, his breathing soft against her hair.

"Are you all right? You slept so fitfully."

It was unfamiliar and lovely, to be held like this after what he'd done to her.

"Yes." Her voice was gravelly, just as he'd promised it would be. "Thank you, Sir."

"You're welcome."

His fingers crossed her back in lazy, unhurried strokes. Lilly stretched and started at the tenderness on her backside, but the hot skin felt good. She looked down at her wrists and stroked the skin he'd cuffed. Shifted her legs at the lingering wetness between her thighs. She'd never been through the aftermath of a scene without humiliation and pain, but Jack hadn't made her feel shameful.

He made her feel beautiful.

Moving purposefully, Lilly lifted her leg over his and brushed it against the bulge in his jeans. Jack's lips parted on a jagged inhale, his limbs going rigid. She smiled, loving the reaction she'd triggered in him, and tentatively reached down to where his cock strained beneath the denim.

"May I, Sir?"

Jack hissed, his hips arching up toward her touch, but then he grunted and took her hand in his. He brought it up to his chest and held it there.

"No, you may not."

The rejection stung. "But, Sir, it's my job to serve you."

"It's your job to do what I tell you to do."

There was a finality to his words, but his breathing was heavy, his eyes flashing. Did he want her to beg again?

"Please?"

"Lilly, stop."

It was a shock to hear her name again. Her face fell. It was over, and he wasn't going to let her touch him. "I don't understand."

"There's nothing to understand. Today was about you."

Jack kissed her forehead and quickly shifted away. He put his T-shirt back on, grabbed his flannel and retrieved a bottle of water from a mini-fridge in the closet. "Drink this. Get dressed and meet me in the kitchen when you're ready. We'll talk there."

She took the bottle and watched him walk out the door. He didn't look back before closing it behind him.

Stunned, Lilly covered herself with the sheet. It didn't make any sense. Jack hadn't seemed displeased with her, hadn't strode away with satisfied indifference like Damien did. He rushed out of the room as if it were on fire. As if *he* were on fire.

She frowned. Why wouldn't he let her touch him? She could tell how worked up he was. She'd felt the proof of it, hard and greedy for her touch. He wanted her, and she wanted to give him the release he hadn't felt in so long.

The kind of release he gave her.

"Oh," she said. "Today was about me."

Everything he did today was for her. He'd never had any intention of asking for anything in return.

Well. Hell, no.

Determined, Lilly stood and reached for her clothes. They'd only planned on one day, but she couldn't stand the idea of not getting to serve Jack, of never hearing his soft curses and groans of pleasure. She didn't want this to only be about her.

She wanted to be back in his playroom, and be his again.

# 17

*J*ack punched his fists through the sleeves of his flannel and clumsily buttoned it closed. He was barely holding on to his self-control. He had to get away from the playroom before he cracked. He reached the first floor landing and scrubbed his hands over his face, but it didn't help. He could smell Lilly on his fingers.

He walked quickly to the liquor cabinet and poured himself a scotch. The glass smarted against his reddened palm, stinging from the spanking he gave her. Fuck, he loved that feeling, the way power coursed through him when he got her to beg. She was everything he'd hoped for, stunning in her vulnerability and then wild in the frenzy of her desire. He never wanted to stop—building her up but holding her off, driving her to a whimpering, pleading mess. And then watching her orgasm take over her when he finally gave her what they'd both been craving.

Jack groaned and took another sip. Seeing her overcome her fears affected him like he never expected. He wanted more. To push her harder, to tan her ass an ever deeper shade of red. To drive into her slick, tight passage and let every dominant urge free.

He needed to get a hold of himself.

Jack set down his drink and gripped the edges of the cabinet.

Damn it, why did she have to look at him like that? It was bad enough to have her sleep next to him with his cock throbbing, to hold and soothe her through what seemed to be uneasy dreams. But when she wanted to touch him—Christ, he'd had no choice but to stop her. There was no way he would've been able to hold back, soft limit or not, and that simply wasn't an option. Not after what happened when they first began. He should've read her better, should've realized that her breathing had been tight and labored from anxiety, not excitement.

Jack leaned over, all that euphoric energy he'd felt during the scene crashing and tumbling into a sea of guilt. It was his own damn fault for forgetting to remind her of her safewords when she'd never used one before, but why did she jerk in fear like that when he'd first touched her? He hadn't pushed any of her limits or used anything she disliked.

There had to be more she wasn't telling him about her ex. More pain she was burying, like a festering wound that wouldn't heal.

He wanted to heal her. To help her see that she should be embracing her submissive side, not fearing it. If only he had more time with her, but that wasn't part of the deal. One day was all they'd agreed to. And what the hell did he know about walking a heartbroken submissive through her pain, anyway? Eve never panicked like that.

*God, Eve. What am I doing?*

A creak on the staircase got his attention, and Jack stood up straight. The plea to his wife for guidance couldn't have been more absurd than at a time like this. He knocked back the rest of his drink and hurried into the kitchen. Lilly lingered in the hallway a few feet away from him.

"Hey," she said.

Her cheeks were rosy in a post-orgasm flush, lips swollen from the bite of his kiss. Her messy ringlets curled over her sweater, and Jack was suddenly angry at her clothes for covering up what he wanted to see. To touch. Taste. Fuck.

*Fuck.*

"Hey back." He fought to keep his voice steady and waved to the island. "Have a seat."

She sat down and shifted, looking like she was trying to find a comfortable position. Jack stifled a groan. He'd branded her with his handprints. She'd be feeling it for days. It took every ounce of restraint in him to move to the opposite side of the island. He needed to keep the block of granite between them, a concrete reminder of the self-denial he had to employ.

"How are you?"

She gave him a tentative smile. "Good. Thank you, Jack."

She was calling him by his name, coming out of her role. That was good. "You're welcome. You did very well."

"Not that well." Lilly leaned on the table and tangled her fingers together. "Is it because I didn't safeword that you didn't want me to...?" She didn't finish, but her eyes skated downward to where his lower body was hidden from view.

"No, Lilly. That isn't why."

*God, please don't push it.*

"It was because today was about me," she said. "You never planned on letting me do anything to you."

"Correct."

Her face fell. God, did she really have no idea how close he was to losing it?

Jack covered her hands with one of his, hoping the small contact would reassure her.

"Please don't think I didn't want you. That wasn't the case at all. But I told you I would respect all your limits, and I had to honor that."

"And you didn't think you could respect my limits if we did... more."

He gave her a tight nod. "That, and I didn't want to push you too much, with this being your first time after so long." Jack let go of her hands and reached up to stroke her cheek. "You were so frightened when we first began. I didn't want to do anything to trigger that reaction again."

Her cheeks colored beneath his touch. She leaned into his hand, a docile kitten asking to be petted.

He wanted to pet her. Cuddle her. Give her a safe space to feel powerless. And then, to ravage her. To feel her come while buried inside her.

Fuck, he didn't think he'd ever wanted something so much.

"I understand," she said. "Thank you for being so respectful of my needs. And it was wonderful." Her lashes lowered when she smiled, a provocative one that made him stiffen to the point of pain. "I really enjoyed it."

"Good." Jack dropped his hand. He liked knowing he'd satisfied her needs, but he needed to put some space between them now. "You're an incredible submissive, Lilly. You shouldn't be afraid of that part of yourself."

She lifted her chin. The waning sunlight streaked in through the windows and shined across her face, creating a kaleidoscope of blue, green and gray in her eyes.

"I want to learn to not be afraid. With you."

Jack went rigid, every inch of his body going tense with desire as her request sank in. "Are you saying you want to continue playing with me?"

Lilly replied with a rapid nod. "I do."

A rush of admiration and surprise washed over him. She trusted him, even after all she'd been through. It was so tempting—the idea of taking that trust and retraining her, showing her how much freedom, power and beauty there was in submission.

He could be the one to anchor Lilly, to guide her back on the path of the vibrant woman she'd lost when her ex destroyed her trust. He could push her boundaries in a way that would heal, not hurt her.

But he had to make sure they were on the same page first.

Jack chose his words carefully. "I'd like that too, but I need you to understand something. There's a reason I've always been very private about what I do. My career is important to me. If anything about this got out..."

He let his words trail off.

*Tell me I can trust you as much as you're about to trust me.*

"Oh. God, no. I'd never say anything." She offered him a meek shrug. "It wouldn't exactly look great for me either. Can you imagine the headlines? 'Paralegal Submits to Venerable Law Professor'. It would be scandalous."

She giggled, and Jack chuckled in response. A playful side was coming out of her, one he hadn't seen before.

A side he wanted to see more of.

"All right," he said. "If we're going to do this, we need to set some more ground rules."

Lilly sat straighter on the stool.

"I'll write up another contract for a period of three months, and we'll see where we are after that. From now on I will discuss each scene with you in advance, and I want you to carefully consider revising your limits."

"Okay."

"I'm serious, Lilly. You have to be completely honest with me. No more miscommunications."

"Yes, Sir."

Fierce desire raged through him at her response. Every scenario imaginable flashed through his mind like a dirty movie, but he held himself in check, and forced the inferno inside him to settle down into a simmer. There were going to be other times with her. Many of them.

He could afford to be patient.

"Is there anything you'd like to change on your checklist?"

"I don't think so."

"All right. We'll leave it as is. I understand your soft limit on sex, and I'll let that be." Jack stared hard at her. "For now."

Lilly shuddered. It made his cock twitch, but he'd found his control. He walked around the island and advanced toward her. "Do Saturdays work for you?"

"Every Saturday?"

"Barring any emergencies or scheduling conflicts, yes."

There was a beat of silence until she smiled and said, "I can do that."

"Good." Jack moved in close. "There's one more thing."

"Yes?" She leaned toward him. He could taste her breath.

"You will not touch yourself during the week without my permission."

She gaped at him. "You mean, I can't at *all*?"

Jack laughed. There was a bratty streak in her that he was going to enjoy playing with. Gripping the sides of the stool, he bracketed her hips with his hands and ran his nose along hers.

"That's right. If we do this, your orgasms belong to me. I say if and when you are allowed to have them."

"And if we do this, will you let me...?"

She glanced downward once again, and Jack's grin widened. Even in the face of denying her pleasure, she was focused on his.

"Yes, Lilly. You will serve me. Repeatedly."

She exhaled and grunted softly. Jack caught her moving her hips, trying to chase the friction she once again obviously craved. He raised an eyebrow and slowly shook his head. She groaned but held herself still.

"Now, let's get you home."

She pouted. "I figured you'd say that."

Grinning back at her, Jack stepped away and strode down the hall, knowing she'd follow. As he retrieved her coat, he felt a blast of bitter air pushing in from outside the front door. It was colder now that the sun was setting. There was no way he'd let her walk to the T.

"I'm driving you," he said, grabbing his own jacket.

"Oh, you don't have to—"

"It wasn't a request."

He backed her up to the wall. She fell against it with a thud. "We may not be in my playroom, but you will obey me while we are in this house. And when I decide something is in your best interest, I expect you to do as you're told. Are we clear?"

A shivery breath escaped her. "Yes, Sir."

"Good."

Jack claimed her mouth and ground his hips against hers. Lilly moaned, whimpering when he ended the kiss. He was tempted to march her back down to the playroom and get a taste of relief, but it would've been a shame to ruin how amped up she was. If he worked this right, he'd be able to seduce that soft limit off her list in no time.

He passed Lilly her boots, then grabbed a pair of winter socks he kept in a wicker basket in the bench by the door. After stepping into his own shoes, Jack led her into the garage. His car purred to life, heat licking from the vents as they set out on the icy streets. Determined to tease her even more, he reached over the gear shift to stroke along the inside of her thigh. She twisted in her seat, legs spreading and seeking out a stronger touch. He removed his hand when he pulled up in front of her building, relishing in the frustrated noise she made.

"I'll call you in the morning," he said. "I want you to think about what we discussed, and be sure it's what you want. Tomorrow, you might regret doing any of this at all."

"I doubt that."

"Do it anyway. And pamper yourself a little. Take a bath and relax."

She raised an eyebrow and smirked. "Is that a command?"

Oh no. He wasn't having that.

He gave her a brief stare of warning. "Don't test me, or you'll get a spanking you won't like as much next weekend. And, yes. It was a command."

She lowered her head in an apology, but the sass was still on her face. Jack tapped the tip of her nose, enjoying the way she crinkled it up in response. "Go. It's cold."

"Yes, Sir."

Lilly stepped out of the car and hurried across the dusk-lit snow, waving before going inside. When she was out of sight, Jack dropped his head against the headrest and exhaled. Waiting until Saturday was going to be a bitch. Maybe eventually they'd play midweek too. There was so much they could do together, so much they'd be able to enjoy, and there was no reason they couldn't keep going as long as they kept things between them.

Between them. Shit.

He'd told Lilly not to tell anyone, while Patrick already knew.

Jack drove quickly across town, parking outside the luxury

building where Patrick owned a river-view apartment. He didn't even
call before going upstairs, but immediately regretted it when he
found his friend leaning against his doorway, a young woman with
cocoa-colored skin fingering his open collar. Patrick met Jack's eyes
and smiled.

"You get home safe now," he said to her.

Jack waited a few feet back and jammed his fists in his pockets,
his jaw clenched with discomfort until the elevator door closed.

"What?" Patrick asked. "You can pick them young. Why can't I?"

"Shut up." Jack brushed past his friend and closed the door
behind them. "We need to talk. Lilly was in my playroom today."

"No fucking way." Patrick punched his shoulder. "I can't believe
you actually went through with it."

"It was your goddamned idea."

"Since when do you listen to me?" His grin widened as he
scratched his goatee. "So, if you finally got some, then why do you
look like you have a pole up your ass?"

Jack walked over to the couch and dropped down onto it. "I
didn't."

"What do you mean?"

"Did you stop understanding English? I said I didn't."

Patrick crossed his arms. "I know it's been a while for you, but
did you forget how it works or something?"

"No, jackass, I didn't forget. But it's a delicate situation." No way
was he betraying Lilly's trust by telling Patrick anything about her
past. "Just leave it that I was worried about hurting her."

"Hurting her? Seriously, Jack, I saw your junk during the locker
room towel debacle of two thousand and two, and honestly you're
not exactly big enough to—"

"That's not what I meant!" Jack shuddered at the memory. Stupid
tiny gym towels. "Look, I've got it all under control, okay? I didn't
come here for your advice."

"All right." Patrick cracked open a beer and offered one to Jack.
He shook his head. "Then why are you here? Other than to turn
down my good booze."

"To make sure you can keep your mouth shut. I asked Lilly not to tell anyone. She doesn't know you know, and I need it to stay that way."

"I always say secrets are the cornerstone of every relationship. Glad to see you're learning from my example."

"This isn't a joke," Jack snapped. "This is important. She's important."

Patrick held up his beer in a toast. "My lips are sealed."

## 18

"*M*an, I've never been so glad it's Friday in my life." Brady yanked open the door to Barrel 'n' Flask and ripped off his coat. "Longest. Week. Ever."

It had been a long week for Jack too. He'd thought about Lilly far too much, picturing all the ways to make her come harder than she could possibly imagine. He was thinking about it again as he looked for her now, finding her by a pool table with Nick. She was laughing loudly, her smile wide, head thrown back.

In a year of seeing nothing at all, now he only saw her.

"Problems at work?" he asked Brady distractedly as they walked through the pub.

"Yeah, we're migrating servers. I had to be on call every night in case they went down. Error messages on websites equals angry emails from our clients." They stopped at the pool table. Brady clapped Nick on the back. "The fun has arrived. Where's Gabe?"

"At the office with Cassie, thank God." Nick snatched a garlic knot off a plate balanced on the end of the pool table. "That way he won't see me eating these. I swear, if he drags me out to another gourmet hotspot, I'm gonna scream."

Lilly grinned. "He's just trying to give you a little culture."

"I don't need culture. I need carbs," Nick said. "Come over next week and cook for us?"

"You cook?" Jack asked. Lawyer-in-training, submissive, track star and chef? What other little gems did he have yet to learn about this girl?

"She makes a mean lasagna," Nick answered for her. "Best I've ever had."

Lilly blushed. It was funny, what compliments seemed to do to her. He wanted to praise her until that blush went from her cheeks to her toes.

"Okay," she told her brother. "Soon. I promise."

Brady snagged a garlic knot, ignoring Nick's sarcastic comment for him to please help himself. "So why'd they let *you* out of the cage?" he asked Lilly. "Shouldn't you be there too, reading books full of legal crap?"

"They're prepping for depositions and didn't need me."

"I have no fucking clue what that means, but if it gets you off the hook for a night, then slap my ass and call me happy."

She nearly choked on her laughter, her gaze catching Jack's. "You've got quite the way with language, my friend."

Brady popped another knot in his mouth and smiled around it. "Yeah, my wife loves it."

Nick turned to Jack. "Will Patrick be joining us?"

"He's got a work thing."

"That makes it an even number." Nick threw Brady a cue stick and held one out for Jack as well. "Siblings throwdown?"

"No way. If Lilly's half as good as you are, I'm not playing against both of you." Brady wedged himself between her and Nick. "Jack, you play with Lilly. At least that way I've got a shot at winning."

"No, you don't." Lilly took a bite of a garlic knot and licked her thumb before smiling at Jack. "Are you up for playing with me?"

A quick, silent exchange passed between them, mirth in her gaze. He grinned at the mischief in her voice. It was a dangerous, delicious thing to share this secret with her.

"I'd be happy to play with you."

Lilly broke, sinking one solid after the next, something Jack enjoyed watching almost as much as the shape of her ass as she bent over the table. It was a test in itself—to see how much temptation he could stand. He was conditioning his restraint, flexing the muscle of control that had become weak in its dormant state. His need was leashed, tethered, and as restrained as Lilly was going to be in his playroom tomorrow.

She won the game with a triumphant smile. Brady bowed his head.

"You are a worthy opponent."

Nick threw an arm around her. "I taught her all she knows."

"Bullshit. Dad taught us. I just happened to learn faster than you did." Lilly checked her watch. "Okay, I'm gonna head out. I need a good night's sleep."

"For what?" Nick asked. "Do you actually have something planned tomorrow?"

She busied herself with putting on her hat, not looking up to meet Jack's careful gaze. "Nope. Just tired from another long week."

*Good girl.*

Nick reached for his coat. "I'll walk you to the T."

Jack felt an odd flicker of jealousy, wanting to do the job himself, but that wasn't part of the deal. And it certainly would've sent up some warning flares to their brothers if Jack had offered to do it. Lilly waved good-bye to him and Brady before Nick led her out of the pub.

Brady started re-wracking the table. "It's really cool that she's finally spending time with us. Nick was worried. Said she had a bad breakup—some shit that went down when she was in law school."

Jack gripped his cue tightly. "Bad" didn't begin to cover it.

"He's hoping she'll meet someone," Brady continued. "Maybe one of these nights we'll be able to find a guy for her."

Jack bristled. She didn't need some guy. She needed a man who could unlock her deepest desires, and tease out the violence and passion of her lust. Someone who would guard her as carefully as he used her, giving her the freedom to be what she wanted without shame. Jack was that man, and the knowledge burned through him.

He didn't answer Brady. He took his turn at the table, ending the conversation.

\* \* \*

When Lilly arrived on Saturday, she was coiled up like a powder keg, and Jack couldn't wait to make her explode.

"Strip."

She pulled her clothes off to reveal gloriously naked skin.

"Kneel."

She complied and dropped to the pillow, her toned thighs open wide, a flush over the perfect curves of her breasts. She didn't seem nervous, but Jack wanted to make sure a repeat of last week didn't happen. He needed to know her body implicitly, and had plans to keep her silent so he could learn her cues—all her signals of arousal and fear.

He ran his fingers through her hair as her breathing settled.

"Beautiful," he said, and she sighed softly. "What are your safewords?"

"Green, yellow and red, Sir."

"And you will use them if you need to. Correct?"

"I will, Sir."

"Good girl. Stand up for me."

She moved to her feet, her eyes on the floor.

"Today we'll work on your behavior. I'll be tying you up, so we don't have any more of those pesky roaming hands. You don't get to touch until I say so. Understand?"

"Yes, Sir."

"You won't speak today, either. If you make any noise at all, except to safeword, you won't be permitted to come. Please me, and you'll be rewarded. Nod if you understand."

She gave him a brisk nod, her eyes clear and bright. Feeding off her obedience and lust, Jack kissed her, and she responded eagerly, catching the pitch that radiated within him like a tuning fork. She was breathless when he stopped, her mouth open, head angled toward him for more. He mimicked her expression, keeping his kiss a few teasing inches away.

"So hungry," he whispered. "Are you hungry for me?"

She nodded frantically.

"You want to touch my cock? Feel how hard I am? Suck me?"

Another nod, coupled with a slip of her tongue over her lips.

"I don't know if I should let you. You were a bad girl last week, touching me without permission. This time you need to earn it."

Jack stepped to the armoire and lifted the coil of rope off its hook. He unraveled it slowly as he walked back to her, studying the way she looked at the smooth twine. Her breathing sped up and her nipples pebbled, gooseflesh rising.

Perfect.

He moved behind her and began the delicate process of binding her wrists and elbows. With every loop and knot, he paused to caress and kiss her skin, whispering how beautiful she was. When he'd finished, he gathered her hair in one hand and twisted it over to one side, baring her skin to his kiss. Testing her resolve, he grazed his lips along her throat and bit down at the junction of her shoulder.

She didn't make a sound.

Jack drew her back against him so his jean-clad erection brushed against her bound hands. She shivered, but stayed silent.

"Such a well-behaved little girl." He squeezed her hips. "Now, we play."

He walked her to the open armoire, reached around and pressed his thumb and forefinger under her jaw, guiding her with his fingers, controlling what she saw.

"Look at all the pretty toys I'm going to use on you."

With his free hand, Jack touched his paddle, then his crop. He stroked down the spreader bar as if it were his cock and read the subtle moves of her body, her hitched breaths of anticipation.

"I will be using many, if not all, of them on you. But some will have to wait until you're ready."

He opened the drawer and felt her breathing pause as he fingered the blindfold, nipple clamps and the sharp spokes of the Wartenberg wheel. He was purposely showing her things she disliked while she was pressed against him. He needed to remind her it would be different with him. That he would protect her as well as push her.

Still holding her face captive with one hand, he brought the other to the stiff tip of her nipple.

"Because you will be ready, my needy little girl."

She jumped when he rolled the tight nub between his thumb and forefinger. He pinched and her legs shifted, caught somewhere between frustration and bliss. Jack moved to the other breast and repeated the motion.

"When it's time to dress these pretty nipples up in clamps, you'll be ready."

She huffed out a strangled exhale. Jack slid his hand down her belly.

"When I want to see the spikes of my wheel crossing your flesh, you'll be ready. When it's time to cover those eyes and plunge you into darkness—" His fingers brushed along her slick opening. Pressed. Slid inside. "—you'll want it too. Badly."

She flexed against his touch, grinding down on his fingers.

"And when I fuck you, you'll be begging for it. I promise you that."

Jack tipped her head back and licked across her lips. Her mouth parted and she welcomed the teasing dips of his tongue. He nipped and tasted, all the while listening to the changes in her breathing. When he focused his attention on her clit, he pulled back to watch her react to the sudden onslaught of pleasure. She shut her eyes. Her body arched into his touch. She was on the edge already, and Jack held her down, his forearm wedged between her breasts, surging with the knowledge that only he could do this to her.

"Does my poor girl need to come?"

She answered by bucking her hips, trembling as Jack worked her faster, his finger swirling in tight circles. At the first hint of her body's spasm into orgasm, Jack stopped. Her bound hands clenched into fists. She was shaking when he turned her around to face him, her pleading expression full of agony that he tauntingly mirrored, shaking his head.

"I know. You need it so bad, don't you?"

She nodded and panted.

"I'll let you come, but not yet. First we have to see how good you can be."

Jack dragged down the fly of his jeans, freeing his hardened flesh. She watched the motion of his hand, her stare hungry.

"Last time, you were practically begging for this," he mocked, stroking himself.

Lilly's face was pained as she watched Jack's hand twist over the tip. He walked backward to the armchair and tugged down his jeans. She stayed put, pouting mournfully from her spot a few feet away. He smiled calmly at her, sat down and resumed the slow path of his fingers.

"You want to suck me, little girl?"

Her brisk nod was her only answer. Chuckling, he crooked a finger at her. Lilly rushed over, and he pointed to the floor between his open legs. She dropped to her knees, her mouth so close he could feel her hot breath. God, he wanted it, but he had to make her want it more.

"Stop." Jack slipped his fingers into her mouth. "Suck."

She obeyed, enthusiastically drawing his finger into her mouth, enveloping them all the way to the knuckle.

"Look at you, craving me. Craving this." He was prying out her wild side, clawing past the walls she'd been hiding behind. "I don't know if you've earned it, though. I could make you suck my fingers while I get myself off."

His threat was empty, but Lilly whined loudly in protest and then froze, her eyes going wide.

Jack's stare turned cold. He pulled his fingers free and held her by the throat. "That was a sound, wasn't it? Didn't I tell you to stay quiet?"

She nodded, repentant. A tear danced at the corner of her eye. Jack grabbed her by the hair and jerked her forward until her mouth hovered above his length.

"Show me how badly you want my forgiveness. Give me that mouth. Let's see how fast you can make me come."

Lilly exhaled in relief. Keeping her eyes on his, she kissed the tip of his cock before licking over it, and then lapped greedily down the shaft. Jack's head fell back with her first slick pass because *goddamn*, it was so fucking good. He glanced down a second later, compelled to watch as she licked her way up. She dipped her tongue into the slit before taking him in again, her eyes on his as she sucked all the way down.

"Yes...*fuck*."

A hint of a smile appeared on her lips, but vanished quickly as she continued to work him. Determined, Lilly hollowed her cheeks, teasing rhythmically at the crown before plunging back to the base again.

"That's it," he choked out as she repeated the move. "Just like that."

He was telling Lilly what he wanted, but even with her hands bound and her voice silenced, she was the one driving him out of his mind. Her mouth was so hot and sweet that he could barely bark out orders over his own labored breaths. Jack shuddered when he nudged the back of her throat. It felt so good, and it had been too long, and he wasn't going to last.

Feeling his orgasm crest, Jack buried both hands in Lilly's hair, keeping her in place and forcing her into a faster rhythm she willingly accepted. He fucked her mouth, taking what he wanted and giving himself over to the rush of sensation and power. He cursed loudly as he came, fisting her hair and spilling down her throat.

Jack dropped his head back, his grip on her hair loosening. When he reopened his eyes, it was to the hazy vision of Lilly sitting back on her heels, her cheeks rosy. There was a lazy grin on her swollen, used lips. The satisfaction she exuded at having given Jack his orgasm was almost as palpable as his own.

"I think you've earned my forgiveness," he said, tracing grateful fingertips along her mouth. "Now, my little girl deserves her reward."

# 19

"*W*hat's the verdict?"

Cassie crossed her arms, impatient for Gabe's answer as he dumped his coat over the wall of Lilly's cubicle. They'd been anticipating his return from the Holbrook pretrial conference all afternoon.

"Bench trial. Third Thursday in May."

"Shit." Cassie slumped down over the partition. "Who's the judge?"

"McAllister."

"Crap."

"A very accurate legal response."

"I call shotgun on not telling Forrester."

Gabe glared at her. "I don't want to tell him, either."

"Don't want to tell me what?"

They turned to see their boss sauntering toward them, holding a newspaper. Lilly grimaced. They needed to get better at seeing him coming. Or start working on applications to practice law in Guam.

"The Giordanos didn't take the settlement," Gabe said. "We're going to trial."

"Of course we are." Forrester held his copy of *The Boston Globe* out to them, his face turned up in disgust. "They said as much to the press yesterday."

Cassie took the paper and started reading. Lilly stood to peek over her shoulder, and Gabe craned his head, hovering next to them. It was an article about the Giordanos, a human interest piece their PR department had obviously paid for, saying Simon had betrayed them, that he was painting himself as David and them as Goliath when they were simply trying to help people.

"This is bullshit," Gabe seethed.

Forrester's expression didn't change. "The Giordanos won't be accepting any settlement offers. They don't want money."

"No," Cassie said. "They want Simon's head on a plate."

"Precisely. To them, it's a matter of reputation. As it also is to us."

A muscle in Gabe's jaw twitched. "We're not going to lose."

Forrester eyed each one of them. "Make sure Mahoney knows that." He snatched the paper back and disappeared down the hall.

Cassie gripped the edge of Lilly's cubicle and dropped her head on top of her hands. "We're screwed."

"We're not. We have time." Gabe glanced at Lilly. "You'd better put the trial date on our calendars. And let's order dinner." He nudged Cassie and pulled his coat from under her, making her stand. "Guess we won't be back at the pub anytime soon. The conference room is about to become our new Friday night hangout."

He started to walk away, and then stopped. "Now that the press is interested, can someone please tell Simon not to talk to any reporters without one of us present? Who knows what he might say."

Cassie hurried to her office. "I'm on it."

When the two of them were gone, Lilly opened the calendar on her computer and entered the Holbrook trial date. She blew out a breath, the wisps that had come loose from her braid flying up with the motion. Three months until they had to go to court. Plenty of time, but with Forrester so angry, it felt like no time at all.

Three months. That was the same length of time as the new contract she'd signed with Jack last week. Tomorrow would be the third time she'd kneel in his playroom. She was already counting down the minutes, eager for his hands on her, for the way he took everything she knew about submission and turned it around. From understanding and sweet in his kitchen, he became demanding and implacable in his playroom, voice low and sinful as he whispered the filthiest things in her ear.

Lilly shifted in her chair. She shouldn't be thinking these things at work.

She found the order form for the local pizza joint. After calling in their dinners, she took out her phone and opened Jack's last message. They'd begun texting on and off, although it was more to check on her than anything substantial. She typed out a text.

*I won't be at the pub tonight. Too much to do. See you tomorrow.*

She waited a few minutes for a response, but there was none. He was probably in class, but even if he weren't, what did she expect other than a quick "okay"? As much as she liked him, this wasn't a relationship. This was an agreement for their mutual benefit. Nothing more.

Hours later, she was sitting with Gabe and Cassie in the conference room, the Giordano files scattered on the table. Lilly stared at the database on her laptop.

"Okay, let's review," Cassie said. "Simon left Giordano last June. He opened his lab, discovered the new formula—"

"Documented in a notebook that looks like it came out of a sewer," Gabe interrupted.

"—then invited Jacqueline to lunch to share his find. He asked her to work for him, but she turned him down. If she was the Giordanos' chief scientist by then, she had to know they had proof Simon took the formula."

"Unless she didn't. She could've gone back to them with the information and constructed the same thing."

"The logs don't show that." Lilly skimmed the entries on her screen, ignoring the column heading she still didn't understand and focusing on the things she did. "There's a timestamp for when each one was generated, and an entry describing Simon's formula dated before he left." She shook her head. "Why didn't the Giordanos patent their formula?"

Cassie searched through the pizza boxes for a last remaining slice. "Because then they'd have to go public with it. With a trade secret, they don't have to disclose the details."

"So they can sue Simon without having to prove they have the same formula at all."

Gabe grinned. "Good system. When they win, they charge. When they lose, they tell the bookies to kiss their rears."

Cassie stopped hunting. "Don't start."

Lilly sighed and rubbed her eyes. If Gabe got Cassie all riled up by misquoting movie lines, they'd never get anything accomplished.

"Someone must know the real formula," Lilly said. "Could we subpoena one of the other researchers?"

Cassie gave up on one box and moved to the next. "They won't talk. They've probably all signed nondisclosure agreements. I'll bet only the Giordanos and Jacqueline know the real details."

"Keep your buddies close but your opponents closer!" Gabe shouted.

Cassie thumped an empty pizza box against the table. "That's not the line!"

Lilly ignored them both. "So if it's their word against Simon's, and we can't get our hands on their formula, how do we win?"

"We have to prove Simon is telling the truth," Cassie answered.

"All I have in this world is my back and my word, and I won't bend them for anyone."

Cassie balled up a napkin and chucked it in his direction. Gabe ducked, yelling from beneath the table, "You mean, you won't say hallo to my beetle friend?"

She grumbled something in Spanish. Gabe sat up and clucked his tongue.

"Oooh, we know we're getting to Miss Cassandra Flores when the Latina comes out in her." He rolled the r in her first and middle names for an added effect. Cassie looked ready to punch him.

Lilly made a last desperate attempt to keep them on track. "So, if there's any possibility the Giordanos aren't telling the truth, then why did they refuse the settlement?"

"It's like Forrester said. It's not about money." Gabe reached for a file, finally back to business. "They have enough funds to pay for Mahoney's fees and give him a trip to the Bahamas to thank him for his time. They don't care about the cash. They want Simon out of business."

"And if *we* lose, *we're* out of business." Cassie put her hands on her hips and sighed. "Why did they have to hire Mahoney out of all the lawyers in Boston?"

"What's the deal between him and Forrester, anyway?" Lilly asked.

"They were rivals all through law school. Forrester graduated with honors while Mahoney didn't. Then Mahoney got a clerkship Forrester had been gunning for, and he never got over it." Cassie reached her arms over her head and stretched. "What do you think Simon is going to pay us in now that we're going to trial? Corduroy pants? Pocket protectors?"

"I'm sticking with the chickens," Gabe said. His phone chirped and he plucked it from the table. "Looks like Nick is on his way home. I'm going to head out."

Lilly's skin heated as she wondered if Jack was leaving the pub too. She reached for her own phone, acting like she was simply checking her email. A new text from him was on the screen.

*Don't work too late. And make sure you get plenty of sleep. You'll need it for tomorrow.*

Lilly struggled to hide her smile as she typed her reply, two words she knew would make Jack's eyes go dark with lust.

*Yes, Sir.*

* * *

"All chained up with no place to go."

Jack ran the edge of his riding crop in a line down between Lilly's breasts. She was helpless, held in place, chained down. And it felt so, so good.

"You like it when pain mixes with pleasure." He circled the tip of the crop around her nipple, then slapped it quickly before caressing again. "Don't you?"

Lilly could barely think with how good it felt. Jack struck her breasts, her belly, the insides of her thighs, then stopped to grip her by the hair with his free hand.

"I asked you a question."

"Yes, I like it," she sputtered. "Please, Sir."

She didn't know why she was begging. For him to stop torturing her. To keep torturing her. To never stop.

"Beg for it." He let go of her hair and slapped her again, this time right above her slit. "Beg for my crop on your pussy."

"Please spank my pussy with your crop, Sir!" He'd reduced her to groveling, a pleading live wire of desperation.

She didn't care.

Jack clasped her throat. Brought his face to hers. Looked into her eyes.

"You're beautiful. And you're mine."

He flicked the crop against her clit with strokes so rapid she couldn't tell what hurt and what would push her over the edge. Jack could, though. And when he brought her there, she screamed.

After Jack released her from the restraints, he curled her up in his arms and played with her hair, massaging her scalp. The gentle movements of his fingers lulled her until she thought she could fall asleep. It was the most peaceful she'd felt in a long time. When he stopped and tapped the tip of her nose, she opened her eyes, drowsy and slow.

"Thirsty?" he asked.

"Very." Her throat was parched and raw.

He handed her a bottle of water, his breathing even, posture relaxed. It was no surprise he was so calm after today's scene. Greedy for her mouth, he'd pushed his cock past her lips before bringing her up from her knees. He'd come even faster than last time, and the guttural *fuck, yes* he'd hissed echoed in her head.

Lilly smiled around the bottle opening. He could light her up like a firecracker, and it seemed she could do the same to him as well.

"Get dressed and meet me in the kitchen," he said.

She nodded from the tangled sea of plush bedding he'd covered her up in. Talking in the kitchen was something he'd wanted to do after every session. She found it a little odd after what they'd done together, but she would've felt cheap too, if he'd done nothing but show her the door afterward.

He really was nothing like Damien at all.

When she padded upstairs, she was greeted by the smell of freshly brewed coffee.

"It's decaf," he said, handing her a cup.

"Too bad. I could have used the caffeine to push me through the rest of the day."

He sat on a stool and motioned for her to join him. "You planning on working?"

"Aren't I always?"

"Workaholic." She grinned as she sat down next to him, enjoying the easy banter between them. "How's the case going?"

"Not so great."

"Give me the highlights."

She hesitated. "You really want to hear?"

"I'm a law professor. Of course I do."

Of course. He taught at Harvard, for Christ's sake. Why hadn't she tapped him for information yet? He might have some helpful ideas.

"To start with, our client is a total mess while the plaintiff's case is totally solid."

"Anything in the depositions that can help?"

"Unfortunately no." She'd sat in while Gabe questioned the Giordanos. With their designer suits and polished testimony, they'd been confident as only people with nothing to lose could be. Jacqueline Broussard, however, had been an incredibly nervous witness. Every answer she gave was coupled with anxious glances to Mahoney and the court reporter. But their stories matched, the documentation ironclad. "It doesn't help now that the press is interested, either. Plus I'm still completely stumped on this database."

"Database?"

"It's a log from the plaintiff. I wish I could find something in it, but I can't seem to. Our opposing counsel is someone Forrester hates, so he's pissed we haven't found anything."

"I think it's less about not finding the information and more about you not believing you can." Jack sighed and looked out the window. "There's so much pressure at these firms. The battle cry to win, win, win."

There was a faraway look in his eyes, one that made her realize he wasn't talking about her.

"We're always pushed to find this one answer, and if you don't find it, then you haven't done your job. It's like you're being set up to fail. It's pretty damn rare that one document will be what backs up an entire case. Legal research is a time-consuming process, not something that you can just turn a page and find."

She'd never thought about it that way before. Then again, she'd never had a teacher like Jack.

He turned to face her, his gaze holding her steady. "If you think your client is innocent, then the evidence is there. You just need the confidence to know you'll find it." One side of his mouth curled up into a half smile, eyes crinkling around the edges. "I have faith in you."

Lilly sat up a little taller on her stool. "Thank you."

"You're welcome." He paused, his tone changing, going softer. "Can I ask you a question?"

"Sure."

"Why doesn't Nick know what happened between you and Damien?"

Her stomach dropped. One sentence, and she was plummeted into the past.

Jack touched her cheek, the backs of his knuckles brushing against her skin. "I'm not judging. I'm only asking because you two seem very close."

"We are, but my family isn't exactly big on acceptance."

"Meaning?"

"Meaning my mother isn't supportive of Nick and Gabe. At all. It was a big shock for her when he came out, and she never accepted it. They were so close, and now she barely talks to him."

"But that's your mother. Not Nick."

Lilly averted her eyes. "I know."

Jack tipped her chin up, not letting her look away. "Do you really?"

"I do. It's just..." she started, not sure how to put it into words. "I can't stand the idea of what happened between Nick and Mom ever happening between him and me. If he thought badly of me for not looking out for myself..." She winced. "I can't let that happen."

Jack studied her for a long moment, then nodded. "I understand. Thank you for telling me. Now finish your coffee so we can get you home. Same time next Saturday?"

He grinned, and the glint in his eyes made her forget about her past, about work, about anything else other than him.

"I can't wait."

# 20

"*W*here did you get your scar?"

Jack paused, his hand frozen as it held Lilly's, halted in the motion of rubbing salve into her wrists. Her skin had gone a deep shade of pink after he'd kept her bound for a session that had been different than all the others. He'd pushed her limits, wanting to show her the pleasure she could get from something she'd feared: the Wartenberg wheel.

She'd trembled at the sight of those gleaming spikes, but Jack promised her she was ready for it, insisting it was for sensation and not for pain or punishment. Knowing she could either let him test her boundaries or keep hiding and stay afraid, Lilly met his challenge, whispering "green". Lilly had remained tense when he ran it over her belly, but the barbs didn't hurt when Jack wielded them. He swept it along the swell of her breasts, and each roll left a tingling path in its wake. She'd gasped in surprised pleasure when he made a thorny dance across each nipple.

The pride in his eyes brought her more gratification than any toy could.

That was probably why she'd blurted out the question, more brave than usual because of what she'd just accomplished.

"I'm sorry, Sir. That was out of line."

141

They were in the playroom, not in his kitchen. Their roles hadn't shifted yet.

"It's all right." Jack finished massaging ointment into her skin. "It was from a whip."

"Someone whipped you?"

"No, I did it to myself. Accidentally." He turned his arm over and examined the scar. "It was years ago. Hurt like a bitch."

Lilly sat up and bent her head, her chin jutted toward his wrist. He held out his arm. She leaned forward and examined the arc of white.

"May I?" she asked, her finger hovering above it. This scar seemed like a doorway to another world.

Jack nodded, and Lilly ran her forefinger along the puckered skin, stroking it like a worry stone. She knew she should've been thinking about the pain he must have endured, but all she could picture was a younger Jack testing the limits of his dominance, seeing what that power felt like for the first time.

"I was so excited when it came in the mail," he said with a quiet laugh. "Eve laughed when I got it. Told me she had no idea she'd married Indiana Jones."

Lilly didn't stop moving her finger, but her breathing went shallow, her mind on high alert. Jack so rarely talked about his wife.

"I tried out a couple of practice strokes, but I had no idea what I was doing, and the whip curled back around and sliced right through my flesh." He shook his head, as if he were chastising his former self. "Once I felt how much damage it could do, I never used a bullwhip again. Making a mistake like that with Eve wasn't an option."

She caressed his injury, the tactile proof of Jack's decision to keep his wife safe. He was so careful with her, so diligent in never causing her harm. Lilly felt a flash of jealousy, but pushed the feeling away.

It was crazy to be envious of a ghost.

She stroked the scar once more, her touch coming to rest on the highest ridge. "You were very good to her."

Jack took her hands in his and turned them over. "It's a lot of responsibility, hurting someone like this."

Lilly could feel her pulse in her throat as he gently swept his thumbs over the red marks on her skin.

"Was it ever too much responsibility?" she asked. "I mean, did you think you'd have to stop?"

She'd wondered how it was possible—how he and Eve had navigated jobs and parenting and family, but still managed...this.

"I went half of my life without realizing I was a Dominant. Something always felt off. I was never satisfied." Although the shadows of the room hid half his face in darkness, it was the closest she'd felt to really seeing him. "Once I started, I couldn't go back. For me, there's no other way to be."

Lilly felt something click inside her, his answer resonating. It was what she'd felt all along—why even when she'd buried her desires, they kept pushing through in her nightmares, refusing to be silenced.

She couldn't stop now if she tried.

A floating, calm feeling stuck with her after he drove her home. When she showered, the hot water was a searing flame against her tender skin, but the pain didn't bother her. The physical reminder of Jack's dominance seemed to bind her to him, a grounding force fighting against the anxiety that used to cripple her.

Odd how getting her skin turned red by one man could wash away the bruises left on her heart by another.

She was stepping out of the shower when her home phone rang. She hurried to pick it up, wet feet skidding over the floor.

"Hello?"

"You're not answering your cell," Nick said. "Are you leaving soon or what?"

"Leaving?"

"To come over for dinner, remember? I got the pasta and everything."

"Right! Of course I remember."

It was a lie. She'd completely forgotten that she'd agreed to cook for him and Gabe tonight, promising to save Nick from another Saturday night at Chez Please Don't Make Me Go.

"I lost track of time while I was working. I'll be there in a bit."

She hated being dishonest, but telling Nick why she forgot was not happening.

The bitingly cold air hit her when she got off the T at Boston Common. Although spring was only weeks away, winter remained a stubborn child, clinging to the ground and treetops. The warmth of Nick and Gabe's Beacon Hill brownstone was a welcome respite, and a short time later she was sitting at their dining room table, their plates scraped clean.

"Now that is a home-cooked dinner," Nick said.

"Yes, thank you so much for the carbo-load." Gabe put a hand on his stomach. "I'll need to detox for a week."

Nick reached over to clasp Gabe's hand. The intimacy tugged at Lilly's heart.

Looking away, she busied herself with clearing the table and suddenly noticed the marks on her wrists. Eyes going wide, she tugged down her sleeves. Grabbing as many dishes as she could carry, she went into the kitchen and put them in the sink. Nick and Gabe's galley kitchen was modern but small—nothing like Jack's, with its gleaming countertops and shiny pots hanging from a rack above the island.

Maybe one day she'd be able to take them down from their idle positions and cook Jack dinner too. After today and the things he'd shown her, anything seemed possible.

Lilly started up the hot water and snapped on a pair of rubber gloves as Gabe arrived with the silverware and cups.

"See, this is why I prefer restaurants. No work."

Nick appeared with the remainder of the table's contents. "That, and because you're a terrible cook. Lilly and I can handle the dishes. Why don't you put a movie on and we'll join you in a few?"

"I feel like a beached whale, so I guess I should be sprawled out on the couch to match."

"No mobster movies," Lilly called after him. Gabe scowled and walked out the door.

Throwing a towel over his shoulder, Nick took the plate she'd finished rinsing and put it in the dishwasher. For a while, they worked in comfortable silence. It was a chore that reminded her of being small, of standing on a wooden stepstool and carefully drying the cups Nick handed her, wanting to prove she wouldn't drop them. To make her big brother proud of her.

"So we never got to talk about the show," he said. "What did you think?"

"You know what I thought of your photos. They were great."

"What about the rest of the show? Did you get to see the ones upstairs?"

She nearly dropped the plate in her hands, certain that all the air had been sucked out of Beacon Hill. She continued rinsing, scrubbing harder than before. "You're my brother. It's gross that you're asking me this."

"It's art, not sex."

Lilly didn't answer. Her worlds were colliding, the one she stole into with Jack crashing into her brother's kitchen. Nick nudged her with his shoulder, and she tried to angle herself out of the way.

"Come on, Lil. What did you think?"

"I don't know. They were—" She shrugged. Shook her head. "—fine, I guess."

Nick sighed. "We used to be able to talk about anything."

She sighed too and looked down at the sink. It was true. Once, she'd shared everything with him, from her first track meet to her first kiss to her first moot court argument. Maybe things would've been different if she'd told him about Damien.

If only she could tell him about Jack, and how happy their Saturday discoveries were making her.

Was it Jack making her happy? Or that she was finally learning to accept who she was?

"Can I ask you a question?" she asked.

"Okay."

"After what happened to you in college, did you ever think, 'this is too hard'?"

"What do you mean?"

She shut off the water and turned to face him. "That being gay was too difficult. That people wouldn't accept you the way Mom hasn't, so it might be easier to try to shut it down?"

Nick leaned against the counter. "I tried to ignore it. I focused on my career for a long time. Pretended that wasn't me and spent most of my time alone. But you can't ignore who you are, Lilly." He shrugged. "Hard or not, it's the only way I know how to live."

*"For me, there's no other way to be."*

His words echoed Jack's. The affirmation made something tight loosen inside her, gave her hope.

"You okay?" Nick asked. "You seem off."

She wanted to say she was great—better than she'd been in a long time actually—but she couldn't. She and Jack had both agreed to keep this quiet.

"I'm fine. Maybe I'm homesick. I miss Dad."

It wasn't really another lie. She did miss their father, even if that had nothing to do with what she was feeling.

He hummed in response and they both went back to work. Lilly flipped on the faucet and watched the suds buoy up—light, like the way her heart felt.

Maybe someday she'd be able to tell Nick everything, and he would understand.

## 21

"*C*an we have ice cream, Uncle Jack?"

Jack opened the movie theater door with one hand while Hope clung to the other, holding it out for Allegra as she scurried outside.

"I don't think so, kiddo."

"Please, please, please?"

"That's three pleases, so you get three no's in return." He rattled them off, snatching her hand before she walked off the curb. "And no letting go while we cross the street."

"That's four no's, not three," she grumbled.

"Thanks, smarty-pants."

A blast of mid-March air cut through Jack's coat as they crossed the street. It was spring break, but the temperature didn't reflect that change in seasons at all. Lumps of slush-covered snow lined the ground, dirty with mud from the street. Half of Harvard's student body had retreated to warmer shores. He almost wished he could've done the same.

Almost. If he were in the Caribbean, he wouldn't have been near Lilly.

He opened the back door and ushered his nieces inside. Allegra insisted on buckling herself while he got her sister situated, and he hoped from the way her teeth had started to chatter that she'd gotten the desire for ice cream out of her system. By the time he got behind the wheel, however, she started another chorus of "please's".

"Allegra Archer," he said, in a tone stern enough to silence her. "Your parents said a movie and dinner, not ice cream. That was the deal this year."

It was a tradition he'd agreed to long ago. One day during each of his breaks, he took the girls for a day to give Brady and Sam some time alone. It had been Eve's suggestion back when she had plenty of activities to bring home from her classroom and enough energy to do them with the girls. She'd upheld her end of the bargain, even when all she could do was smile and watch them from the couch. Last year, Jack hadn't had the strength to do it alone. When he'd suggested a return to the tradition earlier that week, Brady and Sam had hesitated before saying yes, but he'd assured them he was up for it.

What he didn't say was that the days of his vacation were dragging. He needed to fill the time until Saturday.

"Ice cream can be dinner," Allegra insisted.

He stifled his laugh as he started the car. "No, it can't."

"Pretty please?"

"I told you I'd say no every time you said please."

"Bet I can say please more times than you can say no."

"I bet you can't."

Allegra took a deep breath and began repeating the word please in an endless stream until she ran out of air. She gathered another lungful while Hope picked up where she'd left off, and then they both chimed in until they were saying "peas" instead of "please" and laughing too hard to talk. Jack couldn't stop himself from laughing, either. These two seemed to know exactly how to wrap him around their fingers.

"I can't say no a hundred times, but I could get in trouble. What would your parents say if they found out I was getting you ice cream for dinner?"

He caught Allegra's mischievous smile in the rearview mirror. "You don't have to tell them," she said.

Jack let out a dramatic sigh. "Fine. Where do you want to go?"

They cheered in unison and requested a spot on the other end of town. He put on the radio and the girls sang along, off-key and loud and not caring in the slightest. He was halfway there when he turned a corner and realized where they were.

*The hearse idled outside the funeral home and spewed exhaust, fumes curling white in the bitter air. Jack's shoulder burned under the weight of the coffin, even though it was a burden he shared with Josh, Patrick and Brady. The sky was gray, not that he'd looked up to check. Raising his eyes meant reconciling his anger with whoever was in charge up there. Looking down reminded him of where his wife was about to be.*

*He held on to the casket and looked straight ahead.*

The light turned red across from the cemetery, and Jack slowed to a stop. He'd avoided this part of town for ages, yet here he was.

He turned his head slowly to look past the gated stone entrance, a sickening clench in his gut. The gravestones stretched in quiet lines into the dense thicket of trees, but he didn't have to strain to pick out Eve's. He knew exactly where it was. They'd picked out the plot years ago. Eve liked it for its towering trees and the playground at the recreation center nearby. Boston College peeked over its edge, and she'd joked about the tennis courts there, saying they could haunt them whenever they wanted.

He'd never thought "whenever" would be so soon for her.

"Uncle Jack?"

Allegra's voice shook him from his thoughts. His eyes were still on the cemetery entrance.

"Yeah?"

"The light's green."

He looked quickly back at the road in front of him. The windshield was blurry. "Right. Thanks."

He got his act together long enough to get them ice cream, relieved for the patterned placemats and crayons the waitress provided. After wiping their faces clean of the evidence, he took them home, but the sly smile Samantha greeted them with made Jack sure she'd figured them out. She didn't say anything, though, and he hurried to his car with a promise to call Brady tomorrow.

As soon as he was alone and driving again, he was bombarded by memories.

*His house was full of people. Jack went through the motions, shook hands when he had to, thanked them all for their apologies, their flowers, their casseroles left on every countertop. When they left, he was barely able to cough out a thank you to Patrick, Brady and Sam, who stayed behind to clean up.*

*He dragged himself up to Josh's room, and found his son on his bed, laptop balanced on his thighs, headphones plugged in. Jack sat down next to him and looked at the screen. It was a video of Eve taken at Josh's college graduation, before hell arrived in the form of a tumor and another apology.*

*Josh offered him an earbud. Jack took it, closed his eyes and listened.*

*In the video, Eve was laughing.*

He pulled into his driveway and grimaced, hating himself a little, because for some reason, he couldn't remember the exact cadence of Eve's laugh. It was a sound he'd wanted to bottle, to put away for safekeeping and take out on a rainy day. How could he have forgotten it?

He tried to compel the sound of her laughter into his head. Her voice when she said his name, when she called him Master.

He couldn't hear it.

Feeling like the earth had shifted on its axis, Jack went up to his bedroom and sat down on Eve's side of the bed. Opening her nightstand drawer, he picked up the wooden jewelry box with uncertainty. He'd spent weeks fingering the silver collar inside it. Months with his wedding ring still on. Jack ran a thumb over the vacant space on his ring finger. The emptiness there no longer felt strange, and the box in his hands seemed like an old friend he wasn't sure he recognized anymore.

Somehow, something had changed. He'd avoided the cemetery, absolutely certain that going there would drive him back into an unbearable state of anguish, but it didn't. He was sad, sure, but he wasn't devastated, wasn't reeling from the impact of all-consuming grief.

It was unsettling. For over a year, he'd been going through life with one foot in the grave, but now, for the first time, there was some distance between him and his sorrow.

He put the box away and shoved the drawer shut. A sudden influx of nervous energy made him stand and pace, not sure what to do with himself. He wandered downstairs and eyed the liquor cabinet, but it wasn't a disconnect he needed.

He needed to regain control again.

He pulled his phone from his pocket and dialed Lilly's number.

"Hey." She said the word hesitantly, the single syllable coming out a little longer than it needed to. Her uncertainty wasn't a shock. He'd never called her midweek before. "Everything okay?"

"Yeah, fine," he lied. "Just wanted to see how you're doing."

"I'm good." She paused. "You sure you're okay?"

A smile tugged at his lips. She'd learned to read him so well. "Just tired. I babysat my nieces all day."

Lilly giggled softly. "That does sound pretty tiring."

The sound of her laughter settled Jack's nerves in a way he wasn't ready to ponder. He sat on the couch and stretched his legs out. "Your day go okay? How's your week been?"

"Long. Busy."

"Are you working?"

"I was, but I couldn't concentrate."

"Why's that?"

"It's hard to focus like...this."

"Like what?"

A breath. "Distracted."

Her voice was lower. Huskier. Jack grinned.

"Distracted, huh?" She was flirting with him, drawing him in, and he let the pull happen. The focus on Lilly shelved his grief into a far corner of his mind. "What on earth could be distracting you?"

"You know what," she grumbled. "The lack of orgasms is doing wonders for my concentration."

Jack laughed, loving her sarcasm and her frustration. "Good."

Lilly responded with a mixture of a groan and a whine. She must have been burying her face in a pillow because the sound came out muffled. "You're killing me."

"I am. But you like it."

"You're mean."

"You like that too." She whimpered, and he mimicked the sound, taunting her. "Are you wet?"

"Yes." He could almost see the pout on her face. And now that he had her all wound up, he didn't want to stop.

"Touch yourself."

"It's a weekday. I thought I wasn't allowed."

Oh she felt like being bratty now, did she?

"You're allowed when I say you're allowed. Now do as you're told, little girl."

Her breath caught like it always did when he called her that. He'd bet her pupils had dilated too, her expression awash with lust. Jack listened to her shift, knowing the exact moment when she stroked over her clit by the noise she made. He could see her doing it —one finger rubbing in tiny circles. He was hard in seconds.

"Tell me how it feels."

"Good. Wish it was your fingers, though."

"Oh, but I wouldn't give you what you wanted so easily. I'd tease you until you were ready to scream." He would too. Avoid all her sensitive spots, touching her everywhere but where she needed it most. "Push your fingers lower."

"Yes, Sir."

"Do it the way I would, slow and deep."

Jack listened to her breathing quicken and imagined her body surging, her hips pushing up. She moaned, and it was enough to make him have to squeeze his dick to take the edge off. It wasn't enough. He needed more, to push her harder, to see how far he could take this.

"Lower, now," he instructed.

The order earned him a shocked inhale. Jack chuckled. She had little experience in anal, but she'd listed it as curious on her checklist, and he wasn't backing down.

"I *said* lower."

"Y-yes, Sir."

He pictured her doing it, the look on her face as her wet fingers trailed a slow path downward to the tight, puckered entrance below.

"Is your hand where I want it?"

Her swallow was audible. "Yes, Sir."

"Good girl. Now tap yourself there with your pinky, just once."

"Oh. *Oh.*"

"That's my girl," he said, dragging out his words the way he wanted to drag his touch over her skin. "Now rub it the way I'd tease your clit, nice and light."

Lilly grunted as if she were fighting back the pleasure.

"Didn't think it would feel like that, did you?"

"No, Sir." The words came out high-pitched, somewhere between a sob and a sigh.

"Now press your finger down a little. Just the tip."

"Oh, fuck."

The way she said it with her voice so hoarse, he was sure her head had lifted off the bed in surprise, her mouth hanging open, legs shaking. He wanted to see this, wanted his hands on her, his tongue. His cock stiffened, impossibly hard now. He could do this, could tell her to tap her sweet, virgin ass, and fuck her with words until she was completely out of her mind. But if she was going to come this way, he wanted to be there to watch it happen.

"I knew you'd like that," he said. "Now back to your clit. Turn over onto your stomach."

He heard the sheets rustle, reveling in her cry as she started to work herself again.

"I'm lying on top of you, holding you down. Feel my weight. My hand shoved between your thighs. Giving you no choice but to come. You're almost there, aren't you?"

She squeaked out in agreement. Jack smiled and whispered, "Stop."

Lilly sobbed a sound of pure agony, aching and desperate to fall over the edge. He couldn't wait until Saturday to have her. He just fucking couldn't.

"If you want to come tonight, you'll be in my playroom in thirty minutes with your knees on the floor and my cock in your mouth. The choice is yours."

He didn't wait for her reply. He simply ended the call.

Twenty-five minutes later, his doorbell rang. He opened the door to find Lilly out of breath and staring down at her watch. With eyes more wild than he'd ever seen, she ran past him and sprinted down the stairs, tearing off clothes as she went. Jack smirked and closed the door. He'd known she couldn't resist, as drawn to their intense attraction as he was.

Pushing away the thoughts that had plagued him all evening, he followed her downstairs. He didn't want to think about death anymore.

Lilly made him feel alive again.

# 22

The next Saturday, Jack made Lilly watch as he undressed. She'd already stripped, her safewords murmured from her spot on the floor, and now she was staring up at him as he undid each button on his shirt, a look of hunger in her eyes he was sure mirrored his own.

He'd waited a long time for what he'd planned today, and he couldn't wait to start.

"Stand up," he said. "Sit on the edge of the bed. Hands behind you."

She followed his commands as he unfastened the last button on his shirt and reached for his belt. He slid it free from the loops on his pants and snapped it loudly. Lilly flinched, her breathing going suddenly rapid.

"What is it about that sound?" He snapped the belt again. Lilly jolted, but her hips rolled all the same. "Does it scare you, or does it make you even wetter than we both know you are?"

She eyed the belt. "It scares me, Sir."

"What are you scared of?"

"The pain, Sir."

He took a step closer and brought the belt to her chin. She'd become so much more vocal and honest with him, but there were things she didn't understand yet, things she couldn't even admit to herself.

"I don't think that's what you're afraid of." Jack drew the edge of the belt down her throat and between her breasts. Over each stiff nipple. Along the damp skin between her splayed thighs. "Weren't you the girl who was begging for me to spank your pussy with my crop?"

Lilly shuddered. It hadn't taken him long to realize she loved dirty talk, or of being reminded just how lewd she'd been with him.

He changed the angle of his hand so the buckle rubbed against her clit. The silver tip slid easily against her slick skin. She turned her head to the side and squeezed her eyes shut, her face contorting into a mask of pleasure as her hips shifted forward. Jack couldn't decide which he liked better—her face, or the way her legs spread wider, opening her up to more of his steel caress. It was such a high to lure out the kink in her, to watch her get off on something so twisted and corrupt.

"You're not afraid of pain," he said, watching her body move in time with the metal stroking along her flesh. "You're afraid of where I can take you, my perverted little girl. Of letting the deviant inside you come out and play. And it's time for that to stop."

He let the belt fall to the floor.

"No," she whined, grimacing at the ceiling.

He placed his palms on the bed on either side of her. "You gonna fight me?"

Lilly lowered her chin and glared. It was the fight in her that Jack enjoyed the most. Having her challenge him was half the fun. It made her eventual surrender that much sweeter.

She blew out a breath. "No. Sir."

"That's what I thought." Jack stood and took off his shirt. "Look at the toys I've set out for you."

She turned to scan the bed. The nylon restraints had been pulled out from under the mattress, the pillows piled up in a neat line by the footboard. In front of them was a spreader bar attached to a pair of ankle cuffs, as well as his rabbit-hair flogger, the deerskin one and the suede.

Her nipples stiffened to tight little points, a motion Jack's cock agreed with. He couldn't wait to see how she responded to the suede, the sound the falls made when they smacked against her skin. The marks they'd leave behind.

"We'll have a warm-up spanking first, to get your skin ready." He gently clasped her throat, one finger urging her chin back toward him. "Are you ready to play, little girl?"

It was a question he'd gotten in the habit of asking at the beginning of every session. It seemed to settle her, help her find her focus.

"I am, Sir."

"Good girl." He pulled her to her feet and led her to the end of the bed. "Today is about letting go. I don't want you to think. Just relax, obey and feel."

He bent her face down until her torso was on the bed, her hips propped up by the pillows. When she'd relaxed into the position, he spread her arms out to each side so her body made a T-formation and slipped one of her hands into a restraint. Jack wrapped the nylon in a snug embrace around one wrist, then did the same to the other. Lilly tugged at her bonds, testing them.

"Don't even think about trying to wriggle out," he warned. He'd like to see her try, though, just so he could wrestle her back into them. They were more for her to hold on to, anyway. To help brace herself when the real fun began.

Jack hovered over her and kissed the back of her neck, unable to ignore the temptation of her exposed backside. He ground his hips against her, his cock stiff and constrained behind the layers of cotton and denim. He wanted inside her so damn bad, had even purchased a pack of condoms and stashed them in the toy chest in the hopes that she'd lift that damn limit. She wasn't there yet, and until she was ready, he'd need to make her even more crazed than he was. Which was what he'd planned to do today.

Bending down, he fastened the cuffs around her ankles, linked the spreader bar between them and stood back to look at her. She was a work of art, her skin a blank canvas ready for his marking. She must have panicked a little at the distance, though, because she let out a soft cry of distress.

"Shhh. I'm here." He touched her lightly, soothing strokes along her back until she calmed. He liked how he had that effect on her now—that he could soothe her with nothing more than a touch. "Do you know why I've tied you up like this?"

"No, Sir."

"Because it keeps you safe. I need you to be as still as possible. It gives me more control over where the flogger tails land, so they don't wrap around your side and hurt you." He leaned down until his lips were against her ear. "But there's another reason."

Lilly shivered. "What's that, Sir?"

"Because you look so lovely when you're helpless, incapable of stopping me."

The words seemed to roll through her, her back arching as she let out the most delicious little groan. Jack chuckled and retrieved the fur flogger. He fanned it from her spine to her heels, submerging her in its feathery touch until her body sank down, the set of her shoulders relaxing.

He repeated the move several times, letting the falls seduce her, then pushed it through her legs, stroking once along her slit. When he pulled it back, Lilly let out a plaintive whine.

"My greedy little prisoner, always wanting more."

He doled out a sharp spank to her bottom with his free hand. Lilly gasped, her head snapping up in surprise, arms going taut as she gripped the restraints.

"Relax." He kept his palm against the spot he'd struck and rubbed it gently. "You know I won't harm you. Just let yourself feel."

Lilly moaned and Jack's cock hardened even more at the sound. He never felt as dominant as he did when he brought her from pleasure to pain and back. Lifting his hand, he slapped her again, interspersing each smack with a light thump from the flogger, until the swell of her bottom became a symphony of color, her creamy skin layered with the pink echo of his handprints.

He set the fur flogger back on the bed and picked up the deerskin one.

"We're moving on now," he told her, and angled the tails over each pink cheek. When he finally struck her with it, the feeling of the thud against her rear reverberated all the way up his arm. Lilly shuddered and cursed.

"What color?" he asked.

"Green, Sir."

"Do you want to continue?"

"Yes, Sir." She was breathless. It was exactly what he'd hoped for.

Jack started a figure eight pattern, each downward lash leading to the next. Her body undulated with every strike, spilling across the bed in a wave of pleasure. After a few minutes, her skin had flushed to a lovely crimson, and Jack paused when she started rocking against the pillows, the friction she craved unattainable with her legs spread so wide.

"Look at you, trying to work yourself against the bed." He slipped his fingers between her legs. She was soaked, the proof of her desire running down her thighs.

Lilly arched against him. "Please don't stop, Sir."

"Don't stop what? This?" He pumped his fingers once, twice, then pulled them free and slapped her with the flogger again. "Or that?"

She grunted. "All of it, Sir. Please."

Jack licked his fingers. Her taste was almost as satisfying as the sound of her begging.

He traded the deerskin flogger for the suede, and his breathing picked up as he grasped the handle. It was so perfectly weighted, the falls thick and pliable. Lilly lifted her head and looked over her shoulder at him, her lust-filled eyes trained on his hand.

"Face down," he ordered. When she obeyed, a sense of satisfaction and pride charged him up like wildfire. Holding the flogger against her bottom, he asked, "You want this?"

"Please, Sir."

"There's my filthy little girl."

Jack drew it back and waited one more heart-pounding second, letting her anticipation build, before snapping it against the swell of her ass. The force of the heavier tails made her cry out, her body caving in as the first shockwave of sensation surged through her. Jack waited for her to quiet, and then did it again. Her reaction was better than the first time.

"Do you like that?"

"Yes. More. Please more, Sir."

Jack gripped the flogger's handle tightly. He was glad Lilly couldn't see his face because the sound of her need hit him like an avalanche. He'd hoped she'd react this way to his favorite implement of pleasure and torment, and *fuck*, did he plan to torture her with it now.

He began a slow rhythm of strikes, letting the intensity build. The thud of the suede slapping at her skin made his cock throb, made sweat pool in the creases of his elbows and knees. Lilly cried out with each thump, her hips bowing up to meet every smack. When her skin turned scarlet, Jack forced himself to stop and check on her.

"What color?"

She didn't answer. Jack listened for signs of stress, but Lilly's breathing was heavy, deep, her limbs slackened. He touched the small of her back with his fingertips, and she finally murmured, "Green, Sir."

The words came out slurred. It took a minute for Jack to register what he was seeing. It was subspace—that delirious, altered submissive mindset he'd always wanted to witness but never had before. He couldn't believe he'd driven Lilly there with the one thing he'd been dying to do to her. He was torn by the desire to keep a careful watch on her and the perverse need to push her further down the rabbit hole.

"You want more?"

Her head dipped in a slow nod. Jack smirked.

"Such a greedy little slut."

Lilly stiffened, her limbs suddenly rigid, her breath rushing out. She went completely and utterly silent, and Jack had no idea what was happening until she whispered, "Yellow."

He dropped the flogger and moved in close, his hands on either side of her body, his weight surrounding her. "Talk to me."

"That word. Slut." She took a shallow, shuddery breath. "It's what Damien called me."

Jack winced, but felt a niggling sense of discomfort. Why hadn't she told him that?

"Do you want to continue?" he asked.

"I...I don't know."

There was so much uncertainty in her voice. He only had to stop the scene if she said red, but he couldn't tell if she was being honest about her emotional state, or if she could judge it at all.

"I'm so proud of you for safewording, but we need to stop and talk before we keep going."

"Okay." Despite his reassurance, she sounded so ashamed.

He dropped down to free her ankles, then tugged the Velcro off her wrists. He urged her onto the bed, and she'd curled into a fetal position by the time he climbed up beside her. Jack pulled her into his arms.

"Can you talk about it?"

Her breathing was short and tight. Jack stroked her hair, keeping her nestled in the crook of his arm until she'd gathered her thoughts.

"I hated when he called me that," she finally said. "A 'dirty fucking slut' he could do whatever he wanted to. I let him call me that, even when it made me feel like shit, because when he made me feel good all the bad stuff would disappear. And then I started to feel like a slut, because I kept going back to him. Like I was some pitiful whore who was so desperate for what he could do that I didn't even care how I was being treated." She trembled and he held her even tighter. "I'm sorry. I should've told you about it sooner. I just never expected you to say it."

Jack sighed and shook his head. He wasn't even sure why he'd called her that in the first place. It was a word he'd barely ever said before. It just flew out of his mouth. He'd been in too deep, running away with the momentum of the scene.

"Don't ever be sorry for being honest with me."

Lilly lifted her gaze to meet his, eyes wide with something that looked like disbelief. Her expression was heartbreaking. There was so much damage to be undone, caused by a word that left deeper scars than any whip could have.

He could fix that. He could show her how a word's meaning changed depending on who said it.

"We won't use that word again if you're that uncomfortable with it. But first, tell me—is it the word itself or how Damien used it that upset you?"

Her brow furrowed, lines pressing into her forehead. "It's not the nicest word, but I guess it never bothered me before he said it."

"What about when I called you dirty and perverted? Did that bother you?"

"No."

"Why not?"

Her eyes searched his. "I guess it's different, coming from you."

"So wouldn't the same be true for slut if I said it?"

"I...guess."

Jack watched her blink as she worked through puzzled thoughts. He took her hand and brought it to lie flat on his chest, caressing her fingertips. "Do you know why I say the things I do to you?"

Lilly shook her head.

"Because I want to help you embrace this part of yourself without judgment, guilt or shame, and get you to the point where all you do is listen and obey."

"Like you did today?"

"Exactly." He brought her fingers to his mouth and ran the pad of her middle finger over his lower lip. "I want to give you the freedom to let out that depraved, dirty part of yourself. Where all that matters is what you crave, and satisfying that need."

Jack slowly sucked her finger into his mouth. Lilly shifted against him, a subtle move of her hips, her eyes trained on the movements of his mouth. Her skin flushed and her eyelids fluttered as he tongued along the underside of her knuckle. He released her finger and kissed the tip.

"So when I called you those things, did it make you feel humiliated? Degraded?"

"No, Sir."

He lowered their hands and skimmed her wet finger over her nipple, teasing it until it rose up under her touch.

"When I called you my filthy little girl, how did it make you feel?"

The freckles on her cheeks disappeared under a blush that stole down to her breasts. "It made me wet, Sir."

Jack held her hand still. "Then listen to me carefully because I won't say this again."

The discipline in his tone didn't match the tenderness of the moment, but he needed to get her attention.

"When you step in my playroom and become that needy, desperate, begging creature, it's because I make you that way. You're not a slut in here—you're *my* slut," Jack growled. "Do you see the difference? Here, you become my toy. My whore. My perfect, sweet little slut. You belong to me, little girl. And I. Fucking. Love. It."

Jack took her hand and molded it over his cock.

"Do you feel how hard you make me? I love how badly you want it."

He sat up and urged her onto her stomach, playing his fingers over the marks on her ass, admiring the evidence of his branding. "You're bright red and it's all because of me. Because you're my sweet little slut."

Jack pressed open-mouthed kisses to each perfectly rounded cheek. Lilly tried to shimmy away but he squeezed her waist, keeping her motionless.

"Repeat it. Say you're my little slut."

Her reply was halted. Hesitant. "I-I'm your little slut, Sir."

He rubbed his palm over her hot skin. "Again."

"I'm your slut, Sir." This time, it was stronger. Louder.

"That's right. And only my beautiful little slut would give me everything—every opening in her body mine for the taking."

She was his and he was going to prove it. He was going to show her how much of her belonged to him.

Jack pried her legs open and licked over the seam of her ass. Lilly gasped as he circled her rear entrance, his tongue pushing gently at the resistance that greeted him. Her arms flailed out, and Jack grabbed her by her hips, but it wasn't enough to keep her from thrashing around in shocked pleasure. He didn't want to stop what he was doing long enough to order her to stay still, so he found the base of her neck with one hand and clutched her hair, a rough grip holding her down until she complied. When her arms dropped and she grasped the sheets, Jack let go, using that hand for leverage as he parted her slick folds with the other. He worked her with his fingers and tongue, reaping the satisfaction of her short, high-pitched yelps as she writhed beneath him.

"Please, oh please, oh please," she chanted. "Please, make me come, Sir."

Jack slid his hand underneath her desperately flexing hips to find her delicate little slit, but he didn't do it to satisfy her pleading. He'd already decided to drive her to orgasm, unable to make her wait a second longer, because neither could he.

She cried out in a litany of *God* and *fuck* and *yes* and *Sir*. He rubbed her faster, pushing her to shudder longer. Come harder. Scream louder. When the last convulsion rocked through her, Jack ripped off the rest of his clothes, flipped her over and kneeled above her. He laved his tongue between her breasts and braced his knees on either side of her torso. Taking Lilly's hand, he lifted it to his mouth and licked her palm, then wrapped her slim fingers around his pulsing flesh.

"See what you do to me?" he grunted, thrusting into the tight circle of her fingers. "You make me crazy too."

It was too much—the way she was trapped beneath him, hand stroking, looking up at him with those eyes and that mouth, and fuck, he needed to come. Jack tugged her fingers away and pushed her breasts together, driving himself between them.

"Say it again."

"I'm your slut, Sir. Yours!"

"Fuck, yes. You're mine, all fucking mine."

He thrust against her skin, his movements becoming sloppy and fast as his cock took the driver's seat. His eyes slammed shut and he cursed when he came, coating her chest with sticky ribbons. When his body slowed, Lilly was as out of breath as he was. Jack climbed off her, took a towel to both their bodies and covered them with a blanket.

"Thank you, Sir," she mumbled and curled into his side.

Jack laughed quietly, watching her drift off. "You're welcome."

He let his own eyes shut, a first for him. He hadn't slept beside her before—he'd only watched her in slumber—but today he was tired. It was a relief she was too, because he wasn't ready to let her out of his arms.

He wanted too much of her lately.

He shouldn't have given her orders over the phone the other day, shouldn't have beckoned her to his house or called her "little girl" on a weeknight, stepping outside of the carefully constructed lines of their agreement. It was a slip-up, something that couldn't happen again, but it was so hard to feel wrong about something that felt so right.

Lilly's breathing went slow and deep, and he dropped a kiss to the top of her head, nuzzling the soft, sweet-smelling strands of her hair. She was his little secret, wrapped up in his arms. They wouldn't be able to do this forever, but for now, Jack held her close and let himself sleep.

# 23

*L*illy woke up on Sunday morning to the sound of something she didn't recognize.

As her nightmare faded, she blinked in the sunlight, trying to make sense of what she was hearing: it was birdsong, coming from the trees outside her window. She hadn't heard that cheerful noise in months. It heralded the thaw to come—spring was only days away.

Smiling, she kicked off the blankets and stretched her arms over her head. Her body was sore from the day before, but it was a good kind of pain. It served as a reminder of her time with Jack.

She closed her eyes, remembering the sweet safety of his words. *"You're mine, all fucking mine."*

The memory was like silk brushing between her thighs. She had to roll over onto her stomach to stop herself from stroking the ache she'd been forbidden to soothe. Hugging her pillow, she forced herself to focus on something else, and turned to look at the window. Beams of gold were slipping in through the blinds. The sun had turned every wall yellow, the strength of it warming her pillows.

She wanted to feel it shine on her face.

Jumping out of bed, she went to her closet, pushing past the suits and bulky sweaters she'd wrapped herself up in all winter. Some of her lighter clothes were packed in a duffle on the floor, where they'd been in hibernation for months. She shoved her boots aside to reach it, and when she pulled the bag from the corner, her running shoes peeked out from underneath.

Her stomach flip-flopped. Lilly settled onto the floor and picked up the sneakers. They felt like ancient objects, filled with long-silenced secrets. They'd remained untouched since Damien's engagement announcement and the realization of how much he'd taken advantage of her. Of what a fool she'd been.

Lilly sighed and fingered the laces. They were gray from use, proof of how her time years ago had been filled with practices and track meets, blasting through school records and her own personal best. Like everything else she did, she had to excel at it. Another mile before sundown, another paper before bed, driving herself to her next accomplishment, smiling over her shoulder at the trail of glory behind her. She did the same with law school, never stopping when her goals were in sight. But Damien had made her doubt everything she felt confident in. Which was why she'd packed her running shoes away that day, along with her dreams of becoming a lawyer.

She'd forgotten how it felt to never doubt herself.

Jack, however, seemed to know exactly what she was capable of. He'd taken her by the hand and shown her, helping her deal with so many of her fears. These shoes were another block she needed to face, and for the first time in so long, she wanted to.

She put on sweats and unearthed her heart rate monitor, also stashed away in her closet. Once she'd fished her headphones from her bag, Lilly tucked her key and phone into the pocket on her armband and went outside into the surprisingly mild air. Snow was melting into grates. It trickled in rivulets down the street, nature reawakening. Lilly warmed up and took off at an easy pace. When she felt limber enough and there was a straight shot of road ahead of her, she started to run.

It was a challenge getting her heart rate up and fighting against the painful protest in her calves, but by the end of the first mile, her legs began to fly. She splashed through puddles, remembering how once there was nothing as clean as the feel of her feet on the pavement, fresh air on her face and music in her ears. Sweat used to wash away everything until there was only her heartbeat, and for the first time in so long she became a slave to that cadence, obeying its rhythm. It was similar to the state she reached in Jack's playroom, her body moving the way he directed it, her mind silent.

After another mile, she slowed by a park and stretched out her hamstrings. She paced around a bench, her legs tingling as she checked her wristwatch and waited for her heartbeat to lower, once again recalling Jack's words from the day before.

*"My whore. My perfect, sweet little slut."*

She shivered at the memory. He was right—the word she'd hated sounded so different when it came from him. With Jack she felt so secure, so protected. She didn't like the word, but being called *his* slut was different. In fact, if using that word was something he wanted, she knew she'd be able to bear it.

She gripped the bench, finally understanding an aspect of BDSM she never had before: submission didn't mean being coerced, having things forced upon you or suffering the consequences of saying no. It was about intimacy. Trust. And after months of feeling ashamed, Lilly finally felt something else.

Anger.

She took off again, her heels digging at the ground. Damien knew how badly she'd wanted to please him and he'd manipulated her anyway, tugging her however he wanted, making her his own personal marionette. She'd played the part, never breathing a word about what they were doing, accepting the silent treatment when she'd displeased him and how he'd sometimes act like he didn't know her at all. It hurt, but she thought maybe if she withstood it long enough, if she behaved just right, he'd stop making her jump through hoops. That he would realize how much she cared for him and do the things actual boyfriends did. Take care of her when she was sick. Go out to dinner. Hold her hand in public.

But that had never been in his plans.

Her anger escalated into rage, propelling her through the rest of the mile. She'd spent so much time feeling foolish, thinking she was the one at fault, when the truth was it had been Damien's cruelty that made her believe BDSM wasn't for her. He knew how inexperienced she was, and still he kept her in the dark. Literally and figuratively.

And Jack had shined a light on everything.

She'd thought she couldn't do this again—could never kneel and beg and plead, losing herself to the cravings of her body. Yet here she was, already longing for next Saturday to arrive with another opportunity to serve and please him. To listen and obey and become the wanton creature he brought out in her.

By the time she neared home, her clothes were sticking to her, sweat pooling between her breasts. The sensation was a slick reminder of Jack looming above her the day before and the thick, swollen tip of his cock as it dragged over her skin. She'd wanted to feel it inside her. She still did.

Maybe she could put sex back on the table. She'd employed the soft limit to protect her heart, but there was another word Jack said yesterday that might have changed everything.

*"You belong to me, little girl. And I. Fucking. Love. It."*

He loved it. Could he love her too?

No, she couldn't think that way, couldn't confuse Lilly with the little girl or Jack with Sir. It was absurd to try to transfer any thoughts of his ownership in the playroom into love in the daylight, no matter what contract they'd signed.

Lilly unlocked her door, but had to pause when her throat seized up and she started coughing. The tip of her nose was cold, and she rubbed at it with the back of her hand. She'd never had spring allergies before, but maybe there was something in the air here.

Well, she wasn't going to let some East Coast pollen take her down. She'd stop at the pharmacy for some over-the-counter stuff later.

She went into work a short time later, hoping to make some progress while the office was quiet. She walked through the empty halls, her head bent over the *Globe*. They'd printed another story, one that mentioned the firm, and the rivalry between Forrester and Mahoney.

Great. Maybe she should hold on to the paper. See if there were any job postings for paralegals in the Help Wanted section.

She sighed and sat down at her desk. A Post-it note was stuck to her screen, Gabe's handwriting scrawled across it.

*Go to the company site and see what the IT department finally got around to doing.*

She peeled off the note and booted up her computer, navigating to the site. Lilly squealed when she saw the company roster on the homepage, her name finally on it. It had taken a while for it to happen, but there it was in black and white. She sat back with a smile, but then another cough threw her lungs into spasm just as her cell phone rang. Making a mental note to pick up some lozenges when she hit the store later, she checked the screen.

Dad calling. Lilly swallowed a chug of water and thumbed the call button.

"Hey, Dad. It's not our usual day."

"Well, I hear you miss me. Was that true? Or was your brother just trying to get out of talking about himself?"

Lilly faltered, then recalled her conversation with Nick. She *had* said she missed their father. Damn traitor must've told him.

"Of course I miss—" Her words got cut off by another cough. She choked down another sip of water, trying to silence it.

"You coming down with something?"

"No, I'm fine. I was outside running. Pollen or whatever."

There was the briefest pause on his end of the line. "You're running again?"

She took a second to plan her reply. Her father had always been the one to support her, coming to every single one of her meets. Sure, Mom had been there too, but it was her father's raucous applause and whistles Lilly heard over everyone else's.

He must've known there'd been some kind of connection between her refusal to take the bar and packing up her running shoes, not to mention everything else she could fit in a suitcase and bring to Boston, but he'd never asked.

"I started again today, but it's tough getting back into it."

"You'll get there." Lilly could hear the smile in his voice. "Nick was right. You do sound happier."

Lilly froze. Before she could ask what Nick had told him, there was a click and a muffled noise, followed by the sound of her mother's voice. "You're running? You're happy? What aren't you telling us?"

"Oh..." Lilly searched for the appropriate lie. "I've been asked to help out on a really important trial. It's pretty exciting."

They bought it, and she told them what she could until her mother grew impatient and asked if she'd started seeing anyone yet. Hoping to avoid the conversation, Lilly was relieved to see her work phone light up with a call. She was about to tell them she had to go, but the caller ID read out with a number she didn't recognize. Voicemail it was then.

"No, Mom. I'm not seeing anyone." It wasn't exactly the truth. But she couldn't really tell them that, either.

"Oh. Well, let us know when that changes."

Lilly rolled her eyes. "I will. Bye, Mom."

She hung up, but her father stayed on the line. "In case you were wondering, I miss you too. And I'm very proud of you."

Tears sprang to her eyes. She hadn't realized how much she needed to hear that until he said it. "Thanks, Dad."

"Love you, kiddo."

They said good-bye, and she checked her voicemail, but no message had been left. She scanned back through her calls and found the one she'd missed. It was from out of town—an eight-four-seven area code number.

Evanston. The call came from Evanston, Illinois. Near Northwestern.

It could have been Damien.

Her heart stuttered, her skin prickling at the reality that he might be looking for her again. The flimsy barriers she'd put up of blocked Facebook profiles and changed phone numbers wouldn't do much. If he wanted to find her, he would.

Rubbing her hands over her arms, she looked out the window, but as her gaze strayed toward where Jack lived, her heartbeat slowed. His protection was an invisible connection, warming her just as much as the rays of sun had this morning. The cold fingers of winter were losing their hold on the frozen ground, and so was Damien's hold on her heart.

For so long, she'd feared if he appeared in her life again it would be impossible to say no to him. That one look into those enticing green eyes and demanding stare would cripple her back under his power. But she wouldn't ever be lured back to him, not now that she knew how a real Dominant should treat her.

She lifted her head high. If Damien wanted to track her down, he could go right ahead. He didn't matter anymore.

# 24

"*A*nother midweek call?" There was mirth in Lilly's voice. "To what do I owe this honor?"

Jack grinned and rocked back in his chair. He'd missed her fire over the last few days. "Just checking on you."

"Well, don't count on me making another dash to your front door. I'm wiped."

Her words were punctuated with a cough. The deep, guttural kind.

Jack stopped rocking. "Are you sick?"

"No, it's allergies. And lack of sleep." She yawned through her next words. "How's your week going?"

"Fine. My third years are getting anxious. I should tell them to run before it's too late." Lilly's responding laughter bled into another cough. "You sound awful."

"It's just a cough. Don't worry about it," she said. "Will I see you at the pub on Friday?"

Jack didn't like how she was passing off his concern, but hoped if something was really wrong, she'd say so. "Yes, but I've started wishing I could skip over Fridays and go straight to Saturday."

She laughed again—a soft giggle he knew would accompany a glance at the floor, her lashes lowered, her cheeks pink.

"Besides," he added. "I doubt Brady or Patrick would let me out of it at this point."

"They care about you."

"True, but that's not why they started dragging me there."

Another cough. "It's not?"

Jack toyed with the zipper on his sweatshirt, flicking it up and down. He might as well tell her. "They were trying to find me a date."

"Oh." Lilly paused. "Are they...still trying to find you one?"

She was attempting to sound casual.

She was failing miserably.

"No. I told them to stop."

It was only partly true. He hadn't told Brady shit, but Patrick was a different story. Remorse gnawed at him, a hollow feeling in the pit of his gut. She'd told him so much. It didn't seem right to keep the fact that Patrick knew about them from her any longer.

"Lilly, I—" he began, but she started coughing again, and Jack shelved the conversation for another time. Her well-being was more important than relieving his guilty conscience. "I think you should see a doctor."

"I'm fine. I promise."

God, she was stubborn. "Fine, but I'm insisting that you rest. No more work tonight, understand?" He lowered his voice on the last word, making sure she didn't miss the command in his tone.

She sighed, long and drawn out, but he could hear her smile. "Yes, Sir."

They said good night, but the sound of her cough pricked at him in a way he couldn't place, and his unease remained into the days that followed. By Friday morning he found himself needing some kind of confirmation she was feeling better. A quick call wouldn't hurt. Asking about her health was a perfectly normal thing for a Dominant to do for his submissive.

He started to dial, but stopped himself. Too much weekday contact could lead to her expecting more than he could give. He wrote up their contract, damn it. He should know when to stop the lines from blurring.

When he arrived at the pub that evening, Jack pushed through the throng of bodies and scanned the tables in the back. Brady and Patrick were playing darts, their beers on a table next to them. No one else was there.

Anxiety swelled, but Jack kicked the feeling aside. There was nothing to worry about, and it was early. Lilly said she was fine. She'd be here.

"There you are." Patrick handed Jack his darts. "Take my spot. There's a blonde in the corner who needs attention."

"You're impossible."

"No, just opportunistic."

Patrick strode off toward the woman in question. Brady aimed his dart, took his shot and hit the wall.

"Jesus. How could I have been so good at football, but suck at this and pool?"

"Because darts and pool take actual skill, and football, well…"

Brady gave him the finger. "Speaking of skills, it seems I'm going to be trying my hand at tennis this week. Patrick asked me and Nick to join you. Guess he's getting bored with your scintillating company."

"You're starting to sound like him."

"And now my life is complete." Brady grinned and waved over Jack's shoulder.

Jack turned to see Nick and Gabe weaving through the crowd. Lilly wasn't with them. They took a seat at the table and Nick ordered them a round as Patrick settled himself down with them, proudly flashing the blonde's phone number. Jack hurled his darts, feeling frustrated and powerless. Where the hell was Lilly? When Brady stepped up for his turn, Jack palmed his phone, his best poker face on as he texted her.

*Where are you?*

He stared at the screen for several long moments, waiting for her reply.

There wasn't one.

"So what do you think, Jack?" Brady asked.

Jack glanced up to find his brother looking at him expectantly. "What do I think of what?"

Patrick laughed. "I think Jack was having a senior moment. Which is pretty fucking appropriate, considering the topic at hand."

"Shut up. You're as old as he is," Brady said. "We were talking about your birthday. Patrick could host another one of his epic parties."

Jack nodded, barely listening. "Sure. Whatever. Sounds good."

Patrick snorted. "I think that's professor-speak for 'Thanks guys. That sounds great.'"

The withering look Jack shot him could melt glass. It had no effect.

"Two weeks from tomorrow." Patrick lifted his glass in Jack's direction. "Plenty of time for you to practice your grateful face."

Being grateful wasn't on Jack's agenda. He wasn't looking forward to the reminder that he was turning forty-five, or the fact that he'd be another year older than Lilly. He hadn't even planned on telling her it was his birthday. That obviously wasn't happening now.

He checked his phone again. She still hadn't replied.

Screw this. He needed answers.

"Where's Lilly tonight?" he asked, turning to Nick.

"Oh, she's really sick. Bronchitis."

Jack fisted his darts. Damn it. He knew it wasn't allergies.

"She looked like hell yesterday," Gabe added. "Forrester sent her home. She didn't come in today, either."

"Has she been to a doctor?" There was an edge in his voice he didn't bother to hide.

"She went this morning," Nick said. "She hasn't answered her phone all day, but I'm sure she's sleeping. I'll check on her tomorrow if I haven't heard from her."

Jack swallowed, his irritation overshadowed by worry. If she was too ill to even answer her phone, he needed to get to her, but how the hell could he escape this goddamned pub without an explanation?

Patrick pulled his phone from his pocket, glanced at it and grinned. "Must be that blonde calling me already. Be right back."

He strode toward the doorway. Jack flung his darts again, hard enough that one bounced off the wall. When he bent down to retrieve it, his phone buzzed. He palmed it eagerly, waiting for Lilly's name to read out on the screen, but the call was from Patrick.

"Yes?" he snapped.

"Stop being an ass," he answered quietly. "You obviously need to go to her, so I'm out here freezing my balls off and pretending to be on the phone so I can give you a way out. Act like I'm Josh. He's having some kind of PhD crisis and needs to talk to his dear old dad. Now get the hell out of here."

Jack closed his eyes in relief.

"Hey, Josh. What's going on?" He handed Brady his darts, an absent-minded move that made him look as if he were distracted by his son's words. "No, I understand. Grad school is hard... Yeah, sure. Of course, I have time to talk."

He motioned toward the door and Brady nodded. Jack pulled out his wallet, offering to pay for a portion of the beer he hadn't even touched, but everyone waved him off, the illusion complete. He passed Patrick as he walked toward the exit. Their eyes met and Jack nodded.

Jack hurried to his car, dialing Lilly's number as he got inside. Her voicemail picked up, and he punched the steering wheel in frustration. Adrenaline racing, he sped through town, his driving more reckless than it should've been. He found a spot in front of her building, lucking out when someone stepped out of the main entrance. He hurried to grab the door before it closed and took the steps two at a time, pounding on her door the second he reached it.

"Lilly, it's me." When there was no response, he knocked again, louder. "Come on, open up."

He kept knocking until the lock clicked and the door creaked open. Lilly peered out in her bathrobe, one hand on the doorknob. Her hair was a mess, her eyes glassy and red, her face so pale that her freckles stood out in stark contrast.

"Why did I have to hear from Nick you were this sick? Why didn't you call me?"

"I'm fine." Her throat was so swollen her words came out garbled.

"You're not fine. Let me in."

Lilly shook her head. The movement made her wince in pain. "Go home, Jack. You don't have to be here."

"Like hell I don't."

She coughed hard enough to shake her entire frame, then leaned on the door for support. A tear streaked down her cheek. "You're not my boyfriend. It's not your job to take care of me."

Jack flinched. Her words hurt, but they shouldn't have taken him by surprise. Of course she'd shy away. She couldn't admit she needed him because of who they were to one another. But he was her Dom and he needed to take care of her.

"Your welfare is my responsibility," he said. "It absolutely is my job, Lilly."

Her face crumpled. She dropped her hand from the doorknob and wrapped her arms around her middle. "I didn't want you to see me like this."

Jack took her into his arms and hushed her, rocking her gently as he looked around her small apartment. A knitted blanket was bunched up on her couch, the pillows haphazardly strewn across it. Her kitchen table was littered with files and papers. The sink was full of dishes. The garbage can was overflowing with tissues.

"You shouldn't come in," she tried to insist. "I don't want you to get sick."

"I have a strong immune system. And I wasn't asking your permission." Jack closed the door with his foot. "Where's your bedroom?"

"This way." Lilly started down the hallway, and a tiger-striped cat wound around her feet as they walked.

He hadn't even known she had a pet.

It bothered him, that there were things he didn't know about her, but now wasn't the time to worry about that. Jack helped her onto the bed, tucked her beneath the blankets and felt her forehead.

"You're burning up. Have you taken anything?"

She waved toward her nightstand, where a vial of antibiotics, Tylenol, cough syrup and a full glass of water sat.

"That doesn't answer my question," he said sternly.

"I took the medicine the doctor gave me this morning. Then I fell asleep."

"When's the last time you took Tylenol?"

"I don't remember."

"Have you eaten?"

"Today?"

He glared at her. "Yes, today."

"No."

Jack sighed and reached for the painkillers. "I wish you'd called me."

"Can't find my phone. Think Rumbles ate it. Been too tired to get his food."

As if in response, the cat meowed loudly.

"Here, take this." Jack cupped the back of Lilly's head, helping her sit up long enough to swallow the pills with a swig of water. "Close your eyes. I'll be right back."

He went to her kitchen and rummaged through the cabinets until he found tea and a can of soup. He prepared both before searching for cat food and pouring it into the bowl on the floor. When he returned to Lilly's side with the soup, she seemed too weary to even lift a spoon to her lips, so Jack sat next to her and did the job himself.

"My son had bronchitis for the first time when he was five," he said. "It almost turned into pneumonia. Scared the crap out of me."

Hoping to keep her distracted while she ate, he told her a story about Josh and an unnecessary trip to the hospital. He was all bravado, strong and sure as he fed her with a confident hand, but inside he was caving. It wasn't memories of Josh twisting his stomach into knots. There was an echo of Eve's dying form in the way Lilly's eyes slid slowly shut, all her energy and passion drained by illness. Jack drew in a shaky breath, forcing away the ghostly memories.

*This isn't cancer. She'll be okay again.*

"It took a few days, but after some rest and medicine, Josh was back to his old self." Jack spooned out the last mouthful of soup. "You will be too. I promise."

He wasn't sure which one of them he was assuring.

Lilly closed her eyes. "Hope so."

Jack pressed a kiss to her burning forehead. "Sleep."

He listened to her shallow breathing as she drifted off. When her cat curled up at the foot of her bed, Jack realized he wasn't going anywhere, either. Careful not to disturb her, he flipped off the light and went into the living room. He heard the chirp of a phone about to go dead, and found it in a bag slumped on the floor. After finding a plug on her counter, he set it to charge, then retreated to her couch and tried to sleep.

He woke up several times during the night to check on her. By the morning her temperature hadn't dropped. Jack made a quick trip home for a change of clothes and resumed his post. Lilly slept intermittently throughout the day, waking once to field a call from Nick. She was too groggy to manage holding it, so he put the call on speaker.

"Hey, you sound like shit," Nick said. "You want me to come over?"

Jack stiffened, readying himself to leave. Nick should've been the one with her, not him, but Lilly reached for his hand. The pleading look in her eyes seemed to say *"no, you"*.

"Thanks," she told Nick when Jack curled his fingers around hers. "But I'll be okay."

He spent another night on her couch. Her cough started to lessen by Sunday afternoon, but her fever was still too high for him to feel comfortable leaving. He left his secretary a message that his Monday classes were canceled, then insisted Lilly email her boss saying she wouldn't be in the next day.

A few hours later, her fever finally broke. He helped her out of her sweaty clothes and into a bath. She breathed in the steam as he rubbed shampoo into her hair and rinsed her body, watching her revive.

Letting her soak a bit, he asked, "Where are your clean sheets?" She pointed to a closet in the corner, and Jack pulled a set from a shelf. "I'll be right back."

He stripped her bed, replacing the sheets with fresh ones. When he walked by her dresser, he noticed a piece of paper tucked into the mirror above it. It was a printout of her firm's roster. Her name was on it, and Jack swelled with pride. It was a big step—the beginning of a long line of successes she was sure to have. He was quickly distracted, though, by the photo next to it of Lilly with a man who must've been her father. Jack studied the lines on the older man's face, knowing there were similar lines on his own. For the first time in so long, the age difference between him and Lilly felt inescapably clear.

With a sinking feeling in his gut, he returned to the bathroom. She was sitting up, her arms wrapped around her knees, her spine a curved line that disappeared into the water.

"Feeling any better?"

"Yes." She cleared her throat. "But I think my fingertips are starting to prune."

Jack held out a hand. "Let's get you dried off."

He helped her out and wrapped her in a towel. As he rubbed the excess water from her skin, Lilly watched him from the tunnel of terrycloth, her eyes clear and wide. Jack slowed his rough caress as he looked down at her, his heartbeat in his ears. The gratitude in her expression was more than that of a grateful submissive to her Dominant. It was a question and an answer all at once, one he wasn't ready for. What could he possibly say? It wasn't that he didn't return the sentiment in her gaze. He did, more so than he'd been able to admit until this point. Every moment he'd spent in her presence had brought him back from the grave.

He stroked the damp skin of her cheek. Lilly cupped her hand over his and turned her face to kiss his palm. It was so tender and sweet, and it broke his heart to watch. He pulled her to him and pressed his eyes shut. He couldn't keep her, no matter how much he wished he could. That wasn't what either of them had signed on for, and any real future between them was impossible, anyway.

She let out a muffled cough, and he kissed the top of her head. This thing between them would have to end eventually, but not right now. He had to get a hold of himself. She still needed him.

"Thank you," Lilly whispered.

"Nothing to thank me for." He helped her into pajamas, then walked her back to bed. "How does some TV sound?"

Her nod was shy but strong, and he handed her the remote before heating up more soup. They watched a sitcom as they ate, and she fell asleep a short time later with her head in his lap. She whimpered when he moved away, reaching for him in her slumber. He wanted to comfort her, to hold her and spend the night by her side, but sleeping together would only make things more complicated. For both of them.

He leaned in to kiss her forehead. "I won't be far," he promised, and turned out the light.

* * *

Jack awoke Monday morning to the sound of footsteps. He looked over the couch to see Lilly entering the living room. She'd changed out of her pajamas into sweats and a T-shirt. Color had returned to her face.

She offered him a faint smile. "I can't believe you slept on my couch."

"It's a comfortable couch." He peeled back the blanket. "You look much better."

"I feel better. And I'm starving."

Jack grinned. "I'll get you some breakfast."

She offered to help but he made her sit. She was silent while they ate, though, hesitant glances thrown in his direction.

"What is it?" he asked.

Her gaze fell to the floor. "I'm sorry we didn't get to play this weekend. I hope you're not mad."

"You actually thought I'd be upset about you being too sick to play?"

She shrugged. Jack put down his coffee and took her hand. "I honestly couldn't care less about the lost playroom time." He tugged on her fingers until she met his eyes. "There will be other Saturdays."

She gave him a sheepish grin, so adorable and sexy and Lilly.

"Come here." He stood, opening his arms to her. She moved into his embrace, fitting perfectly as he tucked her head beneath his chin. Her skin was no longer clammy but warm and soft again. Jack closed his eyes for a moment and breathed in her scent.

"Thank you," she said. "For taking care of me."

"I told you. It's my job."

She pulled back to look at him, her chin pressing against his chest. Her expression started to shift, eyes growing wider, her cheeks pink, and not with fever.

"I'd like to change something on my checklist, Sir."

Jack's body reacted to the title before his mind could catch up with it, desires he'd forgotten about all weekend reawakening. He tried to stifle it, but it was impossible with how close she was, her breath fanning softly across his chest.

"What do you want to change?" he ground out.

"I'd like to take the limit off sex."

*Fuck.*

A tide of emotions warred through him, a groan rumbling in his chest as he fought the urge to slip into role.

"You don't have to do this," he rasped. "You've been very sick."

"I feel much better, Sir." She began lowering herself to the floor, her eyes pleading. "And I want to."

Jack swallowed, his jaw tight as she settled into her kneeling pose and stripped off her top. She wasn't wearing a bra underneath. His gaze raked across her breasts, dropping lower when she hooked her thumbs into the edge of her bottoms and shimmied out of them until she was naked.

It was nearly impossible to keep his hands fisted at his sides.

"Lilly," he said, purposely using her name. "I don't want you changing your limits because you feel like you owe me something."

"I don't feel like that. I'd been thinking about it already. You've been so good to me, even before this weekend. Please, Sir, let me thank you with my body."

Honesty and hunger shined from her eyes. Jack cursed under his breath. This wasn't how he'd imagined sex happening. They were at her house. It was a weekday. But how could he deny them what they both wanted when she pleaded like that?

Lilly dropped her head in defeat.

"I understand if you don't want to," she said. "We're not in your playroom, and I don't have any bondage toys—"

"You think I need toys to dominate you?"

Her head snapped up, and she seemed to know it the same moment he did—that switch had been flipped inside him, and now there was no turning back. Jack wrapped one hand around her throat, letting her see he wanted this every bit as much as she did.

"Bedroom, little girl. Walk. Now."

## 25

*R*elief coursed through her, not just from the feel of Jack's hands, but from the words "little girl". A shift took over, her mind and body slipping into his ownership in a rush of gratefulness and longing and the undeniable need to serve. She'd never expected him to show up on Friday, never thought he would stay by her side until she was well again. She hadn't understood until now that his being her Dom meant truly caring for her, and in the shadow of her waning sickness, the desire to give herself wholly to him became a powerful urge.

It wasn't just as a thank you—she'd felt the weight of his self-control every time they'd played, pleasure her limit had denied him, and she didn't want him to have to restrain himself any longer.

Jack propelled her toward her bedroom, closed the door and pulled her to him. Lilly whimpered, falling back against the solid line of his body.

"Whining already?" He tugged her hair to the side and grazed his teeth along her neck. "We've barely even started."

She groaned as he nipped his way down to her shoulder, hands cupping her breasts, thumbs teasing her nipples. She reached around behind her, disobediently searching for his zipper. She shouldn't have been trying to take the reins, to make things go faster, but she couldn't help herself.

Jack seized her wrists and chuckled against her skin. "Bad girl. What are you so needy for?"

"You, Sir. I need you."

"You need me to what?"

She swallowed, her breathing tight and fast. "I need you to fuck me, Sir."

Jack laughed again. His hot breath washed over her ear when he whispered, "No."

Confusion punched her in the gut. "No?"

"No."

"But...why?"

"Because I told you when I fucked you, you'd be begging for it. And I don't think I've heard you beg me yet."

He punctuated his words with a thrust against her. She could feel how hard he was, thick and long beneath the denim. His skills with his tongue and fingers had driven her out of her mind several times over already, so the things he'd be able to do with his cock... Lilly shuddered.

"Oh, please, Sir. Please fuck me."

He whipped her around to face him, his smile wicked. "Not good enough, but it's a start. Get on the bed."

Unable to tear her eyes away from that devious smile, she walked backward until she felt the bed behind her. Falling onto it, she steadied herself with her hands and crawled, feet pedaling on the sheets as Jack stalked toward her. He tore off his shirt, revealing the muscular planes of his chest.

"Safewords."

His shirt fell to the floor, and Lilly forgot how to talk. It only got worse when he rid himself of his jeans and boxers. His flesh strained, cock jutting and Lilly's hips flexed at the aching, empty hollow inside.

"Safewords!"

"Red, yellow, green," she fired off quickly in response.

He bent down and kissed her roughly, teeth skimming her lower lip before he kneeled in between her legs and clasped her by the throat, guiding her down beneath him.

"Put your hands above your head and keep them there," he ordered. "Do not move."

Trembling, she stretched her arms up and clasped her hands together. Jack surveyed her body like a starving man being served a seven-course meal. He caressed her lips with his thumb and then plunged it between them. She sucked eagerly, her hips lifting off the bed, her body arching against air. Jack laughed, soft and deep, but she didn't feel patronized or shamed. If anything, it made her even hungrier.

He slid his thumb free and chased it over her breasts, thumbing wet paths over each nipple before fanning his fingers down to her thighs. His touch was so delicate it was almost unbearable. Instinct made her push up, and Jack slapped her side sharply. She gasped in surprise.

"I told you not to move," he snapped.

Alarm gripped in a cold freeze, but as he held her gaze, Lilly remembered this was the same man who cradled her head and fed her soup. Who rinsed her body and washed her hair. Who'd talked her back from every fear that had crippled her for months. Jack wouldn't ever hurt her—not her body, or her heart.

"I'm sorry, Sir. I just need more."

"Poor baby. But begging will get you nowhere if you can't behave."

He pushed her legs open wide, hands bracketing the backs of her knees.

"Stay," he reminded her and bent down, his soft hair brushing against her belly as he leaned in and lapped at her clit.

Lilly gripped her hands together. It was so much more difficult to control herself than it was to be tied up. It was as if he was putting her through the same pain of self-discipline he must've felt all this time, a delicious punishment that only got worse when he released one of her legs and sank two fingers inside her.

She cursed, her mouth dropping open, head tilting back. Her limbs shook with the effort of remaining motionless. Every deep,

187

slow pump of his fingers combined with the rapid movement of his tongue was making it impossible for her to keep still. When he sucked her clit into his mouth, Lilly arched uncontrollably, lost to sensation.

Jack lifted his head and slapped her other hip, even harder.

"I said, stay!" he said, his teeth bared. "Disobey me again and I will stop and leave you like this."

He would too. No matter how much he wanted this, he'd let her suffer.

"I'll be good, Sir. I promise." She strengthened her resolve and Jack tested it, sitting back on his knees to watch his fingers moving inside her, the sound of slick flesh against flesh filling the room.

"Bad little girl. So needy. So wet for me."

She was—drenched beyond belief, ridiculously turned on at being so open and helpless, completely at his mercy. Jack changed the angle of his hand, curving his fingers until they hit a spot that made her sob. She was on the verge of calling out "yellow" when Jack slid his fingers free and palmed her hips, shifting forward until the tip of his cock slipped through her folds. His gaze was trained down between them, stomach muscles bunched, beautiful body working back and forth, arms gleaming with sweat. Her nails dug into her palm.

Jack stopped and smiled. "I can't wait to finally fuck you, but I don't think you've begged me enough yet."

"God, Sir. Please!"

With a quick tug on her waist, Jack lifted her up, twisting her body around until she was on her hands and knees. Poised at her entrance, he grasped her by the hips, then stopped, going suddenly still. Lilly held her breath, anxiety freezing her lungs.

"Shit," he muttered quietly. "Do you have condoms?"

*Oh.* Her breath rushed out, the tightness in her belly softening. It was sweet and endearing, hearing him unprepared like that.

"We don't need one. I'm still on the pill. I never went off it."

He grunted and squeezed her hips, but if it was in gratitude or in silent acknowledgement of what they were about to do, she didn't know. Her questions disappeared, though, when he braced his arms around her, body hovering over hers, his cock nudging her opening as he pressed an opened-mouthed kiss to her cheek.

"Tell me you want this."

His words took her back to that first passionate kiss they shared in her hallway. "I want it, Sir."

He shifted, slipping forward just enough to push the crown inside. "How badly?"

"So bad, Sir," she whined. "Green, green, please!"

His chuckle vibrated through her. "I told you you'd be begging."

Then he finally eased inside her, filling her aching pussy with that blissful hot stretch. When his hips came flush against her ass, Jack stilled, his body rigid and unmoving. His forehead pressed between her shoulder blades as he shuddered and let out an agonized curse.

"Fuck, what you do to me, little girl. You have no idea."

The sound of his pleasure made her walls clamp down around the solid, pulsing weight of him, and Jack groaned.

"So good," he grunted. "You feel so goddamned good."

He brought one of his hands up under her jaw, and wrapped his fingers carefully around her throat. "Don't you dare fucking move."

His momentarily lapse in control had vanished.

Lilly gripped the sheets as Jack retreated, then fucked into her slowly. Withdrew and plunged, over and over, every purposeful thrust a reminder that he was in command of their pleasure. He kept at it until Lilly's arms were trembling and they were both slippery with sweat. Then he changed his angle, lifting her hips so his cock rubbed along a spot so intense it nearly made her weep.

"God, Sir. Please let me move. I can't...I can't."

Jack steadied both his hands on either side of her and brought his lips to her ear. "Since you've been such a good girl, move. Fuck me back. Make your noises and make them loud. They're mine and I want them now."

Her head dipped toward the mattress in relief. "Fuck. Yes. Thank you, Sir."

Lilly ground back against him, surging with that perfect fullness as he slid into her again. She was too keyed up, her need for more a frenzied, debauched thing, and there was no shame at all as she pleaded for him to please take her, harder. Deeper. Now.

He reared up and formed a fist in her hair, yanking her back so roughly she was nearly lifted off the bed. His other hand grasping her hip, Jack started a brutal, pounding rhythm. Lilly moaned and thanked him, her knuckles white as she clenched the sheets, her body arching back to meet his every thrust.

"You like it like this?" he asked, his breathing ragged. "Wet, hot and dirty?"

"Yes, Sir."

"You want me to use you? Until you're bruised and bitten and fucked so hard you can't walk in the morning?"

"Yes, Sir!"

"Who do you belong to?"

"You, Sir. I'm yours."

"Mine."

From the thick fog of her own pleasure, Lilly could hear how close he was. She was careening toward orgasm too, but she needed his permission to fall over the edge.

"Need to come," she begged. "Please, Sir."

"Yes. Fucking do it. Do it now."

She lifted a shaking hand to her clit, thankful for the way his grip kept her upright. It barely took a few swipes of her finger before she was shattering beneath him, her limbs spasming with the force of her release. Jack let go of her hair and bit down on her shoulder, groaning into her skin as he came, each shudder accompanied by short pumps of his hips, his body jerking above hers. The sounds of his climax vibrated through her and she closed her eyes, savoring every second of it.

When he finally calmed, he kissed the spot he'd bitten before pulling out. Sweat ran down her neck as she lowered herself to the mattress on wobbly arms and legs. Jack stretched out next to her and pulled her back to his front, one arm wrapped around her body while the other made a pillow for her head. She smiled, enjoying the simple comfort of his knees tucked behind hers, his stomach against the small of her back, their breathing synced and quiet.

"You should get sick more often, I guess."

Lilly laughed, but her lungs weren't back to one hundred percent yet, and a cough erupted from her mouth, her shoulders jerking up with the force of it. Jack sat up to cover them with a blanket, and Lilly turned over to face him, her hands tucked beneath her cheek.

"I guess so, if it means I get to have you all weekend."

She'd said it as a joke, but then Jack's face went serious. His eyes filled with such startling affection her breath caught.

"I want you for the entire weekend," he said. "Every week."

She blinked, not sure how to respond. Was she Lilly again, or still his little girl?

"What about Rumbles?" she asked.

Jack rolled his eyes. "Bring him. I'll buy him a litter box. We're old friends at this point."

"But where will I sleep? Doesn't sleeping together violate some kind of BDSM rulebook?"

Jack laughed, his eyes shining with emotion he so rarely expressed. "You can have Josh's room. I turned it into a study, but it has a bed and its own bathroom."

"So we'd be like this?" She waved a hand in between them. "The whole time?"

"I'm not implying full weekend play. We'll figure it out so we have time to be ourselves, but I want you longer than a few hours. One day isn't enough for me anymore." He stroked her cheek, then her arm, palm finding a home in the hollow of her hip. "Please say yes."

Lilly felt a stab of anxiety. She was so happy here in the circle of his arms, but her heart was moving toward something larger than the freedom she felt in his restraints, and stronger than the pleasure he brought her body. She was losing a battle she didn't know she was in.

She might have been falling in love with Jack.

She may have already fallen.

But none of it mattered as his eyes fell closed when she whispered, "Yes."

# 26

*J*ack stared at the pile of untouched papers on his desk. He'd meant to work after his last class today, but now it was time to meet Patrick for tennis, and he hadn't gotten a damn thing accomplished.

All afternoon, his thoughts had kept drifting to Lilly.

He'd been like this since he left her apartment two days ago. It had all happened so fast. One minute he'd been chastising himself for letting things stray beyond the bounds of their contract, and then she'd lifted that soft limit, and everything else stopped mattering. He'd wanted to make her suffer before he took her though, to tease her to the edges of her sanity. He'd relived it over and over again in the days since—the memory of Lilly's exquisite pleading and the obedient way she struggled to keep still. It had him jerking off in the shower every morning like a hormone-raged teenager.

The part sticking the most in his mind, however, had nothing to do with how crazed he made her, or the ecstasy of pushing into her warm, welcoming body. It was the deepening emotion he'd seen in her eyes. The proof that she was starting to have feelings for him.

He never should've let things go so far.

Giving up on work, Jack went outside, surprised to find no shock of cold air greeting him. The waning spring sunlight cast its rays over the campus, turning everything orange in its glow. Students milled around in shorts, their shadows forming thin lines across the green as they threw Frisbees around, like new colts in spring.

Jack gazed at them with envy. They seemed so easygoing, absent of any cares, whereas he felt laden down with worries, the proverbial Atlas struggling under the weight of his burden.

When he parked outside the sports complex, Patrick was waiting at the entrance.

"Everything good with Lilly?" his buddy asked.

Alarm jolted through Jack. He slammed the car door shut. "What do you mean?"

"She was sick. You left last weekend to look after her." Patrick narrowed his eyes. "What the fuck did you think I was talking about?"

"Nothing." He needed to be more careful. The sex had thrown him off his game. "She's better now. Thanks."

Patrick remained silent while they changed. Jack thought he was safe until they stepped onto the court.

"You fucked her, didn't you?"

Patrick's words echoed off the walls. Jack whirled around.

"You think you could lower your goddamned voice?"

"Why? So no one finds out you're spending your weekends bringing a beautiful young woman to countless screaming orgasms? Or that you're actually happy for the first time in years?"

"Fuck off." Jack dumped his bag on the bench. "How the hell did you know, anyway?"

"I'm part bloodhound. I smelled it on you." When Jack didn't laugh, Patrick dropped his own bag next to Jack's and yanked out his racket. "Because you didn't look like shit for once, okay? I thought it was a good thing. Christ, what's your fucking problem?"

"It's gotten out of hand."

"Why?"

Jack sighed and rubbed the heel of his palm over his forehead. "She's starting to have feelings for me."

"She said that?"

"No, but I can tell."

"And why is that the worst thing in the world?"

"Do I really have to explain this again?"

"Don't use that Socratic method on me, Jack. I've known you too long," Patrick said. "Answer the question."

He braced his hands on his hips. "Because she's twenty-eight years old. You know how it looks. It could harm both our reputations."

"Oh please. None of those stuffy Harvard directors give a crap what you do as long as they churn out more lawyers than Yale does. And I sincerely doubt Lilly's boss gives a shit who she fucks."

It certainly wouldn't have been the first time someone her age dated a much older man. But he wouldn't be dating her. He'd be owning her.

The idea of what their families would think if they found out was enough to pummel him with nausea.

"You might be right, but Nick would care, and so would Brady." Jack winced. "Josh would hate me."

"It would take some getting used to, but I sincerely doubt he'd hate you."

"Forgive me if I'm not as confident," Jack snapped. "I can barely get him to return my calls as it is, let alone come out here for a visit."

Patrick mimicked placing his hand on an imaginary Bible. "I reaffirm my earlier statement, Counselor. You and Lilly are consenting adults. You're allowed to do whatever you want."

"Consent or not, this wasn't what we arranged. She wasn't supposed to develop feelings for me. Not when—"

Jack winced at the ceiling. If there was any chance Eve was watching over him, she must have hated how far he'd strayed from what she asked.

"Not when I have a promise to keep." Jack retreated to the bench and sank down onto it. "This was supposed to be strictly play. I made that clear to Lilly. I can't give her anything more than that."

"All right. Then end it."

"You make it sound so easy."

He shrugged and offered Jack a bitter smile. "You've said all the reasons why it'll never work, so break it off."

194

Jack shook his head. All the reasons notwithstanding, he couldn't just walk away now. She was still getting over her past and trying to understand her submissive nature. She wasn't ready to be on her own yet.

"I can't. She needs me."

"Bullshit." Patrick poked a finger at Jack's chest. "You need her."

He was about to disagree when someone pulled back the court's flap entrance.

"The competition is here," Brady called out. Nick walked in after him.

Shit, he'd forgotten those two were joining him and Patrick today. What perfect fucking timing. Jack rifled through his bag, taking longer than necessary to get out his racket, trying to compose himself.

"Competition?" Patrick asked, his causal tone returning. "Forgive me if I'm not terribly concerned."

Brady snorted. "That's because you have such an unfair advantage. Don't you guys get a senior citizen handicap or something?"

"Funny," Patrick replied. "Let's see what you've got."

They set themselves up in doubles, and Jack played harder than usual, his serves slicing through the air, his groundstrokes vicious. He couldn't change things, couldn't fix what was happening with Lilly, but he could take it out on the court until his hands went numb. When they reached match point, Jack slammed his racket against the ball with a vengeance, winning the set.

"You didn't even give us a chance," Nick complained.

Patrick grinned. "You have rackets, don't you? We were just waiting around to see if you were going to score."

"That's what she said." Brady chuckled. "Hey, speaking of scoring, will there be any single guys at your party?"

Nick raised an eyebrow. "Is there something you're not telling us? Or Samantha?"

"Not for me, asshat. For Lilly. Haven't you been saying you wanted her to meet someone?"

Jack's pulse hammered in his throat.

"Yeah, I have." Nick glanced at Patrick. "You know anyone?"

Patrick threw Jack a fleeting look. "I wasn't sure I was inviting Lilly. I thought I was throwing a grown-ups only party."

"She's not that young," Nick replied. "She can hold her own. And it might cheer her up. She's been so down lately. She mentioned missing our dad a while back, but I think there's more to it than that. She's lonely."

*She's not lonely. She's mine.*

Bristling over feelings of ownership he had no right to, Jack hid his face by rummaging through his bag for a drink. The thought of Lilly talking to someone else made him see red, but he couldn't expect her to ignore the attentions of other men forever. Not when he couldn't offer her anything permanent.

Patrick looked briefly at Jack again, then back at Nick. "I'm sure I must know some single guys. I'll ask around. And speaking of the party, I assume you and Gabe both have tuxedos?"

"It's black tie?"

"Patrick's parties always are," Brady said. "It's like being in a Bond film."

"Because he's such an international man of mystery?"

Patrick laughed. "Couldn't be further from it, my friend. I just look damn good in a tux." Jack took a long sip from his water bottle as Patrick tossed a ball into the air and grinned. "As long as we're inviting Lilly, let's make sure Cassie joins us too. She's such a little spitfire."

Nick pointed a finger at him. "You are not sleeping with Cassie."

"Who said anything about sleeping?"

Brady shook his head. "Never gonna happen, my man. The girl hates you."

"I like a challenge."

"Well, make sure you invite a bunch of other single ladies as well. We're looking for a date for Jack too, right?"

Jack lowered his water and stared hard at Patrick, Brady scheming by his side.

"We are," he said. "I'll see what I can do."

\* \* \*

The sun was setting when Lilly got off the T in Cambridge on Friday night. She'd skipped the pub that night, too exhausted to even blow off steam. It had been a tense week, with the clock running out on the Giordano trial date and nothing to back Simon's claim.

But she had another, more private reason for not wanting to go out: it was her first full weekend with Jack.

She hiked her overnight bag on her shoulder. Rumbles meowed from his case, and she had to take a break on the corner to shift her loads around. Jack wanted to pick her up, but she'd said no. Getting to his place on her own let her retain one last bit of independence before giving herself to him, and she needed the time to clear her head. It was a nice evening anyway, warm enough that she could keep her jacket open as she walked. Little patches of green were growing bolder, spokes of grass forcing up through the melting snow. Winter was finally over and it felt like a new beginning.

She was sure something new had blossomed between her and Jack last weekend as well.

He opened the door with a smile when she arrived, but there was a strain in his eyes, a tension to the line of his jaw. Before she could ask him about it, it disappeared.

"Hi." He brushed a kiss to her cheek as he closed the door. "I put a litter box in the laundry room. There's food and water there too."

Lilly set Rumbles' case on the floor. The second she unzipped it, he jumped out and scampered away.

"He'll find something to hide under before venturing out to explore," she explained.

"That's fine." Jack moved in behind her. His fingers grazed her neck, sending shivers in every direction. "We have our own exploring to do."

She leaned back against him, her head lolling to the side as his lips found her throat. "Are we—" she hissed when his teeth grazed her skin, "—exploring now?"

She didn't know how soon play started or what the new rules were. She'd hoped he'd make everything clear before their roles shifted, but it was hard to care about semantics when he was touching her like this.

"In a manner of speaking." He kissed her neck. "First, I want to show you where you'll be sleeping."

He led her up the first set of stairs, past the doorway to his bedroom and up another flight to the third floor landing. They stopped at the attic study she'd never been in before.

"Josh's room," she confirmed.

Jack nodded and Lilly walked inside, looking around. There was a twin-size bed in one corner, a desk with a chair in the other, and a nightstand and a small dresser in between. Two windows revealed a view of Cambridge, sparkling and lit for the night.

She turned back to face him. "It's nice. I like it."

"Good. This floor is your space to do with as you please. You should feel free to be yourself when you're up here. The same is true for the first floor."

"And when we're in the basement?"

He treaded closer. "When we're in the basement, you're mine."

Lilly's heart raced, her skin prickling. "How soon do I get to be yours?"

He leaned in and teased her with an almost-kiss, his breath warm and meshing with hers. "You have five minutes to get ready before I chase you down there."

She shuddered. "I'll be ready in three, Sir."

Lilly hurried downstairs, her hands shaking with anticipation when she opened the playroom door. She pulled off her clothes, remembering when she'd feared what lay within this room. Now she felt strong here, eager to be hunted and taken. She knelt at her spot, her arms crossed behind her back. When Jack walked in, he stood in front of her and touched her throat. His fingertips drew a line where a collar would sit.

"Look at me."

She obeyed. He'd stripped, and she took in the flexing muscles of his forearm, the notches in his shoulders, the square set of his jaw. Not to mention every rippling line of strength and masculine prowess below.

"Are you ready to play, little girl?"

"Yes, Sir."

"Who do you belong to?"

His expression shifted, that flicker of darkness in his eyes again. She didn't understand it, and a deep longing clawed at her. If he was doubting that she was his, there was an easy fix for that. She'd be proud to wear a collar for him—something tactile that would prove without a doubt that she belonged to him.

"I'm yours, Sir."

"What are your safewords?"

"Red, yellow and green."

Jack pulled her to her feet and kissed her. He was hungry tonight. She felt it in his grip as he backed her up to the wall. There was no preamble when his fingers found her clit, quickly rubbing her into an inferno of pleasure.

"You're only allowed to come once tonight. It can be now, like this, or after I'm through with you. You choose."

She gritted her teeth, fighting back her release. "After, Sir."

Jack grabbed her legs and lifted her with ease, hooking her knees over his hips as he pushed into her waiting body. He groaned in pleasure, and Lilly closed her eyes in bliss as he found his own inside her.

## 27

"Good morning, beautiful."

Lilly heard Jack's voice before she reached the first floor. Rubbing her eyes, she padded into the kitchen. Jack was sitting at the island, dressed in a white T-shirt and jeans. His hair was damp, his face clean-shaven.

*Dayum.*

She'd never been a morning person, but desire flared as Jack smiled at her over the newspaper in his hands, glasses perched on the bridge of his nose. She'd never known he wore them before.

"Cute pajamas," he said, surveying her flannel pants and tank top.

"Nice glasses. Very sexy."

Jack laughed softly but then pulled them from his face. "Did you sleep well?"

"I passed out as soon as I hit the bed. Somebody exhausted me."

He grinned wider, his gaze lingering. "I'll get you some coffee. Meanwhile, read this. Tell me if there's anything you're not comfortable with or want to add."

Jack stood and pushed a few pieces of paper toward her. Lilly sat and started to read.

It was their new contract.

She glanced up to watch him pour her coffee, momentarily distracted by the way the muscles in his torso stood out in stark relief against the confines of his T-shirt.

"The term is for six months?" she asked.

"Yes. We can reevaluate then and see where we are."

As Jack handed her a steaming mug, she wondered where they'd be six months from now. She smiled at the thought of mornings like this in his kitchen. She could cook for him. Maybe they'd go away somewhere together, and he'd show her sights she'd never seen.

"That works." She flipped to the next page. It was a new addendum stating that the contract could be broken at any time by either participant, terminating their agreement. There were places for the signatures at the bottom.

"And this?" she asked, holding the page up.

"It's standard. In case anyone changes their minds."

She certainly wouldn't be changing hers. Lilly continued to read, catching the things that read differently from the last contract.

"I'll be cleaning the playroom from now on?"

"Yes." He set his coffee on the island and crossed his arms. "It didn't seem fair to ask that of you when you were only here for a few hours. But now it's your responsibility, since you'll have plenty of time."

His smile sparked a hot feeling in her belly that traveled down between her thighs. Cleaning the playroom would give her a sense of belonging. Ownership. In a way, it was as if it was her playroom now too.

Was Jack hers, as well?

She frowned at the thought but shook it off when he caught her expression, masking it by reading a section aloud.

"'Play will commence, and may continue or end at the Dominant's discretion, from six p.m. on Fridays until three p.m. on Sundays. Time will be allotted for relaxation and separation, and as such should be discussed between Dominant and submissive in an open manner.'" Lilly looked up. "What does that mean?"

"What do you think it means?"

She glared at him, then quickly washed the expression from her face, realizing she was being bratty. But they were on the first floor. She could speak freely here.

"It means this is very vague," she said. "Sir."

Jack grinned widely and braced his palms on the counter. "It means I want to leave the option open for play at any and all times, but you should feel comfortable telling me when you're too tired or need some space. I want the freedom to do the same. You'll need time to work or rest, and so will I. We're still human, after all."

A swell of gratitude made her next inhale hard to achieve. Even while creating an arrangement that would take away her control, he was reminding her that she still had choices. That he cared how she felt.

"Can I have a pen?"

Jack opened a drawer and handed her one. She signed and dated it, then pushed it back across the counter. He added his name and put it aside.

"I'll give you a copy later."

He came around the island and picked up a digital timer, setting it for sixty minutes.

"Today we are going to play a little game. When you hear this go off, I expect you to go immediately to the playroom and undress. You'll do whatever I want, for however long I want, but you're not allowed to come until I say so. You may safeword if it gets to be too much."

Lilly smiled, enjoying the way he tested her. She had more mettle than he realized.

"That sounds easy enough."

"You say that now." He set the timer in front of her. "Eat something. I'll see you in an hour."

Not finding much of the breakfast variety to work with in his fridge, or anything else for that matter, Lilly made herself some toast, then gobbled down one of the protein bars she'd thrown in her bag. She was showered and ready by the time the first alarm went off. She waited in the playroom and when Jack crossed to her, he unzipped his pants and stroked his length inches from her lips. She leaned toward his cock, ravenous with the need to serve him, and surrendered as he took her mouth, letting him draw pleasure from her body with as much power and speed as he desired. When he spilled down her throat, she waited for her reward, but all he did was kiss her and say he'd see her the next hour.

The second time the timer beeped, Jack placed her at the edge of the bed and relaxed into the armchair. "Touch yourself."

Sensing he wanted a show, Lilly spread her legs and traced circles over her wet flesh. He never took his eyes off her, which was ridiculously arousing. When her orgasm crested she started to give in, but Jack stopped her.

"Close your legs." He stood, brought her finger to his mouth and licked the moisture off. The only other touch she received was a patronizing pat on the head.

"Be good now," he said, and left the room.

Lilly glowered at his retreating form.

The torture continued throughout the day. Every time he groaned through his release and brought her to the brink, he left her wanting. At three in the afternoon, he folded her face down on the edge of the bed and fucked her hard enough to make her scream, then turned her over and leisurely played with her clit. Her eyes started to close, relief finally in her grasp until he landed two sharp slaps to her pussy. Lilly grunted, the sensation an electric shock to her system, but the pain left an echo of pleasure that ramped her need up several more notches.

Jack loomed over her, his lips turned up in a wicked smile.

"This is called edging. Still think it's easy?"

She could only whimper in reply. By the time the dinner hour rolled around, she was shaking, hunched in a chair at the dining room table. Jack grinned at her over the Chinese food he'd ordered.

"Something you want to say to me?"

His eyes were alight with mischief, but Lilly was so strung out, she didn't even have the capacity for sarcasm. When the timer went off again at nine, she sagged to the playroom floor. The rope and rabbit hair flogger were next to her spot.

"Please," she whispered. "I can't take it."

"Yes, you can." Jack pressed his palm to her sternum, gently pushing her down on her back. "You can, and you will."

He spread her legs, bending them at the knee so her feet were flush against her bottom, then tied her wrists to her ankles. Even the feeling of the twine made her jump. When she was fully bound, Jack chased the flogger over her skin before sliding two fingers inside her. Lilly fought the spasms that ripped through her as he slowly pumped in and out, her toes curled, body straining in her binds.

Seconds before she peaked, he stopped. She snapped her head up in anger.

"Look at the fire in those eyes." Jack's grin was smug as he untied her. "Get on the bed."

Lilly stood on shaky legs and stumbled back onto the bed. She'd never needed to come so badly in her life. She had half a mind to finish the job herself. Jack bent over her, his fists on either side of her hips, grazing her sides.

"You can give me that indignant glare all you want. My will is stronger than your petulance."

She narrowed her eyes and brought a hand down to cup her swollen flesh.

"Go ahead," he said. "I dare you."

Lilly's heart hammered, her chest heaving. Fuck, she needed relief, but she didn't want to defy him. With a grimace that bordered on tears, she tore her hand away.

"That's what I thought." Jack walked to the armoire and plucked something from it. "You know how much I like it when you challenge me, when you show me how strong and feisty you are."

He turned around and kept his hand behind his back.

"But you like having your power taken away. You get your satisfaction from being broken and tamed." He leaned down to whisper in her ear, "And I *will* break you, little girl."

She shivered, sure she could come from his words alone. But then Jack's arm snaked back around, revealing a pair of nipple clamps in his palm. Lilly shrank away, her arousal dampening at the memory of their painful bite.

"I know you're afraid of them, but show me how brave you are."

Jack's tone softened as he caressed her cheek with his other hand. "You showed me before with the wheel. You can do it again. Show me what you can take, and I'll let you come right now."

She moaned in agony. He was going to break her, take her apart until she was nothing but want and need and desperation. She eyed the clamps warily, and Jack cocked his head to one side, asking without words if she was all right.

The sudden intimacy made her realize she *was* all right. She was *more than* all right.

"Green," she said and arched up, the offering of her body prompting a flicker of acknowledgement in Jack's eyes. He dangled the chain over one of her nipples, and Lilly drew in a sharp breath, her hips flexing without her permission. She hadn't expected it to feel good, but the cold metal on her sensitized skin drove a hot spike of pleasure through her.

Jack repeated the motion on her other nipple, then bent down to capture it between his lips, suckling until her head fell back. She was panting by the time he pulled his mouth away, tugged the pert nub with his thumb and forefinger and closed the clamp over it. Lilly hissed at the sharp pinch, but it was nothing like the nauseating agony she remembered. The sensation dissipated into something oddly decadent as Jack nuzzled and kissed her other breast, clamping the tightened point on that one too. He pulled back to look at her, his eyes hungry, but full of admiration too.

"You're beautiful," he said, running a fingertip down her belly.

"Please, Sir," she begged. "No more teasing. I can't—"

"Shhh." He stopped and pulled off his clothes. Lifting one of her legs until her ankle was balanced on his shoulder, he slid into her in one smooth thrust. The feeling of him filling that aching spot inside her was relief and torment at the same time, the release she'd been chasing all day suddenly bearing down on her.

He hooked a finger around the chain between the clamps and gently pulled. Lilly trembled violently, the combination of his slow thrusts and the bite of metal on her flesh keeping her balanced on the pointed edge between pleasure and pain. When he brought his thumb to her clit, she cried out, shaking her head wildly.

"Please let me come, Sir."

"Tell me you're mine."

"I'm yours, Sir."

She didn't say it because he told her to. It was simply the truth.

"Come for me, little girl."

Lilly clenched and flew apart. She was his and she was broken and mended and would never be the same again. She was in too deep, treading waters she told herself she wouldn't swim, but when Jack's eyes met hers before he lost himself inside her, she knew it would be different this time.

It had to be.

\* \* \*

Jack woke up on Sunday to the sound of odd thumps downstairs. Opening his eyes, he recognized it as the kitchen cabinets opening and closing. Still drowsy, his mind sputtered. Was Eve cooking breakfast?

Remorse cut through him as awareness returned. It wasn't Eve downstairs. It was Lilly.

Jack covered his face with his hands and took a breath, trying to force the heartache away, but the memory was a splinter in his skin, pushing up toward the surface, refusing to be ignored.

He washed up and went downstairs, quietly checking the playroom first. It was pristine, the bed made, the toys cleaned and laid out to dry on a towel on the nightstand. Clearly, Lilly was an overachiever on all fronts. He made his way to the kitchen and found her on her tiptoes, her arms stretched above her head as she peered into a high cabinet.

"Searching for buried treasure?"

Lilly spun around in surprise, then put her hands on her hips. "I'm starving and there's nothing here to eat. Don't you ever cook?"

Her question hit home. Hard.

"I'm not usually much of a breakfast person." If she noticed a change in his expression, she didn't say anything. He gestured toward the fridge. "There's some bread in there for toast."

"We finished it."

Her grin was light, but Jack felt lousy all the same. Shame on him. Of course she'd need to eat after how much energy they'd expended the day before. He rifled through a drawer, looking for a takeout menu.

"I can pick something up. There's a good bagel spot by campus."

"Nah, it's okay." Lilly poured them both fresh coffee, something else she'd apparently accomplished before he woke up. "I was going to go for a run anyway. It's not much fun to do that on a full stomach."

"A run?"

A shy, confident smile turned up the corners of her mouth. "I started again."

"Oh. Great." Jack reached for his mug without joining her. "I have some work to do, so if you like, I'll give you a key and we'll figure out food when you get back."

He found the spare key, which Lilly accepted with a polite thank you before going upstairs. Jack suddenly realized the error in his planning—he usually worked in Josh's room, but he wasn't about to invade the privacy he'd promised her. The coffee table in the living room would have to do.

He'd just spread his papers out when Lilly came downstairs, headphones in her ears. She waved and headed out the door. Jack pulled back the blinds, watching as she warmed up and jogged out of sight.

He dropped back against the couch, envious of her youth, of having energy to spare. The stiffness in his body reminded him those years were firmly in the past. The lust-crazed fog he'd been in for the last thirty-six hours was catching up with him. As was the confusion he'd woken up with.

Jack closed his eyes, the heavy weight of guilt like an anvil on his sternum. He hadn't anticipated how Lilly's presence in the house all weekend would make him react. Mistaking her for Eve this morning felt like the ultimate in unfaithfulness.

It was too much to deal with, and he let sleep claim him.

Groggy, he awoke a short time later from sounds in the kitchen once again. There was a clanging and a thump, then the rush of running water, followed by clicking noises he recognized as the gas burner coming on. Puzzled, he lumbered into the kitchen. Lilly was surrounded by pots, bags of groceries halfway unpacked on the island.

"What are you doing?"

She looked up from the stove and grinned. "Making lunch. Or a banquet, apparently. I was hungrier than I thought, and since I passed a store on my run, I thought I'd get some stuff."

Good God, she was cooking for him.

Jack gaped and walked unsteadily toward her, one hand pressed to his chest.

"I had my credit card on me so I grabbed as much as I could carry," she continued. "I bought more than we needed for one meal, but I wanted you to have some decent food in here. You need to eat things that don't come in a paper box."

Her smile was bright, but it disappeared when her eyes met his.

"Was this the wrong thing to do?" she asked quickly, putting down a box of pasta. "You said be myself in here, and I—"

"No, no, no." Jack pulled her into a tight embrace. "It's just I can't believe you… It's been so long since…" But he couldn't finish what he was saying and buried his face in her hair. "Thank you."

She put her arms around him. "You're welcome."

He pulled back and stroked the hair off her forehead, the tug of grief he'd felt earlier vanishing into a feeling of wonder at her gesture. He wanted to kiss her, to find some way to tell her how much she meant to him when the doorbell rang.

Jack glanced over his shoulder. Two tiny faces were pressed against the glass by the front door. His stomach bottomed out. "Shit. It's Brady and the girls."

"What are they doing here?"

"They sometimes come over unexpectedly. Shit!" The bell rang again. "Hide the cat, okay? I'll think of something."

He went to the door, opening it to Allegra and Hope yelling, "Surprise!"

Brady nudged them inside, one hand grasping a bag full of food while the other held his Wii console and games. "It's not a surprise when we've been ringing the doorbell for a half hour. What the hell took you so long?"

"Language, Brady," Sam said as she came up behind him. The girls ran down the hall and her gaze followed them. Her mouth dropped open slightly in surprise. "Oh. We didn't know you had... company."

Jack started to panic, his mind going blank, but then Lilly appeared next to him, perfectly at ease. "Hey, Brady. What a weird coincidence."

Jack's brother stepped into the foyer, his brow pressed low. "It sure is...weird."

Lilly laughed. "I know! I was going for a run—it turns out I don't live far from here—and I passed by Jack when he was bringing groceries in from his car. I offered to help carry them and then we started talking about this awful case I've got at work. He had such helpful advice, I decided to make him lunch."

She was so convincing, her tone so cheerful, that Jack almost found himself believing her too.

"Well, then," Brady said, eyeing Jack. "I guess we didn't need to bring lunch over after all, since you've finally gotten some food for yourself."

Before Jack could answer, Allegra came to Lilly's side.

"You're pretty," she announced. "I'm Allegra and that's my sister, Hope. What's your name?"

"I'm Lilly. My brother Nick is a friend of your dad's."

Allegra tilted her head in consideration. "Do you know how to play Just Dance? Daddy brought ours from home."

"I haven't played it before, but I'd be happy to try after lunch."

She cheered, grabbed Lilly's hand and towed her back toward the kitchen. Samantha followed, and Brady raised his eyebrows at Jack as they brought up the rear.

"She really needed help with this case," he insisted.

Brady finally shrugged. "All right. Cool. Nick said she was a great cook. Let's eat."

Jack closed the door and exhaled quietly, thankful they'd all bought the lie. In the kitchen, the girls were poking through the boxes and jars on the island. Anxiety lurched through him as he scanned it for the contract he'd never put away. Lilly caught his eye and then glanced purposefully at a drawer. She must have slipped it in there when she'd unpacked all the food.

He held her gaze for a moment longer, hoping she could see how grateful he was, but then something unexpected flashed on her face —a brief flicker of pain. He didn't know what to make of it, but she quickly pasted on a smile and turned to Samantha, launching into small talk as they prepared lunch together.

The afternoon passed in a crescendo of conversations, food and laughter. The meal Lilly cooked was delicious, and as she played with the girls, fitting in so easily among his family, Jack sat back in amazement. She danced and talked with a confidence so unlike the wounded, timid woman he'd met months ago, and he loved the way she seemed to shine. It made him hate himself for what they were doing, because as certain as he was that this would never work out in the long run, he didn't think he could let her go.

## 28

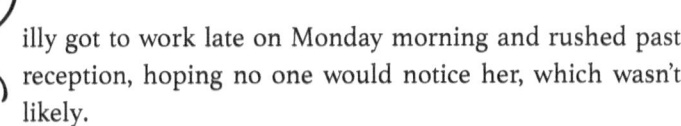illy got to work late on Monday morning and rushed past reception, hoping no one would notice her, which wasn't likely.

No one did. Which was odd.

The office was bizarrely silent. Even the admins were absent from the kitchen and perched dutifully at their desks. Lilly rounded the corner and found Cassie pacing outside the conference room. Gabe and Forrester were inside, Charles Mahoney seated across from them. There seemed to be some kind of silent standoff happening, a staring contest that had probably started when Forrester and Mahoney were in law school and never stopped.

"It's almost nine," Cassie hissed as she pulled Lilly to the side. "Where have you been?"

"I overslept."

She left it at that, not wanting to explain that her brain wouldn't shut off when she'd gotten home from Jack's the night before. Or the fact that she'd woken up disoriented, the sun too bright for the time she'd thought it was, Rumbles' paws on her chest as he stared down at her, waiting for food. Realizing she'd overslept, she'd jumped out of bed, unable to shake the nightmare that blared in her mind.

It was different than the usual fare her subconscious chose to torment her with, and more insidious than any before it had been.

"What's Mahoney doing here?" Lilly asked.

"He was here at eight thirty. Without an appointment."

"Why?"

"No idea, but I'd kill to read lips right now."

They both peered into the conference room as Mahoney slid a stack of papers across the table. Forrester glanced at it, then shoved them back abruptly and stood. Gabe followed suit, but Mahoney took his time, leisurely gathering his things.

He pushed the door open and sauntered into the hall. "My offer stands for the next forty-eight hours. After that, we won't play nice. My clients mean business."

Gabe snorted. "The best way to enter their kind of business is to be made into it."

Mahoney looked amused. "You've groomed this one well, my friend. Is your whole team equally as clever?"

Forrester's gaze darted to Lilly and Cassie. "Some more than others."

"Well, just make sure you've taught them how it feels to lose a fight."

"I've never had to before. Why should I start now?"

"We'll see." Mahoney strode down the hall. "Forty-eight hours, old friend. And then it's war." He turned the corner, and Forrester's knifelike glare settled on Lilly and Cassie.

"Would you two please join me and Mr. Hartley? Now?"

Cassie gripped Lilly's elbow when he turned on his heel. "We're dead."

"Please don't say that."

Inside the conference room, Gabe had returned to his seat. He was slunk down low, eyes closed, fingers pinching the bridge of his nose. Cassie reached for the papers Mahoney left behind and flipped through them.

"It's a settlement agreement."

"Thank you for stating the obvious, Ms. Allbright. I'm glad your contracts class at least prepared you for something." Forrester braced his hands on the table. "What I'd like to know is why Mahoney marched into *my* house, threatened *my* client, and I have nothing to throw back at him?"

His tirade stopped people in the hallway outside the conference room in their tracks. Cassie dropped the papers back onto the table and wilted into a chair.

Gabe's hand dropped from his face. "We've gone through every piece of documentation. Every line of testimony. We don't have anything."

Lilly paged through the abandoned agreement. The conditions were that Simon admit he stole the formula and close down his lab. In return, the Giordanos would drop the suit. Accepting this would destroy everything he'd worked for.

She looked up to find Forrester's cold glare centered entirely on her.

"Then go find me something," he snapped and stormed out. Lilly's face burned.

Gabe sighed. "Ignore him, hon. He just doesn't like being shown up like that. This isn't about you. You're doing great."

She shook her head, her lips pinched tight. This was the first case Forrester had put her on. Her first chance to show her mettle. If she didn't produce something, it might be her last.

"I'll go back through the files," she said, her voice wavering, her coat almost slipping from her hands as she found her way to the door. It was difficult, with the way her eyes had gone blurry. "There's got to be something we missed."

She headed straight for the file room and wrenched the Giordano boxes from a shelf. After placing them on a table, she pulled out a binder full of files and tried to ignore the way her throat felt like it was closing up. It wasn't just because of the way Forrester had spoken to her, though. Her mind remained haunted by the change in her nightmares.

Last night, it wasn't Damien who turned away from her in her dreams. It was Jack.

It was only a dream. A figment of her imagination, her fears from the past morphed and brought into the present.

Pushing the binder she was looking through aside, she took out the next one. Then the one after that. All the depositions read exactly the same as the last seven times she'd looked at them, and none of them showed a single chink in the Giordano armor.

Frustrated, she put the boxes away and went to her desk. She booted up her computer and stared blankly at the screen as yesterday's events flashed through her mind. Jack had taken her home after Brady and his family left. They'd never made it back to the playroom, and Lilly missed reconnecting, missed being "Sir" and "little girl" again after hours playing the part of platonic friends.

There'd been no option but to put up a front with Brady, coming up with that lie and saving Jack from a situation he obviously didn't know how to handle. Still, it hurt to have to pretend—to act like there was nothing between them. It reminded her too much of Damien.

Lilly shook the thought away. The two were incomparable.

Determined to focus, she loaded the Giordano database and scanned the columns, avoiding Simon's incriminating entry and onto the data that followed. She tapped her finger on the mouse, once again wondering what "MOD_dt", and the numbers listed under it meant. It irked her not to know, but it was an insignificant detail and they were out of time.

She put her head in her hands. Forrester believed in her, and she'd promised she wouldn't let him down. So much for that. There was no way she had the skills to investigate everything on a case as big as this. After all, she was the one who'd never done her research at Northwestern, never bothering to look into a single thing about BDSM.

Lilly believed Simon was telling the truth. If only she believed in herself half as much.

Hoping to find some shred of proof, she went back to work. She hadn't moved hours later when Gabe and Cassie found her.

"You're still at it?" Cassie asked. "It's dark already."

Lilly sat up, shocked that the sky agreed with her. "I guess I lost track of time."

"Have you eaten?" Gabe asked.

"Not since breakfast."

"You're done." He picked up her coat and held it out for her. "Nick's meeting us for dinner and you're coming. Shut down the computer."

She complied, too exhausted to argue. Outside, the pavement was wet, the air clean from a storm that must have passed through during the day.

Cassie linked an arm with Lilly's as they walked down the street. "I guess it rained."

"A brilliant deduction," Gabe drawled, imitating Forrester. "I'm so glad you're my associate."

"Shut up. I like spring. The blossoming trees, green grass. Not that we see any of it cooped up in the office all day."

"True. They should put a disclaimer on all JDs," Gabe said. "'Doctor of Jurisprudence, which is conferred with all the rights and privileges pertaining thereto. You will never see the light of day again.'"

Lilly laughed wearily. "Someone remind me why I wanted to be a lawyer?"

Cassie squeezed her close. "Because you're passionate about making sure the bad guys get what they deserve."

The reminder made Lilly stand a little taller.

Inside a bistro on the corner, Nick was seated and waved at them through the window. He gave Lilly a kiss on the cheek and she sat down next to him.

"I'm glad you're here," he said as Gabe flagged the waitress and ordered a bottle of wine. "I need to make sure you know about Friday night."

Lilly propped her head up with one hand. "What about it?"

"It's Jack's birthday."

The announcement was like a club to her head.

"Oh?" she asked, feigning disinterest. "Are we having a cake at the pub or something?"

"No, Patrick is having a big party at his place. It's black tie. I know it's last minute, but you must have something to wear, right? A dress from one of your college formals?"

She knew Nick was talking, but she couldn't hear him over the thoughts stampeding through her mind. Jack's birthday was in four days, and an event worthy of an evening gown was being held in honor of it.

Wasn't that a detail worth sharing with her?

"Lilly?"

She jerked her head up. "I'm sure I have something."

"Well, I don't." Cassie crossed her arms and frowned. "There'd better be some single guys at this party if I'm going to have to buy a dress for it."

"Patrick will be there," Nick said with a wink.

"I said guys. Not pigs."

Lilly forced a smile. The waitress set down a glass of wine in front of her, and she stared at it for a second before downing half of it in one gulp.

Nick eyed her strangely. "You okay?"

"Fine," she insisted on a swallow. The little tidbit of information he'd given her was the big fat cherry on top of today's ice cream sundae of a shittastic day. "I'm great."

Two hours and three glasses later, her stomach not full enough to balance it out, Lilly was home and beyond buzzed, torn between feeling sorry for herself and being pissed as hell.

"Screw this," she muttered, dialing Jack's number. He owed her an explanation. The second he said hello, she dug right in. "Why didn't you tell me it was your birthday?"

Her accusation hung in the silence that followed. It was rude, but it was a weekday and she wasn't on her knees in his playroom. Besides, he'd hurt her. She had some ground to stand on.

"I didn't think it was a big deal," he finally answered. His voice had an edge to it too.

"Really? It seems like a big deal from the black-tie party Patrick is having, which, by the way, I found out about from Nick."

"I didn't ask for the party," Jack snapped, then took a deep breath. "Look, I'm sorry you found out that way. I meant to tell you, but things were a little overwhelming this weekend and I forgot."

His tone was softer now, repentant. "You were so wrapped up in me you forgot to tell me about a party in your honor?"

"I guess I did."

It was almost comical. The knot in her stomach deflated, replaced with a need to smooth things over.

"I suppose seeing you in a tux will make up for it. I'm looking forward to that."

"I wish I felt the same."

"You'd rather be naked with me in the playroom."

He laughed, but it was a tight sound. "Listen, Lilly. You did a great job yesterday of making sure Brady and the girls didn't suspect anything. A lot of my peers will be at this party, so I'll need you to act the same way there. Can you do that for me?"

Her heart sank. It shouldn't have, though. He'd been clear about what he wanted. No one in his life suspected what he did behind closed doors, and the same was true for her. Still, would it be so horrible if people knew they were together, and not what they did when they were alone?

*"This is the way it has to be if you want to keep doing this."*

She pinched her eyes shut and shook Damien's words out of her head. Her ex had entirely different motives when he'd said that, the distance he'd put between them a reminder of how little she meant to him. Jack wasn't rejecting her. He was simply trying to keep his private life private.

"Sure. I can do that," she said. "No problem."

"Thank you." He lowered his voice. "You know, I may not be looking forward to dressing up myself, but I am excited to see what you'll be wearing." His tone dropped another notch. "And taking it off you, after."

Her body reacted to his words, her muscles going slack, but her heart...

*God,* her heart.

"Me too. Good night, Sir." She needed to say that, needed a small verification that this thing between them was real.

And then he gave it to her in words that made her whole again.

"Good night, little girl."

\* \* \*

Lilly's phone rang on Friday night as she was fastening her earring. She threw it on speaker.

"I'm here," Cassie said.

"Be down in a second."

She reached into her closet for her purse and wrap, nearly toppling over in the four-inch heels she hardly ever wore. Rumbles stared from his spot on the bed, tail flicking.

"I'll be back in a few hours," she told him, scratching his head. "And then we'll go to Jack's."

Outside, a taxi idled by the curb. The bottom of Lilly's dress caught underneath her heel, and she reached down to unhook it, feeling like a foal on new legs. She hadn't worn this dress since Northwestern's Barrister's Ball. It was an emerald silk crepe that picked up the green in her eyes, a wash of color that draped from her collarbone to her ankles.

Cassie cooed when Lilly climbed into the backseat next to her. "Your dress is beautiful," she said as the driver pulled away from the curb.

"So is yours."

"Thanks. It cost almost as much as this contraption I'm wearing under it to keep everything sucked in." Cassie dug her thumbs in by the underarms of her sequin-covered cocktail dress and hiked it up. "I'd better not actually meet someone tonight, or I'm going to be pulling a Bridget Jones in some guy's bathroom."

Lilly thought about where she'd be when the party was over and looked out the window at the passing scenery, smiling to herself.

She'd been so upset before she and Jack talked, not sure where they stood, but as today got closer, Lilly remembered she was the person he wanted to go home with. She'd taken a lot more time with her appearance than usual, breaking out her curling iron and shading her eyes in a smoky charcoal. She wanted to be his birthday gift, to be perfect for him, even if it meant keeping up the farce he seemed to need. Then they'd retreat to his playroom, and she'd drop to her knees and take him in her mouth until his hands were knotted in her hair and he was groaning out his release.

"Why are you smiling like that?"

"No reason," she lied, feeling the heat in her cheeks.

Cassie's eyes lit up. "I knew it! You are hoping to meet someone."

"What are you talking about?"

"Gabe said Nick was hoping you'd start dating again, and Patrick's supposedly invited some decent, single guys. Well, hopefully better than decent, but anyway, I'm so glad you're finally moving on from Damien."

Warning bells went off in Lilly's head. She'd only been prepared to pretend so much. Now how far was she going to have to go?

Cassie leaned forward, forcing herself into Lilly's line of vision. "Am I missing something?"

"No, I just—"

"Aw, come on, Lilly. You look awesome tonight. It's time to get back out there. Hey, maybe we'll meet two lawyers who are best friends and they'll fall head over heels for us."

Lilly looked toward the high-rise they were nearing with trepidation. Her palms went sweaty. "Cassie, I'm not—"

"Okay, maybe the odds of that are pretty slim, but it could happen. And then they'd never complain about our long hours or income brackets."

The cab pulled in front of Patrick's building. As Cassie reached for the door, Lilly yelled, "Cassie, stop!"

She froze. "What's wrong?"

"I can't, okay? I can't talk to any guys tonight."

"Why?"

"Because." Lilly rubbed her palms along her dress and glanced nervously toward the lobby. "Because there's someone else, okay?"

"There is?" There was far too much excitement in Cassie's voice as she let go of the handle and slid across the seat. "Why didn't you tell me you were seeing someone?"

"I'm not seeing him. Not really."

"Hey, ladies, you two getting out here or what?" the driver barked.

"In a minute," Cassie yapped back. "What do you mean, not really?"

"I mean, we're not dating. Like traditionally."

"What the hell does that mean?"

"I'm..." Talking about this was defying Jack's request, but it had been too hard, keeping silent for so long. She'd been honest with Cassie before and her friend had understood. She didn't have to go into detail—she didn't even have to say who the guy was. She only had to say enough to make sure she didn't end up spending the party doing tequila shots with some fifth year associates.

Besides, she was ready to own up to this part of herself, to feel confident that this was who she was.

"I'm his submissive."

Cassie's mouth opened, brows pointing together in a look of complete horror. She rummaged through her purse for some cash, threw it to the driver and grabbed Lilly's hand.

"We're walking."

Cassie pulled her across the seat and out the door. She locked her arm with Lilly's and led her quickly toward the edge of the parking lot.

"I don't understand. I thought you never wanted to be in something like that again."

"This isn't like what it was with Damien. Not at all." Lilly tried to keep up with Cassie's pace and tripped in the process. She stopped walking and pulled on her friend's hand until she turned around. "He's made me see how it could be if I trusted him, and I do. I'm completely safe with him."

"How do you know? How can you be sure he didn't read about it in a bad novel or something and decided he could do it too?"

"He has tons of experience. He and his wife did it for years and—"

"He's married?"

"Shh!" She held her hands up, trying to quiet Cassie's screech. "He *was* married. He's a widower."

Cassie glanced at the building behind them, then back at Lilly.

"Lilly," she began warily. "Is he—is he Jack?"

Her pulse pounded, but she couldn't lie anymore. "Yes."

"But he's almost twice your age!"

"He's not. He's only sixteen years older. Seventeen now, I guess." She grabbed Cassie's hand. "Please don't let him know I've told you."

"So he keeps you hidden too, huh? How different is he from Damien, then?"

The words stung, but this wasn't the same thing. Not the same at all.

"It's not like that, I swear. He makes me happy, Cass."

Cassie was quiet for a moment as she looked out at the horizon, where the sun was now a low sliver along the river's edge.

"Diablo," she muttered. "Does Nick know?"

"No."

"Are you going to tell him?"

Lilly rubbed her hands over the gooseflesh rising up on her arms. "I haven't decided yet, so please don't say anything to him or Gabe, okay?"

Cassie sighed and put an arm around her. "All right." They walked back to the building, but Cassie stopped her at the doorway. "Just promise me you're being careful. I don't want to see you hurt."

"Jack would never hurt me."

She was sure of that.

They rode the elevator up to Patrick's apartment and stepped inside a large, open space filled with people and live music. An attendant took their wraps, and Lilly scanned the room for Jack. Her heart picked up when she found him in a black tuxedo, all sharp creases and lines that accentuated his broad shoulders and cinched together at the waist. She stood in the vortex of guests, waiting for him to see her. But when his eyes caught hers, skimming once down her body and back up, he did the same thing he did in her dream.

He turned away.

# 29

---

*J*ack couldn't look at Lilly, not if he wanted to stop himself from throwing her over his shoulder like a caveman. He could already imagine how soft her curls would feel around his fingers. And dear God, that dress. The sluice of green hung so delicately from her skin, pure sin spun out of fabric. It was torture to turn away from her, but he had to. It was the only way he was going to survive.

"It's so good to see you, Jack," Carolyn What's-her-name said. "It's been too long."

Jack squared his jaw and took a sip from his drink. He'd had about all he could handle of conversations like this one.

"I was hoping you'd turn up at an alumni dinner," she added. "But I know it must've been hard without your wife."

Jack forced a polite smile. "It has been, yes. Maybe next year."

She wished him a happy birthday before he moved on, the next group waving him down. The room was filled with former law school classmates, a slew of Harvard faculty and some members of the Massachusetts Bar Association. He managed small talk with them for a mind-numbing hour, all the while keeping his distance from Lilly. At least this ridiculous night would be over soon, and he'd have her all to himself.

When he'd finally greeted everyone, Jack canvassed the room, relieved to find Lilly chatting with Cassie and Nick.

"Having fun?" Patrick asked, suddenly appearing by his side.

"Tons. Remind me why I haven't killed you yet?"

Patrick smiled over the champagne flute he'd raised to his lips. "Incoming."

Brady and Sam were walking toward them, Lilly and the others flanking their sides.

"The entourage arrives." Patrick reached for Sam's hand. "Samantha, you look lovely. It's so good to see you again." He bent down to kiss her hand. Cassie rolled her eyes.

Jack tried to catch Lilly's gaze, hoping they'd share a silent laugh over their best friends' rivalry, but she wouldn't look at him.

Nick bent to the side and looked around Patrick. "There's something different about you tonight, but I can't put my finger on it." He snapped his fingers. "I know. You don't have a woman drooling all over you!"

"That's right," Brady chimed in. "Where are the single women you promised us? I thought we were making sure Jack got some for his birthday tonight."

*Damn it.*

Jack cast a sideways glance in Lilly's direction and caught her blinking back tears. He hadn't told her about Patrick and Brady's renewed pact to find him a date, and there couldn't have been a worse way for her to find out.

"How could Patrick get any single women here?" Cassie's question was directed at Patrick, but her eyes cut over to Jack, sharp as ice. "He's spurned all the ones he knows."

"I got one to come, didn't I?" Patrick asked, flashing her a smug grin.

She glared at him. "I think Lilly and I need a drink."

Jack wasn't sure what had gotten Cassie so riled up, other than Patrick's snark, but he couldn't worry about that right now. He attempted to engage Lilly again, a subtle clearing of his throat he hoped would get her attention, but she kept her eyes obstinately downward.

Cassie linked their arms together, leading her away.

His jaw tightened. Why was Lilly acting like this? She had to know he wasn't interested in anyone else, and she was supposed to be making tonight easier for him, not harder.

"I'm sorry to have disappointed you all," Patrick continued. "But I thought we were much more focused on getting Lilly a date tonight. I've delivered on that, haven't I?"

Jack glanced around the room, noticing for the first time how many men were there. Dozens of them, years younger than himself with no dates by their sides.

His hands curled into fists. He quickly stuffed them into his pockets.

"Yeah, you delivered," Nick replied. "And if Cassie will leave her alone for a second, maybe she'll talk to someone."

He wasn't kidding. Cassie was hovering over Lilly, stuck to her like a barnacle as she led her to Patrick's wet bar where an attendant was mixing drinks.

Brady clapped Jack on the shoulder. "I think the birthday boy is a little crabby tonight."

"I'm not crabby, I'm—"

His words dropped off as he caught Lilly and Cassie knocking back a round of shots. "Well if you're not crabby, then it's time to give a speech!"

Brady hollered the last word, and it was followed by a cacophony of cheers and silverware clinking against glasses. The music stopped and then all eyes were on him.

"Come on, Jack," Brady said. "It's either a speech, or Patrick and I break out in 'For He's a Jolly Good Fellow', and you know you don't want me to start singing."

"Okay, okay." He forced some mirth, giving them the smile that was expected of him. Jack traded his scotch for a glass of champagne offered by a server and held it up in the air. "I'd like to thank you all for coming tonight. By the time someone reaches my age, you'd think they'd be done with parties. I guess I'm not so lucky with a friend like Patrick around."

Everyone laughed. In the corner, Lilly took another shot. Jack tensed but kept talking.

"It's an honor to celebrate with friends and family around me. So I'd like to extend a toast to all of you." He raised his glass, eyes darting to Lilly as her head snapped back a third time. "Cheers."

When the applause died down and the music started up again, Jack excused himself, handed Patrick his glass and weaved quickly through the crowd. He needed to get Lilly alone. He was halfway across the room when she finally glanced his way. Their eyes met, and he gave a curt nod toward the terrace. She turned to say something to Cassie, then lost her balance and caught herself on the wall.

Three shots and she was halfway drunk already.

She righted herself and plucked a champagne glass from a passing server's tray before making her way outside. Jack followed her onto the empty balcony. Lilly's chin lifted as she threw a backward glance over her shoulder, then took a deliberate sip of her drink. Anger prickled in hot waves along his skin. There was no way she should've been drinking so much. Not when he needed her to stay composed.

He stifled the need to rip the glass from her hands and stepped out toward the railing.

"What are you doing?" he asked quietly.

"What does it look like I'm doing?"

"It looks like you're making very careless decisions, and I don't understand why."

"Maybe it's because I dressed like this for you, and you won't even look at me."

That fire he loved was in her eyes, but he couldn't have that now. Not here.

"Jealousy? Possessiveness? That's why you're acting like this?" She flinched at his tone, but she was being defiant now, and he couldn't allow that. "I told you how I needed things to be tonight."

"Right. You needed to look *single*."

She spat the word like it had a bad taste. Jack inhaled slowly. He was the Dom. He needed to be the one to stay calm. In control.

"You know that isn't true, but I can't change what Brady and Patrick are trying to do without risking them asking questions. Stop acting like a child."

"I'm sorry you feel you have to babysit me," Lilly snapped, then downed another gulp of champagne.

"I think you've had enough to drink."

"I don't think I've had anywhere close to enough."

That was it. His patience gone, he seized her arm and walked her along the balcony until she had to stop, her back jammed against the wall. Lilly tried to wrench her arm away, but her brazenness faltered when she looked up and finally seemed to understand how angry he was.

Jack stared her down, furious.

"I said you've had enough. Put the drink down."

Lilly looked at the ground, too crestfallen to notice the balcony door sliding open, and mumbled, "Yes, Sir."

*Shit.*

"I wouldn't exactly say Jack's a 'sir'."

Jack whirled at the sound of Patrick's voice. He should've been relieved his friend was the one walking in on their argument, but he wasn't. Patrick might not have known, and if it hadn't been him, it could have been Nick who'd found them, or Brady, or any of the other dozens of people at the party. How could Lilly have let that word slip? A mistake like that could have unraveled everything.

Patrick sauntered over to them. "Sir makes him sound like a knight. Captain, maybe? No, that would make him Captain Jack, and that doesn't work. I do like the idea of having a nickname for Jack, though. What do you think, Lilly? Maybe Admiral works best?"

She didn't answer. Actually, she looked like she was going to be sick.

Clamping one hand over her mouth, she shoved her champagne glass into Jack's hand, lurched past them and ran inside.

"Goddamn it." Jack started to follow, but Patrick barricaded him with a hand to his chest.

"Stop. She's about to puke and you're too wound up. Let her be for a minute."

"Since when are you the voice of reason? You're the one who made this nightmare happen in the first place. What are you trying to do to me?"

"I'm trying to get you out of your own damn head," Patrick shouted. "But hey, if you're so hell-bent on fucking up your own happiness, far be it for me to stand in your way."

He stepped aside. Jack swept past him and marched toward the bathroom. He waited a minute until he heard the toilet flush. Lilly opened the door, the back of her hand pressed against her lips. She was pale and her eyes were watery. He was concerned, but she was only suffering from the result of too much alcohol, and this night had quickly become a disaster. He needed to stick a finger in the dam, to stop this gash from bleeding all over the floor before anyone else noticed.

"Tell Cassie to take you home," he ordered quietly. "Take Tylenol, drink water and sleep this off. I'll call you tomorrow."

He turned around without saying another word, expecting her to do as she'd been told. A few minutes later, he watched Cassie guide her out the door.

Jack exhaled in disappointment and relief, and reluctantly went back to his party.

* * *

It was the middle of the afternoon on Saturday by the time Jack pulled up in front of Lilly's building. He hadn't called her until noon, wanting to be sure she'd gotten enough rest. He'd needed time to clear his head as well.

The conversation had been stilted, and she'd agreed to his request that he retrieve her himself for once. Jack hoped it was because she was too tired to argue, and not because she wouldn't have come otherwise.

Her face was blank when she sat down in the passenger seat, Rumbles in his case on her lap.

"How are you feeling?" he asked.

"I had a headache. I'm fine now."

227

"Good. I'm glad Cassie made sure you got home okay."

All she did in reply was nod.

He drove back to his place, but tried to gauge her expression whenever the light turned red. Her eyes remained averted, her attention on picking at the corners of the cat carrier. She was so distant and withdrawn; it made Jack uneasy. He wanted to take her hand, to soothe her and see her smile, but that wasn't how this worked. They needed to talk first. He supposed other Dominants might punish her for her actions, but that wasn't something he wanted. There was no reason they couldn't discuss this calmly and move on.

When they were inside his house and her things were put away, Jack asked her to join him in the kitchen. She slumped on a barstool with her legs flopped over the sides. Her heels kicked awkwardly against the rungs, like a child about to be admonished.

"We need to discuss what happened last night." He worked to keep his voice soft, yet stern. "What did you think you were doing?"

"I wasn't thinking. I was trying not to think at all." She sighed. "I just wanted you to notice me."

"I did notice you. I noticed you behaving very irresponsibly."

Lilly frowned and wound her arms around her middle. "I know."

"All I asked was for you not to give anyone a reason to question us, and instead you made me worry like hell about you the whole night. You were disrespectful and rude, not to mention extremely careless. You can't make a mistake like that again."

"I didn't mean to say it, but being there like that, with you...the party was a lot harder than I expected." She sighed again. A heavy rise and fall of her shoulders followed the motion. "Did Patrick suspect anything?"

Jack glanced away. Now was not the time to tell her Patrick knew. "No, he didn't."

She kicked harder at one of the stool's legs. "I wish you'd told me what he and Brady were planning. At least then I would've been prepared."

Remorse flooded his gut. She was right. If he'd warned her about their plot, then she wouldn't have been blindsided the way she was.

Maybe she wouldn't have had to drink to wash away her pain, no different from the way he once had.

"You're right. I should've told you," he said. "But just so you know, not being able to be near you at the party was difficult for me too."

She lifted her head. Her forehead was wrinkled, a deep V between her eyes. "It was?"

"Of course. It was almost impossible for me to stay away. To watch what you were doing and not know what was bothering you. To see you in that dress and not be able to touch you." His gaze swept over her body, swathed in a T-shirt and jeans but a siren call nonetheless. "I should've found a way to get a moment alone with you. Or called you beforehand. I apologize."

Her face softened. "Thank you," she said, but Jack could tell she was still hurting.

He cupped her face in one hand and brushed his thumb over her cheek. "You're welcome. But, Lilly, I told you how important it was that we remain discreet. It's something I've never wavered on and never will. So when we're in public, I need to know you won't call me 'Sir' again."

She winced, and Jack caught it for a second time—the same flicker of pain he saw last weekend. She lowered her head, but by the time Jack nudged her chin up, the look was gone. Instead, her eyes had gone watery, her lashes wet with tears.

The sight of her crying felt like someone had shoved a knife into his stomach, then jammed it up into his sternum for good measure. He wasn't sure what about this conversation was bothering her so much, other than the fact that she'd displeased him, but he couldn't back down now.

"I need you to only call me that when we're here," he continued. "We won't use our names at all in the playroom, either. It'll help keep the lines between us clear. Can you do that?"

She nodded but Jack held her chin steady. She needed to see how serious he was.

"Good, because if you break that rule, I will punish you."

He was shocked to discover he truly meant it, despite his earlier misgivings.

Lilly swallowed. "How?"

Jack considered his options. They'd never discussed punishments, and anything he'd done with Eve was meant more as a way to tease her. As much as he would've liked to dole out the same penance to Lilly, this wouldn't be a lesson he'd be able to teach playfully.

Her gaze dropped to the mark on his wrist, brows pushed together in question. Jack shook his head. As if he could ever hurt her like that. He couldn't endure even the thought of intentionally causing her that much physical pain. Whatever he came up with, it would have to be something else. Something she wouldn't be able to forget.

"It will be unpleasant, but within your limits."

She exhaled a breath, her expression relieved. Satisfied they'd said all that needed to be discussed, Jack was consumed by the need to touch her, reassure her. Claim her.

He leaned down to murmur against her ear, "Playroom, little girl. Go."

Without a word, Lilly slid off the stool and went downstairs. He'd hoped calling her by her pet name would make her smile, but maybe she needed some time to lick her wounds.

Or, perhaps, for him to lick them.

Jack followed her into the basement, power beginning to course through him with each step. In his playroom, everything was clear. In there, he controlled Lilly's every thought, every sensation, every last tingling nerve. They needed to play, perhaps more so now than ever, to remember who they were to one another.

She was naked and kneeling when he stepped inside, her skin lit only by sunlight streaming in through the window. With her head down, she looked so beautiful but also incredibly vulnerable. Jack walked to her side and stroked her hair. She leaned into his touch.

"Safewords," he prompted gently.

"Red, yellow and green, Sir."

"Good girl."

A quiet noise escaped her, her body shifting. Jack helped her up and kissed her deeply, then pulled back to look at her.

"Tell me who you belong to."

His voice was soft, but hers was softer when she whispered, "You, Sir."

"Don't forget it." He kissed her again. "Get on the bed. Lie on your back, arms above your head."

He undressed as she obeyed him, moving into position. Her body was exquisite—all rosy, upturned nipples and smooth thighs, and every inch of it belonged to him.

Jack retrieved his rope from the armoire and placed it next to her, hungry for the taste of her flesh. The sounds of her pleasure. He kissed her throat, her breasts, her belly. Coaxed her open with a slow swipe of his tongue, then dipped his fingers lower, testing her slickness.

"Wet for me already. Such a good girl."

She moaned and Jack pushed her legs up, folding them so her heels met her ass. He looped the rope carefully, strapping her ankles to the backs of her thighs. She'd closed her eyes by the time he lifted her arms, bringing them up over her head and wrapping her hands around the posts of the headboard.

He touched her cheek. "Are you all right?"

Her eyes reopened, lazy and slow. "I am, Sir."

Jack kissed her, no longer tender but demanding, teeth tugging at her lower lip. He knelt between her thighs and stroked himself over her skin, so smooth and soft and his.

Poised at her entrance, he rasped, "Look at me."

Her gaze lifted, and all the pain he'd seen in her eyes earlier was gone. Now they were wide and full of wonder, her body squirming in need. Jack pressed forward, inching inside her in short, shallow strokes. Lilly's hips arched up as she tried to draw him in deeper.

Jack chuckled, loving how eager she was.

"I know what you want, little girl, and part of me wants to deny you. No release at all while I get mine. But I think I'll do worse than that."

"Worse, Sir?"

He hummed in response, sliding forward in one long, deep thrust before returning to his previous torment. Lilly whimpered. Her head fell back against the pillow in frustration.

"Concentrate," he said. "Do you feel what I'm doing?"

"Torturing me, Sir."

Jack grinned, happy to hear the return of her sarcastic side. But there was a purpose to his question. "Bratty girl. You're smarter than that. Now pay attention."

She focused on the way he was working her, and after a few moments, she found the pattern. "Nine shallow strokes, one deep, Sir."

"Correct."

He leaned down to nip at her nipple, and she tightened around him as he licked over the bite. Jack grunted, nearly overcome with the violent need to thrust and take and come. If he wasn't careful, he'd end up forgetting what he wanted to do and fuck her hard enough to make both their legs give out.

Jack drew himself up to his knees.

"I want you to count every thrust. If you don't miss any, I'll give you eight shallow ones, two deep." He drove himself inside and held still. "The next time, you'll get seven shallow and three deep, and so on. You will not stop counting and you won't come. If you get to ten, I'll let you beg for your release. If not—"

He pulled out of her completely and stroked himself.

"Need I say more?"

She shook her head quickly between her locked arms. "No, Sir."

"Good." Jack eased the tip of his cock into her and commanded, "Count."

"One, two, three, four..."

Lilly managed to keep her voice steady at each staccato pulse but struggled through every long slide. Jack didn't give her a break to compose herself before the next round—six teasing ones before four deep plunges.

"...seven, eight, niiiine, ten! Oh, fuck!"

The look of pleasured anguish on her face was exactly what he wanted to see. He pushed her a little further on the next round, reaching down to rub a fingertip along her clit. Her body bucked, head shaking in protest.

"Please don't," she gasped. "I'll never last if you do that!"

"Did you think I was going to make this easy for you?"

Her eyes slammed shut when he started the pattern again. Three shallow strokes, seven deep, and sweat was pooling behind his knees. Two shallow, eight deep, and her legs started trembling. She was a fucking mess underneath him, moaning in agony as he paused before the final round. He rubbed her clit hard and fast, and she cried out in desperation.

"Fuck, please, please, don't! *God*, one, t-two..."

Each number was a test of his control over her, of her obedience to him. Jack gritted his teeth to strengthen his own resolve, his labored breathing belying the shaky tether he held on his own restraint.

"Ten!" she finally shouted.

"Good girl." He picked up his pace, slamming into her. "Now, beg me."

"Please, let me come, Sir."

"Louder."

"Please, let me come, Sir!"

Jack's orgasm began to crest. "Come for me now. Come all over my cock."

His thumb swirled and pressed, faster and slicker and right there, and then Lilly shattered beneath him, thrashing wildly as she screamed, "Yes! God, Jack! Oh, G—"

They both froze at the sound of his name.

Lilly pinched her eyes closed in fear as she rode out the last remaining pulses of her release. Jack's own need to orgasm dissipated, and there was a sick taste in his mouth when he withdrew, knowing what came next.

Punishment.

# 30

*L*illy turned her face into her arm and pinched her eyes shut. Jack heaved a heavy sigh. It was an accident, a slip said in passion, but he couldn't let it slide. Not after what they'd discussed.

He released her from her bindings and climbed off the bed.

"Get dressed."

He didn't wait to see if she'd obeyed as he went to retrieve his clothes. The sheets rustled with her movements, so he dressed in silence, robotically fastening each button and zipper. When he was finished, he flipped the light on and turned around. Lilly's T-shirt and jeans were all askew—one pant leg caught by a sock, shirt hem riding up her waistline, the result of hasty dressing with shaking hands. She stood by the bed with her fingers woven together in front of her, careful glances darted his way from beneath the tangled waves of her hair.

"Do you need the bathroom?"

She blinked several times, clearly disoriented by the question. "I guess."

"Use it."

Once she'd padded quietly out of the room and closed the bathroom door behind her, Jack concentrated on his breathing, willing his anger to dissipate. He had no business trying to control her if he couldn't control himself.

She returned a few moments later without speaking, her head bowed.

"Look at me."

Lilly obeyed, then flinched when their eyes met. Jack had an inkling of what she saw; the withering look he was giving her was the same one he'd given to a few of his students. The ones who'd proved to be massive disappointments.

"Do you understand why you need to be punished?"

She swallowed. Shifted her weight from one foot to the other. "Yes, Sir."

"Tell me why."

"Because I said your name in the playroom, Sir."

"And didn't I *just* tell you not to do that?"

Her gaze dropped to the carpet again. "You did, Sir."

"I didn't tell you to look away," he barked. The startled, sharp lift of her shoulders as her eyes snapped back to his was like an execution. An entire firing squad of Lilly's embarrassment and shame aimed directly at him.

Fuck, he hated having to do this.

"You remember your safewords?"

"I do, Sir."

"Good. Go stand in the corner."

Jack watched as she retreated to the far end of the room and faced the wall.

"You will stand here and think about what you've done, focusing on the importance of following my directions. You may safeword if you're feeling ill or having some kind of emergency." He retrieved a bottle of water from the fridge and placed it within her reach. "Do you have any questions?"

There was a pause before she asked, "For how long, Sir?"

"For as long as I deem necessary," he replied harshly.

He could only see the back of her head, but he caught a faint tremble—the tiniest hitch in her breathing.

The urge to hold her and comfort her was a bug he needed to squash.

"Anything else?"

"No, Sir."

Jack walked out of the room.

Once he was out of her earshot, he scrubbed his palms over his face, then dropped his hands to his sides. What the hell was he supposed to do while she was standing there? Balance his checkbook?

He went upstairs to the kitchen, making sure to listen for any signs of stress coming from the basement as he collected his cell phone and briefcase. Two hours seemed like a sufficient amount of time to keep her like that—with the shape she was in from running, her body could certainly handle it—and that made working in the playroom his only option. He sure as hell wouldn't be leaving her alone down there, but she didn't need to know that.

It wasn't like he was supposed to make this easy for her.

Back downstairs, he stepped quietly through the playroom entrance. Lilly was in the same position she'd been in when he left, her nose to the wall, arms wrapped around her middle. The water didn't seem to have been touched.

God, did she have any idea how much this sucked for him too?

Settling down into the armchair, Jack set a timer on his phone and spent the next forty-five minutes attempting to catch up on case law. He wasn't absorbing a thing. Looking at Lilly in the corner, part of him grew suddenly furious. He couldn't believe this was how they were spending a weekend already cut short by last night's party.

The rest of him just wanted to be near her.

His aggravated exhale must've caught her attention. She tilted her head slightly, an ear turned in his direction. Hoping he'd come to her, he guessed.

Not happening. She still had more time to go.

He left the room again and busied himself with scrolling through work emails as he paced in the hallway, staying within earshot. A hollow space inside him yearned to free her from her sentence, but it needed to be silenced. He was her Dom. Correcting her behavior was part of the deal, and it wasn't as if he was doing her any serious harm. There'd be no broken skin, no bleeding that would lead to scarring. Her punishment was simply a tedious exercise, no worse than an incredibly boring homework assignment.

Which was why he couldn't understand the shift in her behavior when he came into the room. Her shoulders were slumped, her forehead pressed against the wall, her whole body leaning against it for support. Jittery breaths were audible from across the room. It killed him to hear, but it was only natural for her to be upset, and submissives sometimes needed to cry out their pain.

At least the water bottle seemed to have been opened. The last thing he needed was for her to get dehydrated and pass out on him.

One more hour. She could handle one more hour.

Back in the chair less than two yards away from her, Jack watched her the entire time, listening as her tense breathing turned into short, sputtering cries. He ground his fist into his palm, counting down the seconds. His arms ached with the need to hold her. She was crying and she needed him, and he couldn't fix that until her time was up.

What if she hated him when this was over?

The thought had him staring at the timer until the final hour mark was up. When his phone finally buzzed, Jack shut it off and threw it on the bed, crossing to where she was standing in three quick strides.

"It's over now," he whispered. "I'm here."

Her forehead pressed to the wall, Lilly rolled her face to the side. Her eyes were bloodshot, her face streaked with tears. Jack tentatively stroked the backs of his fingers along her cheek.

"You were very brave."

Instead of being comforted, however, Lilly completely fell apart.

Her face crumpled, and she let out a heaving sob. Jack pulled her close, trying to soothe her, but when a minute passed without her arms leaving her middle to encircle his waist, he knew something was wrong. She was like a dead weight, crying and unresponsive.

"It's okay," he said, rubbing her back. "You're okay."

She jolted away from him. With her brows pressed down tight

over her eyes in a look that said *I'm far from okay*, she spat out one single word.

"Red."

She was safing out now? When it was all over?

"Lilly," he started, moving toward her. She took another step away from him.

"I did as I was told, and I'd like to go to my room now, please," she said, then quickly added, "Sir."

Her voice was rigid, her face blank. He didn't like this, didn't want to let her out of her sight. He wanted her with him, to be sure she felt better, but he wouldn't force it. Alone time when they needed it was part of their agreement, and he needed to honor her safeword.

"Of course. Go ahead."

Feeling like he'd been blindsided by a Mack truck, Jack followed her as she walked silently out of the playroom and up the stairs. Remaining a few feet behind her, he stopped when she gathered Rumbles from where he'd parked himself at the first floor landing and made her way to the third floor.

He listened to her footfalls until the door to her room clicked shut.

Hours later, she still hadn't come downstairs. Jack went up several times to check on her, tried to gently insist that she eat something, but she declared that she'd brought a protein bar, and wanted to be left alone. Now it was past nightfall and he had no idea what to do. Retreating to his bedroom, Jack yanked off his shirt and drew on flannel bottoms, pausing when he heard her crying.

Why was she this upset? It was all over. He was no longer angry. She should've been fine by now.

Jack stared up at the ceiling, searching for clarity. Eve had navigated nights like Patrick's party so easily, never struggled in public or in the playroom. Sure she'd misbehaved sometimes, but the consequences for her actions had all been part of the fun, and she'd dutifully seen out her sentences, giving him a sly smile afterward, asking if she'd done her penance.

The smile caught Jack's memory.

Had there ever been a power exchange between them at all?

He looked at her empty nightstand, the truth suddenly so clear: Eve might have worn his collar, but she was always the one holding the reins. The knowing smile she so often wore proved she knew what the game was, even if Jack thought he was the one running it. She'd indulged his fantasies, allowing him to dominate her, but for her it was nothing more than a game.

She'd never been a true submissive.

This wasn't a game to Lilly though, and she wasn't his wife. Nothing bound them together except a short-term contract. How could he have expected her to act the way Eve did, to endure the kind of punishment he'd never given his wife?

Lilly wasn't Eve. Why was he treating her like she was?

He took the stairs two at a time and opened the door to her room without knocking. Lilly was curled up on the bed. Moonlight washed her skin in a blue-white glow, and her eyes were puffy from crying. The pain in her expression cut straight through him. She'd barricaded herself in here all evening when she should've been comforted. Didn't she realize he would've kept holding her in the playroom for hours?

Hell, he'd have held her for a month if he could.

Jack went to her side and brushed the now-damp hair off her forehead. "Why are you crying, sweet girl?"

A sniffle. "What you did...it reminded me of Damien."

"What?" His hand stilled in her hair. "How did I remind you of *him*?"

She sniffed again, unable to answer. Jack cupped her face, one thumb skimming over wet, clammy skin.

"Tell me."

She let out a rushed breath.

"By ignoring me last night. Treating me like I was just another guest, if that. Sending me home and not checking on me all night. And then...downstairs..." Her voice broke. A fresh coat of tears spilled down her cheek. "That's what he used to do to me. Act like I didn't exist."

Jack's stomach roiled. "You never told me that."

She gave him a half shrug, a sad, slow move that hurt to watch.

"It was part of the deal—not letting anyone in on what we were doing. He told me that good submissives always followed orders, and this was how he needed me to be. He never held my hand in public. We never had an actual date. And if I displeased him, he'd stop speaking to me entirely. The one time I said no in a scene, he didn't talk to me for a week."

The realization hit him like he'd run into a concrete wall. She'd had the wool pulled over her eyes. No wonder she hated blindfolds.

He stroked her hair, finally understanding why she'd never taken the bar. It wasn't simply because she was heartbroken. It was because Damien's deception had destroyed her confidence, getting tangled up with her hopes of becoming a lawyer. She'd been driven by a need she couldn't ignore, and that bastard had taken advantage of her innocence, her trust, withdrawing attention just when she needed it most.

And now he'd just gone and done the same thing.

Lilly looked up at him pleadingly, hands coming up to grasp his arm. Her thumb pressed at his scar.

"Please don't do that to me again. I'd rather be whipped than have you ignore me."

Jack shook his head, feeling his own eyes get wet. He'd have preferred the bite of the whip against his own skin than see her hurting any longer.

Without another word, he scooped her into his arms. She clung to him, her face pressed into his bare shoulder.

Then he carried her downstairs and into his bed.

* * *

Lilly wasn't sure how long they lay together in Jack's bed. She drifted in and out of consciousness, exhausted after hours of standing, crying and replaying the past. She felt better now with her head on Jack's chest, her arms around him and his fingers combing through her hair, but she was almost too tired to sleep, her eyes swollen and lower back aching. She curled closer to him, wanting to drown out everything except the sound of their breathing and the gentle thump of his heartbeat.

"Are you awake?" he asked quietly.

"Yeah. Can't sleep."

A deep breath was followed by a sigh.

"Why didn't you tell me?"

Lilly opened her eyes. A sliver of moonlight stole in from the window, ghosting over the firm lines of his chest.

"About Damien ignoring me?" At his nod, she replied, "I guess I didn't see it as a BDSM thing. I saw it as a relationship thing. A *him* thing."

She should've told him about it sooner, but she *had* seen it as separate, even if the last twenty-four hours had twisted everything together. As the minutes of her punishment ticked by, she'd been flooded with memories of Damien, knowing Jack was purposely ignoring her and having no idea when it was going to end. She needed to prove she could get through it, but by the time it was over, she was so lost in her own head, all she wanted was to get away from him.

Funny, how nothing more than standing and thinking had been what finally made her say "red".

"It wasn't a relationship thing, Lilly. It was a power play. Some Dominants do that, shitty ones like Damien. It was another one of his attempts to manipulate you."

Part of her had known that, but having Jack confirm it made her cringe all the same. It was as if she'd been under some kind of spell, lost and drifting as she waited for Damien to dote on her again. And when he did, it was like sunlight shining on her face after years of solitary confinement.

Mind games. That had been his kink. And she'd played along, hooked on sex so good she would've withstood anything to keep getting it.

"There was never any aftercare," Lilly admitted. "And he hated to cuddle. Most nights after a scene he'd leave me alone in his bed. I was supposed to be gone by the time he was done in the bathroom."

Her mouth went dry at the memory. "I have nightmares about it. Even now."

Jack held her even more tightly. "You should've told me all this. I never would've punished you that way if I'd known."

She knew that, but she'd never really reconciled the emotional abuse in her own mind. Not enough to put two and two together and see how being ignored was just as much a trigger as the physical stuff. The clamps, the blindfold, the wheel—they had been easier to talk about because those were things she could explain. Besides, it wasn't as if "please don't leave me alone" had been an item on the checklist.

"I'm sorry."

"No, it's me who's sorry. And you should know I wasn't ignoring you in the playroom. I was watching you very carefully the entire time. I could see how upset you were, but I didn't know why."

She turned her face into his chest, another round of tears threatening. "I should've told you."

Jack rocked her gently. "Shhh. No more crying. I know now and that's all that matters. And I promise never to do that again. But I hope you see there's a difference between what Damien did and what happened today. Cutting you off completely is not the same as my request that we keep this discrete. That's why I gave you that rule about names in the playroom. To help you, not hurt you."

Lilly did see, but it dug down deep regardless. "If I hadn't said your name, you wouldn't have had to punish me in the first place."

She could've kicked herself for saying it. She hadn't meant to do it. It just happened.

She'd been so angry at Patrick's party, being near Jack but not able to touch him, worried about every glance that came their way. And then having him cast her aside, sending her home so she wouldn't cause a scene. She'd only wanted to be with him, to be by his side in that sea of people. It wasn't what they'd agreed to, but Lilly had come to realize she wanted to be more than Jack's submissive. She wanted to be his, for him to mean it all the time when he called her *mine*. That was what made her slip in the playroom today. The sex had been torturous, an allegory for whatever this was between them—how he was almost in her life but not really, a weekend tease of what she couldn't really have. When he'd finally given her what she needed, allowing her to climax, the feelings she'd tried to hold back crashed into yet another colossal mistake.

It felt like making mistakes was all she ever did.

"I'm such a screw up," she said.

Jack kissed her forehead. "Stop. It's over now."

"Not in the playroom. I mean...my whole life."

"Why on earth would you think that?"

Lilly burrowed closer to him, his body protection against the words she didn't want to say. "I used to feel so confident. The athlete, the star student, but I couldn't even figure out I was in a relationship with someone who didn't love me. Who *used* me, and I did nothing to stop it. And now..."

Jack stroked her arm. "And now?"

"Now everything's a mess. I can't get anywhere with work. I'm letting my boss down. I'm buried under the lies I told about the bar, pretending I don't want the only career I've ever dreamed of. And today, with you, I couldn't follow one single instruction. I feel like a failure at everything."

"Hey." Jack angled her body so he could look at her. "You have to stop being so hard on yourself. You're going to be a brilliant lawyer, because you know what it's like to have been taken advantage of." He took her hand in his and placed it over his heart. "And you've never failed me. Not once."

The cloud she'd lived under for so long cleared as she looked into Jack's eyes. She *did* know what it was like to have been duped. And she still wanted to devote herself to defending other people's rights, even if at one point, she'd made the wrong decision and given her own away. Finally, Lilly saw her past as something that would help propel her into her future.

A future she wanted to share with him.

She searched for the right words to thank him, to tell him how much she'd changed since she met him, but then Jack folded his arms around her again, his cheek against her forehead.

"Still, I understand the feeling. I've felt like a failure too, especially when—"

No, it was too soon for him to clam up. He needed to let his guard down. To let her in.

"Especially when?" she prompted.

"When Eve got sick."

Her hand over his heart, Lilly drew tentative circles on his skin. "Tell me?"

A few moments passed before he replied. "Nothing we tried worked. Chemo, radiation, experimental treatments—it was all useless. I felt so helpless, like I was letting her down."

"I'm sure you did all you could," she said, but Jack made a noise, a low sound of disbelief.

"It's easy to say that when you're not watching the person you love the most in the world waste away."

Lilly winced. It hurt to hear him say he loved her. She didn't want it to, but it did.

"After she died, I fell apart. I didn't know how to function. And since—" His voice cracked. She'd never seen him so vulnerable.

"And since?"

Jack took an unsteady breath. "I haven't been to her grave since the day I buried her."

"Never?"

"Not once."

"Don't you think you should?" she asked. "It might help, you know."

"I can't bear it."

It dawned on her then: Jack's love for Eve wasn't in the past—he loved her just as much today. With his heart still belonging to his wife, how could Lilly hope there'd be any room for her in it at all?

He laughed then, but it was a bitter sound.

"You think *you're* a failure? Listen to me. I'm the one who's supposed to be strong, the one who gives orders and doles out punishment, but you have twice the strength I do. You're getting over abuse and blowing through your boundaries, while I don't even have the courage to—"

He broke off again, and this time his entire body tensed. Lilly lifted her head, hoping to be able to read him, but Jack's eyes were closed, his lips folded into a thin, hard line.

"Don't have the courage to what?"

"Nothing. Just something Eve asked me to do before she died."

His walls were back up again. Why wouldn't he let her be there for him? Couldn't he see how badly she wanted to help heal his wounds, the way he'd mended hers?

"You're not a failure," she whispered. "Not with me. You've changed my life."

Jack opened his eyes and gazed at her.

"Thank you. You can't imagine what that means to me."

The feelings came at her, a shower of emotions she could hardly keep to herself. She wanted to tell him what he meant to her, that she never knew what true submission was before him. That—

*That I love him.*

"Will you sleep here?" he asked. "With me?"

She searched his eyes, willing him to open up again. He didn't, but he'd given her more of himself tonight than he ever had before. Part of him remained bound to Eve, but the heart could find ways to let go of the past.

Hers had.

"Okay."

He drew her close and tucked her head beneath his chin. She fell asleep that way, her limbs intertwined with his.

A few short hours later, when the first rays of sunlight danced through the room, Lilly awoke to a change in the pattern of Jack's breathing, his fingers trailing down her back. She opened her eyes, glancing down his body. The blanket was tented with the evidence of his desire.

She sat up. "Should I wait for you in the playroom, Sir?"

"Be my little girl in here," he demanded hoarsely, lips arching hungrily toward hers.

Her heart managed to plummet and fly all at once. Did he realize how much he was blurring the lines? She wanted so much more than their contract offered, and yet, as she looked around the room he'd shared with Eve, she wanted to be Jack's salvation, the anchor in his storm. He was suffering, and this was the only way she could ease his pain.

Lilly answered his question with a kiss, and Jack kicked off the blanket. He let go of her long enough to draw off both their clothes and pull her above him.

"I want you here," he said as he pushed inside her. "Like this."

It was quiet and slow as he rolled beneath her, grinding up in shallow thrusts. He stroked up her back and eased her head down by the back of her neck until their foreheads touched. Her hair fell in a canopy around their faces, and Lilly watched his eyes cloud over with pleasure. They said no names or titles, no words were spoken at all, but when his hands moved to her hips, guiding her faster, he seemed to be saying so much with his body alone.

She took what he gave, urging him closer to climax. When he came, his order for her to give him what was his sent her over the edge as well. As she shivered through her release, she tried to tell him *I'm yours*, but she couldn't. She was his in so many ways now, not just as his little girl, but as Lilly too, and she couldn't tell one from the other anymore.

## 31

One afternoon midway through the next week, Gabe stopped by Lilly's desk and handed her an envelope.

"What's this?" she asked.

"My ticket to tonight's Red Sox game." He yawned dramatically and rubbed his eyes. "I was supposed to go with Nick, Brady and Sam, but I just want to go home and pass out."

"But it's one of the first games of the season. Won't Nick be disappointed?"

"Disappointed he has to spend time with his awesome sister who I get to see more than he does? I doubt it. Besides, I think you could use a night out, Miss Overachiever."

He walked away before she could protest, and Lilly studied the ticket. She had more work to do, but then again, she always had work to do. She'd been feeling guilty over a lot of things when it came to Nick lately, and going to a Sox game was a rite of passage for becoming a New Englander.

She left work with just enough time to feed Rumbles and change. Emerging from the T, Lilly found herself surrounded by the glut of people headed for Fenway. She weaved through the crowd, missing Jack when she passed Barrel 'n' Flask, but since last weekend, her connection to him felt stronger than ever.

They'd spent Sunday morning in lazy ease, cuddling on the couch and watching a movie as a soft spring rain tapped at the windows. When he took her down to the playroom, he had her kneel above him on the bed, coaxing her thighs apart until she straddled his face. She'd trembled as he kissed and licked, never wanting what they had to end. Before the pleasure rushed through her and her eyes clamped shut, she saw something in his gaze—the silent pledge of what she'd always thought was an impossible future.

She was sure he was feeling it too, even if he couldn't say it out loud yet.

She'd left his house that evening feeling contented and calm, and that had stayed with her into the week. The only thing that pricked at her was the way he'd clammed up on Saturday night, holding back on whatever it was Eve had asked of him before she died.

Eventually he'd confide in her, and she would help him through it, just like he'd helped her. Lilly smiled and looked up at the sky. It was painted in a rainbow of blues, pinks and purples, the air almost warm enough to be called balmy. It felt like a promise of things to come.

"So Gabe sent you instead?"

Lilly searched the crowd until she found Nick, waiting on the corner.

She crossed to meet him. "Yeah. He thought it was time I had a little fun, Bah-stan style."

She grinned, the accent rolling off her tongue a little more easily. It felt like home.

Inside the stadium, the atmosphere was buzzing, the energy palpable.

"Gabe did have a good excuse, if you're interested," she said. "It's been pretty much the worst week ever."

"I'm listening." Nick led them to a concession stand selling hot dogs and popcorn. He threw Lilly a conspiratorial smile. "Don't tell?"

She raised an eyebrow. "Only if you're buying."

"Deal. So? His excuse?"

"We refused a settlement agreement on Monday."

"For that big case you're working on?"

"Yup." They were going to turn Mahoney down and take their chances in court, hoping the Giordanos' reputation would help sway the judge in their favor.

She was pretty sure they didn't have a shot in hell.

"Forrester's been an ass about it," she continued. "I think Gabe needed some down time."

Nick pulled out his wallet and grinned. "I know. He called and told me everything before you got here."

She punched his shoulder and he ducked away from her. "Why did you make me go on like that, then?"

He rubbed his shoulder, feigning a massive injury. "Just to rile you up. Hey, you're coming to the pub on Friday, right?"

"I'm not sure." She'd hoped to skip it and get to Jack's earlier than usual, since they'd lost so much time last weekend. "Why?"

If they were in a cartoon, a halo would probably have popped up above Nick's head.

"Just make sure you're there." They received their food and carried it out to the field box where their seats were. Nick waved toward the third base line. "Brady and Jack are already here."

Her stomach flip-flopped. "Jack? I thought Samantha was coming."

"They couldn't get a sitter so Sam gave Jack her ticket instead." Nick threw her a quizzical look. "Is that okay?"

"Yeah. Of course." She nodded, probably a little too quickly. "It's fine."

It was fine. She could do this. She wouldn't make the same mistake again.

As they neared their seats, Brady called out, "I knew we'd make a Sox fan out of you yet, Lilly!" He threw a handful of popcorn in the air, making an unsuccessful attempt to catch it with his mouth.

Jack grinned from the seat next to him, sexy as hell in a light sweater, jeans and a baseball cap. God, it wasn't fair how good that man looked.

"I don't know," she said. "I've always found baseball a little dull."

Brady stopped mid-throw. Kernels showered down over him. "That's sacrilege."

They laughed and sat down, Lilly on one end, Jack on the other, Nick and Brady between them. She glanced over at Jack and caught his careful gaze. He lifted an eyebrow and lowered his chin, the movements silently asking if she was okay. It was so much like the quiet moment they'd shared the first night they met.

She gave Jack a slight nod. A smile flickered across his face, and she mirrored it back at him, sitting back in her seat before their brothers noticed.

The game started, and Lilly let herself fall into the experience, listening to the crowd holler out fouls and strikes, yell fruitlessly at the umpire, and the deafening cheers whenever the Sox scored. At the top of the sixth, Brady stepped away to field a call from work. He didn't return until after the seventh inning stretch.

"Freaking clients," he said as he shimmied back to his seat. "They can't read the dates on their purchase orders, and somehow I'm to blame."

"That's what you get for being the boss," Nick teased.

"Yeah, yeah. All of the grunt work, none of the glory," he grumbled. "My programmers are idiots."

"What happened?" Lilly asked.

"The dates on one of my clients' billing reports are showing up as Unix timestamps."

Nick snorted. "What the hell is a eunuch timestamp?"

"Not eunuch, dumbass. Unix. It's a way of storing dates in a database, but they don't look like dates. It's a quick fix, but man, what am I paying these guys for? Do I have to do everything?"

A way of storing dates in a database. Lilly blinked and turned to Brady. "Tell me more about these numbers."

"They could be anything. There's no pattern. They come out looking like a bunch of random numbers."

"How many numbers?"

"It depends on how old the records are, but if it's current, probably around ten."

"And any field in a database could have information set that way?"

He shrugged. "Sure. Date created, ordered, modified. Any of them could—"

"Modified?"

"To show when an entry has been changed."

Modified date. MOD_dt.

*Oh my God.*

Her mind raced. Could she have been looking at modified dates for the Giordano logs all along?

"Brady, can you show me what Unix numbers look like?"

"There's a site that converts them. Hold on, let me find it." He thumbed over his phone, then tilted it so she could see the screen. "See? They look like they don't mean anything, but they're actually the number of seconds that have passed since January 1, 1970, when Unix was created."

"You're such a dork," Nick said.

"Dork or not, I can whoop your ass."

"That's what he said."

"Oh, don't go there—"

"Brady," Lilly interrupted. "If someone modified an entry in a database log, would you be able to tell when it happened by converting the timestamp?"

Jack's eyes met hers.

"Definitely," Brady answered. "If there's a column that recorded it."

*Holy shit.*

She had to get back to the office as soon as possible. Lilly bolted to her feet. "I've gotta go. I might have figured something out."

"Can't it wait until the game is over?" Nick asked. "I don't like the idea of you walking back to the T by yourself in the dark."

"I'll walk her," Jack said with an indifferent stretch. "I was bored anyway. You guys know I like basketball better."

"Blasphemy!" Brady yelled. "I call the rest of your popcorn."

"Have at it." Jack stood and looked at Lilly. "You ready?"

She nodded briskly and bent down to kiss Nick on the cheek. He held her hand a moment longer, then nodded and released it. Lilly followed Jack out of the stadium.

"I drove," he said. "We don't need the T. You think you found something?"

"I might have. If what Brady says is right, then maybe."

They raced downtown, the city lights sparkling against the endless ceiling of black above them. Jack pulled into a garage and looked over at her.

"Do you want me to wait here?"

Lilly eyed the clock. Most of the office would be empty. The information she was about to show him was confidential, but he was a legal expert, an associate in the field, and they'd talked about the case before. Showing him the database wouldn't breach attorney-client privilege. And besides—she'd trusted Jack with her body and her heart. She could trust him with this.

"Come with me?"

He nodded and cut the ignition. They were silent as they walked through the empty lobby and into the dimly lit hallways of her office.

"I think the database might have been altered," she explained when they reached her desk. She booted up her computer as Jack donned his glasses and leaned over her. Somewhere in the back of her mind, she was aware of how close he was, but she stayed focused, her limbs taut with nervous energy as she opened the database.

"Here." She pointed to the screen. "That's the entry that says our client created the new formula. It's dated June first. I've looked at the digits after it a dozen times. I never knew what they meant, but they look like the numbers Brady showed me."

"What's the column titled?"

She scrolled up to show him the heading. "M-o-d underscore d-t. I think it means modified date."

"And if it had been modified, that means they tampered with the evidence. Do you remember the site to convert the timestamp?"

She copied the numbers and pulled up a browser, typing in the URL Brady showed her.

"Here goes nothing."

Lilly pasted the digits into the website's field and clicked submit. The information popped up below.

November eighteenth.

Lilly stared at the screen. "That's not the same date."

"No, it's not."

She rifled through the files on her desk, checking her facts.

"That's the day our client had lunch with his former coworker, Jacqui. She must've gone back and told the plaintiffs everything, and then they modified the information in the log, not the date it was created. It was such a minor detail I bet they were sure no one would notice." Lilly sat back, stunned. "Simon is innocent."

"Well, what are you waiting for? Call your boss. Tell him what you've found."

She shook her head, excitement dissolving into unease. "I'll email Gabe and Cassie. They'll look over the information and tell him tomorrow."

Lilly reached for her keyboard again, but froze when Jack put a hand on her shoulder.

"This is your find. You deserve the credit here. I've spent my career teaching students how to get to this point. Why would you hold back now?"

It could have been her moment—the opportunity to finally move forward, to show Forrester her worth. The evidence was right there in front of her, but trusting that answer meant trusting herself.

"What if I'm wrong?" Her throat caught on the question. "I've been wrong about so many things."

Jack was silent for a long moment.

"You're letting your past control you, and I won't have that." His voice was lower. The sound drew her gaze upward. "No one controls you but me."

Lilly shivered as she stared into eyes that had become penetrating and dark. He'd shifted into his dominant side, and she felt herself slipping, her mind quieting, body giving over to instinct and obedience.

"Turn off the computer," he said. "We're leaving."

## 32

*B*ack in Jack's car, the doors shut tight in the dark shadows of the garage, Lilly closed her eyes as he wound her hair around his fingers and tugged.

"Don't think about work now. It'll be there tomorrow," he said. "We're going to my house. We will go to the playroom. And you will forget everything but me."

She sank into his voice, his touch. The feel of his fingers in her hair. She didn't care that it was a weekday or that this went beyond the limits of their contract. She'd broken that boundary long ago.

"Yes, Sir."

The drive back to his place felt endless. When they finally stepped inside the playroom, his stare was full of lust and hunger.

"Strip."

Lilly shed her clothes. Her skin tingled as she pulled off each layer, her body aching for his touch.

"Kneel."

She dropped into position. Head down, she heard the sounds of Jack undressing. The click of the armoire as it unlocked. His footfalls as he came back to her.

"So beautiful." His fingers trailed down her throat. "Tell me your safewords."

Her response came easily, the words so familiar now. "Red, yellow and green, Sir."

She felt almost boneless when he pulled her up and guided her toward the mirror. He took his time touching her—a sweep along her shoulders, a squeeze at her hips. His fingertips mapped her spine, scraped against her nipples, drawing out the delicious anticipation that sent blood racing to the ache between her thighs. His touch smoothed over her bottom, and she pressed backward, seeking more.

"Always so eager." Jack reached around to clasp her chin, tipping her backward until the back of her head met his chest. She let herself be pulled, trusting him completely.

"Mine," he whispered fiercely.

"Yours, Sir." She was. All of her was his.

"Are you ready to play, little girl?"

"I am, Sir."

"Then close your eyes."

She complied, feeling him gather her wrists behind her, binding them together with the decadent clasp of his leather restraints. The silky coil of rope around her arms came next, knotted and looped so her elbows met. Then his hands were at her ankles, nudging her legs apart and closing a leather cuff around each one. The heavy scrape of metal clicking into metal sent a thrill through her as he locked her into the spreader bar.

He palmed her breasts, thumbs thrumming over the stiffened peaks. "You have no idea how incredible you look right now."

"More, Sir." His touch was soft. Too soft. "Please."

"You'll have more." He pinched her nipples, sending a jolt through her. "Keep those eyes shut."

His mouth met the tip of her breast with a wet tug, a sharp pleasure-pain she could feel in her clit. He switched to the other while fondling the nipple he'd just suckled, and she was so lost to the sensation she barely heard the tinny rattle of his clamps. He pinched one shut, and the sting only made the throb between her legs that much stronger.

"Fuck, yes," she whispered, then quickly, "Sir."

Jack chuckled and fastened the other clamp. "I knew you'd learn to love this."

The dirty tease in his voice made her smile, but then he pulled on the chain. Lilly's mouth dropped open, her legs nearly giving out. The wide spread of her legs drew her attention to how embarrassingly slick she was between them, her clit so stiff and swollen and begging to be touched. She wanted him with a desire so raw it was razor sharp, wanted the weight of his body on hers, his teeth at her neck, the brand of his slap. She needed him primitive, for him to use her. Mark her.

Own her.

"Please touch me, Sir."

He palmed her belly, fingers spreading lazily over her pubic bone. "I know what you want. But do you know what *I* want?"

"No, Sir."

His lips met her ear. "I want everything, little girl."

Jack slipped his hand down to tease her wet flesh, two fingers sliding inside. Lilly moaned, her head sinking back in relief.

"I want to watch you react to my flogger, hear the sounds you make. See you tremble as I roll the wheel up your back, my crop between your legs. I want you to come all over me."

He was setting a fuse, his words the catalyst to her pleasure, and it wouldn't be long before she exploded.

"But there's something else I want first."

His fingers slipped free, and she groaned, empty and aching. Then she felt Jack's hands at her face, followed by the light pressure of a blindfold over her eyes. She gasped and flinched, her shoulders rising up to her ears.

*No, please not that.*

Lilly's mouth went dry, too dry to safeword. Terror drove the air from her lungs in a full out panic.

"Breathe," Jack said gently. "Do you know why I want to blindfold you tonight?"

Heart racing, she managed to whisper, "Why, Sir?"

"Because, I told you when it was time, you'd be ready for it.

You've faced every fear you've had and overcome them. You're ready for anything, my beautiful, strong, little girl."

She shook her head, but Jack didn't waver.

"Yes, you are. I know you. Trust that. Trust me."

The bubble of dread rising in her chest halted, his words of confidence deflating her fears. Her breathing settled, her anxiety dissipating with each exhale, and she realized she didn't need to safeword. Blindfold or not, she'd never been safer than she was right now.

"What color?" he asked.

Lilly inhaled a deep, slow breath. "Green."

"Good girl."

He fastened the blindfold, then held her for a moment before moving away. He chased the deerskin flogger over her ass, belly and thighs, and the lack of sight heightened every sensation. The crop between her thighs came next, and Lilly's skin grew hot, hips arching, legs shaking, every stroke making her crave another. She'd stopped thinking entirely by the time he rolled the wheel up her spine. Her need was magnified by the knowledge that she was doing as he'd asked, her hunger mixing with a floating serenity that made her mind go quiet.

Jack stepped behind her and stayed silent for a long moment.

"I blindfolded you tonight because you're in the dark about yourself," he finally said. "You hold back, because you don't see yourself as you are. But it's time to change that."

He unfastened the blindfold and pulled it free.

"Open your eyes. Look at yourself in the mirror. See what I see."

Lilly obeyed and took in the sight of her body restrained, bound by rope, leather and metal. Skin flushed, she was sex personified, but her fears and doubts reflected back at her, shining in her eyes.

Her lip quivered. "What do you see?"

"I see someone I've watched blossom from a scared girl into the amazing woman before me. You've been hurt. You have scars from a man you trusted, who destroyed your faith in yourself, but you're so much stronger than you realize. I'm in awe of how courageous and brave you are."

Lilly started to tremble so hard she could hardly stay standing. Jack brought her body flush to his, letting her lean on him, his strength holding her up.

"You submitted to a man who wasn't worthy of you, who treated you badly, but your vulnerability doesn't make you weak. You have to be strong to survive that kind of pain."

The tears swelled, but then he kissed her neck, sweet and soft, palms settling below her belly. Lilly's eyes fell shut as he pressed down gently with the heel of his hand, putting pressure in just the right spot until her hips started to swivel and her head sank back onto his shoulder.

"And even after all you've been through, you're brave enough to admit that you're a submissive. That this is who you are."

Jack dipped a finger down to her heat.

"God, please, Sir."

"See how you beg me now? How far you've come?" He traced her slippery lips, grazing her clit.

"Yes—oh, fuck...please, Sir."

He gave her what she needed, one finger rubbing over her in a rapid, wet swirl. She cried out loudly, feeling like his plaything, but also like she was the center of his universe, used and treasured and adored.

It was how a submissive was supposed to feel.

"I'm amazed by you, by both sides of you. By the woman who has rebuilt her life, and the one you become in here. You feed my passion with your begging and your pleading, your whimpers and your moans. Every time you submit to me, your hunger to give yourself over excites me. It empowers me. You heal me."

"Oh God." Tears welled in her eyes, so many words bubbling up inside her, but pleasure put her on lockdown, stealing any hope of reply.

"I see your admiration, your desire, your lust," he said. "It intoxicates me. Feel the same thing from me now. Feel how much I want you, crave you, *need* you when you're like this. When you're mine."

Her body bowed, so close to release, and Jack helped her chase the feeling, stroking the same spot with a quickened motion of his fingers.

"Come for me now, but open your eyes first. See how breathtaking you are."

Lilly tried to obey, catching their reflection in the mirror, but her eyes squeezed shut again with the force of her orgasm. Jack locked an arm around her, keeping her standing as her legs buckled, whispering words of approval in her ear. When the last spasms left her shuddering, he eased her from his grip and unclasped the cuffs, then the ropes. He bracketed her hands against the wall for support as he released her legs from the spreader bar. Then his hands were on her again, guiding her to sit on the edge of the bed.

"Deep breath," he encouraged before removing the clamps, one at a time. She hissed as the blood rushed back to her skin, and Jack soothed her by kissing the tender flesh. It was too much. She started to cry, needing him inside her. Around her. Above her. Protecting and taking her, blocking out everything else, making her whole again.

"Shhh," Jack murmured, laying her down until he hovered over her and parted her legs with his knee. "I'm here. I've got you."

He slowly sank inside, letting her acclimate to that exquisite burn and stretch until he was seated, deep and perfect, then clasped their hands together. There was no bondage, nothing chaining her to him but her heart to his, every thrust and retreat bringing her closer to him.

It wasn't close enough.

She clutched his hands. "Need you. Please, Sir."

"I need you too, sweet girl." Jack pressed his lips to her throat, kissing the words into her skin. "You may be mine, but I'm yours too."

He was hers. The simple words were so beautiful, made more so by the connection of their bodies. She wanted to tell how much the sentiment meant to her, but her words got lost on a moan of surprised pleasure as another release started to crest.

"I can feel you coming," he rasped. "Give it to me."

She crumbled beneath him, and Jack lost his rhythm too, his

thrusts turning to quick, jerky movements. He shuddered and cursed, groaning into the sweaty hollow between her shoulder and neck. After a few quiet moments, he pulled out and checked her over, fingertips at the places he'd bound and flogged. Jack curled himself around her, and Lilly grew drowsy. The words she'd tried to say floated outside her grasp, sleep taking her.

When the first pink slivers of daylight streaked across the room, Lilly stirred and reached for Jack. He was still asleep, and she turned to watch his face, so peaceful in slumber. She felt rested, the anxious jerk to consciousness that usually that tore her from her nightmares completely absent.

Lilly sat up, searching her memory. She hadn't had a nightmare that night. In fact, she couldn't recall having a single one since the night before Jack's birthday.

Another liberation, and maybe the last shackle chaining her to her past coming free.

With a faint smile, Lilly got dressed and cleaned the playroom as quietly as she could. She picked up the blindfold, amazed at what Jack did for her—how he kept her in the dark only to let her truly see herself. Now she was ready for anything, ready to go to work, to tell everyone what she'd found, and to show Forrester her worth.

Ready to tell Jack how she felt.

She was going to tell him she loved him.

# 33

*a*t the end of a long day, Jack locked his office and took the stairs two at a time, eager to get home. His afternoon had been full of appointments. Two weeks left before the end of the semester meant meeting with frazzled advisees worried about their exams, and for some, the bar in July. He'd counseled and given advice, but he'd been distracted the whole time, wondering how Lilly was doing.

He pulled into his driveway and closed his eyes. Every time he had a moment to himself, the guilt over what had transpired in the aftermath of her punishment tugged at him a little more, like a ripping thread in a piece of clothing. He felt awful for how upset she'd gotten, but how could he have known that would happen? If she'd been honest with him about Damien's treatment, he never would've left her alone like that.

Then again, he wasn't exactly being honest with her, either.

Jack rubbed his eyes and put his face in his hands. He'd nearly had a slip of his own that night, coming close to divulging Eve's final wish.

Nearly. Thank God he hadn't. You don't tell the woman you're naked in bed with that your wife's dying request was for you to fall in love again, especially when you don't harbor those feelings for her.

He didn't love Lilly. He couldn't.

Jack went inside and began the motions of preparing dinner. His kitchen was stocked once again, so different from the barren wasteland it had been before. He was so much healthier now, and it was all because of Lilly. But he couldn't continue to keep her, to hide her from the world when she was just learning how to shine again.

He slammed the fridge door shut. Why did he keep making so many mistakes? When they were in role, everything made sense. But whenever he tried to figure out this non-relationship they were in, he kept screwing up. He'd already crossed so many boundaries—sex in his bedroom, sleeping together in the playroom. When was he going to stop being so selfish, and do what was best for her?

She needed to be in a healthy, complete relationship. One with someone who could give her everything she wanted.

And that person wasn't him.

Jack braced his hands on the counter, forcing himself to face the truth. He could fulfill her sexual needs, but that would only keep her happy for so long. The things she needed the most to heal were things he couldn't give her. And even if he could, even if he could find a way to put his peers' and family's opinions aside, eventually their age difference would become an issue.

She deserved better than that.

When their contract was up, he'd suggest they end things. A simple conclusion to the term of their agreement, nothing more. She'd understand it better that way. He wouldn't hurt her—they'd simply come to a mutual understanding after he'd made her see how far she'd come. They'd have enough time to talk about it so they could move on, even be friends afterward.

His phone rang. Lilly's name came up on the screen.

He heaved a deep sigh and shoved his thoughts onto the back burner. She'd had a big day. "Hey there."

"I did it! I told Forrester."

Jack laughed, happy to hear the exuberant sound of her voice. "That's great."

"Sorry I didn't call earlier. I'm just getting home now. I know you're going to say that it's late and I'm alone, but it's fine. The streets are well-lit and safe. And besides, you're on the phone with me. You'll hear if I get attacked."

"That's very reassuring," he replied dryly. "All right, hotshot. Tell me everything."

She recounted her day, starting from how she'd walked into her boss's office and told him what she'd found, to them subpoenaing the software company for a backup of the database, hoping to find the original tampered entry. Jack heard the jingling of her keys as she talked, the sound of her door closing and Rumbles' meow. The part of his brain that instantly relaxed made him wonder how he was ever going to be able to let go of her when he needed the nightly confirmation that she was home safe.

"Do you think Brady would be willing to be called as an IT expert?" she asked.

"I'm sure he'd get a kick out of that."

"Good, but wait—I saved the best part for last. Forrester came to my desk on his way out. He said if we win this, there's an associate position waiting for me once I pass the bar."

"Congratulations, I knew you could do it," he said, beaming. "I'm so proud of you."

"Thank you."

Jack could hear the word "Sir" hanging from her reply. He wanted to hear her say it, wanted to strike a match to the hunger between them that never seemed to burn out, but he couldn't. He needed to stick to the contract.

"Anyway, I'm beat. For some reason, I didn't get much sleep last night," she said, coyness in her tone. "I'd better get to bed."

"Yes, you need your rest." There was nothing in the contract against encouraging her to sleep. Or in a bit of harmless flirting. His voice was gruff when he added, "For the weekend."

She hummed in agreement. "Oh, about tomorrow night. Nick is acting funny. He wants to be sure I'll be at the pub. I have no idea why. Is that okay?"

"Of course. I think I'll pass, myself. I'm old. I need my rest too, you know."

She giggled. "You're not that old."

Jack's phone pinged, signaling the arrival of a new email. If it was more of his students with frenzied questions, he might have to start reviewing his retirement plans.

"We'll meet here afterward," he added. "Get to bed."

After they said good night, Jack went to his laptop and checked his inbox, finding Facebook comments from Brady and Josh. He'd been tagged in a status of Brady's from the night before at Fenway. Josh had left a comment that said "Go Dodgers", followed by Brady's response that he'd gone over to the dark side. Jack laughed and added a comment of his own: *Didn't the Sox just lose to the Yankees?*

A second later, Brady called.

"I know you didn't mention The-Team-That-Shall-Not-Be-Named."

"Unfortunately for you, it's true."

"Disrespecting the Sox. And you call yourself a New Englander. At least you finally got your ass back online, instead of giving me shit about it."

Jack drew the mouse around Lilly's name on the screen. "Things change. So what's up?"

"I'm just spreading the word. Nick wanted to make sure everyone would be at the pub tomorrow night. Some kind of surprise for Lilly."

Jack's hand stopped moving. "What kind of surprise?"

"Dunno. Nick wouldn't tell me. You coming?"

Jack frowned, the instinct to protect Lilly from the unknown kicking in.

"I'll be there."

* * *

There was no parking outside Barrel 'n' Flask on Friday evening. Jack had to find a space a few blocks down, passing Lilly, Gabe and Cassie as they walked up from the T. She wasn't expecting him tonight, and he was hoping for a few seconds alone with her before this "surprise". He quickened his pace to catch up with them. They were almost at the pub when Lilly glanced over her shoulder.

"Hey," she said, her eyes lighting up.

Gabe turned around and grinned. "You got roped in tonight too, huh?"

"Looks like."

Lilly elbowed Gabe. "Don't bother asking this guy what the surprise is. He says he doesn't know."

"I don't. I swear," he insisted. "It's actually kind of disconcerting how good Nick is at keeping secrets."

"It's not your birthday, is it?" Jack asked, ashamed to realize he had no clue when it was.

"No." She smiled, flags of color rising in her cheeks. "It's in September."

"I'll make a note of that."

They started walking, Cassie and Gabe ahead of them. Lilly looked at Jack and mouthed the words, "Play along."

"Crap, I think I dropped my headphones," she announced. Cassie and Gabe paused, but Lilly waved them off. "I'll go back and look. You guys go ahead. I'll be right there."

It was a ruse to give them some time alone together. Jack suppressed a grin as Lilly took a few steps back, pretending to survey the ground. Gabe shrugged and walked on, but Cassie hesitated.

"I can wait for her," Jack offered.

She didn't respond and eyed him with a wary expression. It almost felt like some kind of standoff until she nodded and turned, following Gabe into the pub.

Lilly hopped closer to him, a goofy smile on her face. "I didn't think you were coming."

Dismissing Cassie's strange behavior, Jack focused on Lilly. He wouldn't have her to himself again until much later. "Blame Brady. Apparently this surprise is too good to miss."

"I'm sorry. I have no idea what's going on."

"Don't apologize. There'll be plenty of time for us after."

Her smile went wider, her eyes glazing over, a soft *Mmm*

escaping her. God, it was such a high to bring out the sexual side of her, then to watch her struggle, trying to contain herself.

"Later," he promised.

They went inside, finding their gang around a large table. Seated in the chair next to Nick was someone new—a man whose back was to them. The entire group seemed to be fawning over him.

Brady looked up and called out, "There she is."

The stranger turned around. He had hazel eyes, surrounded by creases that lifted when he smiled. Jack recognized him instantly.

"Dad!" Lilly shouted, rushing toward him. The other man stood, pulling her tightly into his arms. "What are you doing here?"

"Surprise," Nick said. "I flew him out for the whole weekend."

"You flew me?" her father asked. "I think I paid for the ticket."

"Well, I made the arrangements." Nick turned to Lilly. "You're surprised, right?"

"Completely." She looked so incredibly young all of a sudden, nestled deep in her father's embrace.

Jack tried to hang back, to let her enjoy the moment, but then Brady said, "Jack, come on over and meet Lilly's dad."

He took a step forward. Lilly smiled shyly at him from the crook of her father's arm.

"Henry Sterling," her father said, reaching out a hand.

"Jack Archer."

"Brady's brother, right? It's good to meet you."

They shook hands, and Jack studied the other man's face. There could only have been a decade between them at most. Hadn't Lilly ever realized that? It was a stupid thing to think, because she'd said age was never an issue for her, a fact he'd been grateful for up until now.

God, he was such a hypocrite.

"So, no Mom, huh?" Lilly asked her father.

"She had to work. Lots of orders coming into the shop. You know the drill."

Gabe and Nick looked at one another. Her mother had undoubtedly refused to come, unwilling to acknowledge them. Jack could only imagine what would happen if she found out about him.

It would drive another stake through the family, impossible to repair.

"I know." Lilly smiled through her disappointment. "I'm glad you're here, though."

They all sat down, and Nick ordered them a pitcher. Jack was tempted to drown himself in it. He abstained though, and resumed the same uncomfortable silence he'd enshrouded himself in the first time he came to the pub.

"So, this big case you're all on," Henry began. "You guys get anywhere with it?"

Cassie raised a glass. "Yes, thanks to Lilly. Now we actually have a shot of winning."

"I didn't figure it all out on my own. I had help." Lilly cast a sideways glance at Jack, then turned to Brady. "That reminds me. Can you call me at work on Monday? I've got something to ask you."

"No problem."

Lilly grinned, a more joyful expression on her face than Jack had ever seen before, her cheeks lifting, accenting the heart shape of her face. She looked so damn beautiful, so strong and confident. It was the point he'd hoped he'd get her to when he first met her.

Brady tipped back his beer. "You all got big Sterling family plans for the weekend?"

"How about a billiards marathon, Dad?" Nick suggested. "See if we can finally beat you?"

Henry laughed. "I don't care what we do. I'm just happy to spend a weekend with my son and my little girl."

*She's* my *little girl.*

Shit. This was so fucked up.

Lilly blanched, her eyes meeting Jack's, the term of endearment clearly affecting her as strongly as it did him. This wasn't right. She shouldn't be focusing on him. She needed to enjoy the time with her father. If Jack truly wanted what was best for her, then leaving was the right thing to do.

Retrieving his phone, he hid it under the table and typed out a text.

*I'm going to go. Be with your Dad. Don't worry—there will be other weekends.*

He hit send and stood up. "Sorry to cut this short, but I'm beat."

Henry turned his way, giving Lilly the necessary distraction to read his message.

"It was good meeting you," Henry said.

"Likewise."

Jack caught Lilly's gaze as he walked away. Her eyes were wide with questions, but he couldn't answer any of them.

There were no answers to give her. No easy ones, anyway.

He walked out into the night alone.

* * *

Early Sunday evening, Jack's doorbell rang. He opened the door to the face he'd missed since Friday, her text messages since then frequent, checking in more often than she needed to. He could sense the anxiety in them, but had reassured her everything was fine.

Everything *was* fine. Things would go back to normal now, and when the contract ended, they'd talk.

"Nick took Dad to the airport," Lilly said. "Can I come in?"

"Of course."

She stepped past him and into the kitchen, fidgeting as she settled onto a stool. Jack sat down next to her.

"Did you have a good time with your father?"

"Yes. I missed you, though."

"I missed you too." She crossed her arms before folding them together on the island. She was nervous. "Lilly, whatever it is that's on your mind, tell me."

"You know me so well." She laughed, but it wasn't a happy sound. "Okay. I wanted to talk to you about the other night, in the playroom."

Jack relaxed. This was easy. This they could talk about. "What about it?"

Her voice went quiet. "You have no idea what it did for me.

Everything you did, everything you've *done*; it's made me see that I can be brave. That I can speak up for what I want."

"That's good. That's what I hoped it would do."

She gave him a shy smile. "And what I want is...you."

Jack tensed. "What do you mean, me?"

"I mean, I want to be with you. I don't want to have to hide, or keep this in the dark anymore."

*Shit.*

Jack took a breath. Counted to ten. "Lilly, I told you I needed to keep this part of my life private."

"Not the BDSM part. I don't want to follow you around campus with a leash on or anything. Well, I'd love it if you'd collar me, but that could be something we'd keep between us, so that you'd know I'm yours and I'd know you're mine. I'm talking about the regular stuff. A real relationship, Jack. That's what I want."

She had that look in her eyes, the one that was so wide and hopeful.

He hated knowing he was about to destroy it.

"We can't do that, Lilly."

The color drained from her face. "Why not?"

"Because it wouldn't work. You know that."

"I don't know that."

"Yes, you do. I know how important your family's approval is. Your friends too. They wouldn't understand."

"Cassie knows."

Her admission sliced a hole in the air between them. Jack fought to keep calm.

"You told her?"

"It wasn't on purpose. It was to stop her from making me talk to guys at Patrick's party." Lilly lifted her chin. "Besides, can you look me in the eye and say that you've never kept anything from me? That you've been honest about everything?"

He should've taken her over his knee for the way she was speaking to him, but he couldn't. Not when she was right.

"Patrick knows too."

Lilly's jaw dropped. "He does? What did he think?"

"It's Patrick," he said with a shrug. "Nothing involving sex surprises him."

"When did you tell him?"

Jack stood and walked around the kitchen, needing to put some space between them. "When I first kissed you. I thought I'd made a huge mistake. That I was going to fuck up your life. Patrick convinced me that wasn't the case." He stopped and stared out the windows. "I'm not so sure that isn't true anymore."

"Don't say that."

"Look where it's gotten us." Jack turned back around to face her. "I told Patrick because I needed to make sure he wouldn't accidentally say something. At the time, you didn't seem to want anyone to know, either. That was our agreement," he said, feeling slightly betrayed that she'd changed the game without telling him. "I told him what I did to protect you."

"Jack, don't you see?" She rushed forward and took his hands in hers. "We told people to protect each other, to protect this, and they understood. Patrick and Cassie have accepted us. Nick, Brady, my family—they will too. I know it."

He glanced away, but Lilly tugged on his hands, forcing him to look back at her again. God, the desperation in her eyes. It was killing him.

He squeezed her fingers and then pried them from his.

"You may think that's true, but we don't know for sure. The effect on our careers could still be an issue. And I don't want to risk how my son might react."

"Maybe he would understand—"

"He wouldn't. But say they all accepted us. Then what? I don't want to have any more children, and that isn't fair to you. You have a lot more life left to live than I do."

"That's ridiculous. You're only forty-five. We'd have plenty of years to—"

Jack placed a finger over her lips, silencing her. "This isn't what's right for you in the long run. I want you to have a full life with marriage, children and all the things you could possibly experience, and that's not going to be with me. You have to move on to someone else who can give you all that."

Lilly took his wrist and pulled his hand down.

"I don't want someone else! I want you!" When he didn't respond, her face crumpled. She dropped his hand and wrapped her arms around her middle. "I don't understand how you can act like this after what you said the other night, about needing me, about being mine. Was none of that true? Or was it all just bullshit to get me to submit the way I did?"

"No," he said, horrified she'd even think that. "I meant every word."

"Then tell me how, Jack? How am I supposed to forget the person who brought me back from the dead?"

She stumbled backward until she banged into the edge of the island. Jack winced and reached for her, his instinct to take her into his arms, but stopped himself. He couldn't protect her when he was the one causing her pain.

"I was dead, broken, and you put me back together. You made me whole again."

"And I'll always be honored you let me do that for you, but—"

"But what? If it was all true, then how can it be so easy for you to walk away?"

"It's not easy, Lilly! I'm trying to do what's right here. You need to be with someone your own age. Someone who can provide for you a lot longer than I will."

She sniffled, the fire from her previous words replaced by a soft, sad whisper. "If you really feel like that, then why have you been doing this with me all this time?"

"Because I'm selfish. And I wanted you."

"Wanted?" She laughed bitterly. "Past tense?"

"I still do. You know that. But I can't continue something with you that will only end up hurting you in the end."

Lilly studied him for a moment, her eyes narrowing. "Is that it, or is there something else?"

His lips formed a thin line.

"Because I think the truth is that you're the one who's afraid to be hurt. You don't want to risk losing someone again."

"Lilly," he said. "Don't." But she ignored his warning and took a step forward.

"You're not willing to move on, even though that's what you've been telling me to do. You're too scared to do whatever it is Eve asked you to do. The thing you wouldn't tell me about."

"That has nothing to do with this."

"You sure about that?" She sighed and shook her head. "Jack, whatever it was you said you're not brave enough to do, you can tell me about it. I've told you everything about me. Why can't you do the same?"

There was no way he was talking about this with her. Lilly threw her hands in the air.

"Fine, don't tell me." Tears spilled down her cheeks. "I'm sorry she's gone, I truly am, but I'm here now. I want to be with you, despite the age difference, despite any consequences to our jobs or what our friends and family might think, despite everything. I'm willing to take the risk because..." She paused, treading closer. "I love you."

Oh God.

It was the moment he'd been dreading. He'd known it was coming, but hadn't bargained on it being this soon.

"I don't feel the same way, Lilly."

Her eyes slowly closed and her shoulders jerked in a short, silent cry. Then she started to laugh, a cackle that was almost maniacal.

"I can't believe I'm back here again." Her eyes flew open, an eerie smile on her face. "I'm right back where I was, loving someone who doesn't love me back. I let history repeat itself. I even asked you for the same things I wanted from Damien, and your answer didn't sound any different from his." Her face hardened again. "So I guess you're right. I do have to go."

She glared at him for a long moment. Then Jack opened the drawer in the island, took out their contract and flipped to the addendum that would end their agreement. He handed it to her.

"You need to look after yourself. I don't want to be the cause of any of your heartbreak."

She stared down at the contract. "You already are."

Her words cut, deeper than he'd thought possible.

Lilly signed and dated the bottom line with a flourish. As her pen left the paper, Jack felt it—the moment this thing between them ended. It hit him like an avalanche. She started to walk out, but he couldn't let her leave like this, not after all they'd been through.

"Lilly," he forced out. She turned around. "I'm sorry."

She nodded. "Me too."

He followed her out of the kitchen, wanting to insist on driving her home, but he had no right to put any demands on her now. He stood in the hallway until the door clicked shut behind her.

Jack punched the wall in frustration, but it wasn't enough to loosen the tightness in his chest. He backed up hard against the wall and slid down to the floor, clasped his hands together and pressed them to his mouth. He closed his eyes against the moisture building there, but it didn't help. A tear streaked down his face.

He'd promised to protect her, to nurture her and keep her safe. To heal, not hurt her.

And in the end, hurting her was exactly what he did.

# 34

---

$\mathcal{L}$illy stared out her office window. A rainstorm was in the distance, thick clouds camped out over the horizon, the sky as gray as she felt. It was as if someone had taken out her lungs but expected her to breathe normally, act normally, even though last night she'd walked away from the best thing that ever happened to her.

It seemed like a cruel joke that it had ended up this way, when she'd gone to Jack's house hoping for so much more. Why couldn't he see she'd never cared about their age difference? It was never an issue was when they were in his playroom. Why would it have mattered now?

It didn't matter. Only one thing did, and it felt like a searing knife wound whenever she thought about it—he didn't love her.

She sighed and turned away from the window. Everything she'd thought about their relationship was wrong. For Jack, it had been about fixing her, and only for the duration of their contract, nothing more. If only she could rewind time, and continue staying blind to his feelings, but that wouldn't have been any better. She did the right thing by leaving.

Her work phone rang, and she reached for it, grateful for the distraction. She couldn't focus on the train wreck of her personal life right now. "Lilly Sterling."

"Yo. It's Brady."

Her stomach bottomed out. Was he calling because Jack asked him to check up on her?

"Hey," she replied warily. "What's up?"

"Um, you told me to call you. At the pub on Friday. Remember?"

"Right. Of course," she said, shaking off the foolish hope. Jack would never have asked Brady to look in on her, anyway. "You have a lot of experiences with databases, right? Ones with lots of data, like I mentioned at the game?"

Brady snorted. "I build databases like that."

She laughed and closed her eyes, hanging on to the sound of his voice, the way he phrased his words, the lilt of his accent. He sounded so much like Jack.

*Stop it.*

"Great. I wanted to ask if you'd be our IT expert. The conversation we had about Unix timestamps broke this case."

"Cool. What do you need me to do?"

They worked out the details, and she put him on the calendar for later in the week. When they hung up, she dropped her head into her hands.

Since when did it hurt this much just to breathe?

"Hey, we got the backup database in—" Lilly's head snapped up as Cassie stopped short at the edge of her cubicle. "What's wrong?"

She shrugged and tried to smile, to force it down, to ignore her feelings and bury herself in work. But she couldn't. Maybe if she just let it happen this time, she'd get through it faster.

"It's over with Jack."

Cassie squatted down by her chair. "What happened?"

"I wanted more and he...didn't."

"I'm sorry, honey."

"Thanks." She took a breath and tried to clear her head. She wasn't going to break down and cry here. She had work to do. "So we got the backup? What does it say?"

Cassie held out an envelope. "I haven't opened it. Thought you might want to do the honors."

"It's your case, Cass."

"And it was *your* find."

She stubbornly continued to hold out the envelope. Hesitating for a moment, Lilly reached up and took the package. If she was going to come out of this relationship with another layer of scars, at least she'd do it with her legal footing intact. She tore open the package and pulled out the flash drive inside.

"Plug it in," Cassie said. "Let's see what we've got."

Lilly connected it to her computer, brought up the older version of the database and tabbed down to the entry she'd memorized by now. It was completely different—just a few lines Simon had written on whatever assignment he'd had that day.

"Hah!" Cassie pumped her fist in the air. "We've got you, suckers."

Lilly should've been ecstatic, but a small smile was all she could manage.

"We got them," she agreed quietly.

Cassie tilted her head in sympathy. "Are you going to tell Nick?"

She still planned on honoring Jack's request to keep this between them, and even if she wasn't, there was no guarantee that Nick would understand.

"I don't know."

Cassie put a hand on her shoulder. "It's going to be okay."

Another deep breath. Inhale. Exhale. Over and over until it stopped hurting.

"I know."

She would be. Eventually.

\* \* \*

Jack hunched forward over his desk, his hands clasped together. The sounds of Harvard in preparation for finals wafted in through his open windows. He'd given his final lectures, wished his students luck on their exams and had his last appointments with his advisees.

He had no obligations, save for grading exams in a week. He should've felt relieved, but he didn't.

It was Friday, five days since Lilly walked out his door. On Monday, it had felt like a bad dream. By Tuesday, reality set in. And when Wednesday came, going home to his liquor cabinet felt a hell of a lot more appealing than tennis with Patrick. He'd dragged himself through the workout anyway, hoping the game would beat some of the guilt out of him.

It hadn't.

He'd been in a foul mood and played like shit. With every serve, he remembered Lilly's face falling when he said he didn't love her. The image was seared into his brain. He hated hurting her, but she needed to hear the truth. He'd done what was necessary to get her to end their agreement.

Unwilling to explain himself and risk one of Patrick's pep talks, Jack left the match quickly, insisting he had work to do. Since then, he'd pushed himself through the last few days of the semester. He'd blocked out the picture of Lilly's devastated expression and focused instead on the way she looked at the pub last weekend—the confidence she showed when talking about work, the sparkle in her eyes. She'd come such a long way, and would finally be able to move on to someone who would be able to give her what she needed most. That was the future he wanted for her.

So why did the thought make him sick?

Jack crossed his arms and looked at his desk, finally devoid of paperwork. Once, he'd been happy to be finished with the months of mentoring, advising and teaching. The long days of summer would unfold before him, and he'd spend hours researching, writing articles in the hope of publication. He loved being in scholar mode, burying himself in the questions that fueled his interests, making new discoveries he could share with his students the next semester. It was something he hadn't done for a long time, since before Eve's diagnosis, but he'd hoped to do it again this summer. And in the balmy nights that followed, he'd imagined Lilly with him, their time filled with discoveries of their own.

Now that was never going to happen. He hadn't realized how

much she'd become a part of his life. It felt like he was bleeding out without her.

His cell rang, Josh's name flashing on the screen. Jack tried to shelve his heartache, hoping he sounded normal as he picked up the call.

"Hey, buddy."

"Hey, Dad. Guess what? I have some free time at the end of May and found some cheap tickets home. You'll be done with finals, right?"

A visit from Josh should've been a cause for celebration. He didn't have to worry about keeping Lilly a secret anymore, about telling her they'd need to cancel a weekend or having anything to hide. All the lies were behind him.

He should've felt relieved, but instead he felt...empty.

"Dad?"

"Yes, I'll be done." He forced excitement into his voice. "I can't wait to see you."

He had to stop thinking about Lilly and focus on his son. On his career. His life. He'd told her to move on, and that was what he needed to do too. She'd never get what she was looking for with him, and he had promises to keep.

It was time for him to let her go.

# 35

The sky was waking up in a wash of yellows, pinks and purples when Lilly arrived downtown, the haze of night burning away. The early morning light glittered off the sides of buildings, everything warmed with gold.

Lilly squinted in the sun and smiled, her pace quick in the mild air. She couldn't remember when she'd had so much energy. Maybe it was because of the exciting work she'd done in the past two weeks, helping to craft opening and closing statements, preparing direct and cross examinations, as well as creating a PowerPoint presentation of the evidence.

Or maybe it was because they'd kicked ass in court yesterday.

Lilly bought the morning paper from a vendor on the corner. It was the first time she'd been happy to see the case covered by the *Globe*. Now it was in the *Herald* too. There'd been dozens of reporters in the back of the courtroom, and it brought the firm the kind of press they could've only hoped for.

Lilly scanned the article while she waited for her coffee. There was a not-so-kind portrayal of Salvatore and Francesca Giordano. They hadn't exactly kept their money on the down low in the courthouse, looking bored and dressed more like celebrities than members of organized crime. They hadn't stayed as composed however, when their Uncle Antonio arrived.

Neither had Gabe. He'd practically asked the man for his autograph.

The article went on, naming Judge McCallister and all the counsel involved. Forrester had taken the lead, turning the trial into a face-off between him and Mahoney that felt like a showdown out of the Wild West. The article also named Jacqui Broussard as a witness, and Brady as the expert.

She felt a twinge of victory, remembering the alarm in Salvatore's expression when they put Brady on the stand, the twitch of lips when they'd brought up the PowerPoint presentation of the database. Brady's professional opinion that "M-O-D underscore d-t" stood for "modified date" had made Salvatore's relaxed appearance vanish entirely. Mahoney had been furious.

Lilly paid for her coffee and went inside. She kept reading as the elevator took her skyward, the same apprehension she'd felt the day before returning. She scanned through the reporter's account of the description of Unix timestamps, the slide showing the timestamp converter, then the gasps throughout the courtroom when they revealed the unmodified date. It all went perfectly, but what had finally clinched the case was when they called Jacqui to the stand. Lilly grinned, the article making her feel as if she were experiencing their victory all over again. Forrester's cross-examination ended with Jacqui admitting the Giordanos had falsified their evidence. Then they'd hit home with the presentation Lilly had prepared, which included the subpoenaed original, un-tampered entry.

After that, it had been mayhem. McCallister nearly threw the Giordanos out of the courtroom, insisting they pay all of Simon's legal costs, and at the firm's regular, undiscounted price. Antonio stomped out, leveling his niece and nephew on the way with a glare that had them slumping down into their seats. The judge banged his gavel, and the case was dismissed.

Lilly grinned at the photo at the bottom of the page. The caption read:

*William Forrester of Forrester, Schaeffer and Pierce and his team*

*Gabriel Hartley, Cassandra Allbright and Lilly Sterling win their case against Giordano Diagnostics.*

There it was, her name in print describing a win of her first real case. She was going to have to cut this article out and frame it. Maybe even mail it to her parents. And she'd have to make sure Jack—

No, she wouldn't have to make sure Jack saw it. Sadness descended as she walked out of the elevator and down the hall. There'd been no communication from him at all over the past three weeks. She should've been thinking hateful things, purging all his texts and emails, but the truth was she wished she could've shared the thrill of victory with him. To feel his excitement, and bask in his pride.

"There's our star!"

Lilly snapped to attention as Cassie came toward her and glanced at the paper in her hands. "You got an actual newspaper? How archaic. I read it online last night. There was even a snippet about it on the local news."

"That's crazy. And I'm not a star."

"Like hell you're not." Gabe walked up to them, a bottle of champagne in one hand. Lilly pointed to it.

"Isn't it a bit early for that?"

"Honey, we showed the mob who was boss yesterday. It's never too early to drink when that's the case." Gabe looped his arm around hers. Cassie took the other. "Come on, Forrester's waiting."

"For what?"

"You'll see."

The two of them flanked her sides, her own personal Scarecrow and Tin Man leading her down the Yellow Brick Road. She'd felt like Dorothy months ago, so unsure of herself. Now she had her head held high, even though it felt as if she were the one whose heart was missing.

Inside the conference room, Forrester and Simon were waiting, along with the other managing partners, as well as the associates and staff. Everyone cheered their arrival.

Simon made a beeline for Lilly and hugged her, nearly knocking his glasses off in the process. "You saved everything I've worked for. Thank you so much."

"I didn't really do anything," she insisted, seeing Forrester amble up behind him. "These guys argued the case. I just supplied the evidence."

"But you figured it out. That was absolutely brilliant."

"It was," Forrester agreed. His usual irritated stare was absent, replaced by something that looked like admiration.

Simon pushed his glasses up his nose. "Why exactly aren't you a lawyer here yet?"

"She will be," Forrester answered for her. "As soon as she takes the bar."

Lilly took a breath and nodded. Losing one part of her life hurt like hell, but the path to the other one was finally laid out in front of her.

"Yes," she said. "I will be."

Gabe popped the champagne, and everyone toasted to the firm's success. A breakfast spread had been put out, and an hour passed full of handshakes with colleagues and a conversation with the senior partners that had Lilly buzzing more than the sparkling wine.

After everyone cleared out, Gabe came up by her side. "Did you enjoy that, Counselor?"

"You can't call me that yet. But yes."

"Well, we're going out to celebrate for real tonight. Someplace nice, like that new lounge Neon Bar, with Nick and everyone else."

Lilly went cold, wondering if "everyone else" would include Jack anymore.

Probably not.

"Sure," she said, hoping he didn't notice how sad she sounded. "That'll be great."

The conference room phone buzzed. Gabe hit the intercom button.

"Flowers for Lilly in the lobby," the receptionist said.

*Jack.*

Lilly's pulse went on overdrive. He must've read about the outcome of the trial and had come to congratulate her. Maybe he'd changed his mind. Maybe he'd figured out he really did love her, and this would just be a blip they'd laugh about someday.

"I'll be right back."

The ride to the ground floor was torturous. Lilly paced inside the elevator, ready to race through the lobby, throw herself into Jack's arms and tell him how much she'd missed him. But when she got to the front desk, it wasn't Jack standing there with a large bouquet of flowers.

It was Damien.

# 36

It was like something out of her nightmares, the way he was standing there so casually. She'd forgotten how cruelly handsome he was. Her dreams had edited that fact out, but it was screaming at her now. With dark hair, piercing eyes and a faint hint of stubble lining his angular jaw, he was sex in a sleek black suit.

Her heartbeat kicked up a notch when he swept an appreciative gaze over her. It was infuriating. He didn't belong here, in the world she'd taken so long to build.

Lilly set her hands on her hips and stalked toward him. "What are you doing here?"

Damien tilted his head to the side, that look that said what a silly child she was for asking such a question. "I came to see you, of course."

"You knew I was in Boston?"

"Not until recently."

"How did you find me?"

He smirked and lifted an eyebrow. "Since when did you get so feisty?"

"How?" she demanded.

Damien sighed and gave a little shake of his head, as if he was only answering to humor her.

"When you didn't answer my email on your birthday, and I discovered you'd not only blocked me on Facebook but changed your number too, I needed to know that you were okay. That wasn't very nice of you, cutting me off like that."

Lilly narrowed her eyes. Condescending prick. A lecture from him on what wasn't considered nice was the last thing she wanted to hear. Only she couldn't make the words come out. She dug her fingers into her waist, hoping the move hid how hard she was shaking.

Damien shrugged, nonchalance and sex and power all rolled up into one. "I did a few online searches for your name, but nothing new came up for the longest time. Then a case out here caught my interest. One with some interesting ties to organized crime. The news articles were very entertaining."

He grinned, that charming smile that used to derail her. She didn't smile back.

"My interest was piqued, so I looked up the counsel, and then there was your name on the roster for this firm." He waved a hand, gesturing around the lobby, obviously impressed. His approval was something Lilly once would've given anything for. Something that would've made her stand tall, and then get down on her knees in gratitude.

Her traitorous body responded, even as her stomach churned.

"I followed the case, all the way up to yesterday's win," he continued. "When I saw your picture, I had to congratulate you."

"You flew here to congratulate me?" Lilly laughed, shook her head and tried to imitate his smirk. "You could've saved yourself a trip with a phone call."

"Would you have answered me?" he asked. "I tried to reach you here once, but you didn't pick up."

So that call had been him. Lilly didn't respond.

"A voicemail would've sufficed, but I wanted to do it in person. I wanted to see you."

Damien's voice went lower. Huskier. Lilly recognized the pitch— he'd used it on her a thousand times. It was like a secret weapon.

"I'm proud of you, you know," he said, taking a step toward her. "Of how far you've come. I always knew you had it in you." His gaze dipped to her breasts, then to her hips before drifting upward again. "I taught you well."

She crossed her arms against the heat of his perusal. "You talk like you still know me." Her voice came out small, her shell cracking.

"Don't I?" He moved in close. "Aren't you the same Lilly Sterling I used to know?"

She stepped away, feint to his parry. "Aren't you still engaged?"

There was a tic in his jaw. "No. I'm not."

"You're not," she repeated.

"I broke it off. My heart wasn't in it." Damien's lashes lowered in the same hypnotic stare that once had the power to cripple her. The effect it had on her was muted, but still there, a fire flickering to life in cold coals. "Have dinner with me tonight so we can talk."

"We're talking now."

"Not like this. I'd like to take you out. Somewhere nice."

He closed the distance between them, but even as she took another small step back, evading his nearness, her heart leaped, the Lilly from a year ago taking over. Blind, foolish, lovestruck Lilly who would've grasped at any meager breadcrumb he threw her way. Dinner, in public, just the two of them, was something the old Lilly had always wanted.

It was something Jack never offered her, either.

"Please?" he added, holding out the flowers like a peace offering.

Lilly's hand rose in a reflex, his sudden charm catching her off guard. "Please" was a word she couldn't ever recall him using. As her fingers wrapped around the ornate bouquet, the twisted attraction she suddenly felt for him made her hate herself. The logical part of her head was waving her arms and screaming, but this Damien's behavior was so different from the man she knew.

"I have plans at nine, but I can meet you for a little while before then."

"Where will your plans be?"

"Back Bay area."

"Excellent. I'll find someplace nice nearby. I'd like to pick you up, but I don't know where you live."

"I'd rather meet you there."

His grin turned smug. "Fine. I'll call your office with an address in an hour."

He leaned in close. Too close. As if he was about to kiss her. She wanted to pull back but her body wouldn't cooperate. His lips hovered by her ear, and Lilly held her breath, a shiver slinking down her spine.

"I'm looking forward to it," he murmured, then stepped back and walked away.

She stood there completely frozen, her heart pounding as she watched him disappear outside. Air rushed back into her lungs, too fast for her to catch up with. Whipping around, she punched the elevator button, the bouquet tight by her side. She rushed through the halls to Cassie's office, closed the door behind her and pressed her back against it.

Cassie looked up from her desk. "Why do you look like you're about to puke? Was it the champagne? I told Gabe it was too early."

"Damien." Lilly stumbled and held out the flowers. "Damien is here."

"He's what?"

"Take these? I don't know what to do with them." She dumped the bouquet on Cassie's desk and started pacing. "He flew to Boston to congratulate me. He wants to take me to dinner."

"Holy shit." Cassie looked over the bouquet. "These are really nice."

"Cassie!"

"Right. Sorry. So he wants to take you out? Are you going to go?"

"Yeah. He wants to talk. He's not engaged anymore. He said his heart wasn't in it."

Cassie snorted. "I wasn't aware he had one."

Neither was she. And if his heart wasn't in getting married, where was it now?

"Lilly, you're not exactly in a great place right now. Is this a good idea?"

"I don't know. Maybe." Lilly sighed. "Okay, it's a terrible idea."

She gazed out past the river, its deep blue depths gone pale gold where the sun hit it, toward Cambridge and Jack. The man she wanted didn't want her anymore, and the one she no longer wanted suddenly did. None of it made any sense.

"He's a prick and I hate him, but I need to go anyway. To hear what he has to say." She turned back to Cassie. "I need to get out of here and think. Cover for me?"

"Fine, but I'm expecting you to still meet up with us for drinks afterward. No letting him talk you into going back to his hotel. Understand?"

"Yes." She went to the door, stopping to glance back over her shoulder. "If anyone asks, say the front desk was wrong and the flowers were for you."

"It's been a millennia since anyone's sent me flowers, but okay. I'll say they're from my dad. That's not pathetic at all."

With a grateful smile, Lilly slipped out the door. She tiptoed down the hall as quietly as she could and fled home.

* * *

Jack poured himself a cup of coffee and unfolded his newspaper across the island. The *Globe* was delivered to his house every day, but had been going straight from the concrete to his recycling bin for over a year. For a while, he hadn't had the energy to unwrap it from the plastic. The last few months, he simply didn't have the time.

Now he had too much time on his hands.

Without work to distract him, his days stretched out, his plans sparse, giving him little excuse for avoiding the one thing he had to do before Josh's arrival.

Jack glanced at the clock. He had time before he had to go to the airport. What was another hour?

He sipped his coffee and flattened the paper out, freezing when he saw a photo of Lilly beneath an article on the front page.

He put his mug down and started reading. From the journalist's description, it sounded like their victory had been incredible, even though he could already tell as much from the expression on Lilly's face. She looked so happy. If only he could've been there to congratulate her.

A knifelike pain cut through him. The last few weeks had been hard, her absence in his life a gaping hole. He'd told himself it was natural. That with time, he would readjust. Seeing her like this, however, served as a deep reminder of how her life had veered off and surged ahead on a path he wouldn't ever be able to follow.

He looked at her photo again. Was she truly as happy as she seemed? He wasn't.

God, he never thought he'd miss her this badly.

With the coffee and the paper no longer appealing, Jack stood and headed upstairs to Josh's room. He'd avoided cleaning it, unwilling to face the fact that Lilly would never sleep there again. The room felt like a minefield—everywhere he looked, a memory was waiting, ready to explode.

But as he stepped inside, he realized she'd left nothing behind, not even so much as a tube of toothpaste. It seemed like no one else had slept here at all.

He started to strip the bed but stopped as he picked up a pillow, his throat going uncomfortably tight with the scent he'd sworn he'd just caught. It wasn't possible. There was no way after so many weeks that the bed could smell like her. But if there was any chance it did...

He brought the pillow to his face. Closing his eyes, he breathed in slowly, then dropped it. There wasn't a trace of her scent there, only his imagination playing tricks on him.

Feeling like an idiot, he ripped off the pillowcase, then the sheets, chucking them to the floor in disgust. After remaking the bed, he mashed the linens into a ball, went downstairs and threw them into the laundry room basket.

Needing to escape the prison of memories, he left earlier than he needed to for Logan and sat on the edge of a chair in baggage claim, staring up at the board as he waited for Josh. The flight number was announced, and Jack stood, scanning the crowd coming down the escalator. His son finally appeared, smiling and tan, his curls bleached nearly white from the California sun.

Jack wrapped him in a tight hug. "It's so good to see you," he said, his voice gruff.

"You too, Dad."

He pulled back and held his son by the shoulders. Josh seemed taller. Older. More like a man. And more like Eve than ever.

The guilt of unfulfilled promises pricked at his heart.

"What, did you forget who I am or something?" Josh asked. "I'm Josh." He said it slowly, pointing to himself with a goofy grin.

"Smartass." Jack relaxed his grip and rumpled his son's hair. "You hungry? We could stop somewhere."

"Nah. I ate on the plane. Besides, Uncle Brady is waiting at the house."

That was new information. "And you know this, how?"

"Because he texted us. Didn't you see it?"

Jack checked his phone. Sure enough, he'd missed a text from Brady, asking if they'd be game for going out tonight.

"You've been home for twenty minutes. Can't I have you to myself for a night?"

"You'll have me all weekend, Dad. I promise, by Sunday, you'll be sick of me."

When they pulled up in front of the house, Brady was on the driveway with the girls. He'd positioned Allegra in front of the basketball hoop and was trying to teach her a lay-up.

Josh got out of the car and called out, "Don't listen to anything your dad says, Allegra. He stinks at basketball."

"Josh!" Allegra dropped the ball and ran down the driveway. He bent down to hug her, and Hope rushed in too. When the girls had their fill, Brady pulled Josh into a one-armed embrace, knuckles dug against his head.

"That a spray tan you've got going on there?"

Laughing, Josh shoved him off. "It's the real deal. Got some good color at the Dodgers game last weekend."

"Traitor," Brady muttered and pushed back an inch. They

ducked blows, playing like bull calves as they went inside the house. Josh dropped his bags in the back corner of the kitchen.

"Things going okay with school?" Brady asked Josh as he plopped down on a stool. "I heard you had a meltdown last month. Is my brilliant nephew crumbling under the pressure?"

Josh cocked his head, confused. "What meltdown?"

Jack's stomach lurched. Leave it to Brady to remember the lie Patrick had crafted the night Lilly was sick and ask about it.

"Oh," Jack floundered, trying to think of something. "That was a misunderstanding on my part. Protective father overreacting, you know the drill." He turned to Allegra and Hope. "You girls want some ice cream?"

They shouted with glee and ran toward the fridge. Brady glared at Jack. "Thanks. Now they'll have sugar highs the rest of the night."

Jack shrugged and smiled innocently as he opened the freezer.

"Well, you won't be the one who has to deal with it, right?" Josh asked. "I thought you said we were going out tonight."

"Hell yeah, we are."

Allegra gasped. "Daddy, you said a bad word again."

Brady grabbed the ice cream from Jack. Spooning out their portions, he said, "Don't tell Mommy, and you each can have an extra scoop. Deal?"

They mimed zipping their lips and happily dug into their bowls. Brady turned back to Josh.

"Yes, we're going out, and to someplace nice, I've been told, so first round is on you, Mister Big Shot PhD."

"I'm not a PhD yet. Who will I be buying for, anyway?"

"You remember my buddy Nick? His husband won a big case yesterday." Brady puffed his chest up. "I was the expert witness."

"What on earth could you be an expert at?"

"IT, asshole."

The girls looked up at him, eyes wide, spoons frozen in the air. Without a word, Brady huffed out a sigh and portioned out another scoop for each of them.

"Anyway, they invited us to celebrate with them. You too, Jack."

Jack didn't reply. If Nick and Gabe were going, odds were good that Lilly would too.

"Will Patrick be there?" Josh asked.

"Think so. He wouldn't want to miss a chance to butt heads with Cassie."

"Who's that?"

"Gabe's co-worker."

Josh grinned. "She hot?"

"Yeah, I guess. She's older than me though, and a little rough around the edges." Brady glanced at the paper on Jack's island and held it up. "There, that's her. You'll meet Nick's sister Lilly too. She's closer to your age. Maybe you two will hit it off."

"No!"

Brady and Josh swiveled in unison to stare at Jack. He hadn't been able to help the outburst. Lilly may not have been his anymore, but she and Josh clicking was simply not happening.

He cleared his throat, guarding his expression. "I mean, you're only here for a few days. Why start something you're only going to have to end?"

It was advice he should've followed too.

"True," Brady replied slowly and turned back to Josh. "Anyway, they're all meeting up at nine. You game?"

"Sure. Let me make sure I have something clean to wear." Josh opened his bag. There was nothing but lumpy, unfolded clothes inside.

"Don't tell me you brought laundry with you," Jack said.

Josh pulled out a handful of clothes and grinned. "I'm hoarding quarters out in Cali. Laundry is free here." He ducked into the laundry room, a moment later calling out, "Dad?"

Jack followed to find a puzzled Josh pointing at the litter box and the cans of Rumbles' food. "What's all this?"

Shit.

How had he forgotten about that? Once again, Jack searched for a lie. "I...took a stray cat in for a while, but she, uh, got away."

"That sucks," Josh said. "It would be good if you had a pet, though. For company."

Jack nodded. When they returned to the kitchen, Brady was putting the girls' dishes in the sink. He turned the water off and smacked a decisive palm down on the table.

"Okay, Jack, are you in or out? 'Cause if you're in, then you're designated."

Jack weighed his options. Could he go and keep his distance from Lilly, continuing the farce she'd managed to keep under wraps for him for so long?

He needed to see her. If nothing else, to confirm that she was okay and had put all this behind her.

"We'll pick you up at eight."

## 37

*B*y the time Lilly got home from work, she was no closer to a clear head than she'd been when she left. If only she could talk to Jack. She needed the clarity he always provided for her, but wishing for the impossible was a waste of time, and honestly, what would he tell her to do? *Sure, Lilly, go to dinner with the man who mangled your heart, who proved in five minutes today that he could unravel you with nothing more than words and a look. Great idea. Go for it.*

Yeah, not likely.

But it didn't matter what Jack would say. The only person she could count on now was herself, and there was only one thing that would help her think straight.

Trading her suit for her sweats, Lilly plugged in her headphones and went for a run.

She took off through the tree-lined streets. The feeling of her feet pounding the pavement helped slough away some of the shock ricocheting through her after Damien's arrival. It was disgusting, how he'd shown up at her job like that. He'd probably done it to see if he could still rattle her, and if that was the case, well then, mission accomplished. She should've stopped him from talking so much, should've thrown the flowers back in his face and walked away.

But he never got married. It shouldn't have changed anything, but it did.

Lilly's pulse hammered in her throat, her lungs straining for her next breath. She was running too hard, her legs fueled by her emotions. Slowing to a walk, she crossed her hands behind her head and sucked oxygen deep into her lungs. She'd forgotten how captivating Damien could be, what it was like to be trapped by nothing more than his gaze on her skin and the smooth hum of his voice in her ear. How special it felt to have his attention focused solely on her.

His engagement had been the one certainty keeping the nails firmly entrenched in the coffin of her past. What had changed so much that he'd broken it off and flown out here?

Traffic stopped her from crossing the street and Lilly jogged in place, for the first time taking note of her surroundings. She'd been too lost in thought to notice where she was, but she'd run straight through town, all the way to the corner by Rosie's Diner. She stared longingly at the place where everything with Jack started, the night they finally figured out what had brought them together.

Thoughts of him washed over her, a swell of memories that made Damien's appeal pale in comparison. With Jack, she'd understood what it was like to submit in trust rather than in fear. The sense of security she felt when he had her shackled and helpless was no different from the safety of being held in his arms, drifting off to sleep next to the lullaby of his heart.

He made her feel cherished, wanted and strong. Damien never made her feel like that. Even today as he cornered her in the lobby, he made her feel small. Insignificant.

The traffic moved on, giving Lilly her cue to take off. She needed to flee again, needed to run herself to exhaustion, to silence all the questions bombarding her mind. But as she began to step off the curb, she stopped herself. How many things had she run from? The bar, home, anything that reminded her of Damien. She'd run from Jack too, but Lilly didn't want to run anymore.

This time she wanted to turn around and face her fears head on.

* * *

Hours later, Lilly stepped out of a cab and walked toward Caterina's, a little Italian place Damien had left the address for on her work voicemail. Her hair was up, her heels high, her makeup flawless, and she was wearing her little black dress. There was a lot of history in this piece of fabric, but she'd bought it long ago to congratulate herself for a job well done, and tonight was a night to celebrate another one.

"I remember that dress."

Her head snapped up at the sound of Damien's voice. He was leaning against the door of a shiny red car, a rental that was probably expensive and fast.

She strode past him and the ostentatious car, straight to the restaurant's entrance. "I told you, I have plans after dinner. I didn't wear this for you."

Damien laughed and hopped up the steps after her. "Of course you didn't."

He made a grand gesture out of opening the door, sweeping a hand out as he held it for her. He took in her form, his gaze predatory. Lilly glared and walked inside. He was showing off, flaunting the attributes she'd once found so enticing, but gallant moves and sophistication weren't enough to give him the upper hand this time. The elegant décor of the restaurant was a little more difficult to harden herself against, though. White table linens sat against shining cutlery and sparkling glasses, all of it illuminated by flickering candlelight.

The hostess led them to a secluded table in a corner, and Lilly found her composure as she studied the menu, searching for the most expensive thing on it.

He was paying, after all.

"So they're treating you well out here?" Damien asked idly. "You haven't been stuck with some deadly document review project?"

"You came here to talk about work?"

"No. Just asking about your life."

*My life is none of your business.*

She took a breath and silenced the thought. One needed to be calm when facing poisonous creatures. "Why don't you tell me what you flew here to talk about?"

"Where was this spunky, tough side of you before?" He leaned forward. "I like it."

Lilly ignored his comment and continued perusing her food choices.

"My job is great. My boss has given me some amazing opportunities." She glanced up, adding, "He's offered me a position after I take the bar."

Silence.

"What do you mean, after?" he asked. Then, more quietly, "You never took it?"

She glared at him. "Did you really think I'd be able to after your phone call?"

"Lilly—" he began, but the waiter arrived to take their orders. She chose the pricey filet mignon, flashing Damien her most saccharine smile.

"I'll have the same," he said.

When the waiter left, Damien folded his hands on the table, his expression something that could've been called concerned if she hadn't known better.

"I had no idea my call would affect you so much."

She nearly snorted. "You didn't do it on purpose to manipulate me?"

"Manipulate you?" He leaned back, as if the idea offended him. "No, I called because I didn't want to risk you running into anyone from school and finding out there." He reached a hand across the table. "I was trying to protect you."

"You'll have to forgive me if I find that a little hard to believe."

"You shouldn't." He was still holding out his hand, as if it were only a matter of time before she gave in. Lilly crossed her arms.

"Tell me why you're here."

He pulled his hand back. "I'm here because...I needed to apologize."

Now that was almost as much of a surprise as his saying please.

Damien acting contrite wasn't something she was used to. She'd expected him to say he hadn't gotten her out of his system, and to laugh in his face when he tried to seduce her. But an apology? It seemed like another test, another way to control her.

"What are you apologizing for?" she asked. "Exactly."

He sighed and lowered his head, then leaned in. She wasn't sure if he was trying to get closer to her, or to make sure no one else heard him.

"I'm sorry we ended things the way we did. I didn't want to hurt you."

"Then why did you?"

"Breaking things off was the only way. What was happening wasn't healthy, for either of us."

"What's that supposed to mean?"

"I know you remember. We were addicted to each other." His eyes traced a hot path to where her breasts disappeared into her dress, then back up to her face. "We couldn't stop. It was only a matter of time before someone found out about us."

She felt it again—the pull that used to make it impossible to resist him. Heat flushed through her, and Lilly gritted her teeth against the hot pulse.

"Is that why you'd ignore me?"

He faltered. "That's what you thought I was doing?"

"Refusing to speak to me when we were at the office or at school seems a hell of a lot like ignoring to me. Or would you call it something else?"

He shook his head and laughed.

"I can see why you might have taken it that way, but I wasn't ignoring you. I needed to keep my distance, or you would've gotten too attached. As it was, I knew you wanted more than I could give you."

That stopped the throb of desire he'd set off in her. "You were able to give 'more' to whoever you were going to marry."

Damien grimaced. "She and I weren't...complicated like you and I were."

"So that's why you broke my heart at graduation and got engaged two months later? Because we were complicated?"

"Yes. And not a day has gone by when I haven't regretted it."

Lilly glanced away, hating the way his words affected her. What he was saying—it almost sounded like he actually cared. And that made it hard to believe everything else she'd thought over the past year. Had he regretted what he'd done to her?

Had he regretted all of it?

"What about the rest?" she asked.

"The rest?"

Now it was her turn to lean in. She spoke quietly, her eyes burning. "The rest, as in forcing me to do things I was afraid of. In punishing me for not being able to handle them. In never telling me I was entitled to a checklist. Or limits. Or a safeword."

His smirk returned, one dark eyebrow quirking. "You've been playing with someone else."

She answered with a defiant lift of her chin. "Jealous?"

"No. Impressed, though. And maybe a little curious."

He sipped his water, his eyes amused but calm, then crossed his arms on the table. Lilly drew her hands down to her lap, keeping whatever distance she could between them.

"For the record," he said. "I never forced you to do anything. You enjoyed it. Every. Single. Minute."

He was too close again, filling up her space. Lilly tried to remember how to breathe.

"I wasn't punishing you for not being able to handle things. I was giving you your space, letting you decide if you wanted to come back to me. Which you did, over and over again. And I didn't allow you a safeword because I trusted myself to be able to read you. I didn't want you to have limits because that would've hindered your experience. How else could I have gotten you to the point of complete submission without taking away your safety net?"

Under the table, her hands curled into fists. "That's what you were doing? Enhancing my experience?"

"Yes. And you loved it."

Lilly scrambled for her defense, for anything to diffuse what he was saying, but her thoughts got garbled together. She couldn't disagree. She had loved it. Or else she wouldn't have gone back to him.

"Don't lie to yourself, Lilly. You were consumed by it. Transformed by it—that fine line between pleasure and fear, control and release. Can you honestly look me in the eye and tell me that isn't what you wanted?"

Her nails bit into her palms, her defenses breaking down. Yes, her body had craved that, but she'd never wanted her heart stomped on, her head fucked with.

"I didn't even know what submission was. How could I have known what I wanted?"

"At the time I thought having less information helped you let go. Clearly that was the wrong choice."

"It was."

"Then I apologize for that too."

She frowned, her fingers uncurling. All these apologies were making her even more frustrated. "You should've told me that's what you were doing, so I could have stopped it if I wasn't comfortable."

"What fun would that have been?" Damien's eyes sparkled with mischief. "Sounds to me like the person you're playing with is being a little too easy on you."

"That's none of your business. And he was wonderful."

No matter what Jack had done, she couldn't stomach the idea of Damien judging him.

"Was." He said the word carefully. "I assume that means you're no longer with him?"

"No," she said quietly. "That's over."

"I'm sorry to hear that."

She nodded, her throat painfully tight.

Damien scooted closer in his chair. A slow smile built on his face. "Let me make everything up to you. Come back to Chicago with me."

"What?"

"You don't belong here. Come home. I'll make sure my firm beats whatever Forrester is offering, and you and I can start over again."

She fell back against her seat, her mouth slackened.

"I thought you said no one could know," she managed. "That we couldn't work together and be together. That 'this was the way it had to be.'"

She used air quotes around the last bit, then dropped her hands to the table.

"Maybe I don't care about that now. Maybe I've been going crazy thinking about you, broke off my engagement because of it, and flew all the way out here to win you back. Besides, you're not my firm's summer associate, or my student anymore. We can do whatever we want."

He reached out and took her hand in his. She stared at it, unable to believe he was offering her the simple gesture she'd always wanted.

"Please, Lilly," he said. "Be mine again."

## 38

"There's a spot."

Josh pointed to a parking space, and Jack pulled into it with a glance in the rearview mirror. Brady was practically bouncing in the backseat.

"I thought only Allegra and Hope had sugar highs tonight," he said. "Or did you have some ice cream too?"

Brady gave him the finger and flashed a huge grin. "Sue me for being excited. I'm surrounded by females all the time. You have no idea how much I need a night out."

"Haven't you been going out, like, every Friday?" Josh asked as they climbed out of the car.

"Yeah, but tonight's different." Brady slung an arm over Josh's shoulders. "You're here."

"Screw ice cream. I think you're drunk already."

"Fuck off."

"Oooh, Uncle Brady said a bad word!" Josh teased. "I promise not to tell Aunt Sam if you buy me a beer."

Jack chuckled, his stomach rumbling as they crossed the street. He hadn't been able to eat much at dinner, his appetite replaced by a churning mix of apprehension and dread. He had no idea what to expect tonight.

They'd just reached the entrance to Neon Bar when a red Lamborghini purred to a halt at the curb.

"Nice ride," Brady murmured. "Hey, looks like Lilly finally got a date."

Jack's gaze snapped to the passenger seat. His gut twisted, his pulse racing as he watched Lilly step out of the car, her hair up in a sleek twist, wearing that little black dress he'd once wanted to tear off with his teeth.

Her date got out too, and spoke to her across the roof, his hands folded confidently over the polished metal. He was obviously wealthy, with an expensive suit and an even more expensive car at his fingertips, but he was looking at Lilly as if she were an object he owned too. Jack suppressed the urge to murder the guy.

Brady elbowed Josh. "Guess you won't be getting a chance with her after all."

Josh's head moved as he took in Lilly's form. "Shame."

Jack clenched his jaw, wanting to forcibly yank his son's head in the other direction. Her date got back into his car and drove off, and Lilly turned around, stopping short when she saw Jack. Her eyes flashed with pain.

Brady didn't seem to notice anything and stepped out to hug her.

"The brilliant legal mind arrives," he said, pulling her close with one arm. "Who's the guy?"

"No one important."

"Important enough to be driving four G's on wheels."

She shrugged the shoulder that wasn't smashed against him. "It's a rental."

Jack frowned. Who would she know that drove a car like that, even for a few days? Jealousy seared through him, his hands twitching with the need to touch her, to remind her who she belonged to.

But she didn't belong to him anymore.

Christ, he'd been the one telling her to find someone else. He had no business feeling like this.

Josh cleared his throat and Brady clapped a hand to his chest. "Where are our manners? Lilly, this is Jack's son, the soon-to-be

Doctor Joshua Archer. Josh, this is Lilly Sterling, future lawyer and paralegal extraordinaire."

"It's nice to meet you," she said.

"Likewise." Josh smiled at her. "I guess congratulations are in order. I hear we're celebrating a big win for you guys tonight."

A proud smile blossomed on her face. "Yeah, we are."

The smile killed him. He wanted Lilly's eyes on him. Not on Josh or some stranger with a fancy car. Just him.

"I saw the article in the paper," he said.

Lilly's eyes snapped to his, a move that made the memory of her obedience rush over him, but Jack wanted more than just her attention. He wanted to take her aside, drag her around a corner somewhere and ask her exactly who that man was.

Fuck that. He wanted to press her against a wall and kiss her until she was out of her mind.

Instead, he said, "It sounds like you did a great job. I'm proud of you."

Her gaze softened, emotion cresting. "Thank you."

"You two know each other well?" Josh asked.

Brady stepped in between them. "Yeah, Jack mentored her or some shit like that. But she's not just a ball busting lawyer-to-be. This girl can cook a mean lasagna."

"Aunt Sam let someone else cook in her kitchen?"

"That'll be the day. No, she cooked for us at your dad's."

Josh turned to Jack. "Really?"

There was an awkward silence that nobody filled. Brady studied each of their faces for a moment before getting impatient. "Okay, I've had enough of standing on the street. Are we ready to go inside and toast to my brilliance?"

Lilly laughed. Jack could see her relief in her face. "*Your* brilliance?"

"Of course. Without my incredible genius-ness, how would you ever have won the case?"

Josh snorted. "You do know that 'genius-ness' isn't a word, right?"

"Fuck off."

"That's two curses, so you owe me two beers."

"I don't owe you shit."

"And that makes three."

Brady shook his head and led Lilly through the entrance. Jack hung back, watching her. Seeing her happy, that she'd been able to move on, that she was okay without him—it was what he'd hoped for.

So why did it feel so wrong?

Inside, the club was dimly lit and crowded, music thrumming. Hardwood floors were adorned with smooth leather couches, low tables and high-backed stools. He caught sight of Cassie weaving through the throng. She linked arms with Lilly.

"We've got a table in the corner." She nodded to a spot behind her, then looked at Josh and did a double take. "Are you Jack's son?"

He laughed. "How did you know?"

She eyed Jack briefly. "You look exactly like him."

"I'm hoping that's a compliment?"

"Yeah," Lilly answered, another brief flicker of pain in her eyes before she smiled. "It is."

There was far too much tension in the air, a vibe Jack was sure everyone noticed.

"Why don't you guys go sit?" Cassie suggested. "I need to talk to Lilly for a minute."

Josh and Brady walked off, and Jack watched Cassie guide Lilly to the bar, probably to quiz her about the date. The effort of having to pretend he didn't care was crushing him. He had no idea how Lilly had done this when they were together, acting as if nothing was going on between them, when all she'd wanted was him.

"Now, this is more like it," Patrick said, appearing by Jack's side. "Why have we been going to that shithole by Fenway when we could have been here?"

Jack tried to force a laugh, but it didn't make it to his lips.

"Trouble in paradise?" Patrick asked. "Did you lose the keys to your handcuffs?"

Jack stiffened. He'd forgotten that he'd never told Patrick they ended things.

"I don't want to talk about it."

He plowed through the bar, finding the table where the gang was seated.

"There's the runt." Patrick reached out to hug Josh. "It's good to see you, kid. Glad you could tear yourself away to pay us a visit."

"Thanks," Josh said. It's good to be home."

"So," Brady said, rubbing his hands together. "What are we drinking?"

Patrick's brow lifted. "You're eager to get started."

"The clock is ticking. And Jack is driving so I'm making the most out of it."

"I think a round of shots is in order," Gabe suggested.

"Didn't Cassie say that's what gets her drunk the fastest?" Nick asked.

Patrick grinned. "Definitely shots, then."

Josh started to pull his wallet from his back pocket. "I've been told the first round is on me—"

"I've got it," Jack interrupted.

He walked back to the bar and found a spot not far from where Lilly and Cassie were standing. Her back was to him. Over the noise and music, he could just barely make out their conversation.

"I can't believe it," Cassie said. "You're not going to say yes, are you?"

He heard Lilly sigh. "I don't know. I'm so confused, but right now, with everything he's offered me, and everything that's happened here, going back to Chicago is tempting."

*Chicago.*

Jack saw red. Anger seized him, threatening to boil over. That wasn't some random date. The guy with the car was Damien. And she was considering going back to him.

Before he knew what he was doing, he'd marched straight to Lilly's side.

"Can I speak with you?" he asked through clenched teeth.

Cassie moved to stand between him and Lilly, her lips pressed into a tight slash. Jack's body tensed. It was admirable, the way she wanted to protect Lilly, but she needed to get out of his way. Now.

"It's okay, Cass," Lilly said, putting a hand on her friend's arm.

Cassie gave a minute shake of her head before walking away. Lilly crossed her arms. "Yes?"

"Damien?" he spat. "You were with Damien tonight?"

Her posture went rigid. "You had no right to eavesdrop."

"Why is he here?"

"He offered me a job."

"Is that all?"

She exhaled and looked at the ground. It took every ounce of willpower to stop from capturing her chin in his hand and making her look at him.

"He asked me to get back together with him."

"And what was your answer?"

Her gaze lifted. Her eyes were flat, emotionless. "I don't have to tell you."

She started to walk away, and he grabbed her elbow. "What was your answer?" he repeated, louder this time.

"That I had to sleep on it!"

She wrenched her arm from his grip. Jack backed away, shaking his head, feeling like a hole had been punched through his gut. After all they'd been through, after all he'd done to try to break her of that asshole's hold, how could she even think of going back to him?

"Lilly," he said. "What are you doing?"

Her chin trembled. "Why do you care?"

"Dad?"

Jack whirled around at the sound of Josh's voice.

"I thought you were getting the drinks," he said, looking quizzically at the two of them. "Is everything okay?"

"Everything's fine." Lilly plastered a smile on. "Your dad was grilling me on the questioning techniques we used at the trial."

Jack clenched his jaw. She was lying for him, honoring his request for Josh not to find out. Protecting him, again.

"My dad is a passionate teacher," Josh said, still throwing questioning looks at both of them.

"He's the best I've ever had," Lilly said softly, then stepped away. "I'm going to join the others."

Jack turned back to the bar. He couldn't risk another glance at her. "I've got the drinks," he told Josh, waving down the bartender.

He watched Josh go back to their table out of the corner of his eye, then ordered their drinks, deciding at the last minute to get a shot for himself. Just one. He'd still be able to drive, and he deserved a goddamn drink right now.

He paid and downed it quickly, leaving the glass on the bar as he carried a bevy of small glasses back to the table. "You all ready to drink to your success?"

"Hell, yeah," Brady answered.

"We need a toast." Gabe picked up a glass and looked around the group. "To friendship and love."

"To wins that make our bosses give us bonuses," Cassie added.

Patrick winked in her direction. "To new experiences we might not have expected." She rolled her eyes.

Nick pulled Lilly close to him. "To family."

"Can we drink already?" Brady complained.

Jack kept his eyes averted as they knocked their shots back, sure his poker face had slipped entirely. An extra shot sat on the table. The bartender must have given them one too many.

He grabbed the glass when no one was looking and quickly downed its contents.

Josh picked up the next round, and Gabe continued talking about the case, Cassie adding in how happy Forrester was with them.

Nick lifted a glass in another toast. "Another good thing about this case was that it finally got Lilly out of the house, instead of being at home with her cat all the time."

"You have a cat too?" Josh asked her. "My dad took in a stray for a while. Was that your influence?"

Brady snorted and scrunched up his face. "Jack never had a cat."

Lilly quickly looked away. Josh's brows went down low, his eyes shifting from her to Jack.

Jack reached for a shot without hesitation.

"Dude," Brady complained. "I thought you were designated tonight."

"I'm fine," Jack insisted, but he knew it was a lie. His tolerance had been lowered after so much time off the bottle. Three shots in less than twenty minutes with no food in his stomach had done a job on him.

Everyone was staring. Jack's face burned.

"I think Jack is a little overwhelmed," Patrick said. "Having Josh home and all—it's more excitement than someone our age can handle." He pulled some cash from his pocket and handed it to Josh. "It's time for us old guys to get going. You two take a cab home on me, and tell the driver there will be three stops. I'll take it from your place."

Patrick stood and looked at Jack expectantly.

"Fine." He wasn't thrilled at being parented by his friend, but had no desire to stick around here any longer. Gathering whatever dignity he could scrounge up, he threw a look at Brady and Josh, avoiding looking at Lilly completely. "Sorry about the ride. Have fun."

When they were on the sidewalk, Patrick held out his hand. "Keys."

"Why the hell should I let you drive? Weren't you drinking too?"

"You drank all my shots. Or did you think extra ones magically appeared every single round?"

Jack huffed out a breath. That unfortunately made sense. He slapped his keys into Patrick's palm.

"You could at least thank me for saving your ass tonight. Why the hell are you drinking?"

"I don't want to talk about it."

"You said that before."

"It's still true."

Patrick sighed and got into the car. The entire drive to Cambridge, Jack was consumed with the need to be holding something—the steering wheel. The rim of a bottle. The handle of his flogger. He needed his control back. It was infuriating to feel so helpless.

"You know, I might be able to help," Patrick offered when they pulled onto the driveway. "It's rare that I have a bonus night with a girl, but when I do, I usually know what to say to get them back into bed."

"No thanks." Jack opened the door.

"Hey!" Patrick called, jogging after him. Jack reached into his pocket, but Patrick had his keys. He couldn't even get into his own goddamned house. "Christ, Jack. What the fuck happened?"

"We ended it, okay?"

Patrick didn't speak. He simply unlocked the door. Jack barreled past him and into the living room, opening the liquor cabinet.

"Are you going to tell me why?" Patrick asked.

Jack's hands fell to his sides. "She's in love with me."

"And you don't feel the same way."

He shook his head. "I can't."

There was a beat of silence. Then Patrick said, "You're an idiot."

Jack snapped his head around. "Excuse me?"

"You heard me. You are an idiot."

"Why am I an idiot?"

"Because you were happy with her and you fucked it up."

"I don't want to hear this. You can get the hell out of my house now." Jack retrieved the scotch, waiting for Patrick to see his own way out. Fuck this. Drinking in solitude might not have been better for him, but at least it was quieter.

"Well, that's too fucking bad, because somebody has to talk some sense into you."

Jack coughed out a bitter laugh. "And you're the one to do that?"

"You're damn right I am," Patrick spat. "So what did love for her imply? Was she asking to wear a dog collar and follow you around naked on her hands and knees?"

"No." Jack took a long, burning sip straight from the bottle. "She wanted a real relationship. I can't give her that. She's too young. Being with me is the wrong choice for her."

"But it was the right choice when you were just fucking her."

"Didn't I tell you to leave?"

But Patrick didn't go anywhere. He yanked the bottle from Jack's hands, shoved it back inside the cabinet and slammed the door shut.

"So now you're saying the problem was Lilly's age? That if she were in her forties, you wouldn't have broken up with her?"

Jack faltered. He didn't have an answer for that.

"Because I think this is all complete and utter bullshit," Patrick continued. "It isn't about age, or Josh, or your career, or BDSM. It's about letting Eve go and moving on, and you're scared shitless to do it. It's just an excuse to cover up how afraid you are. Clinging to your memories of Eve is easier than facing your fear of losing someone again."

It was exactly what Lilly said when they broke up, and it definitely was not what Jack wanted to hear from his best friend.

"I thought you of all people would understand," he growled.

"Why is that?"

"You? King of the one-night stands?" Jack scoffed. "I didn't think you'd be the one to criticize when it was time for me to end it."

Patrick's eyes narrowed, and for a moment, Jack saw how deep his words had cut. But he was too entrenched, too angry for being called out on something Patrick did almost every day.

"You're right. I'm not you. I don't have what you have."

"And what's that?"

"The capacity to love and be loved." Patrick's face hardened, lined with regret. It was the most unguarded Jack had ever seen him. "I've never been able to do that. To give enough of myself to anyone that she'd want to give me the same in return."

He leaned in and poked Jack's chest.

"I leave first because I don't think anyone would want to stay long enough to actually be with me. I cut and run because I can't stand the thought of watching one of them walk out the door." Patrick came closer, until they were nearly nose to nose. "I'm the way I am because I'm afraid no one will ever love me."

Jack blinked through his shock. He never imagined this was the reason behind his friend's philandering and finally saw the easygoing smile Patrick so often wore for the mask it was.

"I didn't know that," he said quietly.

"Congratu-fucking-lations." Patrick stepped back and folded his arms. "I've watched you our whole lives. I saw you fall in love with

Eve when you were just a kid. I stood by your side when you married her. I helped you carry her casket when you lost her. And then I saw how Lilly was the first person to put a goddamned smile back on your face."

Jack blanched and looked away.

"You've found someone again, someone who cares enough that she would risk everything to be with you. And you screwed it up for the dumbest reason I've ever heard."

Anger raged inside him as he met Patrick's glare. "And what about Eve? What about what she asked?"

"Do you love Lilly?"

"Did you not hear what I said?"

"I heard. You said you *can't* feel the same way for her, not that you don't. So answer the fucking question."

"It's not what Eve would've—"

Patrick got in Jack's face again. He spoke slowly, enunciating each word.

"Do...you...love...her?"

Jack paused, the word "no" forming on his lips, but he couldn't say it.

Why couldn't he say it?

He scrubbed his palm over his forehead and paced across the room. There were so many reasons why he shouldn't be in love with Lilly, but were they just a way to hide how terrified he was of moving on?

Five months ago, he'd been completely lost. He didn't know who he was or how he would survive another day. He'd been afraid to go near the playroom, sure he wasn't a Dominant without Eve, but Lilly gave him a purpose. He'd told himself he was only in this for her, to retrain her, help her, but that wasn't true at all. He thrived as he watched her push through her fears, eager to satisfy his hunger. She did more than submit to him. She helped him see who he was again.

Jack sank into a chair. He spent so much time trying to fix Lilly, not realizing she'd been repairing him all along. It was clear the last time they were in his playroom. Everything he'd said to her that night was true.

She'd healed him.

He needed her.

He was hers.

"Yes," Jack said. "I love her."

Patrick nodded, as if he'd expected that answer all along. "Then you did what Eve asked. You were just too stupid to figure it out."

Lights flashed against the front windows. Jack heard the sound of an engine idling in the driveway.

"Guess the night ended early," Patrick said, heading toward the door. "Josh is home and my ride is here."

"Patrick," Jack began, but his friend cut him off with a wave.

"We're cool, but you've got some shit to work out, and I can't help you with it anymore." He opened the door and glanced back over his shoulder. "I've always wanted to be you, Jack. Don't choose now to be like me."

He clapped Josh on the shoulder as he left. Meaning to greet Josh, Jack stood and then put a hand to his temple. A headache had coiled up in his skull, and the room was starting to swim.

"I didn't think you'd be home so soon," Jack managed to say.

"I had a question to ask you," Josh said. "When were you going to tell me about Lilly?"

# 39

"What are you talking about?"

"Come on, Dad. I'm not stupid." Josh shoved his hands into his pockets and fixed Jack with a hard stare. "Why didn't you tell me?"

His palms up in a peace offering, Jack took a step forward. The room, however, decided to go with him. Movement was obviously not a good idea.

"Nothing is going on with Lilly," he insisted, but talking made everything worse. His pulse hammered through his temples.

"Don't lie, Dad. I could see it in your face. It was obvious every time the two of you looked at each other."

"Josh, it's—"

"You let her cook here, in Mom's kitchen! And you have litter for her goddamned cat." He spread his arms out, as if the house itself had let him down too. "Jesus, Dad! Could you be any more of a cliché? She even looks like Mom, just half her age."

Jack winced. Josh might as well have hacked into him with a machete.

"I never meant for you to find out, but it's over, okay? It's over." Jack retreated to the couch and sank down onto it. He deserved Josh's contempt, though. He'd earned it.

314

"How long?" Josh asked.

"A couple of months."

"No, how long since it's been over?"

"Three weeks. It seems like a year, though." Jack grimaced as soon as the words were out. Drinking made him too honest for his own good.

Josh took a step into the room. "Why'd you end it?"

"You don't need to hear the reasons. Just know that it's over and nothing will ever happen between us again."

He couldn't believe how much it hurt to say that. Defeated, he fell back against the pillows and closed his eyes. He tried to breathe slowly until he felt Josh's weight settle on the couch next to him.

"You haven't answered my question."

Jack peeled his eyes open. "Which question is that?"

"Why you didn't tell me."

"There was no reason to. It was never going to be something long-term."

"Why not?"

Jack sighed and looked at the ceiling. "Because it was complicated. And I'm sorry you had to find out this way. But, like I said...it's over."

There was a long beat of uncomfortable silence. Jack glanced over at his son. His chin was ducked down, some of the fury drained out of him.

"So you really cared about her?" Josh asked. "This wasn't just about sex?"

"No," Jack replied sadly. "It wasn't."

"That explains what happened after you left."

Jack felt a flash of panic. "What do you mean?"

"Lilly wouldn't talk to anyone, not even her brother. Cassie ended up taking her home."

What a mess. He'd practically pushed her into Damien's arms. At least Cassie was there for her, and no doubt she'd told Lilly exactly where Jack could shove it. She would've been right too. Lilly needed a friend like that. She'd needed it all along.

It was wrong of him to have made her stay quiet. He'd done the exact same thing Damien did—ignoring her in public, keeping her hidden like some dirty little secret. His own selfish need for discretion had trumped his responsibility to her. He was supposed to put her well-being above everything else, and he'd only thought about himself.

What a shitty Dominant he turned out to be.

Josh leaned forward, his gaze on the floor. With his body hunched over, his elbows on his knees, he looked exactly like he did during Eve's last moments.

"Do you know why I don't come home anymore?" Josh asked.

"Because it's too hard without Mom here."

"That's not why."

"Okay. Why?"

"I don't come home because I can't stand seeing you like this." Josh's words hit Jack like a sucker punch, driving the air straight out of him. "I miss Mom, but I made my peace with her death. I'm living my life and doing the PhD program like she wanted me to. I'm doing what she asked. You're not."

Jack's spine stiffened. "What do you mean?"

Josh looked over his shoulder at him. "I heard what she said to you before she died."

Everything stopped. Jack tried to swallow, but his throat clamped shut. "You did?"

"I was standing right there." He nodded toward the kitchen. "In the doorway."

The sudden grief was a painful spike inside him. "I didn't know you heard," he croaked. "I'm sorry."

"Don't be. It was my fault. I shouldn't have listened."

"It's okay—"

"Mom wanted you to be happy," Josh interrupted, and this time, it was his voice that broke. "Did Lilly make you happy?"

Jack nodded, slowly. "Yes. She did."

Josh let his head drop before shaking it and taking a deep breath. "Can you get her back?"

He was stunned for a second time that evening. A wistful smile pushed its way across Jack's lips. "I don't know."

"You should try. If you love her, then you have to try."

"It might be too late."

"Then you'd better do it soon. If you meant what you promised Mom, then you have to let her go and find a way to be happy."

Jack's throat went tight, his mouth dry. "Thank you."

Josh nodded and stood. "I'm gonna go to bed."

"You go on up. I'm crashing soon too."

When Jack heard Josh's footsteps on the third floor, he made his way through the house, turning off lights as he went.

His head spun with Josh's and Patrick's words. All this time, he'd thought he'd been ignoring the promise he made to Eve, putting it aside for his own selfish desires, when the truth was it had been the opposite.

He paused at the basement door, beckoned by what lay behind it, and his memories of Lilly. The wide-eyed wonder in her beautiful hazel eyes. Her blushes and her tears. Her determination. Her love for him, despite the odds.

His beautiful, strong, stubborn little girl.

He loved her, and he wanted her back, not just in his playroom, but in his life too.

Was it too late to fix this?

It couldn't be. He simply wouldn't accept the idea that she'd decided to go back to Damien, or the possibility that he'd lost her for good. His only hope was in showing her he could give her the things she'd wanted so badly. Things he'd refused to give her before.

He was going to show her he could give her everything.

* * *

Early Saturday morning, Lilly arrived at the café she and Damien had agreed on the night before. She'd told him she needed to sleep on it, but he was taking an early flight back, so breakfast had been her only option. It was a good thing Cassie had told the cabbie to stop for doughnuts on the way home last night, or the three shots Lilly had at the bar would've made this morning suck even more.

She'd thought about Damien's offer all night. About how sincere he seemed, dangling what she wanted in front of her like a shiny treat. And then Jack's reaction to everything, how miserable he looked, acting like she was the one hurting him. He had his chance to change everything. He could've said something the moment she told him Damien wanted her. All it would've taken were a few words: *"Don't go back to him. I love you."*

But he hadn't said that. He'd gotten wasted instead, leaving without even a good-bye.

She hated how things were now, but that didn't change the past. Didn't change how Jack's touch and words had rebuilt her, piece by piece. No matter what had happened in the end, she'd been changed by him. She'd learned to believe in herself again because of his help. And after a sleepless night, Lilly knew what she was going to say to Damien.

She found him at a table by the window, dressed in a crisp shirt and his trademark sex-mussed hair. It occurred to her there was no reason he couldn't have hooked up with someone else last night. She wouldn't have put it past him, despite all he'd said about wanting her back.

After all, she shouldn't fool herself into believing he was hers.

Lilly sat down. She didn't even open her menu. "Why do you want me back?"

Damien's eyebrows climbed up in surprise. "I thought I made that clear last night."

"You said a lot of things, but you never actually said why."

His eyes narrowed slightly. He obviously thought he was through with apologizing. Contrite was not a color he wore well for long.

"I'm not sure what else you want me to say."

"How about telling me why you've been going crazy thinking about me? Do you actually care about me, or do you just miss the sight of me on my knees?"

"Lower your voice," he hissed.

"See, there's something I'm waiting for, Damien." She emphasized his name, and his eyes shone with disapproval, his lips pressed together in obvious displeasure, but she didn't care. She had no intention of calling him Sir ever again. "Something I want to hear before I submit to anyone. Because now I know that being a submissive doesn't make me weak. Actually, it makes me incredibly strong. So when I choose to kneel before someone again, I'll do it because that person loves me."

She paused, sure of the answer to the question she was about to ask by the malice in his eyes. "Do you love me?"

Damien closed his menu, sat back against his chair and said nothing.

Lilly laughed. "That's what I thought."

She stood, enjoying the role reversal of looking down at him.

"I'm not the girl you used to know, and I'm not going back to Chicago. My life is here. I have a future here." She started to walk away, but stopped and turned back to face him. "It's funny. I've hated you for a long time. I had nightmares about how you broke me, but now I actually have to thank you for it. If you hadn't done what you did, I would never have realized how strong I am. I'm smarter because of it. And I'll never make the same mistake again."

She walked out without looking back.

Outside, she breathed in the warm air and smiled up at the sun, feeling freer than she'd felt in ages. It was as if she'd thrown off the weight of a thousand rusted chains that had been keeping her shackled to her past. And while part of her wished she could tell Jack everything, there was one person she needed to talk to more.

A few minutes and a couple of blocks later, she knocked on the door to Nick and Gabe's brownstone. Gabe opened it and rubbed his eyes.

"What are you doing here so early?" he asked. "Is it Monday? Did I sleep through the weekend?"

"No, it's Saturday. Is Nick here?"

"He's in the darkroom. Come in."

She waited in the kitchen as Gabe went to retrieve Nick. Her brother emerged from the hallway, wiping his hands, his smile bright.

"What's doing, kiddo?"

"Can we talk?"

Nick's smile vanished. "Sure. You okay?"

"Yeah. Just have some stuff to tell you about."

Nick sat down next to her, and Gabe poured them each a cup of coffee before squeezing both their shoulders and leaving the room. Nerves flooded her system, her knee bouncing under the table. It was a big risk, but she needed her brother's acceptance, and to stop lying for good.

"I need to tell you about what happened back at school. It wasn't just a bad breakup."

"Never thought it was."

Lilly took a breath and told him everything, from when she met Damien to just minutes before when she kicked him out of her life for good. Her tongue nearly stuck to the roof of her mouth when she told him about being Damien's submissive, what he kept from her and how stupid she felt when she figured everything out. The hardest part to say, however, was how she was strangely grateful for the experience, because it helped her figure out a part of herself, that she now understood this was who she was.

But it was also the easiest to say too, because she knew he'd understand.

When she finished, Nick took her hand in his. "Why didn't you tell me all this before?"

"I didn't want you to think badly of me."

"Why would you ever think I would feel that way?"

"People don't exactly accept this kind of lifestyle. You're looked at as a freak, or some kind of twisted sex maniac."

Nick sighed. "Do you have any idea how hard it was for me to tell you I was gay?"

"To tell *me*? Why?"

"One word: Mom."

"I never would've reacted the way she did."

"But I didn't know that. And it was the nineties. People didn't accept different sexual orientations yet. Many still don't. And I didn't want *you* to think badly of *me*. I was the football star, the big brother, the hero. How could I be gay?"

"But you've always been my hero. Nothing could ever change

that. And I never cared who you fell in love with, just as long as you were happy."

"Exactly."

It took a second before Lilly understood what he was saying. She blinked, unable to respond.

He squeezed her hand. "Gay or straight, Dominant or submissive, old or young—it's all the same thing. It's all people, and the different ways we care about one another. That's what I take photos of. That's what my life stands for. You love who you love, Lilly. You can't change that."

Tears pricked, hot in her eyes. "And if they don't love you back?"

"Sometimes people don't know what they want, and you have to wait for them to catch up with themselves. To figure it out on their own."

Nick smiled, and Lilly considered the possibility that he might know about Jack, but didn't say anything. One confession was enough for today, and there was no point in telling him now.

"That's good advice," she said, wiping away a tear. "I guess I'll have to keep hoping."

"That's all any of us have got, kiddo."

Lilly smiled. "There's one other thing I'll need to be hopeful about. I'm going to take the bar exam."

"It's about freaking time." They both laughed. Nick squeezed her hand again. "Did you eat?"

"Nope."

"How do pancakes sound?"

She sighed. "That sounds perfect."

As they stood and started prepping, her phone beeped with a text. Figuring it was Cassie making sure she made it through the morning in one piece, Lilly pulled it from her purse. Her stomach did a somersault when she saw Jack's name on the screen.

She took a deep breath and opened his message.

*Can you meet me this afternoon at Rosie's?*

No "how are you", no emoticon to soften the blow. Great. He probably wanted to talk about how she behaved after he left last night. She hadn't exactly done an awesome job of keeping her emotions to herself.

Lilly replied with as little feeling as he'd put into his own words, saying she could be there around three. She needed time to get her head together. After this morning, she was exhausted. But it would be good to get it over with today. Maybe after they talked, she could find some closure and figure out how to go on with life without him.

## 40

The house was quiet when Jack returned from the store, the sounds of late spring stealing in through the open windows. He placed the flowers he'd bought by the steps and went into the kitchen to scribble out a note for Josh, who was probably still asleep. It was past noon, but the kid was on California time, and yesterday took a lot out of both of them.

Leaving the note by the coffee machine, Jack went up to his bedroom and stood in front of Eve's nightstand. He opened the drawer, took out the jewelry box, flipped it open and studied Eve's collar and wedding rings that lay inside. After unlatching the silver chain, he slipped it free of the rings and dropped it into his pocket. Stowing the rings back into the box, he went to his closet and slid it onto a shelf near the ceiling.

Then he went downstairs, picked up the flowers and headed out into the day.

The drive across the river was calm, little traffic for early on a Saturday afternoon. He found a parking space and cut the ignition. Flowers in hand, Jack walked through the stone archway leading into the cemetery. Sun filtered through the towering pines, the sky a curve of soft, pale blue above him. Birds chirped happily from their perches, and the sound of children's laughter echoed from the

323

playground nearby. When he approached the gentle slope of a small hill underneath a weeping willow, Jack stopped.

"Hi, love."

A warm breath of wind pushed through the trees. Jack placed the bouquet alongside the base of the tombstone.

"I'm sorry I haven't been here. I couldn't. It was too hard."

Another breeze rustled the leaves above him, and Jack looked up at the sky.

"I missed you. Your laugh, your smile. The sound of you in our house. I didn't know how to live without you. I was lost. But something's happened. I finally did what you asked." He took a breath. "I fell in love."

A current of air brushed his face, and he focused on the grave again.

"I stopped myself from admitting how I felt for a long time. I never expected to fall in love with her, but I did. And then I screwed it up." Jack winced and shook his head. "I thought I was doing the right thing by ending it. I was sure she wasn't who you'd want me to be with. But she's a lot like you, actually." He smiled and sighed. "She brought me back to life, Eve."

He reached into his pocket and took out the necklace.

"I understand what you did for me now. That this didn't mean the same thing to you as it did to me, but you did it anyway. For me." Grief swelled, but it didn't hit as hard as it used to. It tightened around his heart, then slowly abated, riding out on his exhale. "I can never be thankful enough for what you did, for knowing what I needed during our life, and after you were gone."

Holding the chain up, he watched the light bounce off the delicate string of metal.

"I know why you made me take this off you, but even with it locked in your dresser, it kept me bound to you. That's not what you wanted. And I'm bound to someone else now, if she'll still have me."

He draped the chain over the top of her grave.

"I'm ready to let you go. I have to, so I can start living again."

Jack stared at her collar for a long moment. The wind rushed through his hair, and Jack had a feeling that this was okay. That it was right. This wouldn't be the last time he came here—Eve would always be a part of him, but she was his past, and his future was with Lilly.

At least, he hoped it was.

He whispered, "Good-bye, Eve."

Then he turned and walked out of the cemetery.

Pulse pounding, Jack drove quickly to Rosie's Diner. A good half hour early, he went inside hoping to find the same booth where he and Lilly sat months ago. Finding it free, he ordered a cup of coffee to help bide the time. The drink did little to occupy his thoughts, and he stared impatiently out the window.

She'd said in her text she would meet him, but he also knew she'd told Damien she needed to sleep on his offer. She might have already spoken to him today, her decision made. The clock ticked past three, and for a minute he worried she wasn't coming. But then he saw her crossing the street. She was wearing a sundress that left her shoulders bare, white cotton skimming her knees. Jack immediately responded, breath quickening, his emotions a mix of apprehension, affection and desire, but he mastered his reaction as Lilly walked toward the diner with a determined step. She looked like she was ready to give him hell.

*That's my girl,* he thought, but he couldn't think of her that way. She wasn't his again yet.

Lilly opened the door. Her firm expression seemed to waver a little when their eyes met, but then she lifted her chin, regaining her composure as she slid onto the seat across from him.

"Hi," he said. "Thanks for coming."

"No problem. What's up?" Her words were clipped and professional. Her walls were back up again, as guarded as she had been when they first met.

"I wanted to tell you that you were right last night. It was none of my business to listen to your conversation with Cassie. I assume by now you've spoken with Damien?"

Her gaze lowered for a fraction of a second, a relic of their former association flickering back to life. "I have."

"Whatever you said to him, there's something I need you to know."

"Okay," she replied hesitantly.

"The thing Eve asked me to do before she died. The thing I wouldn't tell you about. She asked me to fall in love again. And I just went to the cemetery to tell her...that I did."

Lilly blinked several times until understanding colored her cheeks. "You did?"

"I did."

Her face contorted briefly, brows pulling down tight, as if the knowledge that he loved her hurt, but he had to keep going.

"I've been a fool. All the things I thought would make a relationship impossible for us were just excuses. I was afraid to move on, but I'm not anymore. I'm so sorry I didn't figure it out sooner."

Her expression didn't change. He wished she'd smile, give him some glimmer that what he was saying made her even the tiniest bit happy. That it had any influence on her decision.

Maybe it really was too late.

"I understand if you don't want me anymore. And I'll respect whatever choice you make, but if you decide to leave, please don't go back to him."

She frowned and leaned forward, digging a hand into her hair. "This isn't what I expected."

"How so?"

"I thought you wanted to talk because you were angry about how I acted in front of Josh last night."

His lips curled up into a smile. "Who do you think convinced me to talk to you?"

"Josh?" Her eyes widened. "He knows? And you're okay with that?"

"I am."

"Wow. And here I was planning to tell you to fuck off."

Jack's laugh was short and quiet. "I wouldn't have expected anything less from you."

She studied him, her eyes tracking his face, as if she didn't trust what he was saying. "Is this really what you want? Or do you just not want me with anyone else?"

That one stung. "I meant every word. I love you. Don't go."

The look in her face finally shifted, softened, the tension in her body relaxing as part of her armor fell away.

"I'm not going back to Chicago. And I told Damien to shove it."

Another sudden laugh burst out of him. "Congratulations. I'll bet that felt good."

"It did. He's an asshole. And he doesn't love me," Lilly said. "I signed up to take the bar in July too."

"That's great. I'm so proud of you."

"Thank you."

She took a breath. Hope ballooned up in Jack as her eyes searched his.

"I—" She grimaced. Shook her head. "I can't say it back yet."

She didn't have to. The fact that she was here at all was enough for now. They needed to rebuild their trust first before he could ask anything more from her.

"I understand."

She still wouldn't smile, but inched forward, resting her elbows on the table. "So what do we do now?"

"What do you want to do?"

"I can't go back to what we were doing before. It's too painful."

"I agree." Jack leaned closer to her. "What I'd like to do is start over."

She frowned. "I don't understand."

"Right now, you need to be studying for the bar. You need to put yourself and your career first. My suggestion is that we don't play at all for a while."

Lilly shrank slightly, her gaze dropping to the table. Jack lowered his head and tried to catch her eye.

"Hey," he said gently. "Look at me."

She obeyed, but her eyes were shining, the pain of rejection clear.

"I said for a while, but don't think for a second that I don't want you." He let his words sink in, looking at her in a way that gave no room for doubt. "You have no idea how much I want you back in my playroom, but I want more than that."

"You do?"

"Yes. I want us to get to know each other as people, to start over that way. Then, after you've taken the bar, we'll see how we feel."

"I'd like that." Her eyes cleared a little. "So how do we start?"

"Well, what if we try it this way?" Jack held a hand out to her, his palm upturned.

Lilly stared at it, her gaze darting once around the restaurant before returning to his fingers. For the longest time, she didn't move, but he didn't push. He simply waited until she slowly placed her hand in his.

Jack wrapped his fingers around hers. "That's a good start," he said. "And next, I'd like to take you out to dinner."

Across the table, Lilly finally smiled.

# 41

---

*N*ick pulled up in front of the convention center and stopped at the curb. Lilly rubbed her sweaty palms over her shorts and glanced out the window.

"It's going to be fine," he assured her.

"Easy for you to say. You're not the one who has to do it."

She handed him her cell phone. It felt as if she were handing over her lifeline.

Nick put it in his pocket. "Sorry, kiddo, but it's on all your paperwork. No phones in the exam room."

"I know."

"And no being nervous. You're gonna ace this."

Lilly scrunched up her nose. "You know all those times I told you your photos were going to be a hit?"

"Yeah?"

"Did you ever believe me?"

"No, but this is different."

"Why?"

"Because you're brilliant, and you've been studying for three months." He flashed her a smile. "Now go get 'em."

Lilly leaned across the console to kiss his cheek. "Thanks."

She climbed out of the car, the mid-summer heat beating down on her as she queued up with the crowd. It was the first day of the two-day bar exam. As she went through security, she began repeating the acronyms she'd memorized to remember the different legal issues and rules she needed to know. She'd studied for all of May, June and July. Forrester allowed her to change her schedule to three-day workweeks, and she'd spent every Friday morning through Monday evening living off coffee, bent over books and writing out practice essays. She'd resumed running regularly, and some days it felt like her daily outings were the only thing keeping her spine from turning into a permanent curve. As the date of the exam got closer, Gabe and Cassie began coming over twice a week to grill her with practice problems, and on Thursday evenings, Jack met her at the diner for study dates. He was an incredible asset, teaching her tricks until she got to the point where she could sense midway through an answer when she was getting a question wrong.

He'd had every confidence that she was going to pass. He'd said so when he called her the night before, telling her once again that he loved her.

Sitting down at her assigned spot, Lilly laid out her license, seating assignment card and pencils on the corner of her desk, then tucked her plastic baggie packed with protein bars and a bottle of water down by her feet. The last decade of her life had led up to this moment. She was ready. She'd been ready for a long time. She'd just lost sight of that. Now was her chance to prove it.

Lilly closed her eyes and cleared her mind.

\* \* \*

Her cell phone rang, pulling her out of a deep sleep. Groggy, she checked the clock. It was late in the afternoon, but after how exhausting the last few days had been, Lilly felt as if she could use another month of sleep.

The shrill ring pierced through the air again and she rubbed her eyes with one hand as she felt blindly around the bed with the other. She ended up smacking a palm over Rumbles' head instead, and he yelped out a surprised meow.

"Sorry, buddy," she said, finally finding the source of the ringing under her pillow. She'd been so beat when she got home from the second day of the bar yesterday that she didn't remember putting it there. She'd never even plugged it in. Her eyes half glued shut, she hit send without bothering to check who was calling.

"Hello?" she mumbled.

"Good afternoon, beautiful."

A smile washed over her face at the deep timbre of Jack's voice, and she snuggled under the blanket. "Good afternoon—" She cut herself off before adding the word Sir.

It was starting to feel natural to say it again, but it wasn't time. Not yet.

"Or maybe I should say good morning," he continued. "Are you still in bed?"

"Yes. And I intend on staying here for a while."

Jack chuckled. "So how do you think it went?"

"Good. There were a couple of questions that tripped me up, but I think I got them."

"And the essay?"

"Piece of cake."

"Told you so."

Lilly stuck her tongue out, relieved Jack couldn't see her doing it. She'd noticed that acting bratty triggered his dominant side. His eyes would darken with a look that said he'd spank her if he could, and in a way that would leave them both hungry for more.

They'd taken things slowly, their study dates eventually supplemented by Saturday dinners. Jack hadn't done more than kiss her on the steps to her building, although it was often difficult to stop there. He'd pull away, his breathing heavy and fast, voice gruff as he said good night. He never came inside, and she hadn't been back to his house once. They'd stuck to their plan of not playing, enjoying different kinds of games instead, asking each other questions ranging from what their favorite movie was to the most embarrassing moments from their teenage years. She'd been grateful for the break, but now with the bar over, her mind was free for...*other* things.

"Will you be rejoining us at the pub tonight?" Jack asked.

"I was planning on it."

"Good. I have something for you. A congratulatory gift for passing the bar."

"I haven't passed it yet."

"You will."

Lilly's smile was so broad she could feel it pressing at her cheeks. "Well then, thank you in advance. I like presents."

"Would you like to go to the pub together?"

Her breathing hitched. "Are you ready for that?"

"I am. We've waited long enough. I want everyone to know you're mine."

Her whole body warmed in a rush. "I want that too."

"Then I'll pick you up on my way over." His voice was lower when he added, "I was also wondering if I could give you the gift afterward. At my house."

His house. She knew what that request meant.

One evening a few weeks back, when it had been particularly difficult for them to tear themselves away from each other, Jack said that sometime after the bar, he'd invite her over. He'd touched her throat as he said it, making sure she understood what he was saying. That inviting her over meant being in his playroom. He'd said she could decide then whether or not she was ready, and if not, he would respect that, no questions asked. It had been the first night she'd said I love you back to him.

It had taken her some time to get there, but when she had, she'd meant it with all her heart. And she'd missed kneeling for him, missed the sound of his voice in her ear as he gave her commands, the feel of his hands on her body. Hearing him call her little girl. Calling him Sir.

She was ready.

"I'd like that."

Jack exhaled, a quiet sound of relief. "Good. That's good."

There was a gap in the conversation, and for a moment, all she could hear was the sound of their breathing. Lilly smiled, her thighs pressing together in anticipation. In a few hours she'd see his dominant side unleashed again, and would give herself to him, completely.

"I'll see you tonight," she said. When they hung up, Lilly curled back under the blanket, her phone held close to her chest.

Hours later, they made their way through the entrance to Barrel 'n' Flask. The pub was thick with baseball fans and tourists, the air equally heavy with humidity. It was loud, and Jack kept his fingers tightly tangled with hers as he led a path to the back. He hadn't let go of her for more than a few seconds since he picked her up. The gang was waiting in their usual spot, and Jack slowed before they reached it. He glanced over his shoulder and smiled at her. Squeezing her hand once in an unspoken acknowledgement of what they were about to do, he pulled her through the crowd.

Brady saw them first and banged his fist on the table.

"I knew it!" he shouted, standing up and pointing at them. Lilly laughed and hid her face behind Jack's arm. Brady turned to Gabe. "Pay up, loser."

Gabe groaned, took out his wallet and dropped a twenty on the table.

"How are Brady and I supposed to split that?" Nick asked.

Lilly's mouth dropped open. "You were betting on us?"

Nick grinned and held a hand out for Jack to shake. "Why wouldn't I bet on a sure thing?"

"Does Josh know?" Brady asked.

Jack nodded as he reached out to clasp Nick's hand. "He's known for a while. He's actually coming out to visit again in a couple of weeks."

Brady danced around the table, singing, "I knew it," over and over again.

Jack looked at Patrick and pointed to the money on the table. "I assume you're getting a piece of this too?"

"You assume wrong," Patrick said. "I would never stoop so low as to bet on my friend's happiness."

"Pffft." Cassie rolled her eyes at him and turned to Lilly. The rivalry between her and Patrick was obviously here to stay. "They tried to grill me for information, but I told them I didn't know a thing."

Lilly gave Cassie a little nod of thanks. She nodded back and grinned. Jack must have caught the moment because he squeezed her hand once again.

"That's it." Brady grabbed the twenty off the table. "I'm getting us all a pitcher. Any arguments?" He scanned the group. "Good."

As he stalked off, Jack pulled out a chair for Lilly. They sat with their knees touching, their hands joined under the table. She drank and laughed as the evening wore on, and Jack started stroking her knuckles, his fingers feather light. The touch was innocent, yet each gentle brush made her body rush with excitement, the hairs on her neck lifting, her nipples beading under her shirt. It was getting difficult to concentrate, and she started glancing at the clock, more and more eager to leave with him.

Finally, he reached up and touched her chin, then swept a light pass along her neck with one finger.

"I want to take you home now," he murmured.

Lilly shivered and nodded. He stayed close behind her as they said their good nights, his hands on her shoulders.

"Get a room," Brady yelled, but Jack didn't let go, and she loved how affectionate and possessive he was with her.

He held her hand the entire drive back to his house. When he unlocked the door and held it open for her, everything felt different, somehow. Like a weight had been lifted.

Like home.

Jack stepped in after her, his body behind her, so warm and close and solid. "Your gift is in the kitchen."

They walked slowly down the hallway, and Lilly saw a box sitting on the kitchen island. She turned to look at Jack. He leaned against the wall and crossed his arms, his posture relaxed and confident.

"Open it."

She untied the bow and lifted the lid. Inside was a thin circle of shining metal, joined at either end by a padlock in the shape of a heart. A key was nestled into the cotton bedding underneath.

Her heartbeat kicked up a notch. "Is this a collar?"

"Yes. I had it custom made." Jack moved from the wall and advanced toward her. He took the box from her hands and picked up the necklace. "There's an inscription on the back."

He rotated it so she could see the writing. The word "Mine" was engraved in a beautiful script on one line, the word "Yours" beneath it. Lilly stared at it, amazed.

"I thought when you said 'congratulatory gift', it would be a Starbucks card or something."

"I think you've had enough caffeine lately." Jack picked up the key and unlocked the heart in the middle. "Will you wear this for me?"

She ran a finger along the brushed metal. "All the time?"

"Not unless that's something you want." He must have sensed her trepidation, because he nestled the collar back into its box. "I'm not giving you this for taking the bar. And I'm not asking you to wear it because I know it's something you said you wanted. I'm asking you to wear my collar because I love you."

"I love you too," she whispered.

Jack moved in closer. "I never understood the true power and beauty of dominance and submission until you gave yourself to me. You're strong and beautiful, and you trusted me completely. It was through your submission that I remembered who I am."

He cupped her cheek in one hand. Lilly melted into his touch.

"I never want to let you go again."

He kissed her softly, but even through the tenderness of his lips, she could feel the strength coiled up within him. He was holding back, for her.

She wanted to set that power free.

"I'd love to wear your collar, but I have one request."

His thumb brushed over her cheek. "What's that, sweet girl?"

"Put it on me in the playroom?"

A breath rushed out of him. "I was hoping you'd say that."

Jack stepped back and held one hand out to her. Silently, she followed him downstairs, her heart fluttering so fast she could hardly breathe. When he closed the playroom door behind them, she looked at the floor and waited for his command.

Tracing one finger down her spine, he whispered, "Strip."

She quickly rid herself of her clothes. Naked before him, she trembled in anticipation. He lifted her hair and kissed the juncture between her throat and shoulder.

"Kneel."

Lilly lowered herself to the ground. The position didn't make her feel defenseless or weak. She felt stronger than ever, because kneeling before Jack was a choice. A choice she made in love.

He nestled the collar against her throat and fastened it behind her neck. The cool metal felt good against her heated skin. Jack locked it in place and stepped around in front of her. Taking her chin between his forefinger and thumb, he angled her face up toward his.

"Are you ready to play, little girl?"

She closed her eyes. Hearing that name again felt right. It felt more than right. It felt perfect. She opened her eyes again, hoping he could see her adoration and respect as she looked up at him.

"I am, Sir."

He pulled her to her feet, and when he kissed her this time, he didn't hold back. His mouth covered hers, his tongue seeking entrance and sweeping over hers. Every kiss was hungrier than the last, his hands at her shoulders, against her throat over her collar, buried in her hair. He kissed her like she was air, his everything, the only thing he needed to survive.

"Mine," he whispered.

Lilly sighed and smiled. "Yours."

# THANK YOU!

I hope you enjoyed *His Contract*. Lilly and Jack didn't exactly behave while I was writing them, and once they showed up, they had plenty to say.

If they pulled you in, pushed your buttons, or kept you turning pages later than planned, I'd love to hear what you thought. Reader reviews help books like this find their way to new readers who enjoy a little tension, a little heat, and a hard-earned happily ever after.

If you're in the mood to share, you can leave a review wherever you bought the book, or on Goodreads. Even a few words make a difference, and I'm always curious what readers think of these two.

 *Rebecca Grace Allen*

ALSO BY REBECCA GRACE ALLEN

*Legally Bound:*
Her Claim
Their Discovery

*Portland Rebels:*
The Duality Principle
The Hierarchy of Needs
The Theory of Deviance

*Shakespeare in the City:*
Taming Sugar
Hunter Pains

*Decades Duet:*
Find the Cost of Freedom
Smells Like Teen Spirit

# EXCERPT FROM HER CLAIM

*A* glass appeared on the countertop beside her.

"See something you like?" Patrick asked.

He couldn't resist, could he? Couldn't help himself from starting up something, his voice warm and amused.

"Nope," she replied. "Other than my drink."

"It's satisfying you, I hope?"

Cassie threw him a glare, but the move backfired. It only got her caught up in his conniving smile and freshly trimmed goatee, his hair that was a little more mussed than usual, curlier and infuriatingly touchable. Why did he have to look so damn good all the time? "Yes, it is."

"Is that a cocktail to pass the time while waiting for someone to join you? Or is something at work stressing you out?"

Since when did he care how her job was? "Neither, actually, I'm celebrating."

"What are we celebrating?"

"Landing a huge client."

His expression shifted, as if he were considering saying something, before it returned to its normal glib state. "Congratulations. I'm celebrating something too."

"What's that?"

He stared at his drink before taking a sip. "Getting through another week."

As if being a high-powered, extremely wealthy executive was so tiring for him. "And that's how you celebrate. By picking up yet another woman."

"Is that envy I hear?"

Anger bubbled up inside her. She wouldn't dignify that comment with a response. "What do you say to these women to get them to fall into your lap, anyway?"

His eyes glittered. "Wouldn't you like to know?"

Cassie turned away and knocked back a sip from her drink, hoping he would move on.

He didn't. "Come on, Cassie. It's obvious you're pissed because I'm doing something you wish you could. That's why you dislike me so much."

No, it wasn't. She was hard up as all fuck, but she had no desire to go home with a stranger every night.

"Unless..." The way he trailed off forced her eyes back to him. "*You* want to be the one falling into my lap."

Oh, how she hated this man. Pure, one hundred percent loathing. But having him this close, she couldn't tamp down the attraction she'd suppressed for months. He wasn't so much tall but thick, his chest and shoulders filling out his jacket. His suit hid it well, but there was a brute strength behind it. She hadn't noticed before, but there were tiny creases by his eyes and the tiniest bit of salt-and-pepper in his goatee. The small signs of his age weren't a turnoff. He was still all man.

Virile, broad-shouldered, sexy-as-hell man.

Cassie found herself wondering what his torso looked like unclothed, how his skin would feel under her fingertips. If he'd be the one to act out the hungers that haunted her fantasies, to hold her down and whisper menacing things to her, to fight her for dominance until he finally, blissfully won.

Disgust rolled over her. Jesus, she shouldn't want these things in the first place, but now she was thinking about them with *Patrick*, for fuck's sake?

She downed another sip of her drink. "You know, you'd be a lot prettier if you didn't talk so much."

Patrick chuckled. The throaty sound sent dual shockwaves of pleasure and annoyance through her. "You think so, huh?"

"Yep. Maybe I should ask Lilly where I could get a ball gag for you."

Patrick nearly spit out his drink. Placing his glass on the bar and wiping his lower lip with the back of his hand, he asked lowly, "Do you know what I know?"

His eyes were bright, scheming, and Cassie considered her answer. Did *he* know what *she* did? Lilly had sworn Cassie to secrecy on the details of her and Jack's relationship, but that had been months ago, right before the night of that fateful party. The two of them weren't secretive anymore, not about being together, but Cassie wasn't sure Patrick knew what they were into.

"I might," she said. "What do you know?"

"I know that necklace Lilly wears isn't *just* a necklace."

"I know she doesn't call him *Sir* just to be polite."

"Then we both know Lilly would know exactly where to get a ball gag, if you were into that kind of thing."

Patrick grinned, a salacious one Cassie couldn't help but mirror. Her heart rate spiked with a rush of adrenaline. It was like a game, trading clandestine information. Their usual verbal warfare was present, but the vibe was different—without the anger, and a hell of a lot more sexually charged.

"Submission is Lilly's thing, not mine. Being on my knees isn't my number-one fantasy."

"What is your number-one fantasy?"

Cassie started to answer, then paused. What was she doing? She'd already confessed more to him than she ever thought she would, but she was buzzing off their banter. And off a little more than that, if she were being honest. Patrick was close enough now for her to catch his scent, all woodsy pine and vanilla and man. For her to look at his lips beyond his bristled goatee, and wonder what it would feel like to kiss him.

And that, ladies and gentlemen of the jury, was her cue to exit.

She was too turned on, too captivated with the way he was leaning into her, eager to discover her secrets. The risks of following through on this were far too high. She'd never worried what their friends would think if she and Patrick slept together—everyone knew she detested him, and she had a feeling her postfuck attitude toward him wouldn't be any different. But she wasn't about to let her guard down. She wasn't going to tell him her deepest desires, or fool herself into thinking he was actually interested.

Like that night months ago, she was nothing more than another chase.

Repeating Patrick's earlier tone, she tipped her head toward his and asked, "Wouldn't you like to know?"

He chuckled again. Cassie reached for her bag, left some cash on the bar and stood. "I think it's time for me to call it a night."

"So soon? I thought things were finally getting interesting."

"I'm always interesting, Patrick. But you wouldn't have any idea about that, would you?"

"I guess not," he replied with a broad grin.

"Oh well." Cassie hooked her bag over her shoulder. "I hope you're able to find someone half as *satisfying* to spend your night with."

She started out, hoping her words landed the punch she'd said them with and knowing full well Patrick's eyes were on her ass. She glanced over her shoulder.

Yup. Still looking.

Power coursed through her as she sashayed to the exit. He was definitely still interested, and leaving him high and dry was the cherry on top of a pretty fuck-awesome day. Cassie stepped outside and headed toward the T.

"I've always loved your spitfire attitude."

Patrick's voice cut through the night. Cassie stopped and whirled around. He was standing at the doorway to the bar, his arms crossed like a bouncer or a Greek god.

"Have you now?" Cassie cocked her brow and placed a hand on her hip. "Well, you'd love me in bed then. I'm a spitfire there too."

The words popped out before she could stop them, but she didn't regret it. For once, she wanted that bastard to know the chance he'd passed up. Because she might never have been in love and had dated some serious losers, but damn it she knew how to make a man moan.

Patrick dropped his hands to his sides and quickly closed the distance between them.

"Prove it," he said.

"Prove what?"

"That you're a spitfire in bed. Unless all you can do with that mouth of yours is talk."

It took everything in her not to snarl. He was baiting her, seeing how pissed off he could get her, like he always did.

Screw the consequences. She'd had enough of his attitude. This time, she was calling his bluff.

She dumped her bag on the ground and got into his space. "I really don't like you."

"Same here."

Cassie grabbed him by the collar and closed her fist around his shirt.

"Good," she said, and kissed him, hard.

# ABOUT THE AUTHOR

Rebecca lives in southern Florida with three cats who firmly believe they are the main characters. When she's not immersed in fictional love stories, she can usually be found chasing strong coffee, good workouts, and the kind of books that balance heart, heat, and humor. She writes romance for readers who like their happily ever afters earned, their characters flawed, and their love stories a little messy in the best possible way.